YOU
LOVE
ME

ALSO BY CAROLINE KEPNES

You

Hidden Bodies

Providence

YOU LOVE ME

CAROLINE KEPNES

SIMON & SCHUSTER

London · New York · Sydney · Toronto · New Delhi

First published in the United States by Random House,
an imprint and division of Penguin Random House LLC, New York, 2021
First published in Great Britain by Simon & Schuster UK Ltd, 2021

1 3 5 7 9 10 8 6 4 2

Simon & Schuster UK Ltd
1st Floor
222 Gray's Inn Road
London WC1X 8HB

Simon & Schuster Australia, Sydney
Simon & Schuster India, New Delhi

www.simonandschuster.co.uk
www.simonandschuster.com.au
www.simonandschuster.co.in

A CIP catalogue record for this book
is available from the British Library

Hardback ISBN: 978-1-4711-9188-6
Trade Paperback ISBN: 978-1-4711-9189-3
eBook ISBN: 978-1-4711-9190-9
Audio ISBN: 978-1-4711-9192-3

Printed and bound by CPI Group (UK) Ltd, Croydon, CR0 4YY

FSC www.fsc.org MIX Paper from responsible sources FSC® C020471

For my Mom, the MonKon

YOU LOVE ME

1

I think you're the one I spoke to on the phone, the librarian with a voice so soft that I went out and bought myself a cashmere sweater. Warm. Safe. You called me three days ago to confirm my new job at the Bainbridge Public Library. The call was meant to be short. Perfunctory. You: Mary Kay DiMarco, branch manager. Me: Joe Goldberg, volunteer. But there was chemistry. We had a couple laughs. That lilt in your voice got under my skin and I wanted to *google* you, but I didn't. Women can tell when a guy knows too much and I wanted to come in cool. I'm early and you're hot—if that's you, is that you?—and you're busy with a male patron—I smell mothballs and gin—and you're foxy but subdued, showing off your legs as you hide them in opaque black tights, as concealing as RIP Beck's curtain-less windows were revealing. You raise your voice—you want the old man to try out some Haruki Murakami—and I'm sure of it now. You're the one from the phone but holy shit, Mary Kay.

Are you the one for me?

I know. You're not an object, *blah, blah, blah.* And I could be "projecting." I barely know you and I've been through hell. I was detained in *jail* for several months of my life. I lost my son. I lost the mother of my son. It's a miracle I'm not dead and I want to talk to you right fucking *now* but I do the patient thing and walk away. Your picture is on the wall by the lobby and the placard is final, confirmation. You are

Mary Kay DiMarco, and you've worked in this library for sixteen *years.* You have a *master's* in library science. I feel new. Powerless. But then you clear your throat—I'm not without power—and I turn and you make a peace sign and smile at me. *Two minutes.* I smile right back at you. *Take your time.*

I know what you're thinking—*What a nice guy, so patient*—and for the first time in months, I'm not annoyed at having to go out of my fucking way to *be* nice, and patient. See, I don't have a choice anymore. I *have* to be Mr. Fucking Good Guy. It's the only way to ensure that I never fall prey to the American Injustice System ever again. I bet you don't have experience with the *AIJ*. I, on the other hand, know all about the rigged game of Monopoly. I used my Get Out of Jail Free card—thanks, rich Quinns!—but I was also naïve—fuck off, rich Quinns—and I'll wait for you all day long because if even *one* person in this library perceived me as a threat . . . Well, I won't take any chances.

I play humble for you—I do *not* check my phone—and I watch you scratch your leg. You knew that you'd meet me *in real life* today and did you buy that skirt for me? Possibly. You're older than me, bolder than me, like high school girls to my eighth-grade boy and I see you in the nineties, trotting off the cover of *Sassy* magazine. You kept going, marching through time, waiting and not waiting for a good man to come along. And here I am now—our timing is right—and the Mothball is "reading" the Murakami and you glance at me—*See what I did there?*—and I nod.

Yes, Mary Kay. I see you.

You're Mother of Books, stiff as a robot in a French maid costume—your skirt really *is* a little short—and you clutch your elbows while the Mothball turns pages as if you work on commission, as if you *need* him to borrow that book. You care about books and I belong in here with you and your pronounced knuckles. You're a librarian, a superior to my bookseller and the Mothball doesn't have to whip out a credit card, and oh that's right. There are *good* things about America. I forgot about the Dewey Fucking Decimal System and Dewey was known to be toxic, but look what he did for this country!

The old man pats his Murakami. "Okay, doll, I'll let you know what I think."

You flash a smile—you like to be called "doll"—and you shudder. You feel guilty about not feeling outraged. You're part *doll* and part *ladyboss* and you're a reader. A thinker. You see both sides. You make another peace sign at me—*two more minutes*—and you show off for me some more. You tell a mommy that her baby is cute—eh, not really—and everyone loves you, don't they? You with your high messy bun that wants to be a ponytail and your sartorial protest against the other librarians in their sack shirts, their slacks, you'd think they'd be put off by you but they're not. You say *yeah* a lot and I'm pretty sure that a wise Diane Keaton mated with a daffy Diane Keaton, that they made you for me. I adjust my pants—*Gently, Joseph*—and I donated one hundred *thousand* dollars to this library to get this volunteer gig and you can ask the state of California or the barista at Pegasus or my neighbor, whose dog shit on my lawn *again* this morning, and they'll all tell you the same thing.

I am a good fucking person.

It's a matter of legal fact. I didn't kill RIP Guinevere Beck and I didn't kill RIP Peach Salinger. I've learned my lesson. When people bring out the worst in me, I run. RIP Beck could have run—I was no good for her either, she wasn't mature enough for love—but she stayed, like the hapless, underwritten, self-destructive female in a horror movie that she was and I was no better. I should have cut the cord with her the day I met RIP Peach. I should have dumped Love when I met her sociopath brother.

A teenage girl zooms into the library and she bumps into me and knocks me back into the present—no apology—and she's fast as a meerkat and you bark at her. "No *Columbine,* Nomi. I mean it."

Ah, so the Meerkat is your daughter and her glasses are too small for her face and she probably wears them because you told her they're no good. She's defiant. More like a feisty toddler than a surly teenager and she lugs a big white copy of *Columbine* out of her backpack. She flips you the bird and you flip her the bird and your family is fun. Is there a ring on your finger?

No, Mary Kay. There isn't.

You reach for the Meerkat's *Columbine* and she storms outside and you follow her out the door—it's an unplanned intermission—and I remember what you told me on our phone call.

Your mom was a Mary Kay lady, cutthroat and competitive. You grew up on the floors of various living rooms in Phoenix playing with Barbie dolls, watching her coax women with cheating husbands into buying lipstick that might incite their dirtbag husbands to stay home. *As if lipstick can save a marriage.* Your mother was good at her job, she drove a pink Cadillac, but then your parents split. You and your mother moved to Bainbridge and she did a one-eighty, started selling *Patagonia instead of Pan-Cake makeup.* You said she passed away three years ago and then you took a deep breath and said, "Okay, that was TMI."

But it wasn't too much, not at all, and you told me more: Your favorite place on the island is Fort Ward and you like the bunkers and you mentioned graffiti. *God kills everyone.* I told you that's true and you wanted to know where I'm from and I told you that I grew up in New York and you liked that and I told you I did time in L.A. and you thought I was being facetious and who was I to correct you?

The door opens and now you're back. In the flesh and the skirt. Whatever you said to your Meerkat pissed her off and she grabs a chair and moves it so that it faces a wall and finally you come to me, warm and soft as the cashmere on my chest. "Sorry for all the drama," you say, as if you didn't want me to see everything. "You're Joe, yeah? I think we spoke on the phone."

You don't think. You know. *Yeah.* But you didn't know you'd want to tear my clothes off and you shake my hand, skin on skin, and I breathe you in—you smell like Florida—and the power inside of my body is restored. Zing.

You look at me now. "Can I have my hand back?"

I held on too long. "Sorry."

"Oh no," you say, and you lean in, closer as in the movie *Closer*. "I'm the one who's sorry. I ate an orange outside and my hands are a little sticky."

I sniff my palm and I lean in. "Are you sure it wasn't a tangerine?"

You laugh at my joke and smile. "Let's not tell the others."

Already it's us against them and I ask if you finished the Lisa Taddeo—I am a good guy and good guys remember the shit the girl said on the phone—and yes you did finish and you loved it and I ask you if I can ask you about your daughter and her *Columbine* and you blush. "Yeah," you say. *Yeah*. "Well, as you saw . . . she's a little obsessed with Dylan Klebold."

"The school shooter?"

"Oh God, no," you say. "See, according to my daughter, he was a *poet,* which is why it's okay for her to write her college essay about him . . ."

"Okay, that's a bad idea."

"Obviously. I say that and she calls me a 'hypocrite' because I got in trouble for writing about Ann Petry instead of Jane Austen when I was her age . . ." You like me so much you are name-dropping. "I can't remember . . ." Yes you can. "Did you say if you have kids?"

Stephen King doesn't have to murder people to describe death and you don't have to have kids to understand being a parent and technically I have a kid, but I don't "have" him. I don't get to wear him like all the khaki fucking dads on this rock. I shake my head no and your eyes sparkle. You hope I'm free and you want us to have things in common so I steer us back to books. "Also, I love Ann Petry. *The Street* is one of my all-time favorite books."

You're supposed to be impressed but a lot of book people know *The Street* and you're a fox. Reserved. I double down and tell you that I wish more people would read *The Narrows* and that gets a smile—fuck yes—but we're in the workplace so you put your hands on your keypad. You furrow your brow. No Botox for you. "Huh." Something bumped you on the computer and do you know about me? Did they flag me?

Play it cool, Joe. *Exonerated. Innocent.* "Am I fired already?"

"Well, no, but I do see an inconsistency in your file . . ."

You don't know about the money I donated to this library because I insisted on anonymity and the woman on the board swore that she would *spare me the nuisance of a background check,* but did she lie to me? Did you find Dr. Nicky's conspiracy theory blog? Did the lady on the board realize I'm *that* Joe Goldberg? Did she hear about me on some murder-obsessed woman's fucking podcast?

You wave me over and the *inconsistency* is my list of favorite authors—phew—and you *tsk-tsk* in a whisper. "I don't see Debbie Macomber on this list, Mr. Goldberg."

I blush. The other day on the phone I told you that I got the idea to move to the Pacific Northwest from Debbie Macomber's Cedar Fucking Cove books and you laughed—*Really?*—and I stood my soft, picket fenced-in ground. I'm not a dictator. I didn't *command* you to read one of her books. But I did say that Debbie helped me, that reading about pious, justice-seeking Judge Olivia Lockhart and her local newsie boyfriend Jack restored my faith in our world. You did say you'd *check 'em out* but that's what all people say when you recommend a book or a fucking TV show and now here you are, winking at me.

You wink at me. Your hair is red and yellow. Your hair is fire. "Don't fret, Joe. I'll eat the beef and *you* eat the broccoli. No one has to know."

"Ah," I say, because the beef and the broccoli are a reference to the show. "Sounds like someone went to Cedar Cove to check it out."

Your fingertips hit the keypad and the keypad is my heart. "Well I told you I would . . ." You're a woman of your word. "And you were right . . ." BINGO. "It is a nice 'antidote to the hellspace reality of the world right now' . . ." That's me. You're quoting me. "All the bicycles and the fight for equity, it kinda lowers your blood pressure."

On you go about the pros and cons of escapism—you learned my language and you want me to know it—you are sexy, confident—and I forgot about sexual tension. Beginnings. "Well," I say. "Maybe we can start a fan club."

"Yeah . . ." you say. "But first you'll have to tell me what got you into it . . ."

You women always want to know about the past but the past is over. Gone. I can't fucking tell you that *Cedar Cove* helped me survive my time in *prison.* I won't tell you that it was my Mayberry-scented salve while I was wrongly incarcerated and I shouldn't *have* to spill the details. We all go through periods when we feel trapped, caged. It doesn't matter where you suffer. I shrug. "There's no big story . . ." Ha! "A few months ago, I hit a rough patch . . ." Fact: The best prison reads are "beach reads." "Debbie was there for me . . ." . . . when Love Quinn *wasn't*.

You don't badger me for details—I knew you were smart—and say you *know the feeling* and you and I are the same, sensitive. "Well, I don't want to bring you down, but I must warn you, Joe . . ." You want to protect me. "This isn't Cedar Cove, not by a long shot."

I like your spunk—you want to spar—and I tilt my head toward the empty table where you stood with that old man. "Tell that to the Mothball who just went home with the Murakami you suggested. Now that was very *Cedar Cove*."

You know I'm right and you try to smirk but your smirk is a smile. "We'll see how you feel after you've made it through a couple winters." You blush. "What's in the bag?"

I give you my best smile, the one I never thought I'd use again. "Lunch," I say. "And unlike *Judge Olivia Lockhart*, I brought a ton of food. You can eat the broccoli *and* the beef."

I said that out loud—FUCK YOU, RUSTY BRAIN—and you get to hide in your computer while I stand here being the guy who just told you that you can eat my *beef*.

But you don't torture me for long. "Okay," you say. "The computer's acting up. We'll take care of your badge later."

The computer has some fucking nerve or maybe you're testing me. You're leading me toward the break room and you ask if I went to Sawan or Sawadty. When I say Sawan your Meerkat looks up from her *Columbine* and makes a barf signal. "Eew. That's so gross."

No, kid, being rude is gross. She raves about *Sawadty* and you side with her and I don't speak your language. Not right now. You put a hand on my back—nice—and then you put a hand on the Meerkat's shoulder—you're bringing us together—and you tell me that I have a lot to learn about Bainbridge. "Nomi's extreme, but there are two kinds of people here, Joe. There are those who go to Sawan and those of us who go to Sawadty."

You fold your arms and are you really that petty? "Okay," I say. "But doesn't the same family own both restaurants?"

The Meerkat groans and puts on her headphones—rude again—and you wave me into the kitchen. "Well, yeah," you say. "But the food's a little different at both of them." You open the fridge and I stash my lunch and you're being irrational but you know it. "Oh come on. Isn't this small-town quirk what you wanted when you moved here?"

"Holy shit," I say. "I live here."

You rest your hands on my shoulders and it's like you've never been to a sexual harassment seminar. "Don't worry, Joe. Seattle is only thirty-five minutes away."

I want to kiss you and you take your hands away and we leave the break room and I tell you that I didn't move here to take the ferry to the city. You peer at me. "Why *did* you move here? Seriously. New York . . . L.A. . . . Bainbridge . . . I'm genuinely curious."

You are testing me. Demanding more of me. "Well, I joke about *Cedar Cove* . . ."

"Yeah you do . . ."

"But I guess it just felt right to me. New York used to be like a Richard Scarry book."

"Love him."

"But it lost that Scarry feeling. Maybe it was Citi Bikes . . ." Or all those dead girls. "L.A. is just somewhere I went because that's what people do. They go from New York to L.A." It's been so long since anyone wanted to know me and you bring me home and away all at once. "Hey, do you remember those black-and-white pictures of Kurt Cobain and his buddies in the meadow? Photos from the early days, before Dave Grohl was in Nirvana?"

You nod. You think you do, *yeah.*

"Well, it just hit me. My mom had that picture up on the fridge when I was a kid. It looked like heaven to me, the tall grass . . ."

You nod. "Come on," you say. "The best part of this place is downstairs."

You stop short in Cookbooks. Someone's texting you and you're writing back and I can't see who it is and you look at me. "Are you on Instagram?"

"Yep, are you?"

It's just so fucking *easy,* Mary Kay. I follow you and you follow me and you are already liking my book posts—heart, heart, heart—and I like your picture of you and Nomi on the ferry, the one with the best fucking caption in the world: *Gilmore Girls.* It's Instagram official. You're single.

You lead the way to the stairs and tease me about my account. "Don't get me wrong . . . I love books too, but your life strikes me as a little off balance."

"And what would you suggest, Ms. 'Gilmore Girl'? Should I post my beef and broccoli?"

You turn red. "Oh," you say. "That's Nomi's little joke. I got pregnant in college, not high school."

You say that like the father is a sperm donor with no name. "I've never seen that show."

"You'd like it," you say. "I used it to get my kid to think of reading as cool."

I know what you're thinking. You wish there was more of me on my fucking "feed" because here I am, seeing your whole life, pictures of you and your best friend, *Melanda,* at various wineries, you and your Meerkat off being *#GilmoreGirls.* You don't get to learn much about me and it's not fair. But life isn't fair and I won't bore you by humblebragging about being a "private person." I put my phone away and tell you that I had Corn Pops for breakfast.

You laugh—yes—you leave Instagram—yay!—and I feed you the right way, mouth to ear. I tell you about my home on the water in Winslow and you roll up your sleeves a little more. "We're practically neighbors," you say. "I'm around the corner in Wesley Landing."

There's no way you're this way with all the volunteers and we make it downstairs and you graze my arm and I see what you see. A Red Bed. Built into the wall.

Your voice is low. Hushed. There are children present. "How good is that?"

"Oh, that's a good Red Bed right there."

"That's what I call it too. And I know it's smaller than the green one . . ." The green one is too green, same green as RIP Beck's pillow. "But I like the Red one. Plus it has the aquarium . . ." Like the aquarium in *Closer,* and you scratch an itch that isn't there because you want to throw me down on that Red Bed right now but you can't. "My library was nothing like this when I was a kid, I mean these kids have it made, right?"

That's why I wanted to raise my son on this island and I nod. "My library barely had chairs."

There was a little tremor in my voice—stop vague-booking out loud about your shitty childhood, Joe—and you lean in closer as in *Closer.* "It's even better at night."

I don't know what to say to that and it's too good with you, too much, like ice cream for breakfast, lunch, and dinner and you feel it too and you point at a closet. "Alas, some kid peed on it and the janitor's out sick. You mind getting your hands dirty?"

"Not at all."

Two minutes later I am scrubbing urine out of our Red Bed and you are trying not to watch but you want to watch. You like me and how could you not? I do my dirty work with a smile on my face and I moved here because I thought it would be easier to be a good person around other good people. I moved here because the murder rate is low, as in not a single fucking murder in over twenty years. The crime is so nonexistent that there are not one but *two* articles in the *Bainbridge Islander* about a couple of architects who stole a sandwich board from another architect and the population skews older and the Red Bed is good as new and I put my cleaning supplies away and you're gone.

I go upstairs to find you and you knock on the glass wall of your office—*come on in*—and you want me in your den and I like it in your den. I wave hello to your posters—RIP Whitney Houston and Eddie Vedder—and you offer me a seat and your phone rings and I never thought I'd feel this way again, but then, I never thought Love Quinn would kidnap my child and pay me four million dollars to walk away. If unspeakably bad things are possible, then unspeakably good things are too.

You hang up the phone and smile. "So, where were we?"

"You were just about to tell me your favorite Whitney Houston song."

"Well, that hasn't changed since I was kid. 'How Will I Know.'"

You gulp. I gulp. "I like the Lemonheads cover of that song."

You try not to stare at me and you smile. "I didn't know that existed. I'll have to check it out."

"Oh yeah. It's good. The Lemonheads."

You lick your lips and mimic me—"The Lemonheads"—and I want to lick *your* Lemonhead on the Red Bed and I point at the drawing on your wall of a little storefront. "Did your daughter do that?"

"Oh no," you say. "And now that you point it out . . . I should have something she made up here. But yeah, I made that when I was little. I wanted to have my own bookstore."

Of course you did and I'm a rich man. I can help you make your dream come true. "Did this bookstore have a name?"

"Look closer," you say. "It's right there in the corner . . . Empathy Bordello."

I smile. "Bordello, eh?"

You touch pearls that aren't there. You feel it too and your phone rings. You say you have to take this and I ask if I should go and you want me to stay. You pick up the phone and your voice changes, high as a kindergarten teacher in a well-funded school district. "Howie! How are you, honey, and what can we do for you?"

Howie tells you what he wants and you point at a book of poems and I pick up the William Carlos Williams and hand it over and you lick your finger—you didn't really need to do that—and your voice changes again. You murmur a poem to *Howie* and your voice is melted ice cream and then you close the book and hang up the phone and I laugh. "I have so many questions."

"I know," you say. "So that was Howie Okin . . ." You said his whole name. Do you like him too? "He's the sweetest older man . . ." Nope! He's a Mothball. "And he's in hell right now . . ." No one knows hell more than me. "His wife passed away and his son moved away . . ." My son was born fourteen months and eight days ago and I haven't even met him. And he's not just my son. He's my savior.

"That's so sad," I say, as if my story isn't sadder. *I'm* the victim, Mary Kay. Love Quinn's family dipped into their coffers to pay my defense attorneys because Love was pregnant with my son. I thought I was lucky to have money on my side. I thought I was going to be a dad. I learned to play *guitar* in that fucking prison and I rewrote the lyrics to "My Sweet Lord"—*Hare Forty, Hallelujah*—and I told Love that I wanted our family to move to Bainbridge, to real-life *Cedar Cove.* I went online and found us the perfect home, complete with a fucking *guesthouse* for her parents, even though they never let me forget that they were footing the bill, as if they had to mortgage a fucking beach house.

Fact check: They didn't.

Your phone rings. And it's Howie again. And now he's crying. You read him another poem and I look down at my phone. A picture I saved. My son on day one. Wet and slick. A little risk taker. A rascal. I didn't take this picture. I wasn't there when he emerged from Love's "geriatric" womb—fuck you, doctors—and I am a bad dad.

Absentee. Invisible. Out of the picture and not because I'm taking the picture.

Love called two days later. *I named him Forty. He looks just like my brother.*

I went along with it. Fawning. *I love it, Love. I can't wait to see you and Forty.*

Nine days later. My lawyers got me out of jail. Charges dropped. The parking lot. Fresh hot stale air. The song in my head. *Hare Forty, Hallelujah.* I was somebody's father. *Daddy.* I got into a town car. My lawyers all around me. *We need to stop by the firm for you to sign a few papers.* Next stop, the parking structure of a concrete fortress in Culver Fucking City. No sun underground. No son in my arms, not yet. *Just a few papers.* We rode the elevator to the twenty-fourth floor of the building. *Just a few papers, won't take long.* The conference room was wide and indifferent. They closed the door even though the floor was empty. There was a goon in the corner. Thick torso. Navy blazer. *Just a few papers.* And then I learned what I should have known all along. My lawyers weren't *mine.* Love's family wrote the checks. The mercenary attorneys worked for them, not me. *Just a few papers.* No. They were *injustice* papers.

The Quinns offered me four million dollars to go away.

Bequeath all access to *the child. No contact. No stalking. No visitation.*

The Quinns are happy to pay for your dream house on Bainbridge Island.

I screamed. *There is no dream without my fucking son.*

I threw an iPad. It bounced and it didn't break and the lawyers didn't scream. *Love Quinn feels that this is in the best interest of the child.* I wouldn't give up my *flesh and blood* but the goon put his gun on the table. *A private dancer, a dancer for money* can get away with murder on the twenty-fourth floor of a law firm in Culver Fucking City. They could kill me. They would kill me. But I couldn't die. I'm a father. So I signed. I took the money and they took my son and you spin around in your chair. You grab a notepad. You scribble: *You okay?*

I think I smile. I try to anyway. But you look sad. You scribble again. *Howie is the nicest man. I just feel terrible.*

I nod. I understand. I was a nice man, too. Stupid. Locked up in jail mainlining *Cedar Cove,* trying to stay positive. I believed Love when she said we'd move up here together, as a family. Ha!

Again you scribble: *The world can be so unfair. I can't get over his son.*

You go back to consoling Howie Okin and I'm not a monster. I feel for the guy. But Howie raised his asshole son. I've never *seen* my little Forty. Not in real life. I only see him on *Instagram.* Love is a real sicko, yes. She kidnapped my son but she didn't block me. Chills every time I think about it. I lower the volume on my phone and open Love's *live story* and I watch my boy hit himself on the head with a shovel. His mother laughs as if it's funny—it isn't—and Instagram is too little—I can't smell him, can't hold him—and it's too big—he's alive. He's doing this right now.

I make it stop. I close the app. But it doesn't stop, not really.

I became a dad before he was born. I memorized Shel Silverstein poems and I still know them by heart even though I don't get to read them aloud to my son and I miss my son and Silverstein's boa chokes me out, that boa slithers in my skin, in my brain, a constant reminder of what I lost, what I sold, technically, and it is wrong, so wrong, it is *up to my neck* and I can't live like this and you hang up your phone you look at me and gasp. "Joe, are you . . . do you need a tissue?"

I didn't mean to cry—it was allergies, it was William Carlos Williams, it was the saga of poor Howie Okin—and you hand me a tissue. "It's so comforting that you get it. I know it's not my 'job' to read poems when some of these patrons have a bad day but it's a *library*. It's an honor to be in here and we can do so much and I just . . ."

"Sometimes we all need a poem."

You smile at me. For me. Because of me. "I have a good feeling about you."

You're moved because *I'm* moved—you think I was crying for Howie—and you welcome me aboard and we shake hands—skin on skin—and I make a promise in my head. I'm gonna be your man, Mary Kay. I'm gonna be the man you think I am, the guy who has empathy for Howie, for my evil baby mama, for everyone on this terrible fucking planet. I won't kill anyone who gets in our way, even though, well . . . never mind.

You laugh. "Can I have my hand back, please?"

I give you your hand and I walk out of your office and I want to kick down the shelves and tear up all the pages because I don't need to read any fucking *books* anymore! Now I know what all the poets were talking about. I'm doing it, Mary Kay.

I'm carrying your heart in my heart.

I lost my son. I lost my family. But maybe bad things really *do* happen for a reason. All those toxic women won me over and fucked me over because they were part of a larger plan to push me onto this rock, into this library.

I see you in your office, on the phone again, twirling the phone cord. You look different, too. You already love me, too, maybe, and you deserve it, Mary Kay. You waited a long time. You gave birth. You give poems to Howie and you never got to open your bookstore—we'll get there—and you pushed your Murakami on that Mothball, as if that Mothball could ever appreciate being *all but sucked inside.* You've spent your life in your office, looking up at the posters you held onto since high school, the pop star and the rock star. Life never lived up to the lyrics of their songs, to the passion, but I'm here now. *I have a good feeling about you.*

We're the same but different. If I'd had a kid when I was young, I would have been like you. Responsible. Patient. Sixteen *years* in one fucking job on one fucking island. And you'd fight to make things better if you were so alone like me and this morning, we both got out of bed. We both felt alive. I put on my brand-new sweater and you put on that blue bra and your tights, your little skirt. You liked me on the phone. Maybe you rubbed one out while *Cedar Cove* was muted on your TV and am I blushing? I think so. I pick up my badge and my lanyard at the front desk. I like my picture. I never looked better. Never felt better.

I clip the badge to the lanyard—how satisfying, when life makes sense, when things click, you and me, beef and broccoli, the badge and the lanyard—and my heart beats a little faster and then it beats a little slower. I'm not a sonless father anymore. I have purpose. You did this to me. You gave this to me. You placed a special order and here I am, tagged. Lanyard official. And I'm not afraid that I'm getting ahead of myself. I want to fall for you. I've had it rough, *yeah,* but you've had to hold it together for a *child.* I'm your long overdue book, the one you never thought was coming. I took a while to get here and I got banged up along the way, but good things only come to people like us, Mary Kay, people willing to wait and suffer and bide the time staring at the stars on the walls, the bare concrete blocks in the cell. I pull my lanyard down over my head and it feels like it was made for me, because it was, even though it wasn't. Perfect.

2

Yesterday I overheard two Mothballs call us *lovebirds* and today we're in our usual lunch spot outside on the love seat in the Japanese garden. We eat lunch here every fucking day and right now you are laughing, because we're always laughing, because this is it, Mary Kay. You're the one.

"No," you say. "Tell me you did not really steal Nancy's newspaper."

Nancy is my fecal-eyed neighbor and you went to high school with Nancy. You don't like her but you're friends with her—*women*—and I tell you that I had to steal her newspaper because she cut me in line at our local coffeehouse, Pegasus. You nod. "I guess that's karma."

"You know what they say, Mary Kay. *Be the change you want to see in the world.*"

You laugh again and you are thrilled that someone is *finally* standing up to Nancy and you still can't believe I live next door to her, that I live *right around the corner* from you. You chew on your beef—we eat beef and broccoli every day—and you close your eyes and raise a finger. You need time—this is the most serious part of our lunch—and I count down ten seconds and I make a buzzer noise. "Well, Ms. DiMarco? Sawan or Sawadty?"

You tilt your head like a food critic. "Sawan. *Has* to be Sawan."

You failed again and I make another buzzer noise and you are feisty and you tell me that you *will fucking win* one of these days and I smile. "I think we both won, Mary Kay."

You know I'm not talking about a stupid Thai food taste test and you wipe a happy tear off your cheek. "Oh, Joe, you kill me. You do."

You say things like that to me every day and we should be naked on the Red Bed by now. We're getting there. Your cheeks are rosy and you already gave me a promotion. I am the *Fiction Specialist* and I built a new section in the library called "The Quiet Ones" where we feature books like Ann Petry's *The Narrows,* lesser-known works by famous authors. You said it's nice to see books *find new eyes* and you knew I was watching you shake your ass when you walked away. You're glued to me in the library, every chance you get, and you're glued to me here, on the love seat, warning me that Fecal Eyes might rat me out on Nextdoor.

"Oh come on," I say. "I stole a newspaper. I didn't steal her dog. And they're like everyone here. Lights out by ten P.M."

"*You* come on," you sass. "You love being the rebel night owl. I bet you're up all night chain-smoking and reading Bukowski."

I like it when you tease me and I smile. "Now that you mention it, Bukowski might be the way to get Nomi off her *Columbine* kick."

"That's a great idea, maybe I'll start with *Women* . . ." You always appreciate my ideas—I love your brain—and I ask you what you think Bukowski would have thought of my fecal-eyed neighbor and you laugh-choke on your beef, my beef, and you hold your stomach—it hurts lately, what with the butterflies, the private jokes. I pat you on the back—I care—and you sip your water and take a deep breath. "Thank you," you say. "Thought I was gonna faint."

I want to hold your hand but I can't do that. Not yet. You pick up your phone—no—and your shoulders slouch and I know your body language. I can tell when the Meerkat is texting—you sit up a little straighter—and I can tell when it's *not* the Meerkat, like now. I've done my homework, Mary Kay—it's amazing how easy it is to get to know a woman when she follows you back online!—and I know about the people in your life, in your phone.

"Everything okay?" I ask.

"Yeah," you say. "Sorry, it's just my friend Seamus. This will just take a sec."

"Don't be ridiculous," I say. "Take your time."

I know, Mary Kay. You have a "life" here and it's mostly about your daughter, but you also have your *friends,* one of whom is Seamus Fucking Cooley. You went to high school with him—yawn—and he owns a hardware store. Correction: He *inherited* the store from his parents. Whenever he texts, he's whining about some twenty-two-year-old girl who's fucking with his head—ha!—and you are compassionate. You always say that he's *sensitive* because he used to be picked on about being short—I bet the shithead bullies used to call him *Shortus*—and I always bite my tongue—Look at Tom Fucking Cruise!—and you're still texting.

"Sorry," you say. "I know this is rude."

"Not at all."

Making you feel better makes *me* feel better. But it's not easy, Mary Kay. Every time I ask you to get coffee or invite you to *pop over* you tell me you can't because of Nomi, because of your friends. I know that you want me—your skirts are shorter every day, your Murakami is hot for me—and I come in early and I stay after my shift ends. You can't get enough of me and you're spoiled because I'm here almost every day. You never send me home and when you joke about the two of us *loitering* in the parking lot I tell you that we're *lingering*. You like that. Plus, you like all my fucking pictures.

@LadyMaryKay liked your photo.

@LadyMaryKay liked your photo.

@LadyMaryKay WANTS TO FUCK YOU AND SHE IS PICKY AND PRIVATE AND PATIENT AND SHE FINALLY FOUND A GOOD MAN AND THAT'S YOU JOE. YOU'RE THE ONE. BE PATIENT. SHE'S A MOM. SHE'S YOUR BOSS. SHE COULD GET FIRED FOR HITTING ON YOU!

Finally, you shove your phone into your pocket. "Oof, I think I need a drink."

"That bad, huh?"

"Yeah," you say. "I think I told you he has this cabin in the mountains . . ."

You told me about his fucking cabin and I'm not impressed. I've seen his Instagram. He doesn't like to read and he bought his biceps at *CrossFit.* "I think so, yeah."

"Well, he brought this girl up there and she spent the whole trip complaining about the lack of Wi-Fi. And then she bailed on him."

"Yikes."

"Yeah," you say. "And I know it sounds bad, this same old story of a middle-aged guy going for twenty-two-year-old girls, but"—there is no *but,* it's just plain bad—"you know how it is. He's like a brother to me. He's insecure . . ." No. He's just a man. "And I feel for him. He does *so much* for this island. He's a saint, truly. He donates books constantly . . ." ONE HUNDRED GRAND, HONEY. "He's like our own *Giving Tree . . .*"

No man is an island *or* a tree but I smile. "I got that impression," I say. "I saw signs for his Cooley 5K and the Cooley 'street cleaning task force.' But maybe instead of doing so much for others . . ." God, this hurts. "Maybe he should be in that cabin clearing his head."

"Yeah," you say. *Yeah.* "And that's probably the right move because he truly does have the worst luck with women."

Sorry, Mary Kay, but if you knew about my exes . . . "He's lucky he has you."

You blush. You're quiet, too quiet, and you don't want this fucking man, do you? No. If you wanted him, you would have him because *look at you.* You sigh. Sighs are signs of guilt and okay. He wants you and you don't want him—you want *me*—and you shrug. "I don't know about that. It's just second nature for me, you know, helping people, being there . . ."

We are the same, Mary Kay. We just have different styles. "I can relate."

We're quiet again, closer now than we were an hour ago. My whole "Mr. Goody Two-shoes" plan isn't just about me anymore. It's about us being good together. I swore I won't ever hurt anyone for you, not even the guy who owns the hardware store where the *female* staffers swan around in tight jeans and tight shirts bearing the Cooley name. I'm kind like you. I'm good like you. I gulp. I go for it. "Maybe we could get a drink later . . ."

You put your hand on your shirt. Deep V-neck sweater today, deep for a librarian who bends over a lot. Say yes. "I wish," you say, as you stand. "But I have girls' night and I should probably get back inside."

I stand because I have to stand. "No pressure," I say. "Just throwing it out there."

We're *lingering* as if we can't bear to go inside and time is slowing down the way it does before a first kiss and we do *need* to kiss. You should kiss me or I should kiss you and it's fall and you're falling in love with me and I've never felt less alone in my life than I do when I'm with you. There's an invisible string pulling our bodies together but you walk to the door. "Hey, if I don't see you, have a good weekend!"

Six hours later, and I am NOT HAVING A GOOD FUCKING WEEKEND, MARY KAY. I want to spend my downtime with *you* and okay. You didn't lie to me. You're not out with Seamus—he's at a dive bar watching a soccer game because people here like soccer—but you're at Eleven Winery with *Melanda.*

She's your "bestie" and she's @MelandaMatriarchy on Instagram—oy—and she celebrated Gloria Steinem's birthday by posting a picture of . . . *Melanda.* This woman is an English teacher, she's your *daughter's* teacher, constantly harassing your Meerkat to stop romanticizing Dylan Klebold in the comments—Boundaries, anyone?—but you see the best in people. Melanda was the first friend you made in Bainbridge and she "saved your life" in high school, so when she issues Instagram mandates to BELIEVE ALL WOMEN—as in, the mandate is on a T-shirt stretched over her unnecessarily big boobs—well, you like every fucking one of them.

And you do this even though *she* doesn't like all of *your* pictures—you are the bigger person, just like me—and when she wants to go to Eleven Winery and bitch about her OkCupid dates—generally this is every Tuesday and every Friday—you go.

It doesn't take a genius to see that I should be with you, that Melanda should be with *Shortus.* But they're two sides of the same coin. She likes to hate men because she's too guarded to find real love—

your words, not mine—and this man-boy wants a *chick* to suck on his Shortus. And then my phone buzzes. It's you.

You: *How's your night?*

Me: *Hanging in there. How's girls' night?*

You: *You mean* women's *night.*

This is our first text—YES!—and I can tell you're a little drunk. I want to pound my chest and pump my fist because I've been waiting for you to reach out to me and I haven't reached out to *you* because I have to be paranoid. I know how it works in this antiromantic world. I couldn't be the one to hit you up on your personal phone because the Injustice System could take my innocent gesture and frame me as a fucking "stalker." This is life without a Get Out of Jail Free card but it turns out, life is *good.* You did it, Mary Kay! You crossed the line and texted me after hours and the library is closed but you are open. And thank God I dragged my ass to *Isla Bonita* tonight—another win!—because now you're gonna see that I'm not sitting at home pining for you. I'm just like you, out on the town with my friends—the other guys at this bar would appear to be my "friends" on security camera footage—and now I get to make you sick with *FOMOOM*—fear of missing out on *me.*

Me: *Well I'm at BOYS' night. Beer and nachos and soccer at Isla.*

You take a beat. It's killing you to realize that I'm on Winslow Way too, 240 feet away. Come on, Mary Kay. Spill that wine and run to me.

You: *You make me laugh.*

Me: *Sometimes boys and women drink at the same bar.*

You: *Melanda hates sports bars. Long story. Bartender was rude to her once.*

I bet every bartender in the state was rude to Melanda but then, it can't be easy being Melanda. I snap a picture of the bumper stickers behind the bar—MY BARTENDER CAN BEAT UP YOUR THERAPIST and I DON'T HAVE AN ATTITUDE PROBLEM. YOU'RE JUST AN ASSHOLE—and I send it to you and then I write to you.

Me: *Tell your friend Melanda that I get it.*

You: *I love you.*

Me. Numb. Lovestruck. Speechless. Cloud 9000. I stare at my phone, at the dots that tell me there's more to come and then boom.

You: *Typo. I meant I love your picture. Sloppy fingers. lol sorry just . . . yeah . . . wine.*

My heart is pounding and you love me. You said it. Everyone around me is oblivious, but Van Morrison is egging us on from the speakers—this *seems* like a brand-new night and this *feels* like a brand-new night—and what the fuck am I doing?

You want me. I want you. Fuck it.

I'm outside, en route to Eleven Winery, closer as in *Closer,* but then I stop short.

Yes, you told me where you are but you didn't invite me to join you. And let's say I did interrupt your *women's night*. Is this really the way for us to start our love story? Deep down, I know that good guy island etiquette requires that I give you your fucking "space." The walls of Eleven are thin and I hear laughter in "your bar." You're not just with your best friend. You know a lot of flannel-vested townies inside and I want to rescue you from that noisy tedium that can't possibly compare to our lovebird lunches in the garden.

But I can't save you, Mary Kay. Tonight we made progress—you texted me, you started it—and I want that to be what you think about when you wake up tomorrow. It's not easy, but I walk into the alley, away from the sound of your voice. Before I get home, I'm smiling again because hey, this was still a big night for us. You had all those people to talk to, your best fucking friend, but that wasn't enough for you, was it? You picked up your phone and texted *me*. Rude. Obsessed. *Sassy*. And of course you couldn't help it.

After all, you love me.

And you can tell me that you didn't mean it that way. You can point to the fact that you were drinking. You can say that you were sloppy. But anyone with a phone knows that there are very few *actual* mistakes when it comes to the things we put in writing, *especially* after a few drinks. You said it and on some level, you meant it and your words are mine now, glowing in the dark in my phone.

I sleep well for a change, as if your love is already working its magic on me.

3

Everybody *working for the weekend* can bite me. I hate the weekends on this island, the flabby, brunchy vats of time where families and couples convene and revel in their togetherness with no regard for me, alone, missing you so much that I walk to the Town & Country grocery store—your grocery store—just hoping to bump into you at *some* point this weekend while your I-Love-You is still fresh, still new.

Sadly, we miss each other on Saturday and again on Sunday. But fuck you, weekend warriors, because *Monday's finally come*. I look good even though I didn't sleep last night—*There's no doubt, I'm in deep*— and I pull a bright orange sweater over my head. This will make it easier for you to spot me in the stacks and I check Instagram. Last night, I posted some yearning Richard Yates. Did you touch the white empty heart beneath my *Young Hearts Crying* and turn it red?

No, you didn't. But that's okay.

@LadyMaryKay did not like your photo because she likes YOU, Joe.

I lock my door even though the Mothballs tell me I don't have to lock my door and I walk by the movie theater on Madison—I want to go down on you in the dark—and I go to Love's Instagram and watch my son tear up *Good Night, Los Angeles*. I know better than to walk into Love's online family museum when I need to be at my best and I see your Subaru in the parking lot—you're here!—and I quicken my pace and then I slow down—*Gently, Joseph*—and I walk inside but you're not on the floor and you're not in your den. *Grrr.* I shuffle off to the break room, where a married old Mothball tells me about his wife harping on him to take Advil for his lower back pain and I want that to be us in thirty years, but that will never be us if we don't seal the fucking deal.

I fill Dolly Carton and push her into the stacks and boom. It's you. You put your hands on Dolly and your eyes on me. "Hey."

I fight the urge to do what you want me to do, to grab you right here, right now. "Hey."

"Do you want to go get lunch in town or are you attached to your *Cedar Cove* special?"

YES I WANT TO GO TO LUNCH. "Sure."

Your cheeks are Red Bed red and you want to eat food with me and there is a zipper in the center of your skirt and it's a skirt I've never seen, a skirt you broke out today, for me, for our lunch date. You fiddle with the zipper. You want me to fiddle with it. "You wanna go now?"

We are putting on our jackets and we are lovebirds in a movie, strolling on Madison Avenue under a classical score. You want to know if Fecal Eyes introduced herself yet and I tell you she didn't and you sigh. "Unbelievable," you say. "See, if this were *Cedar Cove,* Nancy and her husband would have baked you a pie by now."

I don't want a pity party so I ask about your weekend—code for: *remember when you told me you love me?*—and you tell me that you and the Meerkat went to Seattle. I am bright, interested. "That sounds fun. What'd you do?"

"Oh you know how it is. She's at that age where she walks ten feet ahead of me and if I want Italian, she wants Chinese and if I say that sounds good . . ."

"She wants Italian."

"And she was freezing, she refused to bring a jacket. We popped by to visit some old friends who have a guitar store, they're like family . . ." Your voice trails off. And you shrug. "And lunch was just Danishes on the ferry. Another proud mom moment, you know?" You laugh. "So, Joe, did you . . . do you want kids?"

It's a trick question. Nomi's a senior in high school and if I say I want kids and you don't want *more* kids then you have a reason to push me away. But if I say I *don't* want kids, then you might think I don't want to be a stepfather. "I've always felt like, if it happens, it happens."

"It's the difference between men and women. For all you know, some kid could show up and knock on your door, 23andMe style, like 'Hi, Dad!' "

If only you knew, and I smile. "What about you? Do you want more kids?"

"Well . . . Nomi was the surprise of my life, you know? Lately, it's hitting me that there's this whole new chapter ahead. I don't know about another kid, but opening a bookshop, that I can see." Your voice trails off—you're picturing us in our Bordello—and you dig your hands into your pockets. "So," you say, your voice shaky with first-date nerves. "How was the rest of guys' night?"

I like this new side of you, Mary Kay. Jealous. *Frisky.* And I am sarcastic. "Oh you know, beer . . . nachos . . . babes."

"Ah, so does that mean you met someone?"

God, you have it *bad* for me and I smile. "Well, I thought I did . . ." I have to tease you a little. "But then this woman I work with texted me and I guess I kinda blew it."

You know that you are *this woman* and you shrug, slightly demure, and it's a reminder that as much as we are soulmates, we don't know each other, not like this, on a sidewalk in motion. "Oh come on," I say. "You know I'm kidding . . . I don't go out on the prowl at bars and I'm certainly never, you know, *looking* for *babes* . . ." RIP Beck walked into *my* bookstore same way you happen to work at *my* library. "For me it's always intangible. It's not about looks . . . it's about chemistry."

Did you just arch your back a little bit? Yes you did. "I get that," you say. "I relate."

We fall into a natural, sexy silence and if we were on a busy four-lane street in L.A., I could take your hand. I could kiss you. But this is an island and there is no anonymity and the walk is over. You open the door to the diner and my eyes turn into hearts. Retro red. Red booths like our Red Bed and you chose this place because of the booths. You know the host and he's a gentle man—ring on his finger—and he tells you your booth is open, your booth as in *our* booth.

We sit across from each other and I did it. I got you all to myself. And you did it. You got me all to *your*self.

I open the menu and you open a menu even though you've been eating here for *a hundred years.* "I always get the same thing, but I think I'll mix it up today."

I make you want to try new things and I smile. "Any suggestions for me?"

"Everything's good," you say. "But I wouldn't mind if you got something with fries . . . just saying."

You order a bowl of chili and I go for a club sandwich *with fries* and you smile at me but then something catches your eye. You sit up straight and wave. "Melanda! Over here!"

It's supposed to be you, me, and fries but your friend Melanda clomps up to our booth. Body by Costco—bulk-order boobs—and she moves like a linebacker charging for an end zone, as if life is war. She's sweaty—wash that shit off before you enter a restaurant, Melanda—and she needs a tutorial on Instagram filters because the dissonance shouldn't be *this* jarring. You air-kiss her and tell her she looks great—I don't agree—and why is she here? Are you hazing me? The host brings Melanda a menu and her nostrils flare and she's a *so* person, sucking up the oxygen with a non sequitur. "So I just had the worst row at school with that math teacher Barry who thinks that being 'a father of daughters' entitles him to help me with the Future."

She's not British and she shouldn't say *row* and you look at me. "Melanda's starting a nonprofit for local girls . . ." Melanda bites her lip in protest and you elbow her in response. "A nonprofit for young *women* . . ." She winces and you throw up your hands as in *I give up* and she puts her eyes on me.

"So, what MK means is that I'm building an *incubator* for young women. It's called The Future Is Female. You've probably seen posters in the library . . ."

"I sure did," I say, recalling the mixed messages inviting girls to *establish boundaries* online and commanding them to use her hashtag in all of their posts. *#MelandaMatriarchySmashesThePatriarchy* . . . and the young women who forget to promote her brand!

Melanda laughs. "And?"

"And obviously I'm all for it."

You're different around her, cautious, but that's the story of humans. We shrink to fit. I know Melanda's type. She doesn't want questions. She wants praise, so I tell her it's a *genius* idea. I don't say that there's a way to do these things without being a fucking asshole. But there is. "Well," she says. "I'm past the *idea* phase. We launch early next year." She picks up your water glass. "Which reminds me, MK, did you review my latest mission statement?"

You didn't review it yet and you pull a packet of Splenda from your purse and she grimaces like you pulled out a crack pipe or a Bill Cosby biography. "Sweetie, no," she coos. "You have to stop trying to kill yourself."

That language was telling. On some level, she wants you to die, and you don't know it and she doesn't even fully know it and it's all a little sad.

"I know," you say. "I'm terrible. I have to stop it with the Splenda."

It's not my place to butt in—are you ever gonna introduce us?—and she sips your water and sighs. "So they fired my trainer, *finally*. I wasn't the only one who complained about him."

You say you've never joined a gym and I want to hear more but Melanda cuts you off to bitch about her *toxic trainer* and I wish she'd follow the rules spelled out on her T-shirt—LET HER SPEAK—and you wink at me and . . . wait. Is this a fucking setup?

"Melanda," you say. "Before we get off track, this is Joe. I told you how he's volunteering at the library, he just moved here a few months ago."

I extend my hand. "Good to meet you, Melanda."

She doesn't shake my hand. She sort of pats it and this isn't a setup. My first instinct was right. You *are* hazing me and Melanda's like a wannabe tough frat guy in a Lifetime movie who doesn't want anyone else in the frat. "How nice," she simpers. "Another white man telling us what to read." She slaps her clammy hand over mine. "Honey, please. You know I'm kidding, just having a day."

You make eyes at me the way you did on Day One in the library—*Please be patient*—and Melanda says that her toxic trainer asked

Greg, the barista at Pegasus, to stop selling her cookies and you nod, like a therapist. "Well, I'm glad that Greg told you about it. He's a good guy in that way."

Her nostrils flare. "Well let's not pat *Greg* on the back, Mary Kay. He was laughing, which means he probably laughed about it with my trainer too. *Ex*-trainer."

You nod, Dr. Mary Kay DiMarco. "Okay, but remember. Greg's in there all day and when you deal with the public all day, you hear crazy things. Greg does strike me as one of the good ones. And imagine if he *didn't* tell you about the trainer."

You tamed her without dismissing her—brilliant—and she makes a self-deprecating joke about being *Bitchy McBitcherson* and now you cut *her* off. "Stop it, Melanda. You're allowed to have a reaction."

I want to tear off your tights but for now I just nod affirmatively. "You said it, Mary Kay."

I was beaming when I said that, beaming at you, and Melanda felt it and we are a party of three and she scans the diner and you nudge her, girlfriend to girlfriend. "On a happier note, you're seeing that Peter guy this week, right? The one from Plenty of Fish?"

She grunts. No eye contact with you or me. "Plenty of Fish? More like plenty of pigs. He sent me a dirty joke about Cinderella and a Pumpkin Eater and, needless to say, I reported him."

"Well," you say. "You know how I feel about those apps . . ."

Melanda fixes her eyes on me now. "And what about you, Joe? Are you on the apps?"

She's not stupid. She saw me beam at you. But I don't want to be that asshole pooh-poohing her way of life. "No," I say. "But maybe I'll join just to give Peter a piece of my mind."

It was a joke and you laugh but she doesn't. "Aw," she says. "That's *sweet* but I don't recall asking you to fight my battles. All good here."

I let it slide. Imagine all the dick pics she gets, all the rejection. You take the reins and change the subject. "So, Melanda. How's my daughter? For real."

"Good," she says.

You look at me and tell me that Melanda knows more about Nomi than you do and Melanda is proud—she's one of those *bestie aunts*—

and she says that Nomi is cooling off on Dylan Klebold and you sigh. "Thank God. I was hoping it was just a phase."

"That's what it sounded like to me," I say, because I have a voice too. "Kids go through phases."

Melanda grunts. "Well, I wouldn't diminish a young woman's feelings as a *phase* . . ."

It was okay when *you* said it was a phase and the three of us aren't gonna be at Eleven Winery any time soon. I get it. You take care of Melanda because she's alone. She's telling you about Nomi's ideas for her imaginary incubator and she's not Auntie Melanda. She's *Auntie* Interloper and you almost jump out of your seat.

"Seamus!" you shout. "Over here!"

So it really *is* a hazing ambush and this is Seamus in real life, working the room like a politician, glad-handing the other diners with his masturbation paws. *Did that dryer work out okay for you, Dan? Hey, Mrs. P, I'll swing by and check out your furnace.* He wears a long-sleeve Cooley Hardware T-shirt and a baseball cap with the same logo—we get it, dipshit—and he's too short for you. Too smarmy for you. But he grins at you like he could have you if he wanted.

"Ladies," he says. *Juvenile.* "Sorry I'm late."

I can just hear God in heaven. *We'll make this one short and squat with arms too long for his body and a bombastic voice that turns off women. But it's hard enough down on Earth, so let's give him piercing blue eyes and a strong jaw so he doesn't blow his brains out when the midlife reaper scratches at his door.* But it's not all bad. I slide in to the wall. At least this way I'm across from you. "Joe," you say. "I've been so excited for you to meet Seamus."

You say that like he's not the one who's lucky to meet *me* but I am Good Joe. Convivial Joe. I ask him if that's his hardware store as if the question needs to be asked and the waitress delivers coffee—he didn't even have to place an order—and he laughs. Smug. "Last time I checked."

The three of you gossip about some guy you went to high school with who got a DUI. You're leaving me in the cold and I don't have history with you and this is beneath you, using your friends to ice me out. I sit here like a mute monk and I should step outside and call

Fuck You Slater, Ushkin, Graham, and Powell to file a class action against Marta Kauffman et al., because they made *Friends* and that show is the reason we're in this mess. On a show like *Cedar Cove,* the goal is love. You watch because you want Jack and Olivia to get together. But on *Friends,* everything is an inside joke. They brainwash you into thinking that friendship is more valuable than love, that old is inherently better than new when it comes to people.

I dump ketchup on my fries and you reach onto my plate, reestablishing our intimacy. "Is this okay?"

I nod. "Go for it."

Seamus wrinkles his nose. "No fries for me," he brags. "I'm doing a *Murph* later. You wanna join, New Guy?"

I dab the corners of my mouth with a napkin. "What's a Murph?"

Melanda grabs her phone and Seamus "enlightens" me about the wonders of *CrossFit,* telling me a Murph will kick-start my *body transformation*. "I have more muscle now than I did in high school, and in a couple months . . . six tops . . . you could too, New Guy, if you join up."

Melanda is fully checked out and you're not eating my fries anymore. You're paying attention to *him,* bobbing your head as if exercise is a thing that interests you—it isn't—and this is why people don't bring friends on a first fucking date, Mary Kay.

You pound your fist on the table. "Wait," you say. "We *have* to talk about Kendall."

Melanda cuts you off. "No, we need to talk about my queen. *Shiv.*"

I open my mouth. "Who's Shiv?"

Seamus laughs. "You've never seen *Succession*? Come on, New Guy. You don't have a job. You have all the time in the world!"

Off you go, raving about *Kendall* and Kendall is a stupid name, a few letters away from Ken Doll. It's no fun when three people are talking about a show that one person has never seen. You reach for a fry and your hand lingers on my plate and I can't stay mad at you.

"Hey, guys," I say. "Did anyone see the movie *Gloria Bell*?"

None of you saw *Gloria Bell* and Seamus isn't sold—*sounds like a chick flick*—and Melanda shuts down—*I can't add one more thing to my list*—and you smile. "Who directed it?"

"This Chilean guy," I say. "Sebastián Lelio."

Melanda makes a face. "A male director telling a woman's story . . . how lovely."

"I hear you," I say. "But Julianne Moore is incredible. And the dialogue is top shelf . . . it has a Woody Allen vibe."

Melanda's nostrils flare. "Okay, then," she says. "I think that's my cue."

You tense up and she waves for the check and I will fix this. Fast. "Whoa," I say. "I just meant that it's a smart film."

Melanda doesn't look at me. "I don't condone Woody Allen or his *art*."

You dig your credit card out of your purse and we will not end like this. "Melanda, I'm not defending Woody Allen. I was just trying to say that *Gloria Bell* is a good movie."

"And you think Woody Allen is a synonym for good? Great. White male privilege for dessert! Ugh, where is that check?"

You're staying out of it and Seamus is giggling like an eighth-grade boy in sex ed. "Melanda, I really do think you misunderstood me."

"Ah, must be my lady brain on the fritz again . . ."

Seamus laughs and you show your teeth. "Oh, you guys . . . come on now. Truth is, Joe, I think Melanda and I watched *Beaches* and *Romy and Michele* so many times back in the day that we missed a lot of good movies and never really caught up."

Melanda grunts. "Sweetie, don't bother. We can go."

"Look," I say. "I only mention Woody Allen because say what you will about him . . . his movies have a lot of great female leads. And Julianne Moore is incredible in *Gloria Bell.*" You are staring at me like you want me to stop but I can't stop now. "Melanda, I think you'd like the movie, I'm sure of it."

"Of course you're sure. You know everything!"

I'm taking the heat for all the monstrous men in the world—who can blame Melanda for using me as a whipping post?—and you reach for my ice-cold fries, you're stress-eating and I won't let Melanda Peach me.

"Melanda," I say. "I don't know everything. No one does."

"Pff," she says. "Least of all me, a woman . . ." She shakes her head. "A librarian who endorses a child molester. How nice!"

Shortus drops a twenty and makes a run for it and you pick up the bill and Melanda's on her feet, lecturing me. "I'm sorry I get passionate."

"Melanda," I say. "You don't have to apologize."

"I'm not apologizing to *you,*" she says and she looks at you like *Can you believe this guy?* "As a teacher, I know that we can't separate the art from the artist. And I won't praise a man for telling a woman's story. But you do you, *New Guy.*" She smiles at you. "You ready, sweetie? Do you need a ride?"

You squirm. Message received. "Thanks," I say. "But I feel like walking."

Melanda smiles. "I would too if I ate all those carbs."

You look at me but what can you do? She's your friend, your old friend, and you get into the car with her and I am on foot. In hell. I fucked up my hazing and by the time I get back to the library you're gone—you have a conference in Poulsbo—and I don't think I made your coed frat.

At the end of my shift, I test the waters and post a page from a diner scene in *Empire Falls* and two minutes later . . .

@LadyMaryKay likes your photo.

Okay, you wouldn't *like* it if you didn't still like me and of course you like me. We have our books and the Brooklynites are right. Books are magic. We are magic. You send me a text.

You: *Did you have fun at lunch?:)*

I know it's considered rude to respond to a text with a phone call but it's also inconsiderate to haze a guy before you have sex with him. I walk outside. I call you.

You pick up on the first ring. "Well, hello there!"

"Is this a bad time?"

"I just got home but I have a couple seconds . . . What's up? Everything okay?"

"Well, that's what I was gonna ask you . . ."

"You mean lunch? Oh Joe, Melanda lives to debate and she liked you, she did."

My muscles relax. "Phew, because for a minute there it felt like she didn't . . . but if you say everything's okay . . ."

"Joe, seriously. You were fine. Melanda . . . Well, yeah, she gets fired up. But she's very passionate, very smart and you know . . ."

Your daughter is home. I hear cabinets slamming and you tell me that you *should probably* go and I do the right thing. I let you go. For a moment I consider walking to your house. But if I go and spy on you, I open myself up to busybody neighbors who might "warn" you about a "strange man" lurking in your yard. (Dear Bainbridge: Get a *life.*) Things are supposed to be different with you, Mary Kay. *I* am supposed to be different with you. If I watch you from afar, I am transforming from a person who is in your life to a person who is on the outside, looking in. I don't want that for us and I know you don't either.

I do the right thing and go home, I don't feel at home in my home because the fecal-eyed family is out there, throwing bean bags into holes—yawn—so I grab a coffee and head downstairs to the place that makes my house special, the reason I chose the property over all the others. It's called a *Whisper Room.* You turn on the lights, you close the door and that's it. The world is gone They can't hear me and I can't hear them—long live soundproof spaces—and Love thought this room was *creepy* when I showed her the pictures. She saw padded walls and she called it a cage. But you get me, Mary Kay. You know this house. When you realized where I live, you said you'd had *wonderful times* in this Whisper Room. You knew the guys who owned the place. You hung out down here and I take a deep breath—maybe I'm breathing you in right now—and I have to be patient. You really are one the one. I just have to fight harder.

I do sit-ups and watch a little fucking *Succession.* Your boy Kendall has weak shoulders and basset hound eyes. I bet he never read *Empire Falls,* let alone *Last Night at the Lobster,* another selection for our *Quiet Ones* at the library. The endorphins kick in—Shortus is right about *some* things—and I don't want to sue Marta Kauffman anymore. I want to send her flowers because she and her *Friends* also taught us that real relationships take time, that sometimes you make a baby with the wrong person, you fall in love with the wrong person, but eventually, you get with the right one.

You.

4

It's been two days since you ambushed me with your fraternity siblings and I didn't "stalk" you. I've been good. I went against all my best instincts and joined *CrossFit* to make nice with Shortus (a.k.a. to keep an eye on that fucker just in case) and I'll admit it, Mary Kay. I did judge you a little bit. This adolescent cliquey side of you is not ideal. You're a woman. A *master* of library science. But you've been hunkered down on Land's Fucking End for your entire life. I tear the tag off a brand-new black cashmere sweater—my gift to you, for us—and tonight you'll see the light.

It's date night, motherfuckers!

You were so cute when you asked me out. You were smoothing a sticker on Dolly Carton and I bent over to look at the sticker—THE FUTURE IS FEMALE—and you stayed low, close. I leaned in closer. "Did you get permission to vandalize Ms. Carton?"

You staggered upright and flattened your skirt. "Haha," you said. You looked at your phone. "I should probably get going. I have book club tonight at the wine bar . . ." I smiled—oh Bainbridge, you need to see *Cocktail*—and you wanted me to know where you're going. "Eleven as in the winery," you said, so nervous, so fucking *cute*. "But we'll be outta there by ten."

You waved goodbye and you scratched your tights, drawing my eyes to your legs.

Invitation received, Mary Kay, and I RSVP *yeah* as in yes.

I'm waiting for you in a recessed mini-mall across the street from Eleven and *finally* your Book Club winds down and there are credit cards and hugs, false promises about *getting together soon* and why do you women lie to each other so much? I slink around the block—and I slow down—and you spot me.

"Joe? Is that you?"

You jaywalk to me—no RIP Fincher to issue any tickets—and I meet you halfway, *across the sky.* Do we hug? We don't hug. I nod toward the bar I chose for us, not a fucking winery, just a pub. "Come on," I say. "One drink."

You shift your purse. "I should probably go home. We ran late tonight."

I expected a little pushback and I know all about your *shouldprobably* disorder. Shel Silverstein *should probably* have written a poem about the *shouldprobablies* and the female need to express her awareness of what a *good* woman would do right now. But you're still hesitating and what the hell is there to think about? You're my neighbor. You live *right around the corner* and the pub is *right around the corner* and your daughter isn't six—there's no babysitter to relieve—and your shoulders are tense getting tenser—"I don't know, Joe . . ."—and did you learn nothing from Lisa Fucking Taddeo? Stop feeling guilty, for fuck's sake.

I am the man you need me to be right now. Chill. Cavalier. "That's too bad," I say. "This could have been my very first Book Club."

Your shoulders drop. "Well, I'd hate for you to miss out on your very *first* Book Club. One drink. *One.*"

No one means that when they say it and I open the door to the Harbour Public House and you walk in and we are a couple now. We make our way to a table and I tell you how much I really did like meeting your friends and you are puffed up. "Oh good! See, they're nice, right?"

You sit in a booth and I sit on the other side. "And you were right," I say. "Melanda isn't mad. She followed me on Instagram . . ." White lie. I followed *her* first but she did reciprocate. "And she made me think about a lot of stuff . . ." Ha! "And her incubator sounds incredible . . ." As if her posters are *doing* anything for anyone but her. "You gotta love that, ya know?"

You gotta love *me* and you do. I'm in your circle, at your table. "Yeah," you say. "She's great, she has a powerful voice . . ."

"Extremely. Your people are good people."

You smile. I smile. The heat between us is palpable and you look around and remark on how empty it is and it's just us and a couple of guys in wool hats. Sailor types. Our jackets come off and it's obvious you've been drinking and the barmaid approaches, a soft and pear-shaped pre-Mothball. I ask to see a menu and you look at me. "Oh," you say. "I ate. I should probably just have a water."

I smile, undeterred by another *shouldprobably.* "I don't mind eating alone."

You end up asking for a glass of tequila—*frisky*—and I order a Southern fried chicken sandwich and a local vodka soda and you promise to steal French fries *again* as you lace your fingers together as if you're on a job interview. "So," you say. "How's the house coming along?"

"Shit," I say. "So, it's true. You really don't talk about the book in Book Club. You talk about everything *but* the book."

Your voice is loose with liquor but you're nervous—it *is* a first date—and you're babbling about Billy Joel—you've always loved "Italian Restaurant"—as you text your daughter and tuck your phone into your purse. You tell me about your Book Club, how my fecal-eyed neighbor Nancy picked apart the book. We agree that there is always a Nancy and I tell you about a reading I hosted in New York when a Nancy had *notes* for the author. We're in flow. The talk is small, but we've never been like this, alone in the dark, at night, in a booth.

"Okay," you say. "I have to ask. I know you were done with New York and L.A. But I've been thinking about you . . ." You said it. "And I feel like there has to be more. A single guy moves into a big house on Bainbridge. What's her name? The reason you're here."

I groan the way any guy does when a girl wants to hear about his past and you plead. You endured *three hours* with a bunch of women you've known since high school, most of whom are married to men or women you've known for *aeons*.

"Come on," you say. "Tell me why you really bit the bullet. Who are you running from?"

It's the dream—you want to know everything about me—and it's the nightmare—I can't tell you everything about me. I learned the hard way, with Love, but there is no way for us to move on unless you learn why I am the way I am, handsome, available, good.

I start at the beginning, my first love in New York. I tell you that I fell hard for Heather (RIP Candace). It was lust at first sight. I saw her in a play—pretty as Linda Ronstadt—and I tracked her down at the playhouse.

You wipe your glass with a napkin. "Wow. You went all out for this girl."

"I was young. It's different when you're young. You get obsessed."

You give me a *yeah* and you are jealous, the idea of me *obsessed* with another woman. I sip my drink while you picture Linda Ronstadt on top of me and I tell you what you need to hear, that Heather broke my heart. You perk up. You want to know more and I tell you about the day she dumped me. "I'm checking out this apartment in Brighton Beach because I think we're gonna move in together," I begin, remembering that day on the beach, Candace. "It was a hot summer night. I'll never forget the smell, the gnats . . ."

You're happy because this girl made me unhappy and you pout. "Please don't ruin New York for me, Joe."

I laugh and I tell you that *Heather* dumped me over voicemail while I was *in* that apartment and you gasp—*no*—and I laugh defensively, lovingly, the way you do when enough time has passed and you're ready to love again, in a way you never have before. "Yep."

My chicken sandwich arrives and you pick up one of my French fries and you chew. "Wow. You lost the girl and the apartment."

I take a bite of my chicken and you reach for another fry. We are clicking. You want the bacon, I can tell, and I pull it out of my sandwich like it's a block of wood in Jenga and you pick it up. *Crunch.*

"If you think Heather's bad, oh God, let me tell you about Melissa."

You rub your hands together and this *is* fun. It's cathartic for me to tell you about Melissa (RIP Beck). In this version, I was a waiter at a diner on the Upper West Side and Melissa came into the restaurant, sat in my section, and wrote her number on the bill. You take a big sip—*Well, that's aggressive*—and I say that Melissa was too young for me. Your cheeks turn as red as the Red Bed. You like that I'm the anti-Seamus, that I want a woman, not what our youth-obsessed society would call a *trophy*.

"Yeah," I say. "Way too young, but I thought she had an old soul. Her favorite book was *Desperate Characters*."

You wipe your hands, feeling threatened again. I tell you what I learned from Melissa, that reading doesn't *always* promote empathy. She was a competitive fencer and she was in a love-hate codependent relationship with her best friend Apple (RIP Peach Salinger). "But that wasn't the problem," I say. "In the end, Melissa was in a relationship with one person and one person only."

We say it at the same time: "Melissa."

You feel for me. I endured Melissa's numerous microbetrayals. I tried to love her, help her focus on her fencing (writing). And then she cheated on me. She slept with her coach (psychologist). You bury your head in your hands. "No," you say. "Oh God, that's horrible on so many levels."

"I know."

"A *coach*."

"I know."

I'm eating my sandwich and you're looking at me like I should be crying. "It's really not so bad," I say, realizing that it *isn't*, because look where it got me, to you. "You're lucky to get your heart broken. That just means you have a heart." I'm not ready to talk about Amy, about Love, so I move us past anecdotes into theory. "Everyone is the wrong person until you meet the right person . . ." You rub your empty ring finger. "I'm not bitter, Mary Kay. If anything, I hope they're doing great . . ." Up in heaven, or dust in the wind. "I hope they found the right person." I pray for a remorseful almighty lord—*Hare Forty*—and I take a big bite of my sandwich.

You let the waitress know that we would like another round—fuck yes—and you admire my *healthy outlook* on life. I tell you it's *no big deal.* "So," I say, because the door to your heart is cracked now, the tequila, the details about my life, and you're finally ready for me to enter. "You and Nomi . . . real-life *Gilmore Girls.* What's the story there?"

You let out a deep sigh. You look around the restaurant, but no one is listening to us. No one is close. I know it's not easy for you, being on a date, but you are. You know it. You begin. "I was young but I wasn't *that* young, and my life . . . well, I told you about my parents."

"Mary Kay mom and dear old dad."

You smile. "Yeah."

"Did your dad put up a fight when you moved up here?"

I smell onions, layers peeling away, revealing the truth under the truth. You tell me you didn't understand the divorce. There was no scandal, no cheating. "It was like one day, my mom woke up and she didn't want her pink Cadillac anymore. She didn't want him either."

"Were there signs?"

"I missed them," you say. "Are you good about signs? Reading people . . ."

Yes. "Well, who can say?"

"I think we all see what we want to see." You look around again, so nervous, as if one of these people is going to text Nomi and tell her that her mother is on a date. And then you relax again. "Well, my mom sort of just announced that she was done with Mary Kay, that we were moving to Bainbridge Island, that she was craving nature."

"And you don't know why she left him?"

"No clue," you say. "It was amiable. There was no custody battle, no fight. He was so calm that he drove us to the airport! He's my *dad* and he's kissing us goodbye like we were going away for the weekend. We left him all alone. My mother made me complicit. But then, that's not fair to say because it's like I said. It was all so damn *amiable.*"

I feel for you, I really do. "Jesus."

"One day my mom's harping on me to use more eyeliner and the next thing you know . . . we live here and she's telling me that I don't need lipstick. I didn't ask her why we left, but then . . . what's scarier than your mom becoming a total stranger?"

I think of where I stand with Love, powerless against a woman's blind determination to make our child her own. "I get it."

"And then, after all that, my mom spent every night on the phone with my dad, egging him on to eat better."

"Strange."

"Right? And this was before cell phones. I couldn't call my friends back home. I didn't have any friends here yet. I felt so alone. She was always in her room, taking care of my dad, letting him tell her how *beautiful* she is as if they were still married. I remember thinking, Wow. You leave him . . . You move to another state. But you never leave a man, even when you do."

"Jesus Fucking Christ."

You air-toast me with your empty glass. "And *that,* my friend, is too much information." We've come full circle, inverted the joke, and you signal for another drink and you're in flow, the levee *broke.* "It's like . . . we all know about sham marriages. But what about a sham *divorce*?"

"That's a good way to describe it."

You stare at the table and the waitress plunks our drinks down and you thank her and sip. "I just wish I knew why she left him at all if she was only going to spend the rest of her life on the phone with him, you know? Because why not just stay together if that's what it is? Why uproot my entire life?"

I don't answer your question. It was rhetorical. All you need is for me to listen.

"I look back and I don't know how I survived." You breathe. You are activating the most important empathy, the empathy we have for ourselves. "My mother and I were bickering nonstop. One night I lost my temper and threw my landline at her and she had this huge welt on her forehead, so bad she had to get bangs to cover it up." I smile but you furrow your brow and oh that's right: violence against women is always bad, even when it's you. "It was like *Grey Gardens* minus the fun . . ." I love you. "I guess your *Cedar Cove* fantasy got under my skin because no one welcomed *us* with open arms." You sip your drink. "Then, one day, Melanda asked me to eat lunch together. She told me all about *her* fucked-up family . . ." Foregone conclusion.

They named their child *Melanda.* "I told her all about mine. She said I'd fit in really well because *everyone* on this island is fucked up, they just like to pretend they're not and . . . I dunno. Life just went on from there. Melanda was my buffer. She showed me all that graffiti at Fort Ward. And that graffiti . . . well, it helped. It still helps."

"How so?"

"It's like a conversation that's still alive. My mom and I, we never got around to hashing it out. But I go to Fort Ward and I feel like I can still talk to her even though she's gone. Like maybe one day she'll appear in the sky and tell me that I'm not doomed to mess up my daughter the way she messed me up . . ." That is why you stay away from love and you shrug. "I dunno. I'm probably just drunk."

You're not drunk. You just haven't found anyone to talk to. You look at me—you can't believe I'm finally here—then you smirk. You can't believe I'm *still* here. "Pretty bad, huh?"

"No," I say. "Pretty human."

I said the right thing and you laugh. "Well, I swore I'd never confuse Nomi like that. *Ever.*"

You're self-conscious. You felt so safe with me that you forgot about where we are and you glance around the pub, nervous. You wipe away a half-tear and you snort. "Sometimes I think I got pregnant just to piss her off, to remind her that if you *really* love someone, you know, you *fuck* them instead of just talking on the phone . . ." You *are* a little drunk now. "And once in a while when you're actually having sex, the condom breaks. C'est la vie."

"I get it," I say.

Another anxious look around the bar. "Well, the timing was tough . . . but yeah, I did have this hunger to make my own little family, to kind of show her up."

"And you did."

"Have you met my kid?"

"Oh come on," I say. "Your kid is fucking great. You know it."

You do know it and it's important for you to realize that you *are* a good mother because once you see that, you can let me in all the way. We are still treading water, even after all you said. You're holding back as you open up about your father and explain that he calls you a lot. "I don't always pick up, I mean I have Nomi, I have a job, and every call ends in frustration. I'm not my mother, you know?"

"It's fundamentally different."

"I can't stay on the phone with him all night. I will *not* do that to Nomi."

You think all men are a threat to your relationship with your daughter and I am here to help you change. "I'm sure he understands that."

"I just . . . I will not do that to my daughter. I won't let my life ruin her life."

You think it's your fault that your dad is sad and I know how that feels. I push my plate to the edge of the table. You look at me. You need me. "Look," I begin. "You can't fix someone who doesn't want to be happy." Hi, Candace. "You can't make anyone see the light if they prefer the dark." Hi, Beck. "You try to do that, you end up on a dark road. You make bad decisions." I really did move to Los Angeles for Amy, the stupidity. "And then you get stuck." I have a permanent *bond* with Love Quinn, a son. "It's not easy, but you have to accept that there's no *right* move with your dad. You can't save him from himself."

The *pub* is clearing out and you're rubbing your neck. "Wow," you say. "And here I thought we'd just be gossiping about the Mothballs."

You're officially drunk. Floppy hands and loose lips and *still* I want you. You tell a long-winded go-nowhere story about an old friend in Arizona and you can't remember her name and you say you feel like a traitor sometimes. You don't keep in touch with anyone from your past in the desert and you came here like a *phoenix from Phoenix.*

"I'm the same way, Mary Kay. The ability to move on doesn't make you a sociopath."

You raise your glass and wink. "Let's hope so."

We're closer than *Closer.* You tuck your chin into your hand. "Joe," you say, pulling me in, making me think of your Murakami, *all but sucked inside*. "Tell me . . . Do you like it in our library?"

What I say right now matters and I take my time. "I like it in your library."

You felt my *your.* Your foxy lips are wet. "Do you feel *good* in the library?"

I felt your *good.* "Yes, I feel good in your library."

"And you're pleased with your boss?"

Oh this is *fun* and I stir the ice in my cocktail. "Mostly."

"Oh," you say, and I am the human and you are my resource. "Mr. Goldberg, do you have a complaint about your supervisor?"

"That's a harsh word, Ms. DiMarco."

You lick your lips. "Tell me about your complaint."

"Like I said, it's not a complaint. I just want more, Mary Kay."

"More what, Mr. Goldberg?"

Your bare foot finds my leg under the table and I pay the bill. Fast. Cash. I am up. You are up. You say you need to stop in the bathroom and the bathrooms are off to the left and you go in and close the door and then you open the door.

You grab me by the collar of my black sweater and pull me into the bathroom and press your body into my body, my body against the wall. The art in here is full of passion. Nudity and salt water. A naked woman in the sea on her back. Her hands grasp the shoulders of a frightened sailor, still clothed. It's a shipwreck. It's us. Wrecked. Groping. You kiss me and I kiss you and your tongue is at home in my mouth—land ho!—and the waves wash over your *shouldprobablies*. My hands slide under your tights—no panties, *cotton crotch*—and my thumb finds your *Lemonhead*—and you cling to me. You say it all. You wanted me on the Red Bed and you bite my sweater—this sweater makes you *crazy*—and there are sparks in the water—we are on fire—and you are the last page of *Ulysses*. You grab me. *Oh God, Joe. Oh God.*

But then you break away. Cinderella when the clock strikes twelve.

You remember what you are. A mom. My boss.

And you are gone.

5

I know, I know. It was just a kiss. I barely felt your Murakami and I didn't lick your Lemonhead but then again. *Oh God, Joe. Oh God.* What a fucking kiss.

When you're with the right person you do the right thing and I was smart to let you go home. I went to my Whisper Room and counted my blessings for all the bad women who came before you. I get it now. Of course you ran. Real love is a lot, especially at our age.

I don't go to Pegasus on the way to work—your kiss is my caffeine—and you pushed me away, but this is the nature of grown-up love, especially when kids are involved: push, pull, push, pull. I open the door to the library—*pull*—and you aren't at the front desk and the Mothball on duty doesn't like me. The day we met she asked if I'm *a Bellevue Goldberg* and when I said no she turned her nose up at me. She points at Nomi's chair.

"You mind moving that? It's too cold by that window."

I move the fucking chair into the fucking stacks and I grab my lunch—*WE eat the beef and WE eat the broccoli*—and I tell the Moth*snob* that I'll be right back and she rolls her eyes. Rude. "I hate to break it to you, but your little friend called in sick today."

No. *No.*

The Mothsnob just chuckles.

You're not *sick* and I go into the break room and where are you? Were you really that drunk? Was our kiss made of tequila? I storm away from Silverstein's *Whatifs* and I pass your office and your door is closed. There is no light in the attic and you're not *sick*. You're scared.

I take my post in Fiction and the day drags. I sell a recently widowed accountant on some Stewart O'Nan and I get a day-tripping lesbian to read the first chapter of *Fashion Victim* and I am good at my job but I am better when you're here to chime in. All day I check my phone and you don't text and I don't text and you kissed *me* so maybe I should be the one to text you and I try to find the words.

Hi.

But that's too fucking wimpy.

Hey.

But that's too fucking cocky.

Are you there?

But that's too fucking pushy.

I'm here.

But that's too fucking needy.

I hate cell phones because if it was 1993 I wouldn't *have* a fucking phone and did you tell Melanda about our kiss? Did she get into your head? I walk out to the Japanese garden. I could bail on my shift—I'm just a volunteer—and I could pop by your house and be the Cusack to your valedictorian but I can't do that because Nomi's the one who's graduating this year, not you. And I don't do that. I don't "pop by" and I don't steal phones, not anymore. I check your Instagram—nothing—and I check the Meerkat's Instagram but there's nothing about you, nothing but Klebold. I want to share a picture of *Love Story* but I would never be that lame with you. That blunt. That clingy.

I need to talk to you now because the longer we're apart, the more the kiss seems like a scratch in the windshield that's easily sealed and I want to know why you're hiding.

At the end of my never-ending shift I skulk back to the break room, wondering if I used too much tongue and then the door opens. It's you. Your eyes are puffy and you fake a smile. "Hi."

"Hey," I say. "You're here."

Do we hug? We don't hug. You're wearing a faded green sweater and you don't smile. You gnaw on your lip—you didn't get enough sleep—and you say you just stopped by to pick up a few things. You sit across from me like we're a couple of Mothballs comparing our MRI results, like you weren't sucking on my tongue a few *hours* ago. I lean over the table to get *Closer* and you arch your back. Cold. *Farther.*

"Look," I say. "The last thing I want to do is make you uncomfortable."

"I know," you say. "I feel the same way."

I don't speak. You don't speak. You told me so much last night but I am getting that sick feeling that you didn't tell me everything, that what you told me isn't the whole story, but only part of the story. You are looking at me as if you are warming me up for the news. The bad news. The worst news in the world.

And here it comes. Those treacherous words: "Joe . . . we can't do this. You didn't tell anyone, did you?"

"Of course not, Mary Kay. You know I'd never do that . . ."

You are too relieved. "Okay, good, because if anyone here found out . . . if anyone said anything to Nomi . . ."

"Mary Kay, look at me."

You look at me. "I am a steel fucking *trap.* You have my word."

You calm down a little, but you're still flinching, looking over your shoulder, a paranoid inmate on *Crucible* Island. You don't let me talk. You say that last night was a *drunken mistake*—no—and you weren't thinking clearly—yes you fucking were—and I tell you that you were perfect and you shudder. "I am anything *but* perfect."

My words are coming out all wrong and I know you're not perfect. I'm not perfect, but it would be too cheesy and needy to tell you that *we* are perfect together.

You purse your lips, those lips that are puffy from my kiss. *Me.* "Can we just go back to normal? You know . . . how we were?"

I bob my head like a trained seal that couldn't make it in the wild. "Absolutely," I say. "I wasn't expecting to rush into anything with you. We can take it slow. I *want* to take it slow."

It's a big fat lie and you cluck. "That's the thing, Joe. There is no 'it.' There can't be an 'it.' I have a daughter."

"I know."

"I can't be getting home drunk after midnight. She has to come *first.*"

"Of course Nomi comes first. I know that."

You hide your face behind your hands and tell me that you're not *emotionally available right now* and I want to take a sledgehammer to the chip in the windshield and smash the glass because you're making *our* kiss about *your* daughter. You pull your hands away. "It's her senior year, Joe, and I don't want to miss any part of it . . ." Then don't spend two nights a week at a fucking wine bar with Melanda. "She needs me. She doesn't have a lot of friends." You raised an independent daughter who likes to read and so what if she's not a minisocialite the way you were? Neither was I at that age. "To you she's halfway out the door, all grown-up . . . But time flies and it's almost Thanksgiving and in a few months, she'll be away. And I just can't make any big changes when change is already coming." Ha! As if life is ever that predictable and you should let me in now, right now, so that I'm carving your turkey next week and you are wrong, so wrong and you sigh. "Do you get it?"

"Of course I get it, Mary Kay. You're right, there's no rush. We can put this on hold."

You smile. "What a relief. Thank you, Joe."

You win because you built the boxing ring—Me vs. Nomi—and I can't hit above the belt, in the womb. That said, you came to see me and you wouldn't be justifying yourself to me if you didn't care about me, if you didn't want me eating your mashed potatoes and your Murakami. *Yeah,* there was something off about your little speech, Mary Kay, because deep down, you know you belong with me now, right now.

Our chairs squeak when we stand and you hang your head. "Do you hate me?"

You're better than that. You don't ask stupid questions. But I give you the stupid answer you deserve right now. "Of course I don't hate you. Come on. You know that."

Then you bite your lip and say the worst word in the English language. “Friends?”

You cannot shove me onto a tufted sofa with Seamus and Melanda and we’re not *friends,* Mary Kay. You want to fuck me. But I shake your hand and repeat your hollow sitcom of a word that does not apply to us. “Friends.”

6

I go outside. I walk and I walk and my pinky toes burn—these sneakers are for show, not for this—and I walk away from your house and I want to walk *into* your house and I really did fuck up last night, today. I should have torn off your chastity tights. I should have brought you home or I should have gone home with you and there is no going back and I am the *man.* Bainbridge is safe, but did I text you to make sure you got home okay?

Nope.

You'd been drinking and did I insist on being your escort?

Nope.

I walk into Blackbird and the whole fecal-eyed family is in here—even the grandfather—and this island is too fucking small and there are so many of them and there is only one of me and I get a coffee and sit outside on a bench.

I go on Instagram. Bad Joe. Bad. Night is falling and Nomi posted a picture of you on your sofa and you are asleep in your clothes.

When mom is "sick." #Hangover.

I wish I could like this picture, I wish I could love this picture but I don't feel the love right now. My toes are on fire, my whole body is on fire but you're out cold, dead to me, to the world. I take a screenshot of the photo and examine every corner, every centimeter. I'm not invading your privacy, Mary Kay. We all post our photos knowing that *our followers* will zoom in to grade us. I zoom in. My heart beats.

The fecal-eyed family barges onto the street and none of them say hello—FUCK YOU, FAMILY—and I look down at my phone and what the hell, Mary Kay? There's a bottle of *beer* on the end table that makes my blistered toes pound. You don't drink beer, you don't like the taste and you don't let Nomi drink beer and the bottle is open, half empty. Whose is it, Mary Kay? Who the fuck is drinking beer in your house? I send a text to Shortus.

Hey Seamus! That gym kicked my ass today. Beer?

I wait and I walk. My toes are never going to speak to me again.

No can do, New Guy. Doing a ten day dry out. Remember: That voice in your head that says you can't do it is a liar.

Ugh. I *hate* gym culture and the beer isn't his, but whose is it? I reach the beginning of your street and your house is close but if I walk down that street and look in your window . . . I can't. I promised I would be good and being good means believing in you, in us, and hey, it's just one beer. You did look bad today. I don't know everything about you and it's possible that you drink a half a beer to take the edge off when you're hungover and I go home and watch more *Succession* and you don't call, you don't text and Shortus hits me up to tell me that we can get a beer next week *maybe* and phones have made it so easy to be friends without ever having to see your friends and that's one good thing about today. One.

I did it. I survived the longest most mind-fuckiest day of the year and my mind is clear again. I'm calm. I'm not gonna let one stupid bottle of beer get in our way. All that matters is the kiss, Mary Kay. You broke a rule for me. You swore that you would never get involved with some guy while your daughter lives at home and you did.

And you know what? I need to bend a rule too.

This is a scenic island and I've barely done any exploring—I will not go to Fort Fucking Ward without you—and okay, *yeah.* I went on a couple of nature walks in the Grand Forest when I first moved here, but I was too raw to really breathe any of it in.

I tie the laces on my running shoes—my toes won't hate me today—and I zip up my hoodie and I put on my headphones—Hello, Sam Cooke—and I lock up the house and do what all the well-rounded motherfucking men around here do every day, some of them twice a day: run.

I could run on one of the beaches but the coast is rocky and mottled by McMansions. I could run on the sidewalks but why should I waste my time on pavement when I can run in the woods? I didn't design the island, Mary Kay. And it's not my fault that your house is in a development. It's not my fault that you chose to live in a waterfront home where the only thing that separates your backyard from the sea is a two-foot-wide trail that is open to the public.

Your choice, not mine.

I didn't know you when I moved here and you're the one who told *me* that you live *right around the corner.* You've said it a dozen times and you weren't lying and I'm here, not on your street, but on the trail by the water and Jesus Christ, Mary Kay. There's something almost perverse about this trail, about you and your neighbors in *Wesley Landing*. You're all fearless exhibitionists, aren't you? You all choose to live on land that is the opposite of private. You don't have fences because fences would block *your* access to the trail, your view of the foliage, the rocky coast, the water and I would never live like this.

But you do.

I stop to stretch, as all runners must do to keep the muscles loose. Healthy.

There's a large rock on the property line of your house, engraved with the name of your community. It's wider than the trunks of the trees and this is the perfect place for me to stretch my calves. I plant my feet against the back and lean over and it feels good to stretch and as luck would have it—and at some point my luck did have to turn around—I have a view of your deck. Who knew?

Your sliding glass door is open and you sit on your deck with a half-empty bottle of Diet Coke. See that, Mary Kay? You *do* need me. You sure as fuck don't need any more sugar substitutes. You're on the phone, no doubt with Melanda, and I turn off Sam Cooke and remove my headphones the way a lot of people do when they stretch. I can't hear you and I'm no botanist, but I think there might be poison ivy where I am, so to be safe, I move to another tree. You're used to the people in the woods, on the trails, and you don't flinch at the leaves crunching beneath my feet. I can hear you now. You don't know what to make for dinner. You have salmon steaks in the freezer but they're frostbitten—you need a new freezer, you need to see *my* freezer—and now you're back to counseling Melanda. *Don't text him. You know how it is. If he likes you, he'll text you, and if he doesn't like you, then it's his loss.* She's arguing—can't hear her, don't need to hear her—and the Meerkat is in the kitchen, slamming cabinets. Annoyed. You ask Melanda to hold on and you turn your head.

"Nomi, honey, do you want salmon?"

"Do I ever want salmon? It's like a hundred years old. And before you say it, no, I don't want Mexican chicken."

You laugh—you're sick of your own chicken too—and sigh. Oh, to be a mother and cook every day for thousands of days and be tired of your own Mexican chicken.

The Meerkat slams another cabinet. "Can we cook out on the grill?"

"Well, I guess so . . . Are you already hungry?"

The Meerkat shrugs—whatever—and she grabs a bag of Tostitos and stomps off to her room. You go back to Melanda and I feel for Melanda, who's probably contemplating a singleton cauliflower pizza. "Sorry," you say. "I'm back."

You get a text and you read the text and you respond to the text and is it the man who drank that domestic beer on your end table? You're still counseling Melanda, but what about *us*? When is it your turn to tell her about the Best Kiss of Your Life? And seriously. Who drank that fucking beer?

The acid is cooling in my thighs but it's burning in my heart and you shiver and stand. You go into your kitchen and you close the screen door. You close the slider and it squeaks—you need WD-40—and I can't bear the silence so I put on my headphones. Sam Cooke tries to comfort me but he's wasting his time. I touch my fingers to my toes and the blood rushes to my head and my headphones cancel the noise of the world, but they can't silence the alarm in my limbic system, the one that dings now. Goosebumps crop up on my arms and my legs as the hairs on the back of my neck stand up straight, so many tiny soldiers. Fight or flight. Slowly, I lift my head and the alarm in my brain was right. Someone is here. Three feet away. Armed with a backpack and a cell phone and the two most dangerous weapons in these woods: eyes, blinking beneath unflattering round glasses.

It's your daughter. The Meerkat.

7

On Animal Planet, this is how the lion dies. The lion has no natural predators but an intrusive human on a mission to break the rules of nature shoots him for the fuck of it.

"Hey," she says. "You know that's my house, right?"

I close my eyes. *Please, God. Please don't kill me now.*

The Meerkat remains standing. Emotionless. Still. "Are you okay?"

"Yeah," I say. "I got a cramp."

She nods. Distracted. Good sign. "One time this old guy died out here. It was summer. He had a heart attack."

That stings a little but it also snaps me out of my paranoia. "Well, I'm not *that* old."

"Sorry," she says. "I'm just in a mood because my mom's making me go get charcoal."

Ah, so you were texting with your Meerkat. "You going to the Town & Country?"

She furrows her brow. "We just call it the T & C. God, you're such a newbie still."

That was a little vicious, but it's the same with kids as it is with adults. It's never about you. It's about them. She knows she was rude and she squeezes the straps of her backpack and I smile. Cool Joe. Affable Joe. "I'll head there too," I say. "I could use a Vitaminwater."

Now we're walking and this is normal. This is what people do when they bump into each other and the Meerkat truly isn't alarmed to see me and here comes another jogger—*Hey, Nomi!*—and she knows him too and I flinch at a dog barking in the woods and she laughs. "It's just a dog! Are you scared of dogs?"

"No," I say. I'm still rattled but I have to remember. I was caught off guard, yes. But I wasn't *caught.* "I'm just out of my comfort zone. You grew up in all this but the woods are creepy to me."

I remember taking RIP Beck to the woods and I shudder and the Meerkat grunts. "Oh please," she says. "These aren't *woods*. The real woods are up by my old school. See, when I was in middle school, I found this old Buick there."

I nod. "Cool."

"Yeah . . ." She sounded like you just then. "There were all these empty alcohol bottles . . ." She's so young for her age. *Alcohol.* "And the year before that, there was this big abandoned house in the woods too. *That* place was supercool. It used to be a home for wayward boys."

I raise my eyebrows like a good listener. "Whoa."

"Now *that* was creepy. You go up to the fourth floor and you think the house is gonna fall down and there are old-fashioned wheelchairs and cobwebs. It was so cool. But, whatever. Everything cool here gets destroyed."

"That's just called 'growing up.' See, down at Isla, I listen to these old guys, *actual* old guys, and they sound like you."

"Like me? I don't think so."

"Oh sure, Nomi. They talk about how this place used to be too, how nobody locked their doors and they left the keys in the car and didn't worry about anyone breaking in because there were more crickets and frogs than people."

"I don't think that's true."

"Well, that's the point. Every generation thinks *their* way was the best way."

"But the home for wayward boys . . . that was actually cool. It was a place to go. Then they tore it down and now there's nothing."

We step aside for a set of *cyclists.*

"So you're from New York or something, right?"

That's a good sign, Mary Kay. A show of actual social skills! "Yep," I say. "And it was nothing like this. My library is a good example. We had homeless people in there, crackheads . . . now *that* was scary."

"At least it's real. Everything here is fake, fake, fake."

She tugs on the straps of her backpack and I'm so relieved that I'm an adult. What a nightmare it is to be a teenager, to think there's a place where everyone isn't *fake, fake, fake*. "Sorry," she says. "I'm just mad. My mom always goes crazy before Thanksgiving but this year she's crazy-crazy."

Crazy in *Love*. "Oh?"

"We always stay here but now she's dragging us to Arizona to see my papa."

I wish I had backpack straps to grab because this is news to me. *Be cool, Joe.* "Well, maybe Phoenix will be fun."

She just grunts—*yeah right*. "So what do you do for stupid Thanksgiving?"

Franzen essays and frozen pizza. "I might hop a ferry and volunteer at a soup kitchen."

She waves at a woman raking leaves and the woman waves back and we are normal. This is normal. But then Nomi gives me what the kids call "side eye." "but you said you hated the city. You know there's no *soup* kitchen here, right?"

"*Hate*'s a strong word, Nomi. And I like it here, but on a day like that, it's nice to get out there and help people in need."

She just stares ahead. "People never say that *love* is a strong word."

Is she high? No. She's just overdosing on Klebold poems and loneliness. "Huh. Why do you think that is?"

"Whatever. I'm just annoyed cuz my mom told me not to say I hate her but she took my *Columbine* again and I have all these notes in it and I *do* hate her for that and dragging us to Phoenix. Anyone would. And don't tell me she's just looking out for me. You're wrong. She's a hypocrite. She's mad because it's *Columbine.* She wouldn't be mad if I was into some stupid story about horny babysitters and I'm sorry but *Columbine* is the best. It is *the* book."

And now I miss being a teenager, that salty conviction that you have found it, the thing that makes your mind make sense to you. You'd want me to be compassionate, so I tell her I get it, that I too love that book. She just looks at me. Suspicious Meerkat eyes. And no wonder. Adults lie all the time, but not this one!

"All right," I say. "The part that really stuck with me was all the Eric stuff, fooling his probation officer, how easy it was for him to convince all these so-called smart adults that he was okay. That's the problem with this country, the Injustice System is pretty ineffective."

I want to talk about incompetent social workers but the Meerkat doesn't care about *stupid Eric* and this is why she doesn't have friends, because she doesn't understand that people take turns. She's back to ranting about Dylan's poems and this is my chance to save her, to help her.

"I get it," I say, because that's the first rule of helping any kid. You have to validate their feelings. "But I think your mom's upset cuz . . . well, this therapist I went to once, he told me that sometimes we all get a mouse in our house."

"Are you a slob?"

I picture her going home and telling you I have *mice.* "No," I say. "See, it's a metaphor. The mouse is something you can't stop thinking about or doing."

"And the house is your head. Yawn."

"I know," I say. "It's a little simple but the point is that when you get *really* into something, it feels good. But it's not necessarily good for you. I've been there a buncha times."

She is quiet. Kids are a relief, the way they just shut down and think when they feel like it. And then she looks at me. "What was your thing?"

Women. Terrible city women. "Well, when I was a kid it was this movie called *Hannah and Her Sisters*."

She turns her nose up at me and oh fuck that's right. *Melanda.* "Eew," she says. "That's Woody Allen and he's on Melanda's DNW list . . ."

"Do Not Watch?"

"Yep," she says. "And he's at the top. Like the tippity top."

"Well, your teacher is sure on *top* of things."

"She's more like my aunt."

Melanda is the mouse in *your* house. "Well, my point was . . . that movie was my *Columbine,* the thing that changed my life. See, I lived in New York but I didn't live in *that* New York and I wanted to live in that movie. I stole that tape from Blockbuster, watched it every second I could."

Nomi responds by repeating that Woody Allen is bad, just like his movie and I won't fuck up like I did in the diner. "Okay, but does Melanda think it's okay for you to read Dylan Klebold's poems?"

She growls at the trees above. "There is literally no comparison. He was my age."

"Okay . . . but you have to admit, he did some terrible things . . . Explain why you think that's okay."

No kid wants a pop quiz and she groans again. "It just *is.*"

"Look, Nomi." I am channeling Dr. Nicky. "We got off track. I was just trying to tell you that it's not always good to have a mouse in your house, no matter what the mouse is."

"Did you really read *Columbine*? The whole book?"

I'm not RIP Benji and I never lie about books, especially with my potential stepdaughter. "Yep."

"Did you also read all the stuff Dylan wrote that's online?"

Kids do this. They bring it back to them, especially a kid like Nomi, younger than her age, going to school every day in those glasses—so wrong—and wishing that some maladjusted boy or girl is writing poems for her but knowing it's not possible because she's watching too closely. She picks at a hangnail. "You know how he writes a letter to the girl he loves and tells her that if she loves him, she has to leave a blank piece of paper in his locker?"

"Yeah," I say. "But he never gave her the letter."

"But he wrote it," she says. "And that was sweet." I hope some exchange student with buckteeth moves here this year and rocks her world and she crosses her arms. "Anyway, I'm still not gonna watch a Woody Allen movie."

"Well, that's fine. Do what you want."

"So you don't care?"

I laugh off the question and maybe I'll go back to school and become a guidance counselor. "Look, Nomi. It's like this. Who cares what Melanda thinks? Who cares what I think? You only need to decide what *you* think."

She kicks a rock. "Well I can't watch *any* movie tomorrow anyway cuz we have our stupid *family bonding*."

I'm not a part of your family but I *am* a part of your family and I force my voice to be steady, as if I'm asking for directions. "What's that mean for the Gilmore Girls?"

"Well, first we oversleep. So we wind up on the eleven o'clock even though we said we'd take the ten."

"And then . . ."

"We take the ferry and walk around and look at tchotchkes."

"Tchotchkes."

"We also go to bookstores or whatever, but you know how it is. Mostly tchotchkes."

Your desk *is* crowded with tchotchkes and I laugh. "Yep."

"Then we go to a restaurant with a long line and my mom is too hungry to wait and I'm like 'Just put our name in' and she won't do it and then the people who walked in *after* us get a table and I'm like '*See, Mom?*' . . ." You said that she was the problem and she says that you're the problem and I can't wait to be a part of your fucking family. "And then she wants *pizza* but then she wants dumplings and she's like 'Oh let's go to this place I heard about from Melanda.'"

I laugh. "Been there."

"And then we go and the place isn't open yet cuz she can barely work Yelp and we just walk around starving and look at *more* tchotchkes and then she wants some tchotchke she saw in the morning and she gets paranoid that someone else got it and we run back to the shop and it's gone and she's all *waaah.*"

You're afraid that you're gonna lose your shot with me and I smile. "Then what?"

"She still can't make up her mind about another stupid tchotchke because that would mean making a decision so we go to a coffee shop and she gets mad when I take my book out, like we're supposed to talk *all the freaking time.* But it's BS cuz she's sick of me too and she takes *her* book out and then we come home. And that's our family bonding. The end."

I applaud and the Meerkat laughs, but then she turns into a young version of you, serious. "It's really not as stupid as it sounds. I'm not mean."

"You're not mean. Family is . . . it's a lot."

"It's just weird to like . . . *try* to bond, you know?"

I do know. I remember sitting with Love in prison and trying to feel in love with her and Nomi's done with me. "I'm gonna get a coffee first. See ya."

I wave. "Say hi to your mom."

She heard my request but she's already distracted because she ran into my fecal-eyed neighbors and I can't rely on Nomi to tell you about our great conversation. She runs into people all the time because that's life here and she's mad that you took her *Columbine* away. I walk into the *T & C* and it's bustling. I feel good. I bent the rules and the universe rewarded me, Mary Kay, because now I know about your plans for tomorrow and I am on board.

It *is* time for our family to do some fucking bonding.

8

I know life is ugly. I knew that Bainbridge Island was never going to be *exactly* like Cedar Cove. I'm waiting to board the ferry and this guy in line in front of me is wearing a knit fucking skullcap—someone made it for him, you can just tell—and yellow-framed sunglasses and he's rubbing his son in my face, a lesser Forty with a runny nose. He's also with his wife, the one who knit that stupid skullcap and lied to him, told him he can pull off yellow shades. She's a puffy-jacket sourpuss and she sniffs her coffee—*I think this is oat milk, babe*—and I am alone and they are together and it is absurd.

But not for long, right? Right.

I am taking the 10:00 A.M. ferry to Seattle to get there before you and I'm a little pushy—*Gently, Joseph*—but I want to escape from the in-your-face family that isn't mine so I move to the left side of the boarding throng into a pack of lawsuit-hungry retired lawyers just fucking *hoping* that someone's landscaper mows their lawn because it would give them a project. Yes, it's twee here. If you go to the police station on your birthday, you get a free donut—you don't even have to show ID—but there are twenty-five thousand residents eating locally farmed beets and commuting to Seattle, forming little commuter cliques. Debbie Macomber would feel for me, alone on a Saturday, now marooned with techies talking soccer. I belong nowhere but this is temporary and I'm on board—that's progress—and I put on my headphones and break left for the stairs—two at a time—up to the sundeck. The air helps. The sea, too, a far cry from that heady brown Malibu foam, and I sit on a bench but I'm faced with a wall clock covered by a sign that reads I AM BROKEN.

I find another place to sit—gotta be positive—because it's a big day for us, Mary Kay. I'm not gonna interrupt your *bonding* with your daughter and I'm not "stalking" you. My plan is simple. I'll have some "me time" and you'll have your family time and I'll watch for the signs; when I notice that the two of you are getting sick of each other, I'll "bump into you"—*Joe! What a nice surprise!*—and we'll ride back to the island together. Then, we'll have dinner at my house. (I bought salmon steaks and they're not fucking frostbitten like yours.) Thanksgiving is five days away and that's plenty of time for you to cancel your trip to Phoenix, and you'll do that after you realize that you can date me and be a good mom at the same time.

I walk toward the bow, to another bank of benches, and I zip up my jacket. It's not freezing, but it isn't *springtime for Hitler* and I take off my headphones because people up here are polite, alone like me. No one is forcing a neighbor to overhear one side of a cell phone conversation about a busy boring life and I can't get that clock out of my head.

I AM BROKEN.

I check Love's Instagram—I AM NERVOUS—and Forty is biting his nanny *Tressa,* who says that my son reminds her of Adam Fucking *Levine* and Love is laughing—it isn't funny—and there is nothing I can do. I delete the fucking app and shove my phone back in my pocket but then I freeze. I blink. I wish I could delete my body because what the fuck, Mary Kay?

You're here. You and Nomi are on this boat, my boat, the one you're supposed to miss. You're thirty feet away and you're leaning over the railing and I scoot across the bench, closer to the center of the vessel and I pick up a newspaper and listen to my heart beat between my ears.

Calm down, Joe. This is like yesterday. If you see me, you see me. It's fine. People go to Seattle and I am people. I bend the upper corner of the newspaper and whoever is driving this ship decides that it's time to go and we're on the move.

You pull a fleece hat out of your saggy, bottomless purse and you offer it to the Meerkat and she deflects. I can't hear you, but I see you throw your hands up and look heavenward—help me, Jesus!—and the Meerkat sulks and stares at the horizon. You two are off to a rough start and I watched an episode of *Gilmore Girls* last night. They needed Luke at times like this and maybe I should just walk up to you right now and save your morning. I play it out in my head.

Joe, is that you?

Wow! Mary Kay, what a surprise! Do you want to go fuck in the bathroom?

I know. Too much. And the Meerkat might tell you that she told me all about your plans. *Think, Joe, think.* If you saw me, you'd come say hi. That's what friends do. I'm still in hiding and you haven't noticed me yet—long live print newspapers—and the Meerkat leans over the railing. "Ugh," she shouts. "If you don't leave me alone I'm gonna jump, I swear!"

You tell her that's not funny and she tells you to stop being such a worrywart and this is adorable—I love our family—and then an oaf in a *T-shirt* stomps up the stairs and into the frame and Nomi points at this oaf like she knows him.

"Look at Dad," she says. "He's wearing a *T-shirt* and shorts and he's fine."

The word *Dad* is an iceberg and there is no dad. Dad is gone. Dad isn't on your Instagram and Nomi has never said the word *Dad* and our ship is taking on water. Fast.

"Hey, Phil," you say. "Husband of the Year, will you tell your daughter to put a hat on?"

Dad has a name—it's Phil—and I am Leo in the ice water, I will freeze to death on this boat, in this water. The man you call Phil, *husband*—this is not happening—he shushes you and our ship is cruising, we are sinking—and he's a rock 'n' roll type of ass and you are *Married. Buried.*

No, Mary Kay. *No.*

You don't have a husband—but you do—and this guy isn't *husband* material—but he is—and he's not Eddie Vedder and it's not 1997 so why is he sitting there with his feet up—Doc Martens—wiping his slimy hands on his Mother Love Bone T-shirt while he dictates God knows what into his phone? He pecks you on the cheek—and you let him kiss you—and the ballroom on this boat is flooded and the water is cold—and you touch him. His face. You casually break every bone in my body and pull a sweater from your purse.

He won't take the sweater and I can't take this. Won't take this.

Married. Buried.

You must think I'm a moron. The Mothballs didn't tell me and Melanda didn't tell me and Seamus didn't tell me and your little *community* is a clique of mean-spirited liars but fuck *me* because this is what I get for being Mr. Goody Two-shoes because since when do I rely on strangers to tell me the truth about the people I love? You're married. You really are. He's whining about your upcoming trip to Phoenix right now and he sleeps in a bed with you and we can't hang out like a family today because *he* is your fucking family. Not me.

Married. Buried.

He holds up a bag of chips and Nomi claps her hands and I snap a picture of the motherfucker and there's a tattoo on his leg and the ink is black: *Sacriphil.* I remember that band, barely, one of those nineties, not-quite-Nirvana groups and WHY THE FUCK DIDN'T I GOOGLE YOU ON DAY FUCKING ONE?

Your husband is an overgrown fan boy in dirty cargo shorts and he has bad taste in tattoos and he produces another bag of potato chips like some third-rate magician—I hate magic—and I hate him and right now, worst of all, I relate to Nomi because I hate you, Mary Kay. You lied to me. You want Phil's chips and you wave him on and I remember you in the bathroom of the pub, when you were mine, when you kissed me. He tosses the chips to you and you catch the bag like you're in a bridal party, like it's a bouquet.

Married. Buried.

This is why you ran away from me and *this* is why we've been treading water and Nomi screams at the top of her lungs. "Dad! Come look!"

Your husband is an iceberg and I can't take it anymore. This is the story of my life. Everything that should be mine, everyone, they're all snatched away from me. I lost my *son* and I've tried so hard to be decent. Good. I've tried to forget all the Shel Silverstein poems I memorized when I was incarcerated, when I thought I'd actually get to be a dad, and now you do the same. You steal my shot at family and I can't forgive you, the same way I can't forget those fucking poems. You used me, Mary Kay. Love stole my son, but you have stolen my dignity, my self-respect, and I should have staked out your house the day we met.

Everything looks different now. You weren't hazing me at the diner. You were playing fast and loose, weren't you? You thought one of your *Friends* might say something about your husband in passing. And that's why you were looking around in the pub so much on our date. You were afraid we'd get caught. You're a dishonest woman. You don't wear a wedding ring and you criticize your mother for her sham of a divorce but what the hell do you call *this*?

Your husband's angry teenage boy outfit is embarrassing—you must be the breadwinner—and okay. I never directly *asked* if you're married but that's because you're my boss. And okay, it would have been presumptuous of you to passive-aggressively declare your marital status—*So my husband loved the Lisa Taddeo book*—because that's not your style. But who the fuck are we kidding?

Your husband would never read the Lisa Taddeo book. He's not a reader. I can tell and you are right, Mary Kay. We see what we want to see and I didn't want to see it. Same way I didn't want to believe that Love was capable of stealing my child.

I grab the railing. The ship hasn't sunk just yet. Yes, you're married, but if your marriage was any good, you wouldn't be so into me. I can still save us. I google you—I should have done this weeks ago—and there you are, Mary Kay DiMarco and oh no, oh *no.* Your husband isn't a fan of that fucking band. He is *in* the band, the lead singer—of course—and Google knows his name because Phil DiMarco was that guy who sang that song.

You're the shark inside my shark, you're the second set of teeth and I just die underneath.

I'm the one who *dies underneath* because that's you on the cover of his album and the history is sinking in, sinking our ship. Those are your legs under your black tights and gender-reveal parties are nothing compared to this big reveal—*It's a dad! It's a husband! It's a has-been rock star in shorts!*

We're getting close to the dock and I'm not gonna be *intimidated* by your husband. You were his muse and you're not my muse. I respect you as a *person.* And okay, so he was kinda semifamous but he would never be in a clue on *Jeopardy!* and I'd rather be your work husband than the husband you loathe so much that you can't even speak of him in casual conversation.

He walks up to you and puts his arms around you, and again, the boat is flooded and the water is cold, but I won't let it get to me. I will not fucking freeze to death. You are telling him he needs to put on a sweater—I know you—and it's mind-bending to see you like this. *Married. Buried.* How long did you think you could get away with this, Mary Kay?

We're slowing down and you're searching for something in your purse, and I bet you've been winging it because that's what you do—*Nomi was "the surprise of your life"*—and before I came into your life, you were on cruise control. You *married a music man* and I'm sure you loved him at first. You were his *tiny dancer* and foxes *do* like attention—your body parts are on the cover of his album—but times change. You told me that you never understood why your mother left your father. You called it a *sham divorce.* That's why you're still in the cage with Phil. You don't know how to leave that rat, do you?

Nobody in your family is hungry, but you're rummaging through your purse. You pull an Ani Katz book out of your purse—I told you to read that one!—and you pause. You're thinking about me. You want me. And then you shove it back in your purse and *I* feel guilty because you must be constantly worried about what happens when the book is out of the bag, when I find out about your life, when Phil finds out about me.

Your rat groans. "Emmy, stop it already, *man.* We're not starving to death."

"No," you say. "I know I have a candy bar. It's in here somewhere."

You and I are the same, aren't we? We sacrifice our feelings and our desires for the people we love. The Meerkat is annoyed—*Forget it, Mom*—and Phil is disinterested—*Em, I'm gonna eat with Freddy.* But you're still looking for it, determined to provide for your family, and then you prevail and wave a 3 Musketeers bar in the air.

"Got it!"

It's impossible not to love you right now, the sheer joy on your face, the win. You bite the wrapper of the candy bar that you *knew* was in your purse and you are the girl who dreamed up the Empathy Bordello. You care about everyone and that includes your rat husband. You tear the candy bar in half and I love you for the big things and the little things, the pleasure you take in sharing. But there's a fine line between selfless devotion and self-destruction and you give one half of your 3 Musketeers to Nomi and the other half to Phil and what's left for you?

We disembark and I stay out of the way and let you and your family cross the bridge into the city while I take the stairs down to the street. I watch Phil wave goodbye to you and the Meerkat and of course this rat stayed with you—who would leave you?—and you couldn't leave him. He's too pathetic, exposing his legs so that everyone can see his *Sacriphil* tattoo. You stayed because it wouldn't be fair for Phil to fail as a rock star and a husband.

And I didn't see any of it coming.

I got soft when I moved here, trying so hard to be "good" as if being good is ever that simple. Life is complicated. Morals are complicated. I wouldn't even be here today if I hadn't bent the rules. I slip into a tourist trap restaurant—I really do prefer our small-town life—and I order a cup of coffee and begin my work. Your husband's band is in shambles but he "works" nights hosting his own radio show called *Philin' the Blues*—ugh—and if he's up all night, well, I bet you haven't had sex in a long time.

He doesn't care about you, not really. The man lives his life for his fans—they call themselves *Philistans*—and he encourages these loud, lost losers to keep on rooting for a Sacriphil comeback. Our world is fucked—Phil has fans—and your life is fucked—Phil has you—but now that I'm indoors, on my own, I don't feel so bad about any of it.

I'm happy that the jig is up. We're not teenagers and I have no interest in love triangles—never did—and I'm a New Yorker, Mary Kay. I've dealt with rats all my life. It's nothing personal. I don't "hate" them. But rats carry diseases and you're in luck because I know how to get rid of them.

I go to the rat's YouTube channel. I only know the song about the shark, Sacriphil's legitimate hit. But it's time to get into the liner notes, the deep tracks that tell your story. The first song at the top of the page is ten minutes and thirty-two seconds long—gimme a fucking break—and it's called "Dead Man Running," and oh Phil, my *man*, don't you worry.

Your time has come.

9

In the sixth grade there was this kid in my class named Alan Brigseed. Obviously they called him Alan *Bad*seed and he was portly. Walked with a limp because of an issue with his bones. Wore football jerseys to school every single day and was determined to be a quarterback for the Giants. Real life isn't *Rudy* and back then I knew that poor Alan *Bad*seed would wind up working at a Dick's Sporting Goods in New Jersey—I was right—and two years ago, poor Alan *Bad*seed died in his mother's basement while he was jerking off.

Your husband reminds me of Alan, Mary Kay. I spent the past thirty-six hours learning everything there is to know about Phil DiMarco. I read every profile. I watched every ancient on-screen interview where he talks over the other guys in his band. I dug into the *Philin' the Blues* archives and I went on his Twitter—he doesn't understand hashtags and writes *Peace#* at the end of every tweet—and most of his followers are aging dope whores—apologies to dope and prostitutes—and they tag him in pictures of their implants and sometimes he *likes* those pictures and do you know about this? Or did you just stop caring a long time ago?

Like Alan Brigseed, Phil won't give up the dream. And like Alan Brigseed, Phil would be better off dead. He doesn't work. He makes pennies hosting his graveyard-shift radio show—it's a glorified infomercial—five nights a week and okay, so he does make good money on royalties, it's one of his favorite subjects on the *Blues,* but it's a little less every year. There are few things more tragic than a man hell-bent on becoming something he just can't be. You probably expected more "Sharks" to come along, but like so many artists, that was the best Phil had in him.

He was famous for a second. And fame is poison.

Rock star fame is especially vile. It's a drop of food coloring and one drop—one innocent hungry shark in the water—is enough to turn all the clear water red and make it stay that way. Every Sacriphil album is less successful than the one before and it's some Edgar Allan Poe shit, Mary Kay, the slow demise of his falling, rising star, the way he fights it every night on the air, gaslighting *Philistans,* raging against the *industry,* thanking you for saving his *life* as he blames you for *domesticating* him. He plays his part well, claiming that he put his "art" in the backseat so he could throw his *soul* into being a dad. In reality, Phil just fucking failed. The turnover rate in his band is high—scary high—and if he managed a Dunkin' Fucking Donuts he would have been fired because of his inability to play well with others.

I turn on the heat in my car. It's cold tonight and I'm parked outside of your rat's recording studio. I bent the rules for us and bent rules are meant to be broken. I brought two Rachael Ray knives and Phil's untimely death won't tarnish Bainbridge's reputation as a safe haven. He's just famous enough to be a wild card and when an early morning jogger finds him on the street tomorrow, it will seem like the work of a *Philistan* gone crazy, karmic payback after years of getting close with his *fans,* following them back on Twitter, encouraging them to *pop by and hang.* The cops might also think it's a drug deal gone bad because I've also learned that your husband is in recovery. I listened to every song he ever wrote and I'm sorry to say it, but you are nothing compared to his true love: heroin.

I know it all, Mary Kay. I know that you had to "downsize" a few years ago—it's all so fucking relative—and move to what Phil calls your *sellout, suit-and-tie saltbox* in Wesley Landing. He is pretty funny, I'll give him that, but the privilege of it all! Like he *deserves* a Led Zeppelinesque castle in the woods because he has *one* song that some people know by heart. I'm so happy I'm not famous. And I have a whole new outlook on you.

You got together with Phil in high school. He was in a band. You were into that.

You got pregnant in college. He put a needle in his arm and penned the best songs of his life.

You were his muse and then when he couldn't pull off the magic again, you were the one he blamed.

You're his mother. You're his babysitter. You're his enabler.

But tonight, I set you free.

It's *4:00 a.m. and Phil's awfully lonely*—oh how he would hate that reference!—and I should get out of my car, walk inside, and end his life once and for all. I grip the handle of the knife.

I turn up the volume on Phil's swan song—sorry, *man*—and my timing is good, Mary Kay. The poor guy is really going off the rails tonight, ranting about *Lucky Kurt Cobain.*

As always, his mouth is too close to the mic. "It's true, man . . ." His voice isn't what it used to be. "Nirvana is Nirvana because Courtney killed Kurt. And when you're a guy like me, a survivor . . . well, we worship the dead. We put 'em on pedestals. Music just *sounds* better when the singer's a goner and it's the story of a lot of artists . . . you die, you're not around to feel the love, and here comes the love."

He talks as if Kurt Cobain wasn't a star *before* he died and maybe I won't have to kill Phil. Maybe there's an angry mob on the way right now and I check the rearview. Nothing. And of course there's no angry mob. I'm one of ten, maybe twelve, people listening at this late, early hour.

"Aw, man," he says. "I'm not bitter . . ." Oh yes you are, *man.* "But there was this one night me and Chris were jammin' . . . " Impossible to verify. Chris Cornell is dead. "I had this riff . . . he riffed on the riff . . . and let's just say, a cowriting credit on 'Black Hole Sun' woulda been nice . . ." I grip my knife because you do *not* speak ill of the dead, but then he growls. *"Shut it, Phil! Don't be a whiny little bitch!"* He opens a can of *beer.* "Thing is, I'm not a pretty boy and if I looked a little more like cutesy-tootsie Eric Clapton . . ." Oh dear no. No. "Did you guys see that doc about him? I caught it this afternoon when I was half asleep . . ." What a good partner for you, Mary Kay! "Man, Crapton works that schoolboy charm hard . . ." True. "But the guy could be a real fucking *dick* . . ." Also true. "He'd get nasty and drunk onstage. He went after his best friend's girl . . . and did people hate him for it? Nah. He rode the horse into hell, he couldn't finish *Layla,* and Duane Fucking Allman rode into that hellscape like a white knight and *he's* the reason we have 'Bell Bottom Blues.' Some guys, they *inspire* that loyalty in people. When it comes to me . . . well, no one ever bailed me out . . ." Oh dear. "Chris wouldn't come by while I was trying to finish *The Terrible Twos* . . ."

I scroll down the Wikipedia page and there it is, the third album: *The Terrible Twos.* Don't put the word *terrible* in your title, Phil. It's just too easy for the critics to slaughter you.

He analyzes his fizzling career—*a good marriage is a tough thing to write about*—and I revisit one of my favorite interviews with Phil. Nomi was two years old. Phil was out of rehab, once again, withdrawing from the *pink cotton wool* (he stole that metaphor from Eric Fucking *Clapton*). Anyway, Phil compared you to his Gibson—you are not an instrument—and said he could stay clean for the rest of his life if he got to play with you every day. The reporter told you what your *husband* said and your response was telling: "It's not what you expect when you're a muse . . . but what can you do?"

Spoken like a true battered, trapped woman, and I read the lyrics from "Waterbed," the fourth track on *Moan and Groan.*

I gave you what you want, it's a waterbed
I'm seasick for you, will you gimme head?
Why take 'em off if you won't give it up?
Why lay down if I'm not enough?

You weren't his *muse.* You were his whipping post and you're ashamed, aren't you? You were young, Mary Kay. I made mistakes too—RIP Candace—but I didn't *marry* my mistake. I know, I know. You were pregnant and he wrote his twisted love letters about his fear of commitment when he was young too. But then I turn his show back on and he's digging deep into the past as always, blasting the pity-party dirge he calls "Sharp Six."

Aw you got to do it, MAN
You mute her scream with a RING, they command
A Hustler . . . *You want it*
It's at the newsstand . . .

Summer comes in like a FIRE and it goes
And where she WENT you don't know
Her body . . . You want it
But now it's out of reach . . .

The alarm cuts you UP at sharp six
You're just another TOM, you're a Dick
Your Philstick . . . It's broken
She burnt your wick . . .

You wake up in a CRATE and you're dead
She's in a BARREL in your bed
A crate in a barrel . . . A barrel in a gun . . .
Remember . . . the summer . . .
The end of all the fun . . .
The barrel of a gun (Repeat 10x)

The song ends and he cackles. "Man," he says. "Was I some kinda prick or what?"

Okay, so he regrets the lyrics. But he still plays the song. A *Better Man* like Eddie Vedder would bury those hateful, sexist words, but Phil is no Eddie Vedder and this most hateful album is also the most popular. "Well, Philistans, I gotta drain the lizard."

He's a liar and he doesn't need to take a piss. He cracks a window and he smokes a cigarette—I bet that's not allowed—and he stares at the building across the street and the playlist is a brainwashing exercise. He plays a go-nowhere *Sacriphil* B-side between bigger songs by Mudhoney and the Melvins as if we, the listener, are supposed to think Phil and his cronies are in the same league as those legends, as if we the listener are that fucking stupid.

"Well," he says. "Phil's back and ya know, every time I hear 'Shark,' I gotta give a shout-out to my girls at home. You all know that I'm nothing without them. Hell, sometimes I think, What if Emmy never got pregnant . . . I wouldn't have my daughter *or* my 'Shark.' "

He "loves" you but you don't love him. When you love someone, you scream it from the rooftops but you don't even wear a ring and the Meerkat doesn't talk about him either. Your friends don't ask about him. You think leaving him would kill him, push him off the wagon, and you're trapped in this codependent cycle of abuse and he sighs. "All right, Philistans. Fun fact . . ." Fact as in fiction. "First time I played 'Shark' for Kurt, he tucked his hair behind his ear and said he wished he wrote it. I got the chills, man." BULLSHIT, YOU LIAR. RIP KURT WOULD NEVER. "Maybe that's why 'Shark' is still burnin' after all these years and ya gotta forgive me, my moon's blue tonight . . ." Oh God. "I know Kurt's a god. You know Kurt's a god. He fell for a Courtney and I fell for my girl and . . . well, I'm still here. I got another 'shark' in me. You know it. I know it. Peace out, Philistans, and to all my NA brothers and sisters, I'll bump into you tomorrow."

He plays "Shark" at the end of *every* fucking episode and I hate that I love this song. In theory, it should suck, guitars on top of bass and I forgot about the cowbell and young Phil wails, before cigarettes got the best of his voice, singing at you, at me, at everyone on the planet.

You are the shark inside my shark, you're the second set of teeth
The roses ain't in bloom, the thorns hide in the wreath
On my front door you bang and bang, let me in, lock me out
You hang me up, I twist, you shout
Eat me, bite me, slay me, spite me
Your body invites me and your fire ignites me and
Why are you the flame (the only one to blame, you and your game)

You swell and hide and now you lock me in this frame
Where I can't move, I can't breathe, I just die underneath
Cuz I'm the shark inside your shark, oh I'm the second set of teeth . . .

I kill the volume but I have no choice. I have to finish. I have to sing the rest.

You're the shark inside my shark but I'm the shark inside your shark
You're me, I'm you. What can we do? You're me, I'm you
You gnash, I feed . . . you and your seed . . .
But do you want me in your dreams?
Do you love me when I'm clean?
Do you hear me when I—

(Cowbell)

SHARK!

It's *Rhyming for Dummies* and it's a jumbled mess of mixed metaphors but he was smart to end it with another displaced cowbell and I bet you knew that song was gonna be big. I look at your legs on his album. You want me to think you stayed for Nomi, but everything looks different now that I know about your rat. You like being a muse. You still wear your signature tights every day and his music comes from you. Just once I'd like to fall for someone who isn't handicapped by narcissism, but it's too late. I love you. I can't kill his success, but I can pick up my knife.

Your rat he turns out the lights and walks down the stairs and there he is, thirty feet away, on the sidewalk. He leans against the building the same way he does on the cover of his hit single, posing for a camera that isn't there and he lights a Marlboro Red like he's James Fucking Dean, like his imaginary *Philistans* will summon the courage to emerge from the shadows. He blows smoke rings and watches them fade into the halogen mist and I don't know how to blow smoke rings. Do you like that, Mary Kay? Are you into that kind of shit?

I slip Rachael up my sleeve and I'm ready but he pulls a rabbit out of *his* sleeve. His phone is ringing and he takes the call and it's you.

"Emmy," he says. "Babe, you okay? Why you up?"

I let the knife fall out of my sleeve. You're awake. You were listening. I don't call you Emmy and he says it too many times—*Emmy Emmy Emmy*—and he swears that he got a lot of sleep today—lazy fucker—and he tells you that he's gonna go write through the sunrise—oh fuck you, Phil—before he hits a meeting. He swears he'll pack his own *shit* for Phoenix—liar—and he chucks his cigarette in a puddle. "I'm down to two packs a day, Emmy. And now you want me to quit for a week for your *dad*? Are you trying to make me fall off the wagon? Is that what you want?"

I don't know what you're saying. He doesn't know either because he holds the phone away. But he must be able to hear *a little* because he takes a deep breath and cuts you off.

"Emmy, Emmy, Emmy. Relax. For the nine millionth time . . . it's a *show.* It's an act. The label likes my attitude and Nomi's friends . . . they're not up listening to *me.* Stop caring about what other people think . . ." I wish I could hear you. "Emmy, Nomi doesn't give a *shit* if I go to Phoenix and I told you, I'm going. You win again, babe! . . . What is with you, lately? What is it?" Me. It's me! "Christ, woman, I'm missing a whole *week* of shows and still you're bitching at me. What the hell more do you want from me?" You might be crying. Or apologizing. He rubs his forehead. "Emmy. Baby, come on. Don't do that. You know I love you too."

My blood runs cold. Hot. No.

He gets into his jalopy and turns on one of his own unknown songs and I let go of my knife. *Love you too* means that you said *I love you.* I turn on my car, I blast my Prince, but "When You Were Mine" can't silence *the shark inside my shark.*

You love him. You do.

It's a miserable drive home—*A crate in a barrel, a barrel in a gun*—and I shove Rachael into the glove compartment. This is worse than RIP Beck and RIP Benji. They didn't have a child and twenty fucking years together. I have to be smart about this. *Yeah,* I want Phil gone. But the real problem is you, Mary Kay. In your own stunted adolescent, nurturing, self-destructive, misguided maternal, codependent way . . . you really do love your husband. I can run him off the road, but that would be dangerous. It might even make things worse. I need help—*Hey Siri, how do you kill love?*—but who am I kidding? She doesn't know. No one knows. I have to figure it out myself, alone, while you're in *Phoenix* carving turkeys and reinforcing your dysfunctional family bonds.

I drive to Taco Bell. I can have anything I want, but all I want is you, so I get one of everything.

Happy Early Fucking Thanksgiving to me.

10

It's the most . . . horrible time . . . of the year—mid-fucking-December—and we're in a rut. As it turns out, you're not just beholden to your husband. You're also responsible for your *dad*. You were only supposed to be in Phoenix for a week, but the day after Thanksgiving, your father fell down the stairs. The Mothball Howie Okin knows more about your father's health than I do—we have to fix that—and Howie informed me that your dad has an *osteochondral lesion*, which is Howie-speak for a hole in his bone. Being the good daughter that you are, you put your rat and your Meerkat on a plane and you stayed with your dad to help him move into a new house and I don't begrudge you for helping the old man. I'm not a *what about me* asshole, but your dad isn't the only one in pain. I have a *cardiochondral lesion*, Mary Kay. You don't call. You barely text. Time drags and time flies—November already turned into December—and I walk outside to get the paper and fecal-eyed Nancy is hammering a wreath onto her front door. She doesn't wave and I don't wave and WHEN THE FUCK ARE YOU COMING HOME, MARY KAY?

I have been so good. I didn't kill Phil. I've "processed" my feelings about your secret life. I've given you "space." And on the rare occasion that you *do* text me, I don't harp on you about your return. I asked you exactly once and your response was infuriating. *Soonish, I guess, I think.*

Soonish (adj) FUCKING BULLSHIT, MARY KAY

But I'm just as bad at long-distance relationships. I look at the text I sent you last night.

Me: *How ya doin'?*

I couldn't have done any worse and I know it. You are not *ya* and it's a dorky, broad question, the kind of whining you don't need right now and I pour Rice Chex into a bowl. I try to read the paper but I don't want any more bad fucking news. I go to Love's *Instagram*—I am acing Holiday Induced Self Destruction 101—and I watch my son whip his arm with *another* early "prezzie," a plastic fucking sword and this is no good either so I get up. I put on your favorite black cashmere sweater and the sweater and I go outside and get into my ice-cold car. Nancy's husband is in his car, too, warming up the *Land Rover* for his wife, per usual. I half-wave at him and he pretends he doesn't see me—*Happy Christmas to you too, asshole*—and Nancy swans out of their house. She's on the phone—*Yes, Mom, but we need a fuller tree for our e-card photo*—and I feel like the human equivalent of a fucking *e-card,* destined for an *e–trash bin.* Nancy gets into her nice warm car and she loves her husband and he loves her (maybe) and he's a tool. She's a tool. But they have each other and you won't even tell me how you're *doin'*.

I hit the road and lower the volume on "Holly Jolly Christmas" because you haven't called me once since you've been gone. (So much for *Friends*.) I bet you call your rat *husband* and my phone buzzes—did you read my mind?—but no. You didn't. It's just *Shortus.* He wants to grab a beer again—*CrossBores* are not impervious to the holiday blues—and I won't waste another night with him. He doesn't know shit about you—he's not your *Friend* either—and all he really wants to do is bitch about all the presents he has to buy for his *girls* in the shop.

Halfway to the library, I slow down—I am in no rush for my daily disappointment—and I check your Instagram—nothing—and I proceed to my happy place, which is, oddly enough, your husband's fucking Twitter account. His tweets give me hope. Patience. They got me through the first week of your exodus because he spent his time with you whining about . . . *being* with you.

Hey @SeaTacAirport if I go postal it's on you with the xmas tunes. Peace#

Thanksgiving is the opposite of rock n roll. Peace#

Hey Phoenix. Smoking is legal. Deal with it. Peace#

My sponsor chose the wrong day to lose his cell phone. InLaws# SendHelp#

The wife let me out of my cage. Check me out at @copperblusPHX if you want to hear some REAL music. I'll sign your tits AND your T-shirts JK just the shirts, ladies. Whipped# Peace#

Phil is a sad sack and I have to stay positive, Mary Kay. You were probably *happy* about the hole in your dad's bone because it meant that you got a break from Phil. He's so transparent. *Yeah,* he boasted about his show, but the show must have been a total bust because he didn't post a single picture with a single fan, let alone a woman with *tits.* Even better, your rat appeared in exactly zero of your staged family photos with the Meerkat . . . but that's nothing new. The rat *never* appears in your photos, presumably because he has some rule about tarnishing his image, because he wants people to picture *young* Phil. (Say what you will about drugs, but the lifestyle agreed with him and I get why he's been *TBT1997#* ever since he and the Meerkat got back from Phoenix. The man was at his best when he was high as fuck and skinny as a rail and he's no George Clooney, Mary Kay. He doesn't get better with age.)

Someone behind me beeps and I wave—sorry!—and "My Sweet Lord" comes on the radio as I pull into the parking lot and *Hallefuckinglujah.* You're here. I wore your favorite sweater—yes!—and I want out of this car and into your orbit so badly that I trip on black ice. *Breathe, Joe, breathe.* I don't want to die, not now, before we've christened the Red Bed—ho ho ho—so I take big, cautious steps and I enter the library and you are tan and your cheeks are fuller than they were a month ago and I like you like this. Nourished. Bronzed. *Here.*

I wave at you. Totally normal. "Welcome back!"

You raise a hand. Robot stiff. As if I never touched your Lemonhead. "Hi, Joe. Hope you had a good holiday. Dolly's in History and we're pretty backed up."

That's it? That's all I get?

Yes. Yes, it is. You're already hiding in your computer and I follow your orders and plod to History and I'm worried about you, Mary Kay. Did your rat catch you gazing longingly at the Bruce Springsteen lyrics I posted, the ones you *liked* at 2:14 A.M. Phoenix time? I know you can't hug me but it's *me.* It's *you.* Don't you want to know how I'm *doin'*?

The day is flying by and *soonish,* it's time for lunch, but you eat alone in your office with Whitney and Eddie. I should be in there with you, catching up, reminding you of what it's like to be with me, but I can't push. I have to remember that you've had no privacy for several weeks. You were drowning in dirty dishes and Nomi's anxiety about her college applications—her first pick is NYU, thanks, Instagram!—and then you were the dutiful daughter. This isn't about me. Right now, you're making up for lost solitude.

I take *my* lunch break in the garden because it's cold but it's not New York City cold and finally, here you are, rubbing your shoulders. No jacket.

"Aren't you freezing?"

I swallow the beef in my mouth. "Nah," I say. "Hey, how was your trip? How's your dad?"

Now would be a good time for you to tell me about the *other* dad in your life but you don't. "My dad's much better, thank you, so that's a relief . . . And at least we had a nice Thanksgiving before he fell . . ." Your holiday was not *nice,* Mary Kay. You and the Meerkat looked like marionettes with guns behind your backs in your family photos. "Anyway," you say, as if I'm just another Mothball. "How about you? Did you have a good holiday?"

The worst part about holidays is the way people talk about them when they're over and you know what I did on Thanksgiving. You saw my pictures. You *liked* them. *I follow you and you follow me* and the rules of Genesis are like the rules of jinx. I am allowed to call you out.

"Well, as you saw, it was mostly me and some books, which is to say it was perfect."

You look down at your lap. "I told my dad about you."

I put down my fork. You love me, more than you did a month ago. "Oh, really?"

"Yeah . . . I don't think I ever spent that much time alone with him. I kept thinking that you two would really get along . . ."

You missed me and I smile. "I'm just glad he's okay. I read about osteochondral lesions. They sound tough."

I am *such* a good fucking guy! I don't make it about me and you're talking lesions and moving trucks and I'm here for all of it and then you touch your hair. You *want* to make it about me. "You really would like my dad, Joe. He's old school, obsessive about his books, all of his Tom Clancys lined up in alphabetical order. He airs them out and wipes them down them once a week. All these years, I never knew that about him. I thought you'd get a kick out of it."

I feel for you, Mary Kay. I thought I suffered. But you were forced to be inside of your marriage for a solid week. You played nurse. You dealt with a *move* and how did you get through it? You daydreamed about me. You stored up anecdotes for me and now you feed them to me and I'm happy that you didn't tell me how you're *doin'* in a stupid text. Sometimes you love someone so much that you can't bear a taste or a text because only this kind of moment will do. Shared air. Stillness on a love seat. Your silence is heavy with what you don't say, that you want me to be with you the next time you fly away. I love that you love me. I love that you came out into the cold to see me and we do belong together, but not like this. *Married. Buried.*

I close the lid on my box of beef and broccoli. "Hey," I say. "Do you mind if I cut out early?"

It's fun to watch you fight the devastation in your body. "Big plans tonight?"

I remember Phil's first tweet today: *Xmas lights. Why? No. Aren't we over this? IsItJanuaryYet# Peace#*

"Well, I special-ordered Christmas lights last month . . ." It's not a lie. It's a pre-truth. "It's kind of embarrassing but I love to string lights."

I am the anti-Phil and I am *your* light. "That's so great."

"Lights are a more-is-more situation, you know?"

You squeeze your paper cup. I know it's hard, being with the wrong person when the right person is right here.

I make a pit stop at Cooley Hardware to pick up lights and luck is on my side—No Seamus!—and I get home and there's a box on my front porch. My serotonin surges and Jeff Bezos is a rich man because he knows how much we all just *love* to get a present, even if it's a present we bought for ourselves.

I hang my lights—take *that,* Phil—and I go inside, down to my Whisper Room. I open my present to myself, but it's really a present for you: *Basic Text,* 6th edition. Author: Narcotics Anonymous.

I'm reading Phil's bible for the same reason that you dipped your toes in the *Cedar Cove* series after we first spoke on the phone. You wanted to know what I'm all about. You wanted to speak my language. I don't need a fucking self-help book, Mary Kay, but I will do whatever it takes to help you to follow your fucking heart and *end* your dead marriage. It's the giving season and tonight, I bequeath my time to you, to us.

I want to write to Dr. Nicky and tell him to read the *Basic Text* because it made me realize what we had in common way back when: addiction to toxic women.

I was up all night and my eyes are bloodshot and puffy—perfect—and I choose an old sweater. Lucky for me, your husband likes to *tweet* about his NA meetings so I'm here, in the parking lot of Grange Hall. I will meet your husband and pretend to be a fellow addict slash *Sacriphil* super fan boy. My plan is simple in theory—befriend him, needle him about his failure to produce another "Shark," make him become the worst possible version of himself and undo everything he learned from his "bible." When I'm in Phil's head, when he's in peak monster woulda-coulda-shoulda-been-and-still-could-if-not-for-the-damn-family mode, well, you'll have no choice but to end your sham marriage. If I do a good job, you'll watch Phil come to terms with the fact that he's not a fucking husband and he's not a fucking father.

He's a fucking rock star, *man.*

And you'll feel justified in leaving him. But if I fuck up . . .

I light another Marlboro Red and I'm pacing the way addicts do before they go to a first meeting. This is risky. You could find out what I'm up to, but you started this, Mary Kay. You didn't tell me about him and the best Christmas gifts never come easy. If and when the three of us are in the same room, I'll tell you the truth, that I went to a meeting for the same reason a lot of people who aren't addicts go to these meetings: It was the holidays. I was lonely.

Right now, I have to focus on the mission, like a dad driving all over the city to find that stupid fucking Cabbage Patch Kid. I hear *Sacriphil* music in the distance and it's him. He's in his jalopy and he's pulling into the parking lot, rocking out to his own song. I breathe. I can do this. Christmas is about miracles and transformation—*Hi, I'm Jay and I'm addicted to heroin*—and Phil gets out of his jalopy and I run through Jay's story: I hurt my back in a car accident, got Oxy, got hooked on Oxy, tried heroin cuz it was cheaper and yesterday . . . well, I won't tell my story today—this is one of those *less is more* situations—but a good actor prepares and the *Basic Text* has good advice for all of us: *Find new playgrounds. Find new playthings.*

Here comes my play*thing* now, still a little porky and sunburnt from his time in Phoenix. I freeze up like a starfucker and stare at him as I try not to stare at him. That's Phil DiMarco! Look at him open the door! Stars: They're just as fucked up as *us*! He disappears into the building and I cough all that crap out of my lungs and pat down my mothy sweater. This is it. I'm going in.

My new *playground* is smaller than I expected: There are two rich ladies—one likes Kahlúa, one likes Percocets—a couple of court-ordered resentful old rich people, and a trio of court-ordered teens. A friendly thirtysomething woman picks up a glazed donut. "Hey," she says. "You ever go to this meeting before?"

"No," I say. "You?"

She smirks. She wears two diamond engagement rings—Jesus—and she nods at your husband who is on the other side of the room, just as bombastic in person as he is on his infomercial. He points at his freshly shaven face, laughing at his own terrible joke. "Ya get it, man? I shaved the beard and now it's *growing* on me!"

"Fair warning," says the woman with two diamonds. "Some people in this group like to talk. A *lot.* But hey, at least it's not boring."

Soon we're taking our seats and the rat is so close and the spirit of Christmas is alive in me—it *is* the most wonderful time of the year—and I introduce myself—my voice is shaky but that's normal—and nobody pushes me to spill my guts.

Good.

Mrs. Kahlúa talks about how much she loves Kahlúa, how hard it is to go to holiday parties, and Princess Percocets gripes about her *self-righteous* daughter, and finally, your rat raises his hand. "Can I butt in?"

He rubs the back of his grimy head and takes a long, ten-months-pregnant kind of pause and I try not to picture you on top of him, grabbing his hair until he finally cuts into all that overblown, selfish silence he imposed on us. "So the wife finally got back from Thanksgiving. Felt like she was gone forever." No shit, Sher*cock,* but this *is* pretty exciting. I get to hear Phil's side of the story, a side even *you* don't get to see. "But it's like we're right back to fighting the way we were in Phoenix. It was rough. Thing One was in a *mood,* man." I know we can't name names but seriously, Phil? *Thing One.* "Me and Thing Two . . . we couldn't do right by her . . ." Thing Two is Nomi but Nomi is not a *thing*. "Thing One was all over Thing Two about some book she's reading . . ." Oh come on, Phil, the book is *Columbine.* "And she was all over me about my cigs." *Cigs.* "I'm not gonna say that cigarettes are good for you, but you know what else isn't good for you? Being nagged."

I start to clap and stop. Starstruck. Fan boy. Phil winks. *Thanks, man.*

"Thing One's got daddy issues but lately it's outta control . . ." I've made you think about things, Mary Kay. I've made you grow. "The whole damn week, she's on me to *participate in the family.* I try to 'participate,' man, I do. A local bar invites me to play . . ."

Bullshit. He tweeted that bar and four other bars. He invited *himself.*

"I score us a table and they're cool with my kid and Thing One flies off the handle. *We don't want to go to a bar! My dad can barely walk right now! Thing Two is seventeen!* Man, I know I'm not supposed to say it . . ." Say it, Phil. Say it! "But Thing One . . . she botched the turkey, she can't stay off *Instagram* and for someone who loves to read so much . . . well she ain't reading lately . . ."

You love me too much to concentrate and soon, we'll be on my sofa reading together.

"And Thing Two is seventeen going on twelve. She needs to grow up . . . All she does is ride her bike around on her own in la-la land . . ." Phil shakes his head. "We used to be a dynasty . . . I was her *king*. She was my queen. We were heroes . . ." Another pregnant pause and the woman with two rings bites her lip. She's not alone. Your poor husband is a recurring joke, Mary Kay. "I didn't cave," he says. "But the thing is . . . yes, I fucking *did* cave, man. I didn't get to play for a whole *week*." Lie. "I know I've said it before . . ." Say it again. Please. "But man, is this it? Is this my *life*?" He shakes it off. "Never mind," he says. "You'd have to be in my shoes to . . . Never mind."

The woman with two diamonds starts talking about her two engagements and Phil isn't listening. He takes his *phone* out and he's typing and tapping his foot and is he . . . is he trying to turn this woman's sob story into a song right in front of her? I want to call 911 and report a theft but the meeting is ending and it's time to mingle and I'm nervous again. We're milling around, eating more donuts, and your rat heads outside and if I want your present to be ready for Christmas, I have to do this.

I put down my donut. I chase your rat.

He's on the way to his car and I'm catching up and I can do this. I am JAY ANONYMOUS: SACRIPHIL FAN BOY. I clear my throat—nervous, he's a rocker—and I scratch my head—nervous, he's your *husband*—and he opens the door and I fake a stumble—*ouch*—and he looks over his shoulder and laughs at me, just a little, and I apologize, just a little, and I pull out a Marlboro Red and I'm stuttering when I begin my first official outreach to *the* Phil DiMarco. "'Scuse me," I say. "Do you . . . Do you have a light?"

He leans against his car like he did in the promo photos for *Moan and Groan* and I wish I was wearing a Sacriphil T-shirt but what can I say, Mary Kay? It's a busy time of year and last-minute shopping is tough.

"Hey, man," he says. "You all right?"

I nod, too starstruck to speak, and he passes me his lighter—Zippo with a naked girl, what a good dad—and I drop it on the pavement and he picks it up and lights my cigarette and thank God you can't see us right now. I look at him like he's the Arc of the Fucking Covenant and I breathe in, out. "Wow," I say. "I'm having a butt with Phil DiMarco."

His face is a Shrinky Dink in the oven, expanding, brightening. "Oh shit," he says. "We got us a Philistan."

"I'm so sorry. Shit. I know we're not supposed to use our names."

"Nah, man, it's cool."

"I had to come up to you, man. The whole time in there, I was like, *I can't move, I can't breathe, I just die underneath*!" He likes to be quoted—all writers are pathetic that way—and he laughs and this is painful, but this is the only way for me to get you what you really want: me. "I thought I was tripping. Phil DiMarco, the most horrifically underrated rock star of all time, is ten feet away from me and man, I'm just . . . *man.*" I drop my cigarette—nerves on top of nerves—and he offers me one of his and I take it. "I can't *believe* I'm smoking a butt with Phil DiMarco."

"You're hard-core," he says. "What about you? You got a name?"

"Jay," I say, happy I worked so hard on my character.

He hawks a loogie on the pavement. "No worries," he says. "It's not like you're blowing my cover. Everyone knows who I am. What's your name again?"

I literally just said it but then again he doesn't even know the name of his daughter's favorite book. "I'm Jay," I say. "Jesus Christ, man. What are you even doing here?"

"Same thing you are, man. Day by day."

"But you're you. I mean . . . come on. You don't need this. That shit you said about Phoenix. How do you even stand it?"

He chuckles. "Yeah, Phoenix sucked."

"See, what you said in there made me think. A few years back, you told *Mojo* that you couldn't go six hours without touching a guitar . . ." I smile. "Or getting laid."

He laughs at his own old bad joke. "Well, that was then, man. Things change."

He doesn't *really* think things change and he's right. They don't. I smoke my *butt* and I hope I don't get cancer from these fucking things. I can't stand the idea of dying before you, leaving you here to miss me. He blows a smoke ring and I try and fail—perfect—and I ash on a pile of old freebie newspapers because he ashed on it first but that's a fire hazard, Mary Kay. Your husband is a fire hazard.

"So," I say. "Can I ask . . . Are you working on anything now?"

"Hell yeah," he says. "Always."

"Good, cuz I am *dying* for a new album. And a tour. People say it's not gonna happen . . . I'm like fuck yes it is. Phil DiMarco is gonna come *back* in a big way."

He picks at his dirty fingernail. "You can't push. Every album comes when it comes."

Spoken like a true procrastinator and I nod. "I never thought I'd get to meet you cuz you don't tour anymore."

"We don't tour right *now,*" he says. *Boom.* "Your album's on the way, I promise."

"I gotta ask. Were you . . . were you writing a song in there?"

"You bet I was. See, as an artist, I go to these meetings for the pathos. Not to sound like a douche . . ." As if the disclaimer doesn't classify him as a douche. "But as an artist I get more out of it. Ya got a beast in you, ya gotta feed the beast. I get a lotta good material in there. *Tons*."

"That's so rad." I was right. He's a thief. "You know, I'm thinking I might go get a guitar . . . a Schecter . . ." Find a new plaything. "You can say no . . . but is there any way I can hit you up for advice?"

He gives me his number and says he has to get home as he quotes his own song—*I got a crate in a barrel and a barrel in a gun.* "Here's my advice about finding a good Schecter . . ." Pregnant pause. "Get a Gibson, man."

I laugh as if that was clever and he starts his car and did I do it? Did I get in his head?

I tune in to his show at midnight, and sure enough, he's wailing about the holidays, pining for the good old days when he had time to focus on his true calling, his music. The man is in pain, Mary Kay. And you can't make him happy. Listen to his "show" and look at his body. He has a *Sacriphil* tattoo. He bled for that band. He took a needle for that band. But your name's not inked on his skin, and it's time for you both to realize it.

11

The next day, I walk into the library and I slink into the back without saying hello but an hour later, you find me. You're *frisky*. You put your hands on Dolly and you tell me that Nomi wants to get a kitten for Christmas.

"Are you allergic or anything?"

"No, I love cats, but she's going away soon . . ." You look right at me. "Do you like cats?" You are so hot for me that you are planning our life together and you squeeze Dolly. Nervous. "I ask because our friends . . . they have three kittens, so you know, you could get one too."

You want us to adopt *kittens* together and I smile. "I love cats. It's tempting."

You pull your hands off Dolly. "Well, it's something to think about. Our cats would be siblings." You fiddle with your belt. "Well," you say. "Let's both think about it, yeah?"

I give you a *yeah* and already my plan is working.

The next day, I go to a meeting and Phil bitches to me . . . about *cats*. "Cats are cool. But do I need one more thing to take care of? Already I don't have enough time to play."

In a normal situation, you can't advise someone to leave their spouse because when they don't, you become that asshole who talked shit about the spouse. But nothing about our situation is normal and I am #*TeamPhil*. "You don't need a cat," I say. "You need a studio."

"Tell that to the wife. Man, we're so close to freedom. My kid's on her way to college in a few months and the wife wants to tie me down with a new *cat*."

"Does she not . . . I don't wanna overstep . . . but does she not get who you are?"

He flicks his cigarette into a pile of leaves. "Nope," he says. "Not lately."

The next day I march into the library and walk into your office. "Okay," I say. "Let's get cats. I'm in."

You fix your eyes on your computer screen. He fights you every step of the way and I am on *#TeamYou*. "Well," you say. "That was fast. Do you have a name picked out?"

I sit in my chair and you scratch your collarbone and I latch my hands behind my head and smile. "Riffic," I say. "Little Riffic Goldberg."

"Ah," you say. "I do love me some suffixes."

Suffix sounds like *sex* and you are the smartest, sexiest woman on the planet and you are the fan to my tastic, showing me a picture of your favorite kitten, the one with a natural tuxedo. "Look at *this* little guy. He's all dressed up and he will *find* somewhere to go."

I tell you his name should be Licious and you groan—*anything but Licious*—and I dream of a long slow Saturday, you and me naming our kittens. "Well," I say. "There's three of them, right?"

You nod. "Yes."

"Okay, so after work, let's go pick up Riffic, Tastic, and Licious."

But you throw your empty coffee cup in the trash and tell me that now Nomi's on the fence. You're doing it again, you're protecting your rat. You tell me that Nomi wants a kitten, not a cat, and kittens grow up fast. You shrug. "There's no way around it. It's the fate of all kittens."

You're a fatalist and you need to believe in *fate*. Me. I pick up one of your *tchotchkes* and I make a proposal. "How about I get all three kittens, Tastic, Riffic, *and* Licious and then, when you're ready, you can take one."

"You're so sweet, Joe . . ." Yes, I am. "But three cats . . . what about your furniture?"

"I have plenty of room. And I can get the toys, scratching posts . . ."

I am a homebody and Phil is a home-wrecker and you fiddle with your pen. "I always had this idea that when I had my bookshop . . . well, every bookshop needs a cat."

"Just like every bodega. How about this? I keep one. You keep one. And Licious will live in your Bordello."

You practically purr at me. "Well, on one condition. The little guy in the tux cannot be named Licious. You can't do that to me, Joe. You have to give up on that name."

I purr right fucking back. "Giving up's not really my style, Mary Kay."

Three days later, my arms are all scratched up and I am a man with three cats. I am also the owner of a *Gibson* and I sneeze—my body will adjust to the dander—and Phil waves his hands. Frantic. "C'mon, man. I don't wanna catch what you got."

He was grumpy in the meeting and he's grumpy *after* the meeting. I tell him I'm sorry and he shrugs it off. "It's not you," he says. "The wife's holding a grudge about the kitten thing. Showing me *videos* of the kittens."

I send you my videos and you love that I don't post them online, that they're only for you, for me, for us. And now I find out that you show the videos to him—ha—and he takes a drag of his cigarette. "All right," he says. "I gotta split."

He goes home to you—the injustice—and I go home to Riffic and Licious and Tastic and they're not just exceptionally cute. They also give us a reason to communicate around the clock. You send me links to cat toys and you're "too busy with Christmas" to come over and meet our *future cats* and I'm a busy man, pushing Phil to *man up and put his music first.* Christmas is getting closer—every day Phil is a *little* bit closer to the edge—and every day I send you photos, mostly of Licious. You tell me that you're going to *die* of cuteness and somehow I go to sleep and the next day, I go to a meeting and Phil spends the whole time writing a song in his phone about how his wife is riding him about *cats and bookstores.*

I go home after the meeting and play with my kittens and I check Phil's tweets.

Can't fucking wait to tour. Philistans# Peace#

Did someone say SacriPHIL surprisealbum# ChristmasIsCanceled# Peace#

Fixin' to put another shark inside your shark, Philistans . . . Peace#

What do you do when your wife drives you crazy? Asking for a friend Peace#

Licious and Tastic and Riffic are so cute—they're scratching the Sacriphil albums I bought on eBay—but I can't just sit here. Not tonight. I want to see you. I want to see what your marriage looks like when it's imploding. I put on a hoodie and I pick up my binoculars and I'm out the door.

It's cold in the woods and it's dark in the woods and your windows are bright and I see you, Mary Kay. You're turning the pages of a book and your rat walks into the room and you don't look up. You flip him the bird and he slams the door and you are mine. You don't love him anymore. You love me.

The blow comes out of nowhere.

Something hard hits the center of my back. Binoculars: Down. Me: Down. The blow comes again: A boot in my back and heavy breathing—my poor ribs—and then another kick. POW. I am on my side and I taste blood and another kick knocks me into a rock. Roots punish my back and the boot punishes my front and I know that boot. I've seen that boot. A heavy, militant-but-also-fuck-me Sorel.

In a wheeze, I get her name out of my mouth. "Melanda?"

12

"I knew it!" Melanda grips a pink can of pepper spray, pink as your mother's Cadillac. "I knew you were a pervert the day we met," she says. "Two words: Woody. Allen."

Fuck. *Fuck.* "Melanda, no, this isn't what you think."

She grunts. "For the last fucking time, *you* don't tell *me* what I think. I know what you're doing, pervert."

"You're wrong. Let me . . . please listen to me."

She grinds her big angry boot into my chest and there will be a bruise. "Aw, do you want me to *listen* to you, Joe? Are you gonna tell me you were out here *bird*-watching? Are you gonna tell me that you didn't even *know* that Nomi lives in this house?"

Nomi. No. Not her. NO. I can't breathe and *I* am the bird, dying in the dirt. "Melanda, this isn't what you think."

"He loves books! He adores *film.* And he does love *birds.* Birds as in teenage girls."

My vocal cords freeze up on me. The boot. The lie. "No, Melanda. No, no, I was *not* looking at Nomi."

"Don't even try, pervert." She presses a number on her phone and she thinks I'm a pervert and you don't come back from a *pedo* accusation and I am *not* a fucking pedophile and Melanda may be skilled in the art of self-defense, but she has a lot to learn about offense. I grab her by the *Sorel* and I yank. Hard. She goes down and her phone goes down and I clamp my hand over her big vicious mouth. I pick up the closest rock.

Crunch.

I'm still shaking, Mary Kay. My attacker is locked up downstairs in my Whisper Room and this sort of shit isn't supposed to happen in *Cedar Fucking Cove.* I moved here to be happy. I moved here to make peace, to find *peace,* and now my ribs are flaring, hot like *McRibs.*

My kittens are useless and clueless, meowing and playing like nothing ever happened—thanks, fuckers—and I pick up my phone with my trembling hand. I set up security cameras downstairs so that I have eyes on her, and she's still asleep for now.

I didn't ask to be tangled up in your Blues, Mary Kay. The situation is calm for now, but I can't keep her here forever—she's not a fucking *cat*—and I can't let her go—and I don't want to be the guy who killed your best friend. (Even though it would be self-defense if one thinks of the reputation as part of the self, which it *is.*)

At least I have her phone—thanks for the thumbprint access, Apple!—and I'm getting a Master's in All Things Melanda. She's been scheming to move to Minnesota to chase down *the only decent guy* she ever dated, so I informed the school that she was taking a leave to go out of town for some job interviews. They didn't seem surprised—she fights with everyone at that school—and I *had* to give her an alibi, Mary Kay. We live in America and a single, relatively attractive woman can't just "disappear," because there's nothing women love more than stories about missing women.

But she does have to go, Mary Kay. As it turns out, your "best friend" is a double agent. She's always whining to you about her old friend Netty—they met on Melanda's semester *abroad*—and you are supportive. But then she talks to Netty . . . about *you*. We have to end their toxic friendship—we can't have Netty calling Interpol—so I send Netty a text from Melanda's phone, a text meant for you.

So I'm horrible lol but once again I'm done with Netty. She's whin-

ing about her birthday like she's in sixth grade and it's like Netty honey get a life you know lolol horrible I know.

Netty got the message—oops!—and she snaps right back: *I think this was meant for Mary Kay. Have a nice life. Block. Mute. Bye.*

Netty unfollows Melanda in all the stupid places—that's one achievement unlocked!—and she shares a passive-aggressive meme about *fake friends* and maybe I could do this for a living. Take your phone, fix your life.

My ribs are cooling off and in a sick way, I'm happy that Melanda came after me. See, Mary Kay, you never told me that we have an enemy in our midst. She's been campaigning against me for weeks—I knew it—and you always defend me, and women are on guard when it comes to men—I get it—but never mind me, Mary Kay. You should see what she says about *you.* I screenshot one of the worst entries in her notepad app:

MK and those skirts honestly we get it you have legs lol and *MK shows up with no call bc I live alone as if I have no life HELLO I HAVE A LIFE*—and I know you love her, but this woman is not your *Friend.* This is why I don't try too hard to keep up with Exclamation Point Ethan, Mary Kay, and this is why *Friends* is a lie.

Most people wouldn't like their friends if they got into their phones.

You would want me to have *empathy* for Melanda, and okay. She does try to be a better person. She bought nine meditation apps—they're not working—and you warn her that Alice & Olivia are like her drug dealers and she sends you excerpts of her food diary—*NINE SAFEWAY DONUT HOLES I HATE EVERYONE BUT HATE ME THE MOST RIGHT NOW GRRRR FUCK YOU PATRIARCHY FUCK YOU SAFEWAY*—and you rightfully tell her that she isn't *fat*—fuck you, United States of Body Dysmorphia—but there's a lot you *don't* know, Mary Kay.

Would you still have *empathy* for Melanda if you knew that she manipulated two unpaid, uncredited interns into building her feminist incubator? That's right, Mary Kay. Just ask the interns, Eileen and DeAnn. Your best friend doesn't support other women. She erases them.

And she wants to erase *us* too.

Last week, you told her not to give up on the dream of Minnesota and she *LOL*ed.

Lol MK I'm not moving. Never seeing Harry again.

You just sounded so excited about going there. You never know . . . maybe you will

Right. Kind of like you and your new little boyfriend . . . see we DO know lol

That's not fair. That was . . . that was one kiss.

LOL MK. Face it. I'm not moving to MN. BI is home. You're not leaving Phil. He's home. These are facts. This is why we drink our wine LOL

But she's not honest with *you,* Mary Kay. After she blew you off with an *LOL,* she sent two follow-up emails to HR reps in Minneapolis. She's allowed to make *her* moves but she discourages you from making *your* moves. She suffers and *so* she wants *you* to suffer and now she's wide awake, pounding on the glass walls of my Whisper Room, screaming like a bad actress in a B movie. I crack my knuckles. I can do this. I can take on her voice. And I have to because the two of you text *all fucking day.* You type. Same way you do every fucking morning.

How's life?

IT IS SEVEN A.M. WHY DON'T YOU WOMEN LEAVE EACH OTHER ALONE? I breathe. This is the upside to this mess. I get to *change* your life. I type.

Sweetie omg big news. Fingers crossed. I'm in a mad rush to Minneapolis for a job interview yeeee and I already talked to a couple guys on Bumble lolol who knows but yeeeeee lolol xoxo

My heart is pounding, the sun is up. Did I do a good job? Do you buy me as Melanda? Here come the dots—please, God, you owe me—and here comes your response.

Congrats!

It's a win and I needed a win and you text again, sharing your own news—you're getting a *haircut* today. I put Melanda's phone in my pocket—she told you, Mary Kay, she's in a *mad rush*—and it will be satisfying to see you growing, weaning off your "sister," but now it's time for the hard part.

I have to go and face my attacker.

When I get downstairs, I don't look in the cage and my Whisper

Room was never supposed to *be* a cage. I stand in front of my TV and Melanda's behind me, locked up and screaming—*You're a fucking pervert*—but I owe it to you to *try* and make her see the light. She spits at the glass and it turns out the Whisper Room isn't actually soundproof, which means that I hear every word of her abuse. "You are a fucking pedophile and a psychopath and a fucking sociopath and you will pay for this, you sicko. Let me out. Now."

Ha! That is *not* how we catch flies, Melanda, and I sigh. "Well, make up your mind. Which is it? What am I, exactly? All three or just one?"

I sit in my chair and I take out my flash cards. She is the teacher but I am the professor and I was up all night making a lesson plan. She bashes the glass wall with her fists. "PEDOPHILE!"

I sigh and shake my head. "Wrong."

"Fuck you."

"Come on, Melanda. You're smarter than that."

"I know, Joe. I know about your dirty *Bukowski* book."

You must have told her I thought Nomi might like Bukowski over the phone because I didn't see that in your texts. "For God's sake, Melanda, you should know that reading Bukowski is a good way to learn about vile men. You're an English teacher."

She blinks fast and pivots. "For your information, I'm actually trained to spot pedophiles and using a mom as a conduit, well, that's the oldest trick in the book. Obviously."

"I think your meditation apps are making you paranoid."

"Make all the snide jokes you want, sweetie. I know what I saw. You're a monster. You are a pedophile and *you* will be the one who winds up behind bars."

"Moving on," I say. And I pick up my flash cards. "I found your diary in the notepad app on your phone . . ."

"No. No you didn't."

She bangs on the glass and I choose one of my favorites. "Date," I say. "November first. 'MK calls and expects me to pick up as if I don't have a LIFE but when I call HER does she pick up? Nope! Too busy with her familyyyyyyy. Try being alone you mommy whiner!'"

She makes earmuffs. "Stop it."

I pick another flash card. A real *gem.* "Date: October twenty-seventh."

"You are a child molester, you sicko. These are notes. I get PMS. That is *private.*"

I maintain my composure and I read Melanda's diary. "'Sometimes I just wish I could MURDER MK so smug like she's first woman to ever have a crush at work GET A LIFE GRRR and if Nomi was my kid like just no. Be a role model STOP FLIRTING YOU SLUT HE'S NOT IN LOVE WITH YOU NOT EVERY GUY IS SO CRAZY ABOUT YOU and buy some fucking pants WHERE IS MY PERIOD FUCK YOU WORLD.'"

"Stop it, Joe. You have no idea. Female friendships . . . they're complicated."

I go into her texts and open the history of Melanda and *Seamus.* "Huh," I say. "Is that why you drunk-text Seamus asking who was a better lay back in high school?"

She spits at me, as if *I'm* the one who texts Shortus—I still can't believe you slept with him, it stings, it does—and I sigh. "I'm not judging you, Melanda. I'm just trying to help you see that sometimes . . . you're wrong."

"FUCK YOU, PERVERT."

I pick another card. "November fourth. 'I would be living in Minneapolis by now if not for Married Kay. I HATE HER. Nomi should be living with ME and UGHGHGHGH.' Married Kay," I say. "Clever."

She looks at me. "You won't make me think I'm the bad guy, you sicko. You were stalking Nomi. I *saw.*"

"Huh," I say. "You know, Melanda, I guess what hurts the most, besides my rib cage . . ."

She rolls her eyes. An emoji come to life.

"I get it. This isn't an easy place to be single. Hell, I live next door to a family. You and I . . . we're in the minority. You try to do good . . . *I* try to do good, but you decided that because I'm single, there must be something wrong with me."

"And I was right. You're a pedo."

"Melanda, I am not a pedophile. But after reading your notepad, I gotta say, I do wonder what you were doing in the woods . . ."

"Oh you sicko, I was looking out for Nomi."

"Ah."

"The Bukowski . . . the Woody Allen . . . I knew it then and obviously I *really* know it now. I *see* you."

I pick another flash card. "'Feels so freaking good to tell DeAnn and Eileen that I will be the one taking the credit for the incubator. These young girls are SO FUCKING ENTITLED and someone needs to smack them down because they have NO IDEA how hard it is to be a woman in the real world.'"

She sits up straight as if there's a book on her head. "What's your point?"

"You don't see the hypocrisy? 'Women supporting women.' You're literally *erasing* the women who support *you.*"

"I am not the one on trial here."

"You called me a *pedophile.* You attacked me but look at you. What about *you*? You hate your best friend and you're stealing credit from your fellow *sisters.*"

She folds her arms, indignant. "Nice try, pervert, but you don't know the first *thing* about my life. Eileen and DeAnn are *college kids.* I'm not 'erasing' their work. They don't have a fucking clue about how hard it is to be a single woman in a school system. Let them try going into a school every day where everyone treats you like a leper slash whore because you're not married. And they think you should just be able to work every day all day because you don't have a 'life,' like there's something inherently *wrong* with you if you're alone."

"Christ, Melanda. Just admit it. They're wrong about you and you were wrong about *me.*"

"Well, unlock the door and let me go and I'll know for sure that you're not a predator."

"Melanda, I wish I could trust you, I do, but I wasn't *grooming* Nomi and you attacked *me* and this is on *you.*"

She bangs on the glass, which hurts her hand more than it hurts me. "Let me out. Now."

Her phone is in my pocket and it buzzes. And it's you: *When do you fly to MN?! So excited for you!*

Melanda drops her fists. "Is it MK?" She's trembling now, shaking, and her sizable vocabulary is boiled down to a single word. "SICKO!"

I write back cuz this is what you gals do. *Leaving in a few hours!*

Melanda knocks on the glass. Softer now. She's a teacher again. "Joe, look . . . I'm sorry. I was paranoid and I did judge you, okay? I really thought you were just latching onto MK to get to Nomi . . . I mean MK is old."

You're not old.

"Joe," she says. "I mean it. I'm sorry. And if you let me go . . . Look, you're right. We both overreacted. And no one has to know about this. Now that we're talking . . . well, you're right. We are on the same side. We can be."

I wasn't born an hour ago and I sigh. "There's a remote on the bed."

She kicks the wall as if she's the only one trapped. "Fuck you."

And I gotta say, Mary Kay. I'm a little offended because *I'm* the victim here. I have gone out of my way to be Mr. Fucking Good Guy and now because of *her* my Whisper Room is a cage and Dr. Nicky is right. You can't control other people. You can only control your own actions. Melanda doesn't deserve my help, but lucky for her, when I see anyone trapped in a cage, even if it's their fault, well, what can I say? I'm a good fucking Samaritan.

She screams for help and I nod at the remote on the bed. "Go ahead," I say. "Pick it up. I have a project for you."

She is quivering—it could be an act—and she picks up the remote and the screen lights up and there they are, all of the movies in her iTunes account. See, Mary Kay, Melanda obsessively takes inventory of every calorie she puts into her body. But she needs to take that analytical obsession in a different direction. She needs to think about the *movies* she watches over and over again. I try to explain this to her but she is the same old dog. "Oh God," she sighs. "You're not a pervert. You're a psychopath."

"You call *me* a psycho? I'm the 'pervert.' Melanda, would you look at the size of your Woody Allen collection? You own more of his movies than I do!"

"It's different," she snarls. "I'm a *woman.* You have to know the enemy."

"Bullshit," I say. "You own *Anything Else* and *Melinda and Melinda* and those aren't even in the fucking canon."

She simmers. "Get me out of here."

"This is a teachable moment, Melanda."

"This is not happening."

"Oh, *sweetie,* I think we've established that this most certainly is *happening.*"

"You're a sick man."

"Well, like you, I do appreciate *Crimes and Misdemeanors.*"

"That movie belongs to *Anjelica Huston,*" she snarls. "Not that pig."

I'm on her phone, pacing, and I wish you could see me right now, Mary Kay. "Okay," I say. "Welcome to Melanda's Movies 101."

"Stop it."

"We casually buy movies in the middle of the night, but sometimes our selections say a lot about our underlying issues."

"No."

"You like your female bonding stories—*Beaches* and *Romy and Michele* and *Terms of Endearment*—and you identify strongly with Bridget Jones. You own all three movies, plus *Jerry Maguire* and *New in Town*. Huh. Perhaps the woman you identify with most is Renée Zellweger."

She turns red. "There was a fucking sale, you idiot."

"You're also a fan of the psycho woman genre. *The Hand That Rocks the Cradle . . . Single White Female . . .*"

She sinks to the floor and she's crying now, she's moving forward—yay!—and I hunker down like a counselor, meeting her at ground level. "Melanda, it's okay. We're both in shock. We both lost our tempers . . ." It's not true—I acted in self-defense—but sometimes you have to lie to your pupil. "We need a minute to decompress . . ." And I need a minute to figure out what to do with her. "You were burnt out. Anyone can see that. So just take this for what it is, some time to self-reflect. These movies are your bedtime stories, your comfort foods."

She blows her nose on her shirt. A GIRL IS A GUN. "You're insane."

"Forget about me, Melanda. I'm worried about *you*. You could have gotten hurt out there . . ." She looks at me like *I'm* the crazy one. I carry on. "Look," I say. "Every Sunday you plan a detox from your phone. You turn off your notifications but you never go through with it."

She bites her lip. Then she clocks the Safeway bag I put in her room while she was sleeping. "Can you put the TV in here? I have sensitive retinas."

"Melanda . . ."

She knows not to press me—she's a fast learner, Mary Kay—and she juts her chin at the table. "What's in the bag?"

"Your favorite thing in the world," I say. "Safeway donut holes."

She almost smiles, because what a thrill it is, even under circumstances like this, to be known for who you really fucking are.

13

I'm at the fucking *gym*—gotta be seen, gotta normal the fuck *up*—and Seamus is working out two feet away, singing along to Kid Fucking Rock, who waxes nostalgic-pervert about his whiskey-soaked glory days mounting an underage girl by a lake. Ugh. You and I—well, you and Melanda—are texting and for the second time in five minutes I plant my *kettle bell* on the ground to read your latest missive.

You: *Drink this afternoon before your ferry? What time is your flight?*

Melanda: *Sweetie I wish but I am sooooo busy lol why*

Melanda's phone rings—you're *calling* her, oh shit oh shit—and my stomach muscles quiver like I just finished a fucking *Murph* and I can't talk to you—I'm not her—and I can't talk now—I'm in a fucking *gym.* I send you to voicemail and I type. Fast.

Melanda: *lol sorry but I can't talk, too busy.*

You: *I get it but can you just talk for two minutes?*

NO, MARY KAY, SHE CAN'T.

I type.

Melanda: *Lol sooooo sorry but I'm running so late. Is this more Joe drama?*

My heart pounds. But this is your pattern.

You: *ugh yes and no I just wish we could go get a drink*

We wouldn't be in this fucking mess if you talked *to* me more than you talk *about* me and Shortus yanks his earbuds. "What's up with you, Chatty Cathy?"

"Nothing," I say. "My buddy in New York is having issues with his wife."

Shortus grunts. "Sucks to be him. But that doesn't mean it should suck to be *you* or us, New Guy. Take that shit outside. It's distracting."

I'm not New Guy anymore—I live here—and all these fitness junkies are only here because it provides distraction from their lackluster lives. Shortus reinserts his earbuds and I wipe down the kettle bell as if my hands are dirty and walk outside to deal with you.

Melanda: *I wish we could go drink too but yeeeeee flight so soon!*

You: *And yay flight! You know I always root for you even if the idea of you ACTUALLY moving makes me feel insane. I really felt like a drink today but oh well so happy for you!*

That hurts, Mary Kay. You don't feel insane about Melanda. You miss *me*. And Melanda has no time for you—she's watching one of her favorite Woody Allen movies—and you need a reality check.

Aw, sweetie you'll be okay. Give my love to Phil and Nomi xo

You don't like the patronizing tone—I know you and I don't blame you—and I drive into town and pop into Blackbird—just another normal fucking day, no woman trapped in *my* basement—and the fecal-eyed multigenerational family is here. I bump into the grandfather's chair and Nancy glares at me as if it wasn't an accident and they're all as cold to me as they are warm to each other. Motherfuckers, all of them. But at least they saw me. Normal Joe! Nothing to see!

You're not Nancy, Mary Kay. You're not happily married. But you're not texting *me* to meet up for a drink and that's the problem. I cross the street and head for the T & C and Melanda's phone buzzes. It's you again—shocker—and you want to know what she'll wear for the big job interview. This is sadly normal for you two. She sends you her date outfits and you weigh in—*I like the red*—and she argues with you until you eventually give up—*What matters most is how you feel in it. Gotta run. Phil's home and as we know this is a miracle*—but right now you're in the salon, you're bored, and you badger Melanda a second time.

Need pictures! Let me live vicariously through you.

There are so many problems with this statement, Mary Kay. Melanda can't send you a selfie. She's wearing the T-shirt she had on when she attacked me—A GIRL IS A GUN—and you are too young to feel like the only living you have left to do is vicarious. I turn the screw.

lol that is so sad. No offense but I feel like the Joe stuff is making you crazy.

You deflect and say that you might get bangs today—*just fully become my mother*—and that's a cry for help but Melanda is a bad friend. I read enough to know what she would say so I lie to your face: *Do it. You can rock bangs! You have the face for them and you are NOT your mother. Send me pic if you do gotta run so busy before flight lol*

You give a smiley face. *Send pics! I'm here! Excited for you, M!*

You're acting out. Cutting your hair instead of coming clean with *me* just because your best friend is about to get on a plane. You text again.

Pics please!

Melanda has 24,985 *pics* in her phone, most of them pictures of her, standing in front of a full-length mirror. I choose a recent selfie and send it to you with the shrugging brunette girl emoji—her favorite—and you are typing. A lot. This isn't a fucking essay contest. It's a yes or no question and then here you are.

Wait I thought you returned that blue dress last week? When we were in Seattle?

My heart alarm goes off and no. NO. This would be easier if there weren't ten thousand texts between you two and so many fucking pictures of so many fucking outfits and I close my eyes. WWMD.

Ugh long story but more like get me off this rock no offense lol just excited to go

That was cruel, maybe too cruel and you're silent. I send another photo of Melanda in mustard pants and a green sweater—was she trying to be vomit for Halloween?—and once again: nothing. I studied your conversations and this isn't how it goes. Radio silence is bad and it makes me nervous for me, for you. Are you telling the stylist about what just happened? Did I fuck up?

I type for Melanda: *You there? Sweetie I'm sorry just frazzled lol you ok?*

More silence. You're in the salon, in the chair, exactly 1,058 feet away from me. You have nothing to *do* but write back to your friend and are you suspicious? Do you have a sixth sense? Did you run out of the salon? Are you pounding on Melanda's front door? So help me God if a *selfie* that isn't even mine brings me down and I can't take this silence from you. I need to know that you're not on a paranoid mission to *find your friend.* I need to know that you're not at the *police station,* where they're not used to this kinda thing and I have to find you because it's not like you to drop off. I walk toward Firefly and I *loiter* by the gazebo—I miss lingering with you—and then the door to the salon opens.

It's you. And you didn't get bangs.

You wave at me and I wave at you and I'm holding Melanda's phone but you don't know that. Thank God I took off the FEMALE FIRST case—Smart Joe!—and you put your hands in your pockets and you're heading my way and you're *Closer* every second and now you're here. You touch your hair. "It's a little much, right?"

"Well, Mary Kay, you did *just* step out of a salon."

You laugh and I'm safe. We're safe. You don't suspect anything—I can tell because if you did, you'd be holding your phone as if it contains evidence—and you don't think it's weird that I'm here because this is Cedar Fucking Cove. We live here. "Well," you say. "It's good to see you, but I should probably get home . . ."

Liar. You just told Melanda you want to drink. "Oh come on. How about a drink?" I took a blow to my *ribs* for you and I hold your eyes. "Hitchcock?"

You nod. "Hitchcock."

Your hair bounces when you walk—we are in motion—and I tell you I need a haircut and you say that Firefly takes walk-ins and I open the door for you and you thank me and we sit up front by the window. You bring your hands together.

"Okay," you say. "I feel bad that things have been so weird."

I take a sip of my water. "Don't be ridiculous, Mary Kay. I get it."

You pick up the menu and act like I meant what I said and you don't know if you want wine or coffee and this is new for us. This is a first for us. You're ordering a glass of *Chablis*—last time we drank the hard stuff—and pulling your turtleneck over your chin. You just said you felt bad that things were weird but look at you now, such deliberately tiny sips as you run your hands through your hair, as if I'm blind, as if you're hungry for a compliment, as if I'm in a position to tell you that you look good.

You're a fox. Foxes know they look good. I stare at you. "Hey, are you all right?"

"Yeah," you say. "Just tired." Bullshit. "I woke up on the wrong side of the bed." More bullshit and that's a lazy answer, a child's answer, a stranger's answer. "And I'm a little weirded out. Melanda says she's headed to Minneapolis today."

I'm tired and spent and now I long for you to go back to your bullshit because YOUR BEST FRIEND IS IN MY FUCKING BASEMENT and why didn't I just let you go home? I nod. "Vacation?"

"She says she's going on a job interview."

Red flags abound. If you believed Melanda's story, you would have said that she's leaving town, not that she *says* she's leaving. I sip my water. You rub your forehead. "Maybe it's just me . . ." Yes. Let's go with that theory. "She's always talked about moving there one day . . . but the timing feels off. Or maybe *I'm* off."

"Maybe we should get something to eat."

You ignore my suggestion. "Last week, we took one of those quizzes to find out which *Succession* character you are . . ." I know. I already read the texts and I was surprised that Shortus got Roman. "Anyway," you say. "Melanda got *Ken Doll* as you call him . . ." God, I love you. You remember everything. "And I got the evil ogre dad."

"I don't think Logan's an ogre."

"Ah, so you watched it."

"Yes I did and Logan Roy is a good man. His spoiled kids are the evil ogres."

"No," you say. "Logan Roy is a monster. His kids have issues *because* of him."

"That's a cheat," I say. "You can't go through life blaming your childhood for the way you are as an adult."

You shut down on me and maybe you and your husband belong in my Whisper Room with your friend Melanda because maybe you're all broken birds, busted beyond repair. You rub your eyes and your hands are trembling and it's just a stupid TV show. I have empathy for you. I want to take care of you. "Hey," I say. "I think we should get you something to eat."

"Joe, I'm married." A beat. "Seriously."

You did it. You told me the truth. And now you won't look at me, only at the table, and I should be relieved—we're in a new place—but if we go deep right now, you're gonna want to hash it all out with Melanda. I pray for a kitchen fire but it's no use.

We're here. Melanda is in my basement. And you're staring at me. Waiting.

I do what anyone would do at a time like this. I stay silent. I don't acknowledge the waiter when he drops the check as if he's pushing us out the door and I stare at the table. I remember the *Titanic* ferry.

You sigh. "Well?"

"Well what?"

"Well, say something."

"What do you want me to say? I know."

"You *know*?"

"Mary Kay, come on. You can't be all that surprised . . ."

You sip your water. "How long have you known?"

I don't want you to think I'm a liar like you and I don't want you to feel worse than you already do and you *are* part fox. You want to feel clever. You *like* to feel clever. So I lie to you. "Only for a couple days."

You snort a little. It's not becoming. It's not you. "Wow. I guess I'm a really good liar."

"I wanted to be in the dark."

You want to have all the power and this is why Melanda resents you, because you think being in a shitty marriage makes you superior. "Joe, let's not fight."

"We're not fighting." We are fighting.

My heart isn't in my body. It's on the table. Right in front of you. Bloody. Raw. Beating. "Joe," you say, and you say it the wrong way. "I didn't come here to tell you I'm leaving him. This isn't a date."

Yes you are and yes it is. "I know that."

"And I'm not a cheater."

Yes you are, but things will be different with me. "Of course you're not."

"My daughter . . . if she knew about that night . . ."

You loved that night and I did too. "I mean it, Mary Kay. I didn't say a word."

"And I didn't come clean because I'm about to make any changes in my life. And if that were to happen . . . which isn't to say that it *will* happen . . ." Yes it will! "Well . . . that's why I can't do this with you on any level. You cannot be the man who wrecked my marriage."

Everyone knows that the people *in* the marriage are the ones responsible for the marriage, everyone except married people, and I sip my water. "Agree."

"And I am sorry. I should have told you that night at the pub. Hell, when 'Italian Restaurant' came on . . . I mean why didn't I just say it then? What's wrong with me?"

I tell you there is nothing wrong with you and you tell the waiter that we want another round—yes!—and you stand—*be right back*—and I take out Melanda's phone and sure enough, there you are.

I'm a horrible person aren't I?

Melanda ignores you because you need to think for yourself. I put her phone back in my pocket and a minute later, you come back. Your hair is flatter and you take a deep breath like you were using one of her meditation apps. "Okay," you say. "What do you want to know?"

"It's none of my business. We're okay. I'm glad you told me and I know it wasn't easy."

You clench your napkin. "Please stop defending me. You've always been up-front with me. You told me everything about your past . . ." Everything that matters. "And I let you think that I'm alone. Remember that first day, when you said *Gilmore Girls* . . ."

I remember everything about you. "I remember."

"I should have said it right then. But I admit it. I wanted to pretend. You were so . . . new."

You want me to say nice things to you but I can't say nice things or you'll call me a *marriage wrecker*. I nod.

"My husband's name is Phil. He's a musician. You might even know who he is . . ."

You say it like he's George Fucking Harrison. "I mean it, you don't have to do this."

"Phil DiMarco . . . He was the lead singer of Sacriphil."

It's fun to tell you that I don't know Sacriphil and you wish I did—foxes like attention—and you tell me he's not just your *husband*. "He's Nomi's dad."

I nod as in *I fucking knew that* and you hiss at me. "Well? Aren't you gonna tell me I'm horrible? I don't wear a ring and I ran around with you . . . flirting with you . . ."

"Well, all we can do is take it from here."

"But see, that's the thing. I'm not here, Joe." Yes you fucking are. "I can't *be* here." Yes you fucking can. "Joe, I *lied* to you, stringing you along, letting you adopt all those kittens."

"I wanted those kittens."

You pull an ice cube out of your drink with your fingers. You hide it in your palm. "Look, no marriage is perfect . . ." According to all the people who should have gotten divorced ten fucking years ago. "But part of the reason I never even thought about making any change is . . ." You open your palm. The ice cube glistens. "Joe," you say. "I didn't think someone like you existed."

I want to kiss you. *This* is our moment but you bulldoze over it with your words, telling me how selfish you think you've been, as if you wish I would walk out on you and make it easier for you to stay in your rut. You don't owe me an explanation but you *want* to explain. You love talking to me because you can be honest with me. You don't come out and say it, but it's true. Look at you, relaxing and thinking out loud. I'm the only one you can talk to. *Me.*

"See," you say. "It sounds trite and Melanda would be *horrified* . . ." You say her name so casually. You can't hear the alarms going off in my head because WHAT THE FUCK DO I DO WITH HER, MARY KAY?

I can't think about that right now so I breathe. *Be here now.* "How so?"

"Well," you say. "I got married so young. I've never been through anything like this . . . meeting an available man, spending time with him, getting to know you slowly . . . And Melanda's stories about being out there are always so grim. But you . . . I built my life around the idea that I wasn't gonna meet anybody like you."

But you did. "Really, Mary Kay, it's okay. Nothing has changed. We can wait."

You shake your head no and you fight my collective plural with your collective plural—*We're a family, Joe, it's not that simple*—and I let you win this battle. There's no point in arguing with you right now. Melanda's only been "gone" for a few hours, and already you're changing. Growing. You're not there yet, I know. Your maternal instincts have overwhelmed your basic need for love, for self-preservation, and soon your phone buzzes and it's him.

We both know it's time to go.

On the sidewalk, we don't embrace. You say you *should probably* go and bells are ringing on the shop doors as they open and close. The holidays are all around us. You thank me for being *such a grown-up* about all this and I tell you the truth, that I just want you to be happy. You think this is goodbye. You think this is the end. But I walk away with a smile on my face.

I didn't think someone like you existed.

Oh, Mary Kay, yes I fucking do exist and deep down you know there is no going back.

14

I trot downstairs and I'm basking in a cloud of smug. Melanda tried to turn you against me and she failed and even though I should kill her for putting me in this position, I admit it, Mary Kay.

I want to fucking gloat. I want the teacher to know she failed.

She greets me and the donut holes in my hand with a blank stare. "Melanda, there are handcuffs in the drawer of the end table. Cuff yourself to the bedpost and I'll bring you a snack."

She bickers as if *I'm* not the one in hell right now and my sugar high is fading. She's here, she really is—am I fucked?—and she finds the handcuffs—the cops should have locked her up, not me—but life is a shark that moves forward—even *Phil* knows that—and my time away was productive. I saw you—you love me—and things are different in here too now. Melanda is slower. She's slouching, almost apologizing for her inability to get the cuffs on. She'd never admit it but she gets it now: I'm the fucking boss. And she cuffs up because she works in a school system. She's conditioned to respect authoritative ranks so I enter the room like the professor, like the principal. "Okay, Melanda. What have we learned today?"

She eyeballs me. "Well, you're in a good mood. I suppose you saw MK, huh?"

That's none of your fucking business, Melanda. "I thought we'd start with a deep dive into friendship narratives."

"If you're so obsessed with Mary Kay why didn't you kidnap *her*?"

"I didn't 'kidnap' you. You're not a child. Now come on. Friendship movies. *Romy and Michele*. *Beaches*. Let's dive in."

I don't want to be Melanda's Dr. Fucking Nicky but you know what, Mary Kay? I *do* want your friend to cop to her sins. It's only now that I realize *just* how much she hurt us. If you had a real best friend, you would have told me about your husband several *weeks* ago and her phone buzzes. It's you: *I did it. I told him. Calling you now ahahahha*

You are a woman of your word and Melanda's phone is ringing and I send you to voicemail—what fucking choice do I have?—and now *Melanda's* gloating, smoothing the wrinkles in her sweatpants. "Uh-oh," she says. "I'd say someone has a big problem."

"Yeah, you own a library of movies about female friendship but you're not a friend."

"Oh please," she says. "Most women our age love *Beaches* and *Romy and Michele.* But I'll tell you what *is* unusual. Me sending MK to voicemail. Gimme the phone."

"No."

"Suit yourself. And FYI . . ." Is she this patronizing with her students? "My movies are just bedtime stories I turn on after I pop a Xanax, sweetie."

Her phone buzzes. It's you: *Can you talk? I promise I'll be fast! Or set a time for later?*

I know you don't mean to hurt me, Mary Kay, but for fuck's sake TAKE A FUCKING HINT. I write back: *Sorry I am insane busy lol will call you later!*

You don't write back—you're mad—and Melanda says that I'm playing with fire and I hate her, Mary Kay. I hate her for being *right.* I pop a hole in my mouth—so help me God if this woman makes me get love handles—and I ask her if she's the Hillary Whitney or the C. C. Bloom—and she sighs. "I know you work the 'loner' angle pretty hard, but here's a heads-up about friends. When I go out of town, MK waters my plants. We talk, Joe. We talk a lot."

FUCK MY LIFE. "Are you the Hillary Whitney or the C. C. Bloom?"

"When I need to talk, she picks up. And when she needs to talk, *I* pick up."

You text again, as if you're on *her* side, not mine—*You okay? Can I do anything?*—and I wish you weren't so kind but I know you have an ulterior motive—you want to talk about me—and Melanda snaps her fingers at me. "Just let me talk to her."

"You know that's not an option."

"Be real, sweetie. I'm a single woman. MK is a mom. She checks up on me. One time, my phone died when I was out with this guy . . . She has the code to my place. She was at my condo that *night.*"

Why do you have to be such a good damn friend, Mary Kay? "Let's focus on you, Melanda."

My voice is shaky—how could it not be?—and there's a crack in my cloud of smug.

Melanda eyes me. "Do you *want* to go to prison."

I may not know what to do about Melanda, but I am not going to prison and you are not going to Melanda's fucking condo and you text again—*Sorry to be a stage nine clinger but I really need to talk*—and I know, Mary Kay. I get it. But Melanda is FUCKING BUSY RIGHT NOW and she sprawls out on the futon and lectures me in her sing-song tone about how all women are C. C. Bloom *and* Hillary Whitney and all women are Romy *and* Michele and I need you to not *want* to talk to her so I have no choice, Mary Kay. I have to be mean. Well, Melanda has to be mean.

Sweetie I am so happy you told him but I'm one person trying to take care of myself and I just . . . lol you can tell me about your side-piece boyfriend when I get settled into my hotel okay?

You're so mad that you don't respond for a full minute and you're so benevolent that when you *do* respond you're kind: *I get it. I will water your plants tonight. Is the code the same?*

I prefer keys to codes and you're antsy. You don't really care about her *plants* but you want to hide out in her condo and think about me and pretend that you're single and Melanda grins. "Even for her, this is a *lot* of texting." She sits up on the futon. "What's your plan, Joe?"

I DON'T FUCKING KNOW and you text her again—*Let me*

know if the code changed, love you—and I love *you* so I nip this in the fucking bud: *Lol same code but no need to worry about the plants. I tossed them a couple days ago. Would LOVE if you could scoop up mail next week tho xoxo.*

You give Melanda a thumbs-up but I know you, Mary Kay. You won't wait a week and what the fuck am I gonna do about her?

"It's not as easy as you thought, is it, sweetie?"

"Do you cry when Hillary Whitney dies in *Beaches*?"

"You didn't realize that real best friends talk every day. And I do not mean text. I mean *talk*. As in out loud."

"You're happy for C. C. Bloom when she gets custody of that little girl, aren't you? You always wanted something like that to happen to you, so that you could have Nomi all to yourself."

"Honey, enough about the movies. You're in trouble. MK *will* go to the police if I don't call her back. I mean yes, your little Minnesota story is cute, *absolutely,* but if I *did* fly to Minneapolis, I'd call her from the airport to bitch about a loud 'businessman' and I'd call her from the hotel to bitch about the sheets. You don't know how it is with sisters."

"You're not her sister."

She huffs. "Fine. You won't be the first overzealous man to dig his own grave."

You see the best in people—always a dangerous approach to life—and this why we're a good team, Mary Kay. I see the worst. I tell Melanda that I don't care if I go to prison. I tell her that *she's* the one behind bars, that her whole life is a loveless fucking lie. She rolls over—I'm getting to her—and I tell her that I am here to protect you from *her* and that no matter what happens, I have all the evidence. I know that she resents you and I tell her that she's neither a feminist nor a sister and that you're not gonna be her prisoner anymore.

And now she sits up and looks at me. "So Phil and I went out in high school."

It's so sad, how *puffed up* she gets by mentioning ancient *high school* history. "Ah," I say. "So Mary Kay stole your boyfriend. No wonder it's so toxic between you two."

"Hardly," she says. "I only tell you because obviously, I never moved on. Phil is . . . well, he's a rock star . . ." Mick Jagger is a rock star. Phil DiMarco is a rocker. "And honey . . ." She puts her hand on her chest. "It's sad that you think that she'd ever leave him for you."

"Tell me the code to your condo."

She grins. "Ah," she says. "I got to you, didn't I?"

"I'll get in there one way or another, Melanda."

"I know," she says. "You'll get into my condo. But you'll never get between MK and Phil . . ." She smirks again. Vicious as an eighth-grade queen bee. "It's so cute. You swagger in here because she finally told you about Phil. You break into my phone . . . you think you know us . . . I don't know your deal, but you've obviously seen *Beaches* and *Romy and Michele.* You know that best friends talk about *everything.*"

"Give me the fucking code."

"But you don't have transcripts of our wine nights . . . our phone calls . . ."

I hate my skin for turning red. "Just tell me the code."

"Pound 342," she says. 342 as in *You love me.* Ugh. "You can write it down."

I should just fucking kill her, Mary Kay. "Thank you."

I turn to go and she baits me. "I wish you were there the night she told me about you."

I say nothing.

"How you didn't go to college . . . how you don't have any friends . . . and I *definitely* wish you had been there the night she told me about what a bad kisser you are. Too much tongue."

I won't let her see my face. I know better, Mary Kay. She's lying. She *has* to be lying.

"It's so sad that you actually think you're in competition with Phil . . ." My teeth are chattering. "And she's right, Joe. You read too much." No such thing. "You overdose on *beef and broccoli* . . ." You would never say that about me. "That's the only possible explanation for why you could believe that she'd ever leave someone like him for someone like you. She's too kind for her own good. *Obviously* she said *something* that put a pep in your step today but my God, honey, get a clue. MK is nice to everyone. She's a *librarian,* a public servant. A people pleaser. It's just a shame when guys like you take kindness so personally."

She yawns like my mother and she reminds me of my mother, who would turn up the volume on Jerry Springer when I got home from school, when I wanted to tell her about my day. When I was dead to her *because* I was happy. That's what's happening right now, Mary Kay. You put a "pep in my step"—you told me I *exist*—and your friend wants me to stumble. She's not smart like you and me—she can't be happy for other people, not really—and she won't ever learn her lesson and fuck it. Do I do it right now? Do I kill your best friend?

"Sweetie," she says. "Could you move the TV in here? I have sensitive retinas and the glare from the window really is *killing* me. I'd also love a steak. I am simply dying for some real red *meat,* you know?"

I want to, I do. But no. I don't have a plan and I'm not going down over *Melanda.*

I slam the door and on the way upstairs, my tongue pulsates in my mouth. *Fuck you, Melanda.* My tongue is just fine.

Isn't it?

15

I did not give her my fucking TV and I am not going to get her a *steak*. Bad dogs don't get treats. Everyone knows that. And that's what she is, Mary Kay: a bad dog. Territorial and violent. She attacked me and I brought her home. I fed her. I tried to train her and she turned around and assaulted me again.

I definitely *wish you had been there the night she told me about what a bad kisser you are. Too much tongue.*

Now I'm pacing in my backyard (watching my estranged son run around on Instagram to remind myself of how fucking good I am. He's toddling. He's cute. I made that). I trip on an exposed root in the *natural landscape* and I hate Bainbridge Island because there is such a thing as TOO FUCKING QUIET. We're not in the desert and no one has to be on the factory line at 7:00 A.M. so why is everyone but me asleep?

I wasn't gonna hurt anyone. I'm a good goddamn guy but I'm a lonely guy, bullied and used. *She* attacked *me*! It's her fault that she's in that basement, that I'm in this mess, and did you really make fun of my kissing? Did you mean it when you said you never thought you'd meet someone like me? Or is Melanda right? Was that your *kind* way of telling me I'm not good enough?

I can't be here. And no I don't want to get on the *ferry* and ride to Seattle and stuff my face with salmon ampersand quinoa and visit a bookstore underneath a market—we get it, Seattle, you have *history*—only to be hungry an hour later and hunt down some restaurant with a twee pink door. All of that is really only fun if you're doing it with someone you love and I love you but you're like the rest of the islanders right now.

You're in bed.

I put on my gloves—no fucking prints, no DNA—and I unlock the door to Melanda's condo and set the stage for her departure in case you do pop by. I go in the bathroom—the door is propped open by a copy of *The Thorn Birds* that she cut in half—and it's a foul mess of O.B. tampons and *Fitness* magazines and monogrammed towels: *MRS.* Wow. Melanda Ruby Schmid really is a very bad dog. Her parents knew it, burying the ruby because they knew she wasn't a gem, saddling her with initials she could never live up to. I pick up a framed photo of you and your *best friend* and even when she's happy, she's miserable. Hiding behind sunglasses while you squint in the sun.

I check my phone. Melanda is tearing the sheets off the bed and she isn't capable of appreciating a surprise movie-binge staycation because she isn't capable of love. She only sleeps in one half of her bed at home—the other half is littered with mini Dove wrappers and oh for fuck's sake, Melanda, you're not a supermodel. Buy a candy bar.

She's reading Sarah Jio's *Violets of March* and no, Melanda, that book isn't about you. It's about a *nice* woman, a divorcée who got married because she believed in love, unlike *some* people.

Was she right, Mary Kay? Are you never gonna leave him?

I open the junk drawer in her kitchen and she has dozens of *Women's Fitness* exercise calendars and they're glued together by time and self-loathing. I look in her mirror—it rests on the other half of *The Thorn Birds*—and it lies to me and makes me taller and thinner than I am. I look above her mirror where there's another big fat lie in the form of a cheery sign: YOU ARE BEAUTIFUL. I pick up her computer and the last thing she googled was *young Carly Simon* and no, Melanda. You don't look like Carly Simon because Carly Simon has a soul. I turn on her TV where it's nothing but *Real Housewives.* She didn't watch the documentaries made by women for women that she praises on Twitter and she listens to "Coming Around Again" so much because if no one ever stays—and who could stay—then no one ever leaves and thus no one can ever return to play the game again with her.

But this is the burden of being a good guy. I would never say any of that to her.

The person I need right now is *you*. And it's late but it's not that late.

I pick up Melanda's phone.

Melanda: *You there?*

You: *Yep. Can't sleep. How's the trip? Did you get in safe?*

Oh, Mary Kay. You could sleep if you were with me and so could I.

Melanda: *Yes and sooooo . . . okay so I met someone lol*

You: *Already? You just landed, no?*

Melanda: *Well . . . we actually started talking a couple months ago but long distance I mean I didn't say anything because who knows but now I'm here and well . . . NOW I KNOW lol*

You: *Wow. Well that's . . . great?*

Oh, Mary Kay, you are greener by the bubble.

Melanda: *lol yes with him right now so gotta scram but yay for meeee!*

You: *Wow! Details? Tell me he's not married.*

Jesus, you are jealous and as well you should be. You see now that Melanda took a leap of faith so she gets to be happy and *this* is how I make you see the light.

Melanda: *Nope! Divorced. Totally free . . . no offense lol*

You: *Ha.*

I grin. It is a *little* fun to get under your skin.

Melanda: *wow INDEED and he can KISS lol speaking of which . . . how's your little friend?*

You: *That's so great M!*

You didn't bite the bait but on a good note, I hear the pain in your voice.

Melanda: *I forgot about just kissing someone who like really really really knows how to kiss lol am sorry I am in seventh grade right now woo hooo lololol*

You: *Yeah. Nothing like a kiss.*

I miss your *yeah* and do you mean *our* kiss?

Melanda: *You ok with stuff?*

You: *Yeah. Just trying to get Nomi to do her college essay. Maybe I'll go back to college too! When do you find out about the job?*

Jesus, Mary Kay. Life moves forward. You went to college. You married Phil. Get with the program and move on. Don't pine for the past and don't make it all about the future. Be here now and give me your Lemonhead.

Melanda: *Haha you could not pay me to go back to school I am so happy right now. I mean Carl . . . my interview is tomorrow but I feel really good about it you know?*

You: *So happy for you M. Seriously.*

Seriously. Take it in, Mary Kay. I know that divorce used to seem like a bad idea, like you'd be at wine bars eight nights a week with Melanda. Squabbling over horny Shortus types, men you don't even like, regretting every decision that led to that barstool. But you met me. It's time to leave that fucker and *be* with me. Carl did it. He left his wife and you can too.

Melanda: *Ok seriously back at you ARE YOU OK you can talk about joe. I won't yell at you and make fun of his sweater lol I promise*

I wait. I watch the screen. Nothing. Nothing at all. And then a minute later:

You: *Melanda you don't have to make a dig at him every time I mention him. I know you don't like him. Message received.*

Melanda: *I'm sorry I'm just like CARL CARL CARL ONLY GOOD MAN ON EARTH*

You: *Well that's great. Can't wait to meet him if things work out.*

If. Ouch! Is that the issue? You want the sure thing over the risk?

Melanda: *Oh it's more like whatever happens, being with him is a game changer you know? He went through the fire and he left his wife and even if it doesn't work out I am just so happy we met you know? That said ok yes we are totally getting married lolol*

You: *Ha.*

You never do the isolated *ha* and Melanda's really getting to you. *Good.*

Melanda: *r u mad at me?*

You: *No. Just feel like shit tonight. And I know. I'm married. I made this mess and I have a husband but I don't need a lecture right now so please spare me.*

Melanda: *Only love you sweetie. And on that note . . . I know I was hard on Joe.*

Mary Kay: *Eh. I should probably just forget it. It was just a kiss. A good one. I was living in a fantasy. Cliché but true, ya know?*

I have my answer. You *do* like the way *I* kiss and Melanda was right about one thing. I'm nothing like Phil. I'm *better* than Phil. And Melanda may not have *come around* and seen the light just yet, but I'm in control now and it's time for her to be a real friend.

Melanda: *No MK. Look pre-Carl I was in man-bashing mode. I can admit that. I mean you know that . . .*

Mary Kay: *I know he wasn't your favorite . . .*

Melanda: *Do me a favor. Give it a chance. I'm not saying to leave Phil and I'm not saying Joe is anywhere near the man that Carl is . . . lol gush gush gush . . . but I just . . . I want you to be happy. There's no law that says you can't just get to know him I mean you told him about Phil. Don't push him away.*

Mary Kay: *Um who is this and can you send my friend Melanda back* ☺

A chill runs through my body. I stare at the phone and fuck you, Steve Jobs *and* Mother Nature, because this is the flaw of all communication. Why can't we take things back? The pressure is increasing every second and I have to say something but did I go too far?

Melanda: *Oh believe me I'm grossed out too and fully aware that in seven days I will probably hate Carl and Minnesota lolol*

You are typing. Slowly. The dots appear and the dots go away and people who go to bed early wake *up* early and I need to finish packing up for Melanda's imaginary trip and I need to get the fuck out of here before the joggers awake and boom.

Mary Kay: *I was just kidding. Very happy you're happy. And yeah . . . about Joe, we'll see.*

Oh yes we fucking will, Mary Kay.

16

It's Christmas Eve and all day long, I live like a Mothball. I don't make eye contact with you unless you address me, which you do twice, both times for *professional* reasons. At noon, I go out to the love seat, because I always go out to the love seat. I know how to take a hint, Mary Kay. "Melanda" told you to give me a chance, but the last time we spoke, you told me to back off.

The door opens at 12:13 and you're wearing your coat—you mean to stay—and you make a sad face at my lunch. "Well, that's not beef and broccoli."

"No," I say. "This is what we call a peanut butter and jelly sandwich."

You sit on the love seat. Not close as in *Closer.* But you're not shoved against the armrest. You smile at me. Playful. "Is it okay if I tell you that Nomi likes the Bukowski you suggested?"

"I think that's okay. Is it okay if I tell you that I'm really happy you came out here?"

"Well, I think that's okay. But I should ask you if it's okay for me to say that I was up all night because I couldn't stop thinking about you."

"I think it's okay for you to say that . . . as long as it's okay for me to say that I was up all night thinking about you too."

We are on fire and you scratch your messy bun. Red. Gold. *You.* "Is it okay for me to say that I thought about you in the shower?"

"Only if it's okay for me to say that I *always* think about you in the shower."

You turn red. "Is it okay for me to say that I've been hoping that you do?"

"Only if it's okay for me to say that I fucked you in my head in every square foot of this library."

You glance at me. Did I go too far? You smile. "Is it okay for me to be a little insulted that you haven't imagined what we could do right here?"

"I said every square foot of the library, Mary Kay."

"Yes, but in my head, we've been on every square foot of the *property.*"

Now *you* went too far and you turn red and I want to hug you but there are Mothballs inside and there's an invisible ring on your finger. "See," you say. "This is the catch-22. We both know that a lot of this is about the boundary. I mean who's to say that all the tension between us isn't *about* the boundary? I'm thinking of both of us here, Joe. Because look at us. Yesterday I was a nervous wreck about telling you and it turns out you already know . . . joke's on me . . . and today, ten seconds into it and it's . . . Well, my God, our IQs are dropping a million points a second."

You're the one who's married and I'm the one who's not and I wouldn't respect you, let alone love you, if you weren't so torn up right now, but it's time for me to show off for you the way you showed off for me. "You're right," I say. "And we should probably go back inside."

You look at me like you were hoping I would kiss you. As if I can fucking do that. "Is it okay if I say I'm sorry for imploding?"

I stand up. You're still sitting. At this height, you could unzip me and put me in your mouth and that's what you want but you've convinced yourself that it's *all* you want when it comes to me. I leave you on the love seat and go back into the stacks and wait three minutes and text you from Melanda's phone.

So?

So what?

So did you see Joe yet? Sorry lol I'm in love mode!

You're spending the rest of your lunch break hiding from me in your office and you sigh.

Well I just offered to sleep with him in the parking lot. He probably thinks I'm insane. THIS is insane.

You're talking yourself out of it and I'm sick of the way you women call out everything natural and reasonable as *insane.* But I'm not me. I'm Melanda.

Well maybe you should lol kiddiiiiiiing

You pick up a candy cane on your desk and bite into it. *Crunch.* Like the rock hitting Melanda's head in the woods. And maybe there is a little holiday fucking magic just for us. Maybe something good will come out of this mess after all.

What if I'm just really horny or what if HE'S just really horny? What if I'm just building him up in my head. I mean look at Seamus. Nice pig, but a pig. We know men. Joe is probably too good to be true. You're the one who said it. No friends. No ties. He spent Thanksgiving alone and you know what they say. People show you who they are.

I want to storm into your office and dive into your Murakami because sexual frustration is poisonous.

Sweetie Carl's here so I have to go but honestly . . . I was moody that day at the diner. You like him. He likes you. Deal with it. xoxo love youuuuu

Melanda's right, Mary Kay. You like me. You do need to fucking deal with it and I know how to force you to deal with it. There's a seminar in one of the glass-walled conference rooms. It's a setup for disaster—Mothballs teaching Mothballs how to operate their *iPhones*—and you forced Nomi to help out but she's the only one in there under sixty. She's not even doing her fucking job, Mary Kay. She's holding *her* phone, forcing one of our patrons to look at her pictures. "See," Nomi says. "This is the shed at Fort Ward. The moss on the roof is like the floor of a forest for Barbies. When I was little I wanted my dad to steal it."

I know Phil's her dad but *ugh* and the Mothball glares at me and

Nomi clocks me and grunts. "So my mom roped you into this too? Nice. Real nice."

"Not at all," I say, rolling up my sleeves and wiping belVita fiber cookie crumbs into a napkin. "I'm here because I want to be here."

Nomi makes room for me at the table and Mrs. Elwell remarks on your Meerkat's *demeanor* and I am a pro, defending your daughter without excusing her behavior—I love to play both sides!—and before you know it, we're in a groove. We help Mrs. Elwell "connect" with her family on Facebook—remember when slide shows were universally acknowledged to be torture?—and Nomi is softening her approach, learning to be more patient, more like *me.* She's not the fastest learner and she snorts when a Mothball in a sweater set can't access her *Budussy* books. But I catch her eye—*Be nice, Nomi*—and what can I say, Mary Kay?

I'm good with kids. I'm selfless. I know my way around a cell phone and I'm paternal but not *patriarchal* and you have a front-row seat. You see me and I see the wheels turning in your head as you remember that I'm not just a good kisser. I'm a good *person*. And I don't rest on my laurels because I had one hit song *twenty* years ago—get over yourself, Phil—and when it's over your Meerkat sighs. "Well," she says. "We survived."

"Oh come on," I say. "You had some fun. I know I did."

Nomi won't admit it—that's kids—but when I'm packing up to go home, she cracks a *Budussy* joke. You see that we bonded—another score!—and I wave. Friendly Joe! Well-adjusted Joe! "You guys have a great holiday! Gotta go meet some friends in the city!"

Sure enough, you send a text to Melanda while I'm walking home.

Okay he's good. It's like I almost forgot how smart he is because it was so surreal to be so open with him about the other side of things and . . . okay. Okay wow. Aahahhahah.

Melanda's busy with Carl, and she *is* jealous at heart, so she just likes your text. And you don't text again and that's just as well because I may not have *friends* and I may not be unhealthily attached to my family that I secretly hate—I'm talking to you, my fecal-eyed neighbors—but I do have Melanda in my basement—and you know what, Mary Kay? I'm actually happy she's there.

This has never been a good night for me. When I was a kid, I wrote letters to Santa telling him I'd be a good boy and wait for *next* Christmas, when things would be better—ha!—but now the lie of my childhood is true. I have a future with you and this really is the last shitty Christmas of my life, the darkest hour before our permanent dawn. I won't make it worse by giving myself a *body* to deal with when everyone else on this rock is opening their fucking presents so I warm up some fried chicken I had in the freezer and I grab a gallon of ice cream and head downstairs. She sees me. She smells the chicken. And before I even ask, she handcuffs herself to the bed and tosses the key at the door. Such a good dog suddenly, and I enter the Whisper Room and she does a little upper body ladies' night kind of dance on her futon.

"Oh honey, I *love* fried chicken!"

I hand her the tray and she tears skin off the chicken and pops it into her mouth. "Scrumptious," she coos, as she licks her fucking fingers. I know what she's doing, Mary Kay. She's playing me. As if she thinks this is the first time I've been cornered into quarantining a dangerous, unstable person in my fucking personal space. I play right back. "Well, you seem happy."

"You know what? I actually *am* happy. And omigod, I really did forget how much I *loooove The Hand That Rocks the Cradle.*"

"Oh yeah?"

She eats more skin. She licks her fingers. "It does make me *kind of* sad though . . ."

"Oh yeah?"

She tears the lid off the ice cream and digs her fork into the gallon. This is part of her game. "Yeah," she says. "I feel like you think Mary Kay is the Bridget Fonda, the Annabella Sciorra. You buy her barn jacket demeanor and the whole holier-than-thou good woman thing . . ." You *are* a good woman and Melanda smacks her gums. "Sweetie, you should know that Mary Kay is just . . . Well, she's not what you think."

Poor Melanda. If only she knew that you and I had a banner day. I tell her to hold that thought and I go upstairs and make us two mugs of hot cocoa and by this time next year, I'll be doing the same thing, making cocoa for *you*.

Melanda claps when I return to the Whisper Room. "Ooh, yes. I miss carbs so much."

You're allowed to have this one last nuclear holiday with your unchosen family, same way Melanda is allowed to have a sugar high. The steam turns her skin red and she purrs like one of my cats. "Mmmm," she says. "Yummy."

"So you were saying . . ."

She puts her mug on the end table and she picks up the remote and pauses *Anything Else* and it's just me, Melanda, and Jason Fucking Biggs. She picks at the GUN on her shirt. "So I got pregnant in high school."

I remain calm. I am the fucking key master. "Is this another lie? Because I know that Mary Kay never said I'm a bad kisser."

She bats her eyelashes, what's left of them. "I know," she says. "I said some *really* icky things when I was detoxing . . ." Always with an excuse. "But you were right . . ." Stop trying to mind-fuck me, Melanda. I'm too happy to be stupid. "And you should know why I was *really* in the woods the other night."

I sit in the chair and sip my cocoa. "Well, go ahead."

"So I was fifteen and I barely knew the guy and I took care of it."

"Okay."

"And Mary Kay was amazing, totally there for me, real hard-core best friend stuff."

"Well, that's no surprise."

She dips a finger into the melted vanilla. "True," she says. "And I was there a few years later for *her*. When *she* got pregnant."

"And . . ."

Melanda flaps her wings. "And she was older. It wasn't *dramatic* . . ." You're not a drama queen. A drama queen wouldn't have been so responsive to all my good doings in the library today. "And I go to the hospital the day she goes into labor. I'm in the room with her holding her hand because Phil . . . well, I mean, he wasn't that kind of guy . . ." There's one true thing. "So Nomi arrives and she's beautiful. Perfect. This feels like our baby, you know? And MK looks at me and goes, 'Thank you, Melanda. If you hadn't showed me how hard it was to give up a pregnancy, I might not have my baby.' "

Very well played, because as a man, I can't say anything. "That's a lot to take in."

"So she put Nomi in my arms. I held that little girl and I was fine with my decision. I have no regrets. I did the right thing at the right time . . ." I know the feeling. "See, I was in the woods that night because Nomi *is* part mine. Mary Kay knew what she was doing when she put Nomi in my arms, when she found a flaw in every guy I *ever* even tried to date. Yes, I've had my moments. Maybe I'm not the best friend at times . . ." Ha! "But Mary Kay uses me, Joe. *I've* been the one looking out for Nomi. In *The Hand That Rocks the Cradle,* Annabella Sciorra practically *lives* in that barn jacket. Like Mary Kay in her tights. But that's the male director's gaze for you. In reality, no woman wears that barn jacket every day. You should know that you've put yourself in jeopardy for a woman who only exists in your head." She looks at the TV. And then she looks at me. "You look like him, you know? Jason Biggs. A handsome version, *obviously.*"

I don't look like Jason Biggs and she licks her fingers and goes back to watching her fucking movie and I do *not* wish her a Merry Christmas. She was supposed to see what's wrong with *her* but instead she's trying to make me think there's something wrong with *you.*

I go upstairs and I am fuming, trapped, fucked. *Ho Fucking Ho* and everyone on this rock is asleep except me and Melanda. I read my stupid horoscope on one of her *astrology apps*—no, Joe, no—and I go to Love's Instagram and watch Forty open his fucking presents again—no, Joe, no—and I miss my son, my son I never met and right now the bitch is right.

You really aren't here with me. You only exist in my head.

But then my phone buzzes. It's you: *Merry Christmas Eve, Joe. Just thinking of you.*

I needed you and you knew it—our connection is like me, it *exists*—and I settle into my sofa and my cats gather and romp. I spend the rest of the night texting with you about Christmas stories and the Bukowski you bought for Nomi and it's calming and cozy—you send me a picture of your bare legs, your fuzzy sock slippers—and our phones are magic. *We* are magic and we light up the wee hours of the long, heavy night but eventually you do *have* to get some sleep—big day today—and I wish you sweet dreams. I am content. Loved. It's almost like your friend Melanda ceases to exist, like Santa Claus finally did me an overdue solid and schlepped into this house and dragged your friend out of here, onto his fucking sleigh.

Almost.

17

It's the day after Christmas and I've been living in a fantasy, texting with you when you manage to squirrel away from your family. This power imbalance wouldn't work with anyone but you, Mary Kay, constantly empathetic—*I hope you don't mind me only having a minute here and there*—and though we don't say it, we both know that this is the last holiday we'll spend apart.

My present to Melanda was giving her exactly what she wanted: no fucking food. But it's been almost two days and I don't want her to starve to death—that takes too long—so I'm on my way downstairs with a bowl of food—she really is like my dog—and lucky for me, she's asleep. No more *film school* today because she'll make up more stories to stay alive. And it's not entirely her fault for thinking she has a chance. Last night, I told you about how I gave the fecal-eyed family a wreath and you said I'm too nice for my own damn good. And you're right, Mary Kay.

I am. But I'm also a fucking procrastinator. I know I have to kill Melanda. But I just keep putting it off.

It's not just me, Mary Kay. Most "normal" people in America are in the same boat right now, torn between wanting to save the people they're stuck with and wanting to fucking kill them. I don't know if her story about you is true, but I know that I don't care. So what if you had a callous moment in the delivery room? You had just created a child with *Phil*. We're animals. Animals eat other animals alive. That's the way the system is designed. And so what if you manipulated Melanda into being your unofficial co-parent? You were stuck with *Phil* and mothers do crazy shit. Love lets my son chew on Christmas lights—I don't even let my cats do that—and the fact is, motherhood is the hardest job in the world. I love the person you are now, Mary Kay—*you wished me a Merry Christmas, you wished me a Merry Christmas*—and if someone from my past attacked *you*, well, you might hear things about me that would put you off.

I'm a lot of things, Mary Kay, but I'm not a hypocrite.

I'm on my way to the library when Melanda's phone pings in my pocket.

Christmas wasn't the same without you. Hope you had fun with Carl! Would love to see pics!

LOL no pics cuz his kids were with his wife and we were pretty much naked the whole time bwaahahahahha

Well that's great. I can't stop thinking about Joe . . . We're talking nonstop like teenagers.

I pump my fist. Well, not really, but I want to.

Sweetie don't think. Just do! Lol love you! Hope you guys had a fun holiday too!

There's a big difference between telling someone that you hope they had fun and asking if they had a good time. You know it too, and you don't write back to Melanda. *Good.* You're right. We have been texting *like teenagers* and we're not in high school and it's time for you to step up and make room for me. I get to the library before you and I am shelving Richard Scarrys by the Red Bed when I hear your voice.

"Hey," you say, and what a rush, to finally hear your voice out loud in person, to see your face. You murmur now, as if things changed for us over the past few days, because they *did* change. "I am . . . I have a little something for you."

You're holding a white box and there is a red ribbon wrapped around the white box and you motion toward the door and I follow you outside, where it is gray. Drab. As if January can't fucking wait to get here. We didn't go more than two hours and twelve minutes without talking over the last five days but now we sit on our love seat like strangers on a bus.

You hold your box. "Is this weird?"

"Only if there's a bomb inside."

You laugh. I always make you laugh. "Yeah . . . I got you a little something . . ." Because we bonded over Christmas. "You were so great with Nomi the other day and that meant a lot to me."

"Well, that was nice of you."

You nod. You're still married and you feel guilty, which is why you can't speak the truth and I get it. We're at work. We have to pretend the last few days never happened, not because someone might be eavesdropping—we're alone out here—but because you too are procrastinating. You look down at the box that sits on your lap. A corduroy skirt today. Black tights.

"So how was it? How was Christmas with the family?"

You look at me—you can't fucking *believe* how good I am—and you crack a smile. "Well, it was our first Christmas without Melanda. So we didn't have a buffer."

You really do believe it's her texting you and I smile. "And how was that?"

You rub the ribbon on my box, my box that is your box. "I don't know why I'm telling you this. It doesn't feel fair."

"We're just talking. And I do care about you. You know that."

"Yeah," you say. "I guess it's that thing where even when someone is like family, which Melanda really is, well it's still company. So you dress up a little, you know? You have a *guest*. And it was different without her. There was this moment, after we ate. Phil . . ." You gulp. "My husband's playing his guitar, blasting his music, and Nomi's wearing her headphones and reading her *Columbine* and I almost . . ." Got in the car to come see me. "Well, open your present already."

You hand me the box and a car passes by and the windows are down and Sam Cooke serenades us—*Darling you send me, honest you do*—and Love sent me away but you *send* me and I *send* you. You nudge me. "Well come on. Open it."

I pull the ribbon and I open your box—if only—and I count six red strawberries, all of them doused in chocolate and I bet *Phil* didn't get any fucking strawberries. I look at you. "I wish I had something for you."

Your cheeks are flushed and your eyes are glued to me and you *missed* me. "Yeah," you say. "I wish a lot of things lately . . ."

I want your Murakami and I want your Lemonhead and we both stare at our tree. "I don't want to be selfish, Joe."

"You're not being selfish."

"Well, that's not what Phil says . . ."

I can't be the one you talk to about the rat and you're the one who made the rules. I nod.

"See, Joe, I think Melanda's mad at me. I think that's why she blew me off at Christmas."

I can't talk about this either and my heart is pounding. *Melanda.* "Why do you say that?"

"It's ancient history, but in high school . . . God, I'm too old to start stories with that sentence . . . Anyway, when we became friends, she told me that all these people like your neighbor Nancy . . . Well, she told me they *hated* me. And then one day I go into the bathroom, and I overhear her telling Nancy that *I* hate Nancy."

So that's why you stole her rat and that's why you weren't exactly sensitive about her pregnancy when you got pregnant. And you don't know she's in my basement. You really don't. Do you? "You never told her you overheard her?"

You shake your head. "It's weird to miss her and yet *not* miss her, you know? She might not even come back for a few months . . ." I know. "Melanda" texted you that. "She's gonna start this new job. She met this new guy . . . I'm not so good with change. And it's strange to feel almost jilted, as if I was being 'possessive' or something when I know I should just be happy for her and I know we were both dragging each other down. But it stings in some weird way, to feel . . . left."

RIP Beck . . . RIP Candace . . . Love. I nod. "It is," I say. "But ultimately, the distance gets you to a more honest place, you know?"

You're contemplative. You need me because I'm the first person in your life that really fucking *listens.* I give you the silence you've been craving and you want me so much that you're shaking. "Come on," you say. "It's getting cold."

You open the door—you're not cold, you're hot, hot for me—and you look at the Red Bed and *I* look at the Red Bed and you blush. "Have a good rest of the day!"

I have a *great* rest of the day because of you. You love me and I oughta buy Melanda some chocolate-covered strawberries—ha!—because look what she did for you, for me, for *us*—and I carry your box under the crook of my arm and Sam Cooke's "You Send Me" is on repeat in my head and the world would be a happier place if more people would lift their souls with music instead of *ugh*-inducing podcasts. I make it into town and I take off my headphones and there is music in the café today—Bob Dylan in Pegasus—and there really is *revolution in the air,* strawberries in my hands. I get the chills.

We were tangled up in *Phil's* blues and you *were* married when we met but you gave me a gift and you are *soon to be divorced* and I'm helping *you* out of the jam that is your bad, blue life. I'm saving you! It's almost like you *knew* about my situation with Melanda, and now I don't have to feel bad about it because you don't want things to go back to normal.

Why would you? You have *me.*

I open my box and look down on my six, Red Bed red strawberries, *Murakamis* cloaked in chocolate. I reach my hand into your box that is my box but some asshole body slams me. The box goes flying and the Adidas–sneakered ass who did this mad-dogs *me* like I did something wrong.

"Dude," I say. I am so mad I'm saying *dude.* "What the fuck?"

He doesn't speak or move and I don't like this, Mary Kay. I don't like him.

"Sorry," he says. "Small sidewalk . . . small world, too, my friend."

I am not his *friend* and he's not one of us. He doesn't live here. I can just tell. I step toward him—this is *my* town—and he shakes his head slowly, like a B movie gangster, as if someone wearing Adidas sneakers and a battered old long-sleeve T-shirt—SOMETHING BOATHOUSE—could ever be remotely intimidating.

A kid on a skateboard runs over one of my strawberries and the man who knocked the strawberries onto the sidewalk steps forward. “Nice gift,” he says. “Nothing says forever like a fruit box. You really know how to pick ’em, Goldberg.”

The sky falls down. He said my name.

Is he a cop? Is this about my dog back home?

I give nothing. I say nothing. I know nothing and he laughs. “Calm down,” he says. “They never taste as good as they look, do they, Goldberg?” I could punch his lights out right now. I make a fist. “All right,” he says. “I know you have a temper . . .” No I fucking don’t, not anymore. “So I’ll cut to the chase. I’m just here with a message from our friends the Quinns.”

The Quinns? Love’s family? No. It’s a new year. A new life. “Who are you?”

“It’s pretty simple, Goldberg. Stay away from Love. Stay away from Forty.”

“I don’t know who you are, but obviously you’re ill-informed because I *have* stayed away.”

“Oh, Goldberg,” he says. “Mind your Instagram activities or you’re gonna wind up like your little strawberries. Capiche?”

I looked at Love’s stories because IT WAS FUCKING CHRISTMAS AND SHE STOLE MY SON AND YOU TELL ME HOW TO NOT LOOK AT YOUR OWN FUCKING SON and I ask him who sent him and he chuckles.

I pick up my empty box. “Well, you stay the fuck away from me. And my family.”

He steps in front of me. “I wouldn’t talk that way to me if I were you, Joe.”

“You walk up here. You start shit with me and I don’t know who the hell you are and you talk about my *family.*”

The motherfucker snorts. “‘Family,’” he says. “Well, that’s one word for it, my friend.”

“Who are you?”

“Look, you’re not a member of the Quinn family, Goldberg. See, *I* work for the Quinn family. I’m here on *behalf* of the Quinn family. Think of me as your co-worker.”

"But I don't work for the Quinns."

"Huh," he says. "How'd ya pay for your house?"

I don't answer the question because he knows the goddamn answer and he laughs. Pig. Snob. "See," he says. "The difference between you and me is that the family is on my side, not yours. Understood? So, stop stalking your ex, my friend, and stay offline. Because if you don't stop . . ."

He smashes a strawberry with his shoe and looks at me. "Got it?"

He flips his hat around and walks away and I let him. I have no fucking choice.

18

I can't get those mutilated, bleeding strawberries out of my mind—What *else* does the Strawberry Killer know?—and Melanda is doing jumping jacks and what the fuck happened? I was with *you* and you were with me and now your strawberries are gone—I didn't get to eat one—and Melanda never ate the food I brought her. She claims she's *still fasting her body and her soul* and that's a lie. There's nothing spiritual about her fucking hunger strike—she just wants to be thinner than you—and I don't want her to be here.

But she is.

And she's different, Mary Kay. She just finished *The Anjelica Huston Story* (a.k.a. *Crimes and Misdemeanors*), and she's high on endorphins, sounding off on Rebecca De Mornay in *The Hand That Rocks the Cradle—Who wouldn't go nuts working for a barn jacket mommy who gets to be married to the nicest man on the planet?*—and she takes a punch at *Single White Female—Who wouldn't go crazy shacking up with Bridget Fonda and her stupid swan neck?*

She won't stop talking and I can't stop thinking about the Strawberry Killer and why is every fucking person lining up to get in our way? Finally, she stops jumping and sighs. "You were so right about *Beaches*, Joe."

"I'm gonna go back upstairs. You seem okay for now."

"Wait," she says. "I mean it. You were right, Joe. You were right about a lot."

Sorry, Melanda, I'm not some dumb asshole who gets off on a woman telling him he's right. "See," she says. "I don't cry when Barbara Hershey dies. You want to know why?"

I didn't care then and I don't care now. "Why?"

"Because she *deserved* to die, Joe. She stole her roommate's boyfriend." She touches her toes and rises, Jane Fucking Fonda, and now she's jumping again. Clap. Swish. Clap. "I want to go to Minnesota, Joe. I'm ready." This should be good news. She wants out and I want her out—LIFE IS SUPPOSED TO BE EASY WHEN PEOPLE WANT THE SAME FUCKING THING—but she's *here*. She knows things. She jumps and she jacks and she pushes. "I'm tired of this island, where women are expected to go around forgiving the women who shit all over them. Right now, I just want to forgive *you*, Joe." She stops jumping and takes her pulse and her poor parents, no wonder they died early. "And I promise you, Joe, I will never breathe a word of any of this to anyone . . ." She's saying my name *way* too much. "You helped me. And I'm ready to move on." She flops onto the futon with a "*Woof, I'm dizzy*" and she picks up the gallon of water and drinks directly from it even though there's a plastic cup on the nightstand. She's relaxed and I'm tense, riddled with Silverstein's *Whatifs*—What if someone saw me with the Strawberry Killer? What if you see your strawberries mashed on the pavement?—and why didn't I scrape up that mess and what am I gonna do about *this* mess?

"I fucked him," she says. "I fucked Phil."

"In high school. I know."

"No, Joe. I'm talking about a few weeks ago, when MK was outta town. Go back to my condo. I dare you. I am *so* behind on laundry so you can take my panties to a lab. They'll find Phil's DNA, I promise you."

Another story, no doubt. I want your panties not *her* panties and I take her phone out of my pocket and she laughs. "Oh come on," she says. "I'm a teacher. I don't *sext* with him. It's an affair. You just have to trust me . . ." She rubs her calf, as if she's pretending her hand belongs to a man, to your fucking rat. "Remember when Jennifer Jason

Leigh mounted Bridget Fonda's boyfriend in *Single White Female*? It's kinda like that. We are talking a *ton* of blow jobs."

She drinks directly from her jug.

"Melanda, this doesn't matter."

"Wrong," she says. "This changes *everything*. Now you know my dirty secret. You can let me go because I don't *want* Mary Kay to find out about me and Phil. And you don't want her to find out about you and me."

I don't want there to be a *me and Melanda*—why can't your friends be normal?—and she crosses her legs. "You don't believe me."

"I didn't say that."

"So, it started after my thirtieth birthday, not the best time in my life, as you might imagine . . . MK wanted to throw me a surprise party, but you know how it is . . ." What the hell would I know about surprise parties and would you recognize your strawberries if you saw them on the sidewalk? "I told her no, but she insisted. So I got all dressed up, figured we'd be at the pub, maybe somewhere in Lynwood . . ." Oh, Melanda, learn how to tell a story and oh, Mary Kay, I am sorry about your fruit. "But then MK picks me up. She drives us to her *house* . . ."

Is she making this up as she goes along? "Can you just get to the point?"

She twirls her hair. "Go on my Facebook. Look at the pictures. It wasn't a party for me, Joe. It was a fuck-you to me. All families. All kids and babies and it's not like I don't like kids and babies, but come on. I'm thirty years old and I don't even have a boyfriend and Phil was supposed to bring this guy from his band who seemed decent and he's not there and I'm literally the only person at *my* birthday party who doesn't have a husband or a kid."

I dig up the pictures on her fucking Facebook and I see you. I see all the children, but like most pictures, these don't tell the whole story. Melanda curls up like a college kid in an emotional circle jerk. She says she got drunk and passed out on your sofa before the party ended.

"I woke up . . . I didn't know where I was. I didn't know what year it was. You know that kind of drunk?" No. "That dirty thirty kind of drunk . . ." She's Bridget Jones now, she's fucking *British*. "Anywho,

Phil comes downstairs." She gulps, in a way that makes her story seem legitimate. "He whipped it out. I could have told him to bugger off. But I was just so mad at MK. I wanted to suck his cock, Joe . . ." Bridget didn't talk like that. Too crass. "And I wanted to do that because of what she did to me with that pretend party. So I did it." She arches her back, a mix of pride and shame and joy and you deserve better, Mary Kay. "And that's that. Our ten-year anniversary is coming up and I do *not* want to be here to 'celebrate' it. I also don't want to be forced to come back here for some stupid court hearing about all this . . . so this is where we are."

"You expect me to believe that Mary Kay has *no* idea about you and Phil . . ."

"I'm a *very* good liar, Joe. You of all people should know that."

I shove her phone in my pocket. "This has nothing to do with our situation."

"Are you kidding? Don't you get it? I want *out.* I hate the person I've become. I hate that I slowly, unconsciously settled for this man just because he calls me *Ruby* and I hate that I became someone who got off on pulling one over on my best friend. I hate my condo. I hate my job. I hate my noisy fridge and I hate the guilt and I hate that I'm actually *happy* I missed Christmas because it meant that I didn't have to sit in their house like some overgrown orphan and go home and gorge on Hostess Cupcakes while I sit on my couch just *hating* myself. I swear to you, you are in the clear because *I* want to be in the clear. I want out."

I see your strawberries on the sidewalk. I see the rain washing them away.

"Okay," she says. "You don't believe me. You need details . . ." No, Mary Kay. No. "So, a few years ago he got this day job . . . I mean the man does *not* belong at a desk . . ." She says that like it's a good thing. "I would sneak out of school at lunch and park a block away and go into his office and . . . you know. He said he couldn't live without me and it's terrible, but it was so exciting, sneaking around, sucking him off, and going back to teach all the kids about Zora Neale Hurston." She's waving her arms as if this weight has *finally* been lifted and it all *feels* real but she might be faking it. She has been studying some of the world's most phenomenal actresses and you're a fox. You would know if your best friend and your husband were boning. Foxes see things. "I don't know, Melanda . . ."

"Oh, come on," she says. "Barn jacket Goody Two-shoes wives are *always* blind. These past few days . . . Being away from my *life* . . . well now I get it. Phil's married to MK. You're in love with MK. That's the story of my life here. And here's the kicker . . ." The long dramatic pause and I am the Bonnie Hunt to her Zellweger in *Jerry Fucking Maguire.* "You're right, Joe. I'm not a woman supporting women. I don't want to leave. I *have* to leave."

She takes a stage breath and I feel played. "Melanda, I think you need to eat something."

"You're judging me. And you're allowed. I was dumb like Anjelica Huston. Who knows? Maybe I'm too romantic . . ." Oh, for fuck's sake. "And yes, Joe, yes, I *have* dreamed about Mary Kay catching a rare heart disease or a fast-moving cancer but that was only because I wanted Phil to be free." She rubs her eyes. "And now I'm just . . . tired. Now I just want out."

I picture her in Charlize Theron's apartment in *Young Adult,* drunk and alone, calling you up in the middle of the night and telling you what I did to her as she underplays what she did to *me* and I knock on the glass and she sighs, ever the condescending teacher and she says she *hears* me. "Look at it this way. If there's one thing you can be sure about, well, I know how to keep a secret. I never gave Phil an ultimatum. I never threatened to tell MK. And I don't want to hurt her anymore. And this time around . . . this is a secret that I would hold on to because I don't *want* her to know. I've done enough damage to them."

"You're not the one who's married, Melanda. He took advantage of *you.*"

She looks me right in the eye. "No, Joe. I took advantage of *them.*"

She kicks the wall with her bare foot and now she's rubbing her foot and she reminds me of my son, always banging himself on the head, his mother begging her Instagram audience of cunts for advice. *How do I get my little boy to stop beating himself up? Do I put him in a helmet?*

I tell her this is a *very creative story* and she accuses me of saying she's not *hot enough* for Phil because she doesn't *prance around in miniskirts* like you and I tell her she's twisting my words and she tugs at the GUN on her T-shirt. "Did you read that book *The Beloveds*?"

"The Maureen Lindley? No, I haven't read it yet."

Her face is the reason people like RIP Benji lie about reading books and her eyes fill with judgment. Thick, ugly snobbery. "Well, it's this theory. Some people get to be loved and some people don't."

"That's a crock of shit. You just said that Phil 'loves' you. So which is it?"

"You're a kidnapper. I'm a husband fucker. Let's agree that we're not model citizens. You want in, I want out." She makes it all sound so simple, Mary Kay, like a bizarro-world Pacific Northwest fairy tale where it's happy endings all around. But that's what teachers do. They simplify things. She rubs her eyes. "Well, if you won't put me on a plane right now, can you *please* bring the TV in here? I have *such* a migraine."

I'm tired too, Mary Kay. And I can't deal with her remains, not with the fucking Strawberry Killer out there. I'm a nice guy, and she's starting to cry, so I bring the TV into her room. She rolls over and picks up the remote. "Thank you," she says. "And if it's not too much . . . I'd love a nice big fast-breaking last supper. Steak or salmon. Or even chicken."

"It's not your last supper, Melanda."

She cues up the third and last Bridget Jones movie. "Can you just let me watch in peace?"

I leave her to be loved vicariously through Bridget Fucking Jones and there are moments when I want her to be happy. Maybe she's right. Maybe she really does want a fresh start. I imagine a world where you and I are living together. Phil is gone, finding new women to suck on his *Philstick* and Melanda calls you once a week from her new life in Minnesota. She never tells you about that night in the woods and you never find out that she betrayed you. We take our secrets to the grave and people do that. I *want* to do that because I want to be the man who fixed your life. Not the man who killed your best friend.

But then I remember her Sorel boot in my ribs. I remember how the corners of her Carly Simon mouth turned up as I left her just now. I can't fucking trust her, Mary Kay. I have to fact-check her soap opera saga so I throw a salmon on the grill. I pop a steak in the oven—Nice Joe! Chef Joe!—and I play the Sacriphil songs from the year Melanda turned thirty. It's no use, Mary Kay. This is a *concept* album about a day in the life of a ghost—oh, Phil, you should have quit after your Shark—and I turn off the fucking "music" and text Phil from my burner phone: *Hey, you around?*

A good five minutes later my *man* Phil responds: *Hell yeah Joe!*

I step on Riffic's tail and he hisses and my veins shrink up on me. Phil called me Joe. To him I'm *Jay.* Does he know? Am I fucked? Ten seconds later: *I mean Jay. Sorry man!*

Fucking prick.

I write back: *Question. Banging the girlfriend's best friend. Am I going to hell for that, or is that kinda shit good for the music?*

Phil responds with an all caps warning—FOR YOUR EYES ONLY, HAVEN'T LAID DOWN THIS TRACK YET—and a page of his notepad. The title of the song is "A Diamond for You, A Ruby for Me" and I scan the lyrics and he's *mining rubies at Fort Ward* and Jesus, Mary Kay. It's true. Her story wasn't "creative" and sometimes truth really is more repugnant and useful than fiction.

I'm mad for you and I'm sad for you. Of all the places they could have gone, Fort Fucking Ward. The salmon is sizzling and the fat in the meat is bubbling and Melanda is right. She knows my secret and I know hers. Could I do it, Mary Kay? Could I let your best friend go?

I never *wanted* to kill her—I don't want to kill *anyone*—and okay. It's insane to imagine her walking up the stairs, going to an airport, and starting over. But once upon a time, it was insane to imagine a woman like *you* walking into my life and I want to do right by you.

I placate your lying, cheating rat with all the caps I can manage—*YOU ARE THE KING*—and I put Sam Cooke on repeat to sanitize my eardrums.

And then my doorbell rings.

That's not a thing my doorbell does and is it the Strawberry Killer? Is it Phil? Did he somehow find out where I live? I don't like the sound of my doorbell and there it goes *again* and now there is knocking and what if the rat found out my address and now it's the doorbell *and* the fists pounding on the door and my skin crawls.

I don't look in the peephole and I don't run. My hand sweats as I grip the doorknob.

And there you are.

19

You are wet—it started raining—and feral—you barge into my house.

Your hair is dripping on your blouse and your blouse is soaked—I see the outline of your bra—and you pace around in my living room—did I close the door to the basement?—and you are quiet. Wordless and airtight, like my Whisper Room, and do you know about Melanda? Do you know about *Jay*? I never should have knocked out Melanda and brought her home. I should have let her try and ruin my name—*A Girl Is a Gun*—because you would have come to my defense. You would have told her she was wrong. But I let my fear get the best of me and you drop onto my red sofa and you look at me like I'm a cheater.

You point at my big red chair. "Sit," you say, as if I'm a dog. "Sit."

You don't speak to me. You pull your shirt over your head and it feels like the first time I ever jerked off—Blanche DuBois, I love you forever—and it reminds me of the first real-life woman I saw naked—my mother fell in the shower, there was hair down there, there were breasts up there—and the first time I had sex—Mrs. Monica Fonseca—and it's Sam Cooke in that passing car, it's the Eagles on a summer night when even people who get off on hating the Eagles have to kind of love them.

You didn't come to arrest me and you don't know how hard I've worked for this but here you are, dropping your skirt, peeling off your tights—*Oh God, Joe. Oh God*—and your Murakami is so close I can smell it and you sit on the sofa and I start to stand and you order me to sit and you stare at my pants so I unzip them and is that okay? Yes, that's okay.

Your eyes are on the road and your hands are on the wheel and we are going to the fucking roadhouse in our own way and your nipples pop for me—*Oh God, Joe. Oh God*—and the pages of your book were stuck together. Sealed off like your legs below your tights but look at you now. Unglued. Slick. *Oh God, Joe. Oh Joe.* You are inside of you, but you are there because of me.

I move again. I want to be *Closer* and again you shoo me off. *Sit.*

You won't let me in today—you're still married—but I am inside of you, inside of your mind—and you came here to teach me and I am your pupil and I'm a fast learner—*This finger goes there. The thumb belongs here*—and your knees buckle and your toes curl and you finish first—*Sisters before Misters*—and you roll up in a ball and hide your face in a red pillow. You know I'm getting close and you peek and your eyes are just above the red pillow and I finish because of your eyes.

You sigh. "Oh God, Joe."

Again we don't speak. We don't move. Our bodies hum. The air is musty with our sweat, our fluids. Do I hug you? Do I high-five you? I know you so well but I don't know you naked and you came here, in more ways than one, and are you grossed out? Am I becoming an anecdote in your head—*So this one time I showed up at this guy's house and touched myself while he jacked off, I mean that's how you know it's time for couples counseling*—and the serotonin is crashing. What do I say to you? What do I do? Do I bring you water? Do I feed you?

And then you laugh. "Okay, I'm a little embarrassed."

"Don't be. That was very hot."

"Yeah?"

"Yeah."

You're a fox and foxes need to move so you pick up your tights and you tell me you've never done anything like this—you think you have to say that—and I walk across the room. I take your tights in my hands. I breathe in the white cotton center, the part that breathes you in, day in, day out. I am a gentleman. You want your clothes so I hand over your tights and you laugh.

"This is just never an elegant activity, putting on tights."

I run my hand up the back of your leg. "Agree to disagree."

You pull away and I take my hand off your leg. You pull up your tights and you fix your bun. "Huh," you say. "I didn't know you play guitar."

"A little." I should have hidden that fucking *Philstick*. "But not in a serious way. I have an oboe too. And a flute."

You smile. "And you play them all at once, right?"

We're smiling again and I got us out of the jam. I bring you down to the red sofa, *the Red Bed.* We are spooning. We are one. Your voice is small, scared. "I don't know what to say right now."

"You don't have to say anything."

Silence falls on us like Guterson's snow falling on cedars. We are learning what it feels like to be alone in private. You feel what I feel. Warm. Safe.

I shouldn't tell you this but you're here. You came. "So the day after we first talked on the phone, before I started working at the library . . . I bought a cashmere sweater."

"Yeah?"

"Yeah," I say. "I didn't know it in the moment, but I got home and put it on and realized it . . . it felt like you."

"I think you're aware that I like that sweater."

Licious saunters into the room and you light up. "Oh God," you gasp. "Licious is even cuter in person. Come here, baby."

Licious leaves the room—fucking cats—and you nestle into my chest and I kiss your head. "All of our cats are cute."

You stroke my chest. "I like the way you say that. Our cats."

We could be teenagers on a beach in the nineties and we could be in the hospital beds in our nineties and there's something old about us together, something young. And then you pat my hand. "Joe, I should probably go."

I hold you. "You should probably not say 'should probably' so much."

I get an F in pillow talk and you're wiggling away, you're on your feet and you're putting on your skirt and what do I say to make you stay? You pull on one boot and then you reach for the other and then you flinch. "What was that noise?"

The Whisper Room is *almost* soundproof and it better not be my dog. "I think I have a mouse."

"Well, don't worry. Riffic will take care of that. He's the toughest one in the bunch."

You are fully dressed by now and I'm still lying on the couch, a big spoon with no little spoon underneath and I can't read your face. Is that guilt? Regret? You mumble something about humane mousetraps like we're in a fucking Facebook group chat about exterminators and I nod, like I give a shit about mice right now.

I stand up. Do I touch you? Do I hug you? "Do you want something to eat?"

You shudder and tell me again that you *should probably* go and then you laugh because of what I said about your *should probablies* and I *should probably* build a time machine because I ruined it. The afterglow.

"See, Joe, this is the problem." You open the door and you open your mouth and you look at me and you look away and just say it, Mary Kay. "You *should probably* stop being so perfect . . . I'll um . . . I'll see you soon, yeah?"

"Yeah," I say. "Soon."

Tastic creeps up on us and rubs against your leg and you pick him up and coo. "Oh God, Tastic, you are the cutest, you are! You are my perfect little baby, yes you are."

You're wrong—Tastic is the neediest and Riffic is the cutest—but I don't question your judgment and you go before I say something stupid and YES! You called me "perfect" and that's what I'm going to be from now on. If I were your cat, my name would be *Perfect*.

When you're gone, I lean my head against the door. I want you to pound on the other side and beg for more, but that's not gonna happen. Perfect men aren't greedy. They're grateful. I go into the kitchen and I like the idea of us in split screen, opening cabinets and going through the motions as we replay every nanosecond of our first (almost) time. I put the overcooked salmon and the blackened steak onto a plate. I get the Heinz ketchup. I grab a couple Hostess Cupcakes and the tray is ready.

I glance at my red sofa. You were there. You'll be there again.

I open the basement door. The tray is heavy and each step is a challenge. But at the same time I have no fear of falling. I'm not walking. I'm floating. *Perfect*.

But then I make it to the bottom of the stairs and I stop short. Something is wrong. The room is silent. Lifeless.

And then I see her. Melanda's facedown on the floor of the Whisper Room. There's blood on the floor, on the glass wall, and the TV is down too. Shattered.

I drop my tray and I scream her name. "Melanda!"

I grope for my keys and I'm in the Whisper Room on my knees and I'm too late. She used the *television set* and there is blood, so much blood, and I grab her shoulders and I whisper. I hope. "Melanda, can you hear me?"

But her heart is silent—I am wasting my time—and that's when I realize the blood on the wall isn't spatter. It's writing. She used her own blood as ink. Finger paint. Her last words, her goodbye:

Single White Female.

20

This isn't a misdemeanor. This is a crime and Melanda's *the shark inside my shark,* the body in my *house* and it wasn't supposed to happen like this. If you hadn't come over tonight . . .

No. This isn't your fault. She did this. Not you. Not me. *Melanda.*

I can't let my empathy get the best of me right now. She chose to end her life on my *property* and she left me to do the dirty work, to clean up the mess. I turn off the security cameras and delete my files—I don't like snuff films—and if some twisted voyeur techie already saw what she did, well that's the point, isn't it?

She did it. Not me.

She will never be *coming around again* and as it all sinks in, well, in some ways I could kill her for what she did to us. Her blood is on my fingertips, it's on the walls of my Whisper Room and she was in this room because she attacked *me.* I grab her phone. I can't call 911. I can't trust the Injustice System—if only you knew—and I can't bury her in my yard. Fecal-Eyed *Nancy* is a nosy *Nextdoor* app–addicted gossip and I crack a smile. Is there something wrong with me? No. Laughing at funerals is a common phenomenon. We laugh at death because we have to, because what is more ironic than being stuck with a very smart, opinionated woman who can't weigh in with her thoughts at a moment when I could really use her fucking help?

I could take her to the dock and let her sink to the floor of the bay, but the tide gets low. I could put her in the trunk and drive to the footbridge by 305 but I *like* that footbridge. I could dump her in Murden Cove—the smell is bad enough there as it is—but once again with the low fucking tide . . . For her it was easy—*Single White Female*—but this is hell on me and unlike that daytime-soap-loving sociopath in *Fargo,* I don't have access to a wood chipper. And why would I fucking want a wood chipper? It's not like things worked out for him and we all know how it ends—chills—and I will not end up in the back of a fucking police cruiser.

Goddammit, Melanda, why me? Why my house? I know she had her reasons. I've read the phone—I had to know everything about you—and I read her journals—I had to know everything she won't put in the phone. I know that as recently as two weeks ago she was sick about never having had a baby.

I want to have one but then I go into Blackbird and those mommies are so smug as if giving birth makes them more of a woman than me and they're so BORING and they think they're so INTERESTING and how can I want to be one of them? UGH MK is lucky she did it early before all these women turned into martyrs and HELLO they have husbands and ok so the husbands don't unload the dishwasher unless they're asked to do it but they do it, you know? MK is lucky and I'm not lol I know. Get over it! Sigh.

But she didn't get over it and now look what she did to us. *Single White Female.*

It's hard to be alone, I know. We all need to let it out. But she listened to that Carly Simon song about the hardships of relationships almost nine *thousand* times and did any of it sink in? That song is about crimes and misdemeanors. You break a window, you burn a soufflé, but you don't *break yourself.* You get a new shrink. You move. Seattle's right there and isn't that what you all think is so *great* about this island? You walk onto the ferry and into the city and find Frasier for fuck's sake, or even Niles, but don't do *this.* Don't leave the planet and don't go in Blackbird when you damn well *know* there will be fecal-eyed mommies in there wearing their babies in a circle jerk.

I'm sad for Melanda—she just couldn't come around—and I am sad for me.

What do I do with her now?

I'm frozen—the Seattle freeze is officially real—and I can't bring her to her house. I can't allow headlines in *The Bainbridge Island Review*—LOCAL FEMINIST SLITS WRISTS—because headlines will lead to investigations and whispers. You are all that matters and you can never know that she ended her life. Same way you can never know that she was down here while we were up there and I wish Melanda had never attacked me in the woods. I wish she'd moved to Minnesota years ago, when the time was right.

I roll her body onto a duvet and I wrap her up like a burrito and it helps. I don't have to look at her corpse anymore. But then my eyes land on her bare feet—*nothing stays the same*—and oh, Melanda, why?

I take out her phone. She left me with no choice, Mary Kay. I have to make you despise her. I have to burn the bridge and tell you what you shouldn't have to know so that you never want to speak to her ever again. She's been your best friend for a long time. You didn't fight over Phil. You remained close as sisters, jumping off the pier at Point White, spending Mother's Day together, sharing your daughter, the way you unknowingly shared your husband.

I close my eyes. I picture Melanda falling in love with Imaginary Carl. It's new for her. She tells him everything and he tells her that she has to end this toxic friendship. You stole her boyfriend and you were young—I know—but at some point we all have to own up to our past mistakes. People do this when they fall in love, when they think they finally found their person. I did that with Love. I told her everything about me. And now Melanda's going to reach into the bottom of her oversized broken heart.

Me as Melanda:

Sweetie this isn't easy for me and it isn't going to be easy for you but that's part of the problem. Life is easy for you. You breeze into things. Phil wanted you the second he saw you and I said it was ok because what could I do? He didn't feel that way about me. He felt that way about you. You can't make anyone love you. I know that.

And that hurt. But I was there for you. I said to myself you know what, she's a good friend. I love her. So on we go.

After you had Nomi you told me you were happy I had an abortion because if I hadn't, you might have gotten cold feet with Nomi.

And that hurt. But I was there for you. I said to myself you know what, she's a good friend and I love her.

My thirtieth birthday and you threw me a surprise party and it was all families and I was a third wheel on my own birthday and you could have had the party at a bar.

And that hurt. But I was there for you. I said to myself you know what, she's a good friend and I love her.

The night before Mother's Day. You invited me to "tag along" with you and Nomi but you didn't call the restaurant and change the reservation and I had to sit at that table in the way of all the waiters and spent the whole meal apologizing.

And that hurt. But I was there for you. I said to myself you know what, she's a good friend and I love her.

Last fall I told you I wish I had a boyfriend or a kid just so I had someone to drive around with when the leaves are changing and you said aaww and the next day you posted a picture of you and Nomi on the way to Fort Ward.

And that hurt. But I was there for you. I said to myself you know what, she's a good friend and I love her.

I read that Sarah Jio book and I told you it made me feel hopeful because look at these sexy men lusting after this woman close to our age and you laughed and said "Good luck" and then you asked if I ever heard back from that job in Minneapolis.

And that hurt. But I was there for you. I said to myself you know what, she's a good friend and I love her.

Christmas. I told you I had the flu and you knew I was lying because you know me and you didn't come over and force me to come over even though you knew I wasn't sick.

And that hurt. But I was there for you. I said to myself you know what, she's a good friend and I love her.

I don't want the pain anymore. I am not a good friend. So I can't blame you for not being a good friend to me.

I'm not gonna dress it up and I'm not gonna make excuses because it is what it is and you need to know it.

Phil and I have been sleeping together for ten years. At my place. In his car. At his studio and at that wealth management place by the pub. The bunkers at Fort Ward.

I betrayed you. And I am sorry.

You betrayed me. And hopefully you are sorry.

Please respect my decision to walk away and save my own life. Nomi will miss me but she has a mom and a dad who love her and she'll be okay. Goodbye, good love. M.

Send. Vomit. Breathe.

I carry my poor dog up the stairs and my pet is heavy and my house smells like salmon. Licious and Tastic and Riffic are running around, lazing about, cold as the grammar that inspired their names, acting as if nothing is wrong, as if I'm not holding a dead fucking *body*. But in a way, nothing *is* wrong. I didn't kill this woman. I carry her body into my garage and I pop the trunk and I get in the car and I start the car.

I turn on some Sam Cooke—got to stay positive—and I break the speed limit, but only by five miles—the Injustice System better not fuck with me, Mary Kay. Not tonight—and you told me to go to Fort Ward before we even met and tonight, I'm finally doing it. You like Fort Ward and Melanda fucked your husband at Fort Ward so that's where Melanda will rest. I know how to get there and I know where to park and I wanted to come here with *you*, not her.

It isn't fair. None of this is fair. I kill my headlights. My heart thumps in my chest. All it takes is one cop, one restless rambler, one set of horny teens. But it's January and it's after midnight and time is the only thing on my side and thank God for that.

I get out of the car. There are no cameras in the lot and I spot the tiny shack the Meerkat talked about when we were coaching Mothballs with their iPhones—*the moss on the roof is like the floor of a forest for Barbies*—and there's the opening to the trail you told me about—*quickest way to the bunkers is the first entrance*—and there's the entrance I need: the long way up.

I strap the flashlight on my head—thanks, Cooley Hardware—and I ease RIP Melanda out of the trunk. I don't belong here. I did not kill her and Fort Ward is not the Grand Forest and I hear you in my head, in my soul—*When you do go to Fort Ward, make sure you don't walk off the trail because there are some surprisingly steep drop-offs*—and the trail *is* steeper than I anticipated and damn you, Melanda, because this is the definition of injustice.

I didn't kill her. I didn't.

I struggle to stay upright and you weren't kidding. This isn't the Grand Fucking Forest—*the first part of the trail is paved, thank God*—and it helps to have you with me as I climb, as pavement gives way to rocky terrain. My thighs burn—Sorry, Seamus, but this is harder than a *Murph*—and the endorphins kick in and I am angry. I am sad.

I didn't kill her. I didn't do this.

But my heart is thumping faster and louder and my forehead is a sweaty foul place and every time I put one foot in front of the other, I am steadier, my muscles are adjusting. But then I am angrier by the second. An anger that taints every endorphin in my body.

I didn't fucking do this, Mary Kay. I didn't.

I pass a chain-link fence, I'm getting there, and the black rocks work against me, unstable enemies on the floor of the forest trying to take me down with every step, and I am deaf with pain until finally the trail bends and to my left I see the abyss—not as deep as I expected but deep enough—and I break away from the trail. I'm a gentleman and I try to carry her but it is steep—you were right—and eventually I just can't hold on to her any longer.

"Sorry, Melanda."

I drop her body and let it roll down into the core and she loses her duvet along the way and it all comes back to me, the horror of what she did.

I run down the hill to wrap her up. I don't like an open casket.

The ground is wet and loose as you said—*I'm telling you, Joe, don't walk off the trail*—and I dig into the earth with a trowel—thanks again, Cooley Hardware—and my bare hands. I remember pottery in third grade and a field trip to the beach when I was eight—nine?—and I dug and I dug but I didn't find any crabs. I dig like a dog, like a child, like my son, like a young Melanda by the sea, sunburnt and full of hope for her future, resembling a young Carly Simon, assuming they were on the same track in life and there is dirt in my fingernails and the dirt is tainted by blood.

I didn't do this, Mary Kay. I didn't do this.

I help Melanda into her bed and I cover her with muck and large fat orange leaves. She would want to be here. She wanted to give back to the community—*the future is female*—and her incubator will come to fruition. I can't help but feel proud of my work. I laid her to rest and she'll fertilize the land she loved so much that she couldn't leave it behind.

And this part, this I did do. This resting place is my work, my empathy, my sweat.

I kiss my hand. I touch a leaf. "Sweet dreams, Ruby. Watch in peace."

I wipe my hands on my shirt, my shirt I need to burn, and then white light blasts me and it isn't lightning. It isn't nature. It's man-made light. And where there is man-made light, there are men.

"Say cheese, Goldberg."

21

I know that voice and the Strawberry Killer followed me. He's alone. I'm alone. And this is the dark version of the poem about the second set of footprints in the sand, when God is carrying the lonely, besieged man on the beach. The Strawberry Killer didn't save me. He followed me. He's armed with a camera and a flashlight and a gun and this is what I get for caring about Melanda so much that I forgot to watch my back. This is what I get for trying to let her rest in peace. I reach the trail and I'm out of breath and is this how I die?

"I didn't . . . This isn't what it looks like," I say.

Even I know that's a stupid thing to say but this is why people say it in the movies so fucking much. Because it's true. The Strawberry Killer points his gun at me. "Turn around and put your hands behind your head, my friend. One step at a time."

That's what a cop would say but a cop wouldn't call me his friend.

I look up at the starry sky and as I take a step forward, I feel the press of metal in my back. We pick our way down to the parking lot over divots and ruts in the path. Is this it? Is this how it ends? Does Love win? My foot lands on a stone and I lose my balance and the Strawberry Killer seizes my shoulder. I fall back into line, marching in the dark. Am I going back to jail? I want to marry you but this soft-shouldered preppy goon is going to *bury* me, isn't he?

Finally, the parking lot comes into view, just two shadowy outlines of cars. I want to make a run for it but the road ahead is wide and I am a fish in this motherfucker's barrel. Then, before I can paint a full picture of us in my mind, before I can take one good shot at an escape, the back of my head explodes and all the Christmas lights in the sky disappear at once.

I wake up with a lump on the back of my head and my throat is dry. It's dark, *too dark to see* but I'm not knocking on a door to heaven. I smell old blood and I taste donuts and I wanna go home but I *am* home. I am in my Whisper Room and the welt on the back of my head throbs.

I am groping in the dark and I might be bleeding. RIP Melanda only just died—am I next?—and no I'm not *next.* You need me right now. It's been hours—has it?—and you must have read her fuck-you message by now and you must be devastated, tearing at the walls, desperate to see me and I am on my feet. I knock on the bloodstained glass wall—*Gently, Joseph*—and my cry in the dark is met with singing—*Some people call me the space cowboy*—and the Strawberry Killer is the kind of asshole who knows all the words to that preppy ditty. SK is playing my guitar in the dark—trying to anyway—and I pound on the glass like RIP Melanda and the guitar stops and the lights come on all at once.

His hair is slicked back—no Figawi hat down here—and he shakes his head. "My, my, my," he says. "Looks like someone's got some cleaning up to do."

It's not my blood and it's not my mess and a woman *died* in here and look at her note. *Single White Female.* It's almost like she knew this was coming, like she knew I'd need a reminder that I'm not psychologically damaged like her.

"Okay," I say. "I think there's been a big misunderstanding."

"So you didn't just dump a body in the mud, my friend?"

Yes but no, and Mr. Mooney would tell me to know my enemy. "Who are you?"

He waves like a bougie hippie at Pegasus on open mic night. "Oliver Potter," he says. "Any requests?"

I don't make a request and I don't like the joke and he thumbs my guitar and he's a full-blown Angeleno, Mary Kay, ice water in his veins, smug as Patrick Bateman with an *American Psycho* thin-lipped smile. He's laughing at me—*who tuned this guitar?*—and I need to focus.

I've been here before and I got out before—*You set yourself free, Joseph. I just turned the key*—and he strums and the feedback zings and he covers the mic and winces. "Apologies, my friend."

A real psycho wouldn't be so considerate; Oliver is just someone who aspires to *be* a psycho. He has a Glock—*a gun in a barrel, a barrel in a gun*—and my weapon is superior: my brain.

"So," he says. "Walk me through it, Goldberg. You kill off the stage-twelve clinger bestie . . ." Lie. I didn't kill Melanda. "And then you win your little MILFy librarian over with a six-string? And then you set a jealousy trap and just like that, boom, you're back in Pac Pal with Love?"

His theory is a scratch on the record and he is wrong. I don't want Love. I want you. And this is why I'm in the cage, to learn, to face the reality that I've been fighting, that I *do* feel guilty about shifting gears, not missing my son as much as I once did, accepting our fate to be apart. You see it in memes all the time. *Life is change.* But change is hard. Look at RIP Melanda's blood letter. She couldn't do it. She couldn't come to terms with the person she was, the person she wanted to be. But I can. Oliver tunes my guitar and sneers—*Your D string is about to pop, Goldberg*—and I won't pop. I study my enemy; his T-shirt is old, not vintage. He didn't drop four hundred bucks for it in some Hulkshit man-boutique in Venice. He grew up in that shirt. There are pit stains. Grease stains. The logo is BAXTER'S BOATHOUSE and that's probably some waterfront dump in Florida and I shrug. "I don't really have a plan, honestly."

"Well," he says, really going for that aspiring sociopath—psychopath?—vibe. "If you ask me, my friend, your MILF's not worth it. Too much baggage. And Love's not really the jealousy-trap type. You would have been better off with your first plan, which I can only assume was to win her back with your *music*."

You are not a *MILF.* You are a fox. And I am not Phil. "What's Baxter's?"

Oliver looks down at his shirt as if he forgot that he was wearing it and he's insecure. That's good news for me and he pulls at the hem. "Well, actually," he says. "I used to work at this place in high school, the first family that ever owned me, pre-Quinns. Seems you and I have that in common."

"The Quinns don't own me."

"You keep telling yourself that, my friend. See the key to life is knowing that you are owned and maximizing the potential of said ownership. I wrote a pilot about Baxter's. Shitty script, but it got me my first agent because the bones were there."

I think of RIP Melanda's bones, the animals that might be finding her at this moment and oh God, Oliver is a *writer.* I play along. I tell him what he wants to hear, that I never thought about it that way, that I worked at a bookstore in high school, that the owner *did* kind of own me. He nods, pleased, because writers don't want to write. They just want to be right about every stupid fucking thing in the world. "Well, yes, my friend. Oh also . . . cute cats you got. Three of 'em. Quite a statement."

They're *kittens,* asshole, and I hang my head in fake shame. Writers are narcissists who want to tell their stories, so I ask Oliver where he's from and he says he grew up on Cape Cod, Massachusetts.

"Do you know where that is, Goldberg?"

Fuck you, I'm not dumb. "Yep. How did you meet the Quinns?"

He wants control—typical writer—so he tweaks a knob on the guitar. "How do you *deal* with this, Goldberg? Your G string is mad fucked."

His hand slips on the guitar and he blames my string, the way a bad tennis player blames a racquet and then he puts the guitar on the floor and now I guess we're supposed to pretend he never touched it. "You seem pretty calm for someone in a cage, my friend."

"Well," I say. "You made a good point . . ." Praise the writer. "The Quinns own this house, technically, so it was only a matter of time."

"They really screwed you with this shit box."

"Are you kidding? Did you see my view?"

"Yes, Goldberg. You live in a house on an island. And you have a view of . . . the other side of the island. Well done there, my friend."

STOP CALLING ME YOUR FRIEND, YOU PIECE OF SHIT.

I calmly tell him that I found the house myself, that Winslow is ideal because you can walk to everything. He strokes his chin—why do bad guys always have strong jawlines?—and he says that *he* would have chosen Rockaway or Lynwood and that's another thing about sociopaths, Mary Kay. They like to talk about *real estate.* I am patient. The goal is freedom so I tell him that I agree—I don't—and he picks up the guitar—no—and whines about my B string and guitars really do bring out the worst in men, don't they?

"Come on, Goldberg. Let's be real. What is there to walk to around here?"

"Everything. The main drag is right down the street. You know, where you saw me."

"Main drag? You mean that strip of menopause wine bars that shuts down at eleven? You call *that* a main drag? You lived in L.A., my friend. Come on now. Be real with me."

My heart beats for you, for the power to shatter this glass and throw *him* in the water for daring to slander our home.

Oliver pulls my keys out of his pocket. "All right," he says. "I know your story so I suppose it's only fair if you know mine. Basic chords are as follows. Born and bred on the Cape. Burnt my wrists on the fryolator. Went to Emerson, wrote some good plays, wrote some not so good plays . . ." His plays are all shit. "Hightailed it out to L.A. when I got a gig on a *Law & Order* spin-off . . ." That word should be banned: *gig*. "Banged out an episode of *Law & Order: Los Angeles* but the show went away . . ." As did his career. "Waited tables. Kept in touch with a consultant from the show who was a PI. He convinced me to get into that game, which he said would actually be better in the long run, in terms of my writing . . ." Like I give a fuck and writers assume readers are stupider than we are. "Got into the PI game, got my brother Gordy into it when he came out west . . ." It's a turning point when he mentions his brother because for the first time, Oliver doesn't seem entirely deluded and narcissistic. He is proud of what he did for his brother and he sighs. "I had a mentor. I had it made. But the Quinns did to us what they did to you, my friend."

"What's that, Oliver?"

"Gordy and I were doing really well with Eric. Eric was my mentor . . ." Say it again, Oliver and I hope I don't repeat myself this much. "The Quinns wanted Eric's help with their piece-of-shit son, Forty. Eric had a rule. He would do anything for the Quinns, anything but help that piece-of-shit Forty."

I stare the fucker down. "You know my kid's named after him, right?" And this is why I told Love that saddling our son with that stupid, tainted name was a bad idea.

"Yes, my friend, and I feel for you. I do." And then he sighs, wanting to get back to *his* story. "Long story short . . ." It's a little late for that, Oliver. "Eric turned down the gig. The Quinns turned around and offered the job to me and Gordy. And we've been working for them ever since."

"What a nice story."

"Joe, Joe, Joe, I'm not the bad guy here. I hate the Quinns just as much as you do. You should see where they're putting me up, this second-rate motel with powdered eggs in the lobby and a mattress so thin I can barely sleep, which is why my back is fucked up and I can't get the right angle on the strings on this piece-of-shit Gibson."

"Well, maybe you should file a complaint with HR."

"Look, my friend, I'm trying to make you see that the Quinns have me locked up, just like you. They gave me a job. They gave you this shit box. But they own us, Joe."

I go into RIP Melanda mode. I can't help it. "Oliver, you locked me up in here. Our situations are nothing alike."

"Are you kidding? I saved Forty's ass on a rape charge before he kicked the bucket. You got in through the sister. We saved their precious fucked-up kids. We *both* took their money."

"I didn't get in *through* the sister, Oliver. I loved her."

He smiles. "Does your MILF know that?"

I ignore the question and he sighs. "You say you want out. But do you mean it?"

"Yes, I mean it. Let's talk out there. It reeks in here."

"I'm talking big picture, my friend. Why are you living on this poor man's Nantucket?"

"I *chose* to move here. That has nothing to do with the Quinns. I wanted to leave L.A. and I wanted to live here and I *chose* this house."

"Ah," he says. "So you wanted to abandon your son?"

"Fuck no, Oliver. That's different. I didn't have a choice about that and you know it."

Oliver nods. Smug. "And finally, light dawns on Marblehead."

Oliver's just like RIP Melanda, Mary Kay. He doesn't believe that people can grow and change their minds and I don't want to be analyzed by this failed writer turned Privacy Invader and I tell him he's right—it hurts—and I ask him what happens next. Any good writer should be able to answer that question but Oliver failed as a writer.

"We'll get to that," he says. "First, I gotta know. What was your magic number?"

"You mean what did they pay me? Oliver, they pointed a gun at my head. I had to sign the contract."

"Yeah, yeah, yeah. What was it? Eight mill to leave your kid? Ten?"

This is why I'm in the cage. Oliver isn't entirely wrong and I did it. I took the money. But I didn't *sell* my son.

"Four million," I say. "Plus the house."

"The house they bought for you."

"The house is in *my* name."

"Well, isn't that nice of them? My Benz is in my name too. Thing is though, I can't afford the payments if I quit working for them."

I don't want to be like Oliver and I am *not* like Oliver. "Okay," he says. "Brass tacks. I have video of you and the dead chick . . ."

Woman not *chick* and I tell him I didn't kill her and he sighs. "Well, my friend, if I called the local yokel cops right now and they saw you in that room with her blood on the walls . . ."

"I didn't kill her."

"It doesn't matter, Goldberg. All that matters is how it looks. Now listen up. I sent those pictures to Gordy but Gordy has *not* shown those pictures to Ray . . . If he does that, you'll get thrown in jail, and they won't need me to watch you anymore. I'll be out of a job. The Quinns will win."

"What do you want?"

Oliver settles into his chair like any aspiring writer about to pitch his shitty story and I am the executive so I lean forward because I have to lean forward. I want to buy his pitch. I want to get the fuck out of here and be with you. "You and me are from the wrong side of the trust fund, my friend. The Quinns found us. They see our potential, our brains, and they like to squash it because their own kids never had what we have. We're not a part of the old boys' club and we never will be, but what we have here is an opportunity to create a *young* boys' club. A *poor* boys' club, if you will."

"Oliver, I don't follow. What do we do in this 'club'?"

He's a defensive writer so he tells me that I don't have to *follow* as if it's my fault that his pitch is muddled. "We help each other out. I don't show Ray what you did to this chick and you help me because you got paid a helluva lot more than I did, my friend."

"You want money."

"My mom's sick, so my cash flow is a bit tight." He's human again, the way he was when he first mentioned his brother, and he breaks eye contact. "My mom has cancer and fuck cancer is right because that shit is expensive."

"I'm sorry."

"And my girlfriend Minka . . . she's a ten . . ." I hate it when men do that, when they rate you like they hold the cards and you're all in swimsuits. "And a ten has certain expectations of a man and I want to hold on to my ten and we just moved in and the walls are a little bare for her tastes and she's all about the reno, she's way into antiques and she's going for this *Sweet American Psycho* vibe . . ." I knew it. I knew his hair was on purpose. "So you help me keep my ten in antiques and I help you keep those Quinns off your back."

I can't say yes fast enough but then Oliver makes a face that reminds me of his failed screenwriting aspirations. He stares at the blood on the windows. "I know you, Goldberg. And it's important that you know me. Gordo and I communicate in a very unique way and if he contacts me and doesn't hear back in our *very unique* way, he shows Ray the pictures and you're in a cage that smells a lot worse than this one. Point is, you make me go away, you go away too. You feel me?"

"I get it. I'm in." And then I say what he wants to hear, the name of his show. "Poor Boys Club is on."

Oliver puts the key in the door but then he hesitates. It's a myth about cages and I've been where he was, I was just there a few hours ago, holding the key, aware that *my* life was at stake too. "When I was a screenwriter"—No, Oliver, you wrote *one* episode of television—"we had this phrase *on the nose.*" I'm not a moron but it's kind of like hanging out with Seamus. Sometimes you have to let your *Friends* think they're broadening your horizons so I nod like that phrase is foreign to me. "What you did to this chick tonight was too on the nose, too on brand. So when I let you outta here, you're gonna *behave.* No more of the bad shit. No Instastalking Love, no dead chicks in the dungeon. Nada. Zilch. Nothing. You so much as steal a plastic fork from Starbucks and you're done."

Oliver turns the key. "Wait," he says. "Do you have a 1stdibs account?"

I shake my head. "No."

He lets me out of the cage as if it isn't in my house and he hands me my phone.

"Download the 1stdibs app," he says. "Pronto."

I download the rich-people shopping app and I open an account and I look at him. "Now what?"

"Search for 'Mike Tyson,'" he says. "There's a portrait by Albert Watson and you're gonna buy it for me."

I blow twenty-five thousand dollars on a photograph of Mike Fucking Tyson and Oliver stretches his arms—those pit stains are worse up close—and he asks me where I store my cleaning products. "Amateurs don't know how to clean up after a crime. We don't want the Poor Boys Club to end before it starts."

I give Oliver a mop and I find a bottle of bleach and soon we're scrubbing Melanda's last words from the glass wall. Oliver sneezes into his elbow. "At my first job back home, I had to clean the women's bathroom at the ferry dock. Nothing will ever be as nasty as that."

"I worked in a bookstore," I say. "This guy used to jack off on our *National Geographics* and my boss made me scrape off his jizz with a letter opener."

"Jesus," he says. "Maybe the Quinns aren't that bad." And then he winks. "Kidding, Joe. Kidding."

Finally, we finish the job and the Whisper Room is spotless. Oliver is on his way out the door—*See you on Menopause Avenue*—and in an ideal world, I would call you right now. But we don't live in an ideal world, Mary Kay.

I pick up Melanda's phone and I enter the pass code and I prepare for the worst. You know it all now. You've had time to read, obsess over every detail. Your heart might be broken . . . if I did a good job. Did you believe it was her? And if you did, is this betrayal going to put you off men? Off *me*? What do you say to the woman who violated your trust for ten fucking *years*? I open Melanda's text messages and . . .

22

Nothing! Your best friend shocks you with a revelation about fucking your husband and she breaks up with you via *text message* and all you said was: *Be well. Xo.* I go to Instagram and Nomi still follows Melanda—maybe you didn't tell her?—but you *unfollowed* Melanda.

Women are strange. You're in the library all day acting as if nothing has changed, like you didn't climax for me in my house. Nomi comes in with muddy boots and you are Carol Fucking Brady. "Nomi honey, can you wipe your boots?"

And she is Cindy Fucking Brady. "Sorry, Mom."

Last month, when you told her to wipe her muddy boots off she barked at you and flipped you the bird and you flipped her the bird right back. But today she's calm. You're calm. It's all way too fucking *calm* and does Nomi know that you unfollowed her *aunt*? Are you pretending that you and your Murafuckingkami didn't put on a show for me in my living room? Every time you're within ten feet, I brace myself for you to tap me on the shoulder and ask if we can talk. We almost had sex! We *have* to talk. But you remain calm, distant. I poke the tiger. I leave Dolly in the middle of Cookbooks—you hate that—but you just move the cart out of the aisle and eat lunch on your own at your desk. The Meerkat comes back before we close up shop and knocks on the desk—you hate that too—and you smile. "Hi, sweetie."

"Did Dylan's mom's book get here yet?"

"Sorry, honey, I'll text you when we get it."

She storms out the door without saying goodbye and still you are calm. Dead calm.

This is the calm before the storm. I know that foxes are stealthy and you're busy designing your escape. I see you, Mary Kay, I see you on the cusp of blocking out what happened between us because it's too much, on top of that *note* you got from RIP Melanda.

But I am busy too. It's not easy having a stalker and Oliver Fucking Potter *is* a stalker, and I need to get off this rock and pick up some supplies if I'm going to save you from your overly active guilty conscience. *Think, Joe, think.* Oliver's motel is across from the Starbucks and I tell him I'm placing a mobile order and I ask him if he wants to meet up. He asks for a *tall hot blond*—such an asshole—and I place the order and tell him I'll be there in ten minutes.

Now he's at Starbucks, blowing up my phone—*where are you*—and I tell him that I had a change of plans—*Sorry Oliver, I have to go to Seattle for an interlibrary loan issue.* He'll never catch me now and he knows it. His response is terse but respectful: *Well played, my friend.*

Amen to that, Oliver, and I board the ferry with all the passive-aggressive cliquey commuters. I sit in a chair and a limp-dick Amazon drudge juts out his jaw.

"You're gonna sit there?"

"Yes, I'm going to sit here."

"Well, sometimes one of our friends sits here."

Fascinating. I smile and put on my headphones. "I guess not today, then."

In the city, I use my Quinn cash to buy cameras and that's one good thing about Oliver Fucking Potter. He reminded me that I have money. And money is power.

I book a hotel room in a Marriott and I send Oliver a picture of the receipt and then my phone rings. Oliver.

"Not cool, Joe."

"Oliver, I'm too freaked out to be in my house. I just need one night."

He hangs up on me—all friends fight—and sends me a link to an

Andy Warhol print on 1stdibs called *Peaches*. And then a text: *Don't fuck with me again, Goldberg.*

I buy him the *Peaches* and I leave the Marriott and hop back on the ferry—no cliquey commuters, just lonely lost souls hoping that the cutesy ways of Winslow lift them out of their misery—and it's a relief knowing that Oliver won't be tailing me for the rest of the night.

I buy a beer from the canteen—it's stressful, having a stalker—and I check Melanda's phone when I disembark. I can't use her to get to you anymore—I miss our talks, me as Melanda, you as you—and you didn't write anything more. The beer is cold. *You* are cold. You don't reach out to me and I wish you would, Mary Kay. I worry about you. Did you sleep last night? Are you crying in the shower like Glenn Close in *The Big Chill* or are you attacking your rat husband like Glenn Close in *Fatal Attraction*?

I have to know how you are, Mary Kay. I know Melanda's message was a lot to take in. I know you probably think you're a bad person and you're not a bad person. I relate to you more than ever. I couldn't worm my way into my family with Love and you're *still* trying to find your place on this rock after twenty years but your place is with me.

You need me to watch out for you and I jog on the Eagle Harbor trail and it's a little unnerving, to be honest. I'm still not over what happened—damn you, RIP Melanda—and I step off the trail onto your lawn and I pause. The quiet. The stillness. You and the Meerkat went to Costco after work—Nomi calls it *#RetailTherapy*, buying paper towels in bulk to clean up the mess of your life—and your rat is in Seattle waiting for a former Sub Pop photographer to show up. Alas, that's not gonna happen because I'm the one who sent the fake email and I'm the one apologizing to Phil, assuring him that I'll be there soon, *man*. In the Richard Scarry sense of the world, everyone in my life is busy being busy. And I'm busy too.

It's only ten steps to the sliding glass door and it's a good thing that your husband is such a devout we-don't-lock-our-doors kind of asshole because that means your door is open. I grip the handle and the door squeaks—Jesus, Phil, take care of your home—and for the first time in our life together, I am in your house.

Nomi wasn't kidding, Mary Kay. You really do like your tchotchkes and your shelves are littered with literary toys. I spy a Shakespeare doll and a Virginia Woolf puppet—who makes that, who?—and a tiny *Bell Jar* and I know what this is all about. You buy tchotchkes so that you can pretend that your home is the Empathy Bordello Bar & Books. It's how you cope. You've been living in denial for nearly twenty years, trying hard not to see the horror around you—RIP Melanda playing footsie with Phil at the pub while you all eat *brunch*—and Phil's passive-aggressive refusal to let his old songs go—*a crate in a barrel, a barrel in a gun*—and you've spoken no evil, throwing salmon steaks into the freezer, onto the grill, repeat infinity.

And it's not just the tchotchkes that alarm me, Mary Kay. Your house is a shrine to the nineties and the early aughts, when you all lived up by Hidden Cove in *Manzanita.* It's like the two of you are sending a dangerous message to your daughter, that everything good, every memory worth preserving was almost twenty years ago, before she was even born.

You have his debut album framed, but all the other albums are in your garage, as if they don't exist. I pick up a picture of you that's almost nineteen years old. I recognize the background, the tiny one-home island they call Treasure Island. You cradle your newborn baby and you look like a child bride. Your smile is a cry for help and you are trying to hide *a second set of teeth* while you just *die underneath* and I see what no one else wanted to see. A woman trapped, held at gunpoint but in this case the gun is your husband's *Philstick.*

I could spend hours exploring your photographs, tracing the disintegration of your love and your marriage, as spontaneous photos of your family *bonding* by the bunkers at Fort Ward—RIP Melanda—give way to uncomfortable staged shots on holidays—*Say cheese for the timer on the iPhone and everyone be sure and mask your misery!*—but Costco's not *that* far away and I'm not here to visit your family museum.

I'm here to help you shut it down.

I set up cameras in the living room—one across from Phil's chair—and I set up cameras in the kitchen—this is where you hide from your rat's guitar—and I put cameras in the most fetid part of your house: your bedroom.

It smells like him, not you, and the rat has a bunch of his own scratched-beyond-repair compact fucking discs and what is it with you people and the past?

My phone buzzes and I flinch. It's Oliver: *Update.*

I'm so sick of that word. He's requested *eight* updates already today. The rule is simple: When he asks for an update, I have to give him a fucking update.

I leave your house the way I came in and I'm on the trail and the trail is empty and I send Oliver a picture I took earlier of the view from my hotel room—and I follow up *that* picture with a link to *Mackintosh chairs* on 1stdibs. He sends me an order—*Good eye, buy 'em*—and I purchase the fucking chairs and send him a screenshot of the confirmation. It's another eight grand gone but I've noticed a pattern. The more I *lean in* to my role as Oliver's personal shopper, the more time passes between his fucking *Update* texts.

I stop into T & C and pick up spicy popcorn—gotta nosh while I watch the Very Special Episode of your family sitcom tonight—and I put the popcorn into my reusable tote bag—we save the planet together—and I walk home and head down to my Whisper Room—cleaner now than it was when I moved in—thanks, Oliver!

The cameras are A-plus level of good and it's like magic. There you are in the kitchen! Here comes Nomi with her backpack.

"I'm going to the bookstore."

"Now? They close soon."

"Well, *you* forgot to order my book at the library."

"Nomi, the loan system is tricky . . . I don't want to fight but can you at least consider reading something that isn't Columbine-related? It's getting a little . . . Nomi, please."

Nomi stares at the stove top and my cameras are high def. Top shelf. "Soup's on fire."

The soup's steaming but it's not on fire and the Meerkat is gone and you pour that goddamn soup into the disposal and the door slams as Nomi leaves and Phil walks in. The TV show is about to get real and I shove a handful of popcorn in my mouth.

Phil doesn't sit at the table and he doesn't ask you what happened to the soup. He just stands there. You rinse out the pot. You don't greet him. It's a Mexican standoff and this is it. I can already hear you saying it in my head. *Phil, I want a divorce.*

You drop the pot in the sink and clench the edge of the counter with both hands. He doesn't move. As if he knows you want to kill him.

"What now, Emmy?"

"I have one of your songs stuck in my head."

He smiles and oh you're *good.* "Oh yeah, which one?"

"Well, the one about the shark, of course."

He's a little disappointed because *everyone* knows that one. "Ah," he says. "Well, I'm working on something now that's gonna put that shark to sleep. Something way better . . ."

"You know, Phil, I always loved that song . . ." You gaze at him and he smiles. "I loved it because it was so raw. It was about us, the tension of a new baby . . . the feeling of your life changing from the inside out. It's funny, though. I never knew that it was actually about Melanda."

BOOM. I turn up the volume and Phil digs his hands into his dirty pockets. "Shit . . . Emmy. Hang on now. That song *is* about us."

"Oh for fuck's sake, Phil, I don't give a *shit* about the fucking song right now. You and Melanda? Behind my back? For how many years?"

"Emmy, let me . . . *shit.*"

"Yeah," you say. "That's what you are. Both of you. A couple of pieces of *shit.*"

You pick up a sponge and squeeze the dirty water. Sponges are filthy by design and you can run it through the dishwasher but it will never be clean again. You pick at the dirty grout on your counter. "The worst part is . . . Jesus, all this time I think of myself as the person who makes you happy . . ."

"You do."

"Oh fuck you, Phil. You do *not* get to say that right now. She was my best *friend* and you . . . I want you out."

I clap my hands. YES.

"Emmy, you don't mean that. You know there is no me without you. Baby, I'm a fuckup, okay?"

He drops to his knees and he's pawing at your legs like the dog that he is and he's crying and I want you to kick him in the face but now *you're* crying and I drop my popcorn on the floor and no. Don't cry, Mary Kay. This isn't your fault. He's bellowing that he deserves to be *dead* and you're taking care of *him* as if he didn't FUCK YOUR BEST FUCKING FRIEND.

You help him to his feet and he's blubbering and shaking and sobbing in your soup-stained pot and he *pukes* in your pot and you rub his shoulders.

"Emmy, I'm the worst piece of shit on the planet."

"Phil, stop it." Your voice is soft.

"I never deserved you. You think I don't know that? And Melanda . . . she . . . she threatened to ruin our life. She got *off* on hurting you and I didn't . . . I'm a piece of shit."

"Phil, come on. You're making yourself sick."

You hold a paper towel up for him like he's a child and he blows his nose and you wipe his tears away and I throw my popcorn at the TV because no. You need to get mad. He's casting aspersions on *Melanda* and you're assuring him that she's *out of our lives* and *she* wasn't the bad guy.

Phil is your fucking *husband,* Mary Kay. And if Tyler Perry were here he would tell you to grab that pot and fill it with hot grits and smash it over his head. If Melanda were here—Goddammit—she would remind you about the fucking *sisterhood.* But look at you, mopping up his tears as you soak in his manipulative words.

"I don't deserve you, I don't know what the hell is wrong with me. It's like, my old man's been telling me I'm not good enough since I'm a kid, and then I get clean but I gotta find another way to get dirty to prove my old man right. I should blow my fucking brains out."

"Phil, stop it. I mean it."

This can't be happening, Mary Kay. You're forgiving him for what is unforgivable. Ask the Bible. Ask anyone, Mary Kay.

HE FUCKED YOUR BEST FRIEND AND THAT IS WRONG THE END.

You blow your nose into his flannel and your marriage is ugly, unhygienic. "Okay, Phil . . . Look, I can't be a hypocrite. I'm not perfect either."

He pulls away, slightly, and I zoom in, slightly. Your empathy is your own worst enemy right now. And he knows it. Don't you see that?

"What do you mean you're not perfect?" he says. "Is there something I should know about? Some*one* I should know about?"

He's not crying anymore. He can fuck your best friend and demand immediate forgiveness but you say *one tiny thing* about your own life and he shuts down on you. Opposites attract. But opposites destroy.

"God, no," you say. "I only meant that I should have figured this out sooner."

You're not a very good liar and you can't compare our *relationship* to what he did to you.

He grabs a *Ulysses* saltshaker and throws it at a cabinet—broken! Broken as the clock on the ferry!—and he exits stage left screaming at you, calling you all kinds of names. He's in the living room stomping back and forth—what a big strong man!—and he says he always *knew* you'd do this to him and you want to know how he can say that after what you just found out about him and he spits at you.

"You're a fucking tramp. Look at the way you dress."

"The way I dress? I wear a skirt so I'm *asking* for it? Do you really wanna go there right now?"

"Do you see other women around here wearing skirts?"

"Fuck you, Phil."

That's more like it and he growls. "Who is it?"

"Well," you say. "I'll tell you this much. It's not your best *friend.*"

He grabs a ceramic Brontë sister doll and throws it at a picture frame—BAM—and he wants to know who it is. "I told you. I deserve the same honesty, Emmy."

"Do you hear yourself, Phil? You didn't tell me *anything.* I'm the one who confronted you. And I'm trying to be compassionate. I'm trying to be reasonable."

"Who the fuck is it? Is he here? Do I know the bastard?"

"That's your question? *Do I know the bastard?* Oh Phil, I just . . . That's all you care about. If you know him. I tell you that I have feelings for another man and you don't want to know what I'm missing . . .

you just want to know if you can talk about him on your fucking show. And the answer is no, by the way. Unlike you, he doesn't air his grievances five nights a week. Unlike you, he *reads*."

That was for me! An Easter egg just for me and I'm off-camera but I'm on the only screen that matters, the one in your head. "Yes! You go, Mary Kay!"

Phil kicks at the carpet like a bull in a pen. "Who is he, Mary Kay? Who's your fucking boyfriend?"

"This isn't about my *boyfriend* and this isn't about Melanda either. This is supposed to be about us. About *me*."

You called me your boyfriend and I pop a little more popcorn into my mouth and Phil picks up *another* tchotchke but this time he doesn't throw it. Hopefully it will break in his hand and he won't be able to play guitar anymore. You're tense. You're walking in circles. And then you stop. "Hello."

He says nothing.

You slap your thighs. It's so over. "So that's it? You're gonna shut down and act like nothing happened?"

"Well, that's me, Emmy. You hide in your books. I play my guitar."

"Oh right. Shame on me because I like to read. Shame on me for wishing I had the kind of husband who wanted to go to the meadow *with* me and curl up in the bunkers with our books."

"That was high school."

"So was your fucking music."

Down goes another tchotchke and I love this show. You do too. You clap your hands. Disgusted golf claps. "Well done," you say. "More for me to clean up. Tell me, were you off with *Melanda* when I was reading and being stupid enough to believe that you were writing your fucking 'songs'?"

Phil huffs and he puffs. Literally, he's lighting a cigarette. "It's always the same," he says. "You wanna hide from life and I wanna *live* it."

You gawk at him as well you fucking should. "Oh, that's rich, Phil. Really, really rich. So I suppose you're the hero because you're the *writer*. You humiliated me with your fucking songs and you fuck my best *friend* and somehow that's okay because oh right! Phil is an *artist*!"

This is it, the end of your marriage, and I pump my fist in the air. "You tell him, Mary Kay!"

"And as we all know, artists are *gifted.* And they need things to write about so I guess I should just bow my head and stock the fridge because music comes first in this house! Never mind me, never mind oh I don't know . . . never mind *loyalty.*" You are trembling now. "She was my best *friend.* She was like my *sister.* She was Nomi's *aunt* . . . and you wrecked it. All of it."

He flicks ashes on a dirty plate. "Yeah," he says. "Well, that's one thing the three of us have in common. We deal with you, Emmy. And being in it with you . . . well, that's the loneliest kinda lonely there is. Ask Melanda. Ask Nomi. They'll back me up all night long, babe."

You march up to him and slap his face and I want to give this show a thousand stars and Phil just shakes his big fat head. He reaches for your hand. You let him hold it and he starts to cry—fake news, fake tears—and he's groping you and he's *all apologies* and he says he didn't mean it—yes he did—and he's begging you to forgive him and over and over he says the same thing: "I never wrote a song about her, Em. I'm sorry, I'm sorry."

That's a lie—he sent me the song—and you know that sorry doesn't cut it but the man is a performer. He's a good crier. You rub your forehead. You know this man doesn't understand you and how could he? You're staring through your glass doors and you've wasted the bulk of your life with this *artist.* You want a new life. A life with me. You said it at Hitchcocks. *I didn't think someone like you existed.* I am your fresh start. *Me.*

Tell him, Mary Kay. Tell him you love me.

Tell him you would be happier in the Nirvana meadow *in the tall grass with the one you love,* being innocent with me, forever young, forever old, feeding our hungry souls with words, with stories. Tell him you've outgrown him and that you can't go on pretending that any of this fits. Tell him that you wanted it to work for Nomi's sake, but now you have this friendless unfiltered daughter who wants to read about teenage serial killers and you see the light.

You walk away from him. It's a step. Literally, metaphorically. You are even closer to the window.

Tell him, Mary Kay. Tell him that he was the love of your young life, that you don't hate him. You wanted to be on a pedestal and tell him that what hurts the most isn't that he cheated with Melanda, but that deep down you don't really care because of how you feel about me, the partner you want, the lover you deserve. *Me.*

Phil walks to the CD player—you live in the nineties, in the past—and he digs around and he finds what he wants and he plays what he wants and it's Jeff Fucking Buckley's voice and it's Leonard Cohen's words.

"Hallelujah."

This is not where we were headed and he cups your face in his hands. "I need you."

"Phil . . ."

"I miss you."

This is why we *should* have had a full-on fucking affair. He's getting to you. You want me but I'm here and he's there. His hands move along your body and you close your eyes and from your lips he draws a kiss and *you don't really care for your rat, do ya?* He habitually abuses you with his own lyrics and now he seduces you with Cohen's, whispering in your ear about faith and there you are, letting him croon a better man's words as he slides his hand under your skirt.

I clench the bag of popcorn. He is a boa and he unzips your slutty skirt and tightens his grip on your neck and he tells you that you're *a bad girl* and he bites your ear and he shreds your tights and somehow he has six hands, eight hands. Your shirt is off and his jeans hit the floor and he's inside of you—*he breaks your throne and pulls your hair*—and you moan as if you want that, as if you like that. You pretend to finish—there is no way you liked that—and he lifts you up like the pipe-smoking captain to your legless mermaid. That was *our* Normal Norman Rockwell painting at the pub and now you're in it with him, in the cage of his arms, your marriage. He lights another cigarette and he spoons you on the sofa and his ashes hit your tits. You wince and he kisses the places where he burnt you and you do not go together. We do. He puts his *butt* out in your half-empty cup of coffee and he strokes your Murakami with his nicotine-stained hand, callused fingers. "All right," he says. "Are you gonna call Layla or do you want me to?"

You laugh like that was funny and you sigh. "Oh come on, Phil. We both know that you're not gonna call. Can you do tomorrow at one?"

He squeezes you in a way I never have, with his arms and his legs. "I'll do whatever you want me to do, Emmy. You're my girl. I'd die without you. You know that, right?"

You're gonna let him fuck you again—*you're the second set of teeth*—and I turn off my TV but I still see him—*the thorns hide in the wreath*—and spicy kernels tickle my throat. I choke and up comes all that indigestible popcorn, shooting out of my mouth, and *I can't move, I can't breathe, I just die underneath.*

Phil isn't Leonard Cohen and he isn't Jeff Buckley but I've never moved in you the way he has, the way he does and it's a cold and broken clock of a *Hallelujah.* I pour Woolite onto your favorite black sweater and I google "Layla" and "couples counseling" and "area code 206" and there she is in Poulsbo, your licensed sanity killer: Layla Twitchell. She's your enabler, your enemy in plain sight, the woman who tries to save your marriage, the woman you *pay* to save your marriage. It's tempting to get in the car and drive to Poulsbo and make *Layla* pay for her sin, but I'm not that guy anymore.

I'm a good fucking guy and your rat is passed out in his chair. You took a shower—I didn't put cameras in your bathroom, I don't need to see that—and now you're in bed reading your Murakami, closing the book, writing in your journal, going back to your book. You are like my jeans in the washing machine and you need me to pull you out of that chamber and end this vicious cycle and you look into the lens and I zoom in and our eyes meet. Fuck it. Tomorrow, I will ask you to join me in RIP Kurt's Meadow and tomorrow you will say *yes.*

23

You are skipping lunch to go to Poulsbo to see the dentist—nice lie, Mary Kay—and I am on the way to Sawatdy to pick up beef and broccoli. I pull into the strip mall—even Bainbridge isn't perfect—and the island is turning against us. There was a death in the family and the restaurant is closed and I drive to Sawan but oh that's right. The family that owns Sawatdy owns Sawan and that's the problem with an island. There is no beef, no broccoli, and I can't get it out of my fucking head.

I keep picturing you with that rat. You let him rip off your tights. You let him cum inside of you. But you don't know that I know about that and good guys move *forward*. I won't let *one* moment of weakness between you and your manipulative ball and chain get in the way of our family. I drive to Starbucks. I buy two lattes, one for you and one for me—*Be the change you want to see in the world*—and I blast Sam Cooke. Positive Joe! I drive to the library—remember when I thought I was moving to a walker's paradise?—and I barge into the library with a big fat smile on my face, as if you didn't permanently ruin Jeff Fucking Buckley for me.

I knock on your door. You look up and you don't invite me in. "What's wrong?"

"Nothing," I say. "I did a mobile order and I got two by mistake. You want?"

You gulp. You want. "You should see if Ann wants that. She's downstairs."

I smile at you. "By the Red Bed?"

You do not smile at me. Too much. "Joe . . ."

"Sorry," I say. "It was just a joke."

You look so sad, and I bet Layla is on Phil's side—maybe *she's* fucking him too!—and you are getting it from all angles. Come on, Mary Kay. I know you're in hell. Open up to me. Tell me about your no-good, very bad week. Tell me about Melanda. Tell me about Phil. Tell me about Layla. But you don't. You just tell me that you're *so busy* right now. Bullshit.

But I remain positive. Rosie Joe the Riveter. "So I might head up to the meadow and read." You gulp and that was too much and too little. "Or who knows? Maybe I'll finally go check out Fort Ward."

"You should do that."

"You wanna join?"

You look at Eddie Vedder and then you look at the clock. "You should head out early before it gets too dark. And the meadow's probably a better idea. It's closer."

I inch closer. *Closer.* "Maybe *you* should cut out early and hit up the meadow. I can cover for you if that helps . . ."

"Joe . . ." Dot. Dot. Dot. "That sounds nice and I know we . . ." You can't even finish the sentence. You just exhale. "We'll talk later, okay?"

I catch your eye, which is no easy thing, the way you're trying so hard to avoid me. "You know where to find me."

You nod. "Have a good time up there."

I walk out of your office and you know where I'm going and it's my job to go there. But then I hear laughter in History. The hairs on my neck stand up. It's *Oliver* and he sees me and I see him and he's talking to a Mothball, as if he's a resident, as if he's allowed to check out *books.*

The Mothball distracts him—thank you, Mothball—and I get in my car and I drive to the forest because you said it.

It's *Closer.*

I am on foot. Oliver wants an *update* and I snap a picture of the sign—Barn or House—and send it to him. Oliver is placated, for now, and I post my *Barn or House* photo on *Instagram* and twenty seconds later there it is.

@LadyMaryKay Likes your photo and she can't wait to join you in the meadow.

I hike up the hill and I wait for you in the tall grass and the light in the sky won't last forever. I hear noises. Humans. I pull on my sweater and no. It isn't you. It's my neighbor and your frenemy Nancy and her entire extended fecal-eyed family and they brought their large yellow Lab and she's charging me and I let her kiss me.

"Flowerbed," I say. "How you doing, girl?"

Flowerbed slobbers all over me—she knows I'm good—and I let her give me sloppy kisses. It's an open display of affection and positive thinking is easier when there's a dog wagging its tail for you. I know you're on your way. You love me, you do. But then Papa calls—*Flowerbed!*—and he wants the dog to leave me and I want you to leave Phil and this whole fucking island is against us.

Flowerbed disobeys—good girl—and she wags her tail even more, smiling at me, as if she knew I needed a pick-me-up. "Good girl," I say. "Very good girl."

But now Master "Papa" Doofus is stomping up to us in his *Columbia* pullover and his man-leggings and his Timberlands. He blocks what's left of the sun and he doesn't smile or say he recognizes me from the neighborhood, even though he fucking does. His fecal-eyed family members are whispering about me, as if it's so sad and grotesque to be alone up here. They should do the decent thing and wave hello, *fuck* you, and you should do the decent thing and show the fuck up already. He whistles at *Flowerbed* and she obeys her doofus master even though she likes me better, even though she wants a new life with me and possessive, overbearing men like him and Phil ruin *everything.*

My phone buzzes. Is it you? No. It's just another bossy man—fucking Oliver—and I buy him another present on 1stdibs. It's been sixty-three minutes since you liked my photo and the fecal-eyed baby is crying and Nancy is clapping her hands—*Let's get a move on*—and it was bad when they were here but it's worse now that they're packing it in.

My phone buzzes—serotonin surge, is it you?—but it's just Oliver.

I text you a picture of the meadow—fuck it—and you don't write back and you're not going to write back and I can't do this anymore, Mary Kay.

I pick up my blanket and walk—it's just me and the trees—and I stop and stare at that sign that offers everyone a choice because it is impossible to walk on two paths at once. *Barn. House.* I am the barn, the home of all that is natural and you choose the house, prefab, phony. You're like Flowerbed, programmed to obey your "master." I know it now. And I know what I have to do.

An hour later, I am in my driveway, staring into the trunk of my car.

It's time for me to run. Your best friend is dead. You fucked your husband. I talk more to *Oliver* than I do to you, the woman I love, and I deserve better, Mary Kay. I don't want you to be some woman who gets off on being treated like shit but that's what you are, and it's like Dr. Nicky says on his blog, like Melanda said to you. When people show you who they are, it is your job to pay attention.

My phone buzzes, but it's different this time. I don't get that burst of serotonin—my brain is too smart—and I trudge back inside for one last bag. I check my phone and I was right. It's not you. It's never going to be you. It's Oliver, hitting me up about another "antique" on 1stdibs. I drop my reusable tote bag on my muddy floor—this is why rich people have mudrooms—and I bid on taxidermy for Minka, for Oliver and he doesn't thank me. He just asks if I ponied up for expedited delivery and sends me a picture from the house on Rockaway that he moved into—*Now THIS is a view Goldberg*—and he's right. You can see Seattle from Rockaway and I can't see shit from my house and you love me but it means nothing if you won't act on it. I tell Oliver that I'm heading for Seattle because I'm too creeped out to be in this house and he says to keep my notifications on and text him my new address when I'm settled.

Fucker.

I fill the food bowls for my kittens—practically cats—and I don't feel good about leaving them, but the side door is ajar. They'll find their way.

I pick up the last box, the one that hurts the most—tights you left in the trash can at work, a cardigan that carries your scent—and I carry the box outside. A woman in a Cooley Hardware pullover is walking her dog, glaring at me without saying hello—oh, Bainbridge, lighten up—and I pop my trunk and drop the box.

"You're leaving too?"

I know that voice and I turn around and your Meerkat is in my driveway, eyeing the box in my trunk and I didn't *seal* that box and your tights are right there—no, no, no—and can she see them?

"Nomi," I say. "How you doing?"

"So are you moving or what?"

Your teenager is such a child right now, pulling at a cowlick. I close the trunk. Safer that way. "I'm just going away for a few days. Business trip."

I sound like a dickhead in a John Cheever short story and she huffs. "Okay then. Have fun in your brand-new life."

She turns her back on me and I can't leave like this, not with her mad, losing her aunt and the cool guy from the library in the same fucking week, bound to tell you about what she saw. My plan was to disappear on you, not to crush your daughter's spirit and she's halfway down the driveway and fuck you, Bainbridge, you fucking fishbowl. "Nomi, hang on a second."

She turns around. "What?"

"I'm not moving away."

"It's a free country. Do what you want. My aunt left. I mean I guess I would too if I were you guys." Her aunt tried to *kill* me but she doesn't know that. She kicks a rock. "I just came by to tell you that I went back to the library and helped more old people. I was gonna write about Dylan for this senior seminar thing . . . but now I guess I'll write about the stupid joys of community service and old people or whatever. But whatever. I know you don't care."

"Hey, come on. Of course I care."

"Is that why you're leaving without saying goodbye?"

"I told you. I'm not leaving."

It's the truth. I'm not fucking leaving. Not anymore. This is about our family and Nomi needs me and thank God that Bainbridge is a tiny, nosy rock. Thank God you live *right around the corner.* Otherwise, I'd be on the ferry by now. "Do me a favor, Nomi. Don't call 'em 'old' people."

"All they do is talk about how young I am so how is that fair?"

"It's different and you know it."

"If it's rude to call someone old then it should be rude to call someone young."

"Point taken," I say, and I was overreacting today, same way she is overreacting right now. This is how you drive a rat insane. You trap it on an island, fuck with its head. Nomi and I are in this together and my phone buzzes. It's *Seamus* and that Cooley Hardware handmaid acted fast. He's blunt: *Heard you're splitting. Is that for real?*

Bainbridge Island: Where Boundaries Go to Die—and Nomi squints. "Who's texting you?"

She has no right to ask about my private communication and it's time to teach this kid a lesson. "Nomi, don't take this the wrong way, but there's this thing called privacy . . ." I'm talking to her, but the lecture is for me too. I planted those cameras in your house and it's my job to deal with the consequences. "And privacy is good for us. We all need it."

"Ah," she says. "So you're defending old people because you *are* an old person."

"Believing in privacy doesn't make me old. It just means I think some stuff is private." I hold up my phone. "And if you're really that curious . . . It's just Seamus."

She shudders. "Ick. He's so annoying."

True. "Oh come on," I say, emboldened by his outreach, as if he and Nomi and this whole fucking *community* are coming through for us, begging me to stay. "He's a nice guy."

She shrugs. "I used to work at his store. But just for a few months."

The Meerkat waves at Nancy, who is pulling an Athleta catalogue out of her mailbox.

"See," Nomi says. "I'm not *anti*-privacy. But you grew up somewhere where you can be anonymous. Bainbridge is freaking impossible. You can't have privacy here. I mean, you run a stop sign and you don't get a ticket but someone sees you run that stop sign and before you know it, your mom's like *I heard you ran a stop sign* and the guy at the T & C winks at you and tells you to drive safe and you *have* to drive safe cuz obviously your mom told him to keep an eye on you. I can't *wait* to live in New York, assuming I get into NYU."

I laugh and this *is* Cedar Cove and you couldn't join me in the meadow, you're punishing yourself for what you did in the *privacy* of my home. "I get it, Nomi. I do."

She grips the straps of her backpack. "I'm outta here. Have fun with Seamus but please don't tell him I said hi. I'm supposed to be at the library and he'll tell my mom and . . ."

I zip my lip and she walks away, happier than she was when she arrived. I unpack my car and I shoot a video of Riffic and Licious fighting over the smallest box. I send you the video and you send me a smiley face and that's all I need today, Mary Kay. I pick up a tchotchke I lifted from your home. A Phil Fucking Roth doll. I stuff it with catnip and toss it to the kittens and they go wild, thrashing, tearing off his limbs.

God, I wish I could kill Phil for you. But no.

I check your Instagram—nothing, you're in shame mode—and I check the Meerkat's. She shared a picture of herself with a few tech-challenged Mothballs—she didn't tag me or thank me—but you know who got her in that room. You gave me chocolate-covered strawberries—and my phone buzzes. Oliver wants an *update* and I tell him I was just being a pussy—it's the truth—and that I'm gonna stay in the house.

I am a good man, Mary Kay. Good men don't run away. I'm not an avoidant wimp who runs out on you to play *Xbox.* I buy Oliver a present for Minka—a bottle of fake perfume called *Chanel Fucked Up No5* by Axel Crieger—and that buys *me* time to fix dinner before your show tonight. I wasn't crazy about the first episode—too much graphic nudity and emotional violence—and I know that you would be devastated and embarrassed by your behavior in that house. I know you don't want me to see the ugly part of your home life. But tonight's episode will be better. And if not, I'm just the man to retool it.

24

I did it, Mary Kay. I am the mouse in *your* house and you can't figure me out. You keep trying to get my attention. Your rat had a *gig* on New Year's Eve but you stayed home to be with your Meerkat. You sent me glad tidings after midnight and I responded with a *you too* and I watched you stare at your phone, typing and deleting, ultimately tossing the phone on the couch. You've also been angling for my attention in our library. You replenished *The Quiet Ones* with a few short story collections and a Richard Russo novel that came and went too fast, according to you. But I didn't knock on your door to give you an *atta girl.* A day later, you announced that you were walking to Starbucks, an obvious play to get me to follow, but I stayed right where I was.

You carry the frustration into your home every night—good job, me!—and you're going through withdrawal, which means that your show is *getting better all the time*. In Episode 3, you were grumpy. You miss me and you can't have me—ha—so you were slamming cabinets. Apologizing to the Meerkat, retreating to your bedroom and avoiding your rat and tonight—Episode 104—you are in full-on Stepford mode. You don't sulk and stare at the walls and think about me. You are in nonstop motion, rifling through the rat's nightstand and his drawers because you live in fear of him falling off the wagon and you think he's hiding heroin in his guitar case, in the bottom of his amp.

He isn't hiding drugs, which means you're not *finding* drugs and you want to find drugs because that would make it easier for you to force him to check into rehab, which would pave the way for the two of you to split up. It wouldn't be about the drugs. It would be about the lying.

So now I'm off-island at a bar in Poulsbo called Good Old Daze, which is poppin' as bars like this are on Thirsty Fucking Thursday. It's easy to spot Aaron the drug dealer (a.k.a. Ajax. A.k.a. not *all* kids who grow up on Bainbridge turn out to be angels). I read about him on the Bainbridge Island Community Facebook page. People blame Ajax for the untimely death of a guy named Davey and Ajax holds court at a table in the back with an overall lack of shame about his purpose here. He wears a brown leather jacket that screams 1987 and Bruce Springsteen wails about hungry hearts and the barmaid pours stiff drinks in dirty glasses. I met Seamus for a beer at Isla and pretended to get a booty call and sneak out the back so Oliver won't see—the work I do for you, Mary Kay—and then I drove into Poulsbo.

I order a shot of Jack and make my way to Ajax, who mad-dogs me when I stand there at his table. Shaking. "What of it?" he says.

"I heard . . . Are you Ajax?"

Ajax scans the bar to make sure this isn't a sting and I tell him I knew Rudy—thanks to Facebook, I know all about RIP Davey's bad-influence buddy Rudy—and before you know it, I have a seat at the unsteady table with Ajax. A couple quick exchanges about the shitty scene at the bar—Ajax was hoping to get *laid* tonight—and then we're in the bathroom and just like that, I am the proud owner of ten highly toxic, no-good little M30s.

It's bone chilling, Mary Kay. A man is *dead* because of these poison pills and Ajax doesn't warn me about the fentanyl. He really doesn't care about me or the dead guy but then, that's the world, isn't it? The fecal-eyed family doesn't care about me either and this is why we need to find our tribe and take care of each other.

He tells me I can go now, and so I do, out the back door, into the rain, past a girl sucking a guy's dick in a Honda, past a woman crying in her car—*Bell Bottom Blues, you made me cry*—and into my car. I'm shaking for real now. It's scary to be in possession of all these fatal little pills and Ajax's paranoia is infectious. I adjust the rearview and turn on the interior light and I put the fucking pills in the trunk.

I know it's irrational, but I don't want to die from M30 fumes.

It's a straight shot home once I hit the 305 and I play Simon & Garfunkel to wash the Good Old Daze out of my brain but I drive too fast or too slow. I can't stop checking the rearview. It's really raining tonight, not drizzling, and Shortus is going home—*You were luckier than I was tonight*—and my wipers aren't working quite right. It's a two-lane road, always quiet and dark at night—it's fucking Bainbridge—and I tell myself that the set of headlights a few car lengths back is nothing to worry about because this is the way to the ferry. I turn up the volume and focus on bridges over troubled waters but my heart is beating fast.

Can you catch fentanyl by touching a tainted plastic bag? Am I ill?

Home at last and sweaty as fuck—I shouldn't have worn your favorite sweater—and I walk into my house and I call out to my cats but my cats aren't dogs. They don't come when called. I grab some paper towels and head back outside. I stare at my car, my car full of poison. I don't want an accidental contact high and I sure as hell don't want anything to happen to my cats. I pop my trunk and the paper towels aren't plastic, but at least they'll provide *some* boundary between my skin and the fentanyl.

I fold four paper towels and pick up the bag of death and my heart thumps faster—is fentanyl airborne?—and I walk back to my house. And then I hear the sound of my guitar. I clench the paper towels.

Oliver.

"In here," he says.

I walk around the corner, down into my sunken living room, and there he is, on my couch, strumming my Gibson. Chills. Flashbacks. All of it. "Did you have a good night, my friend?"

"It was okay."

He's tuning the guitar again and he's pure Angeleno. He's not a great writer. And he's not a great private detective and he probably put his detective hat on tonight because he hit a snag in the *spec script* he's no doubt writing in his downtime.

He eyes the wad of paper towels. "What's that, Goldberg?"

"What's up, Oliver? Did my bid on the Frank Stella not go through?"

I dump the paper towels in the trash bin—I pray my cats don't find a way in—and he tosses my guitar on the floor and man-spreads on my sofa in the spot where *you* sat.

"I saw you in Poulsbo," he says. "And needless to say, I am not pleased, my friend."

Of course he followed me. Of course tonight had to be the night that he threw himself into his work. "I don't know what you're talking about."

He just shakes his head. "Don't mess with me, Goldberg. We had a deal. You stay outta trouble. And that means you stay clean. Away from trash like *Ajax*."

In some fucked-up way I forgot that he is what he is, a private fucking detective, *a dancer for money.* But that's not my fault. It's easy to forget the origin of our relationship because most of the time he's just on me about *art.* I flop into a chair. "Oliver, I'm telling you. It's not what you think."

"Oh, so I suppose you got the pills for a 'friend'?"

Yes. "No. Look, I heard a rumor that bad stuff was going around . . . I just wanted to get it off the streets so some kid doesn't OD again."

"Saint Joe of the Stockyards."

"I'm not calling myself a saint . . ."

But it's true, Mary Kay. I did save a life tonight, maybe more than one. Oliver lectures me about the danger of drugs and people who deal in narcotics as if he's my tenth-grade guidance counselor and he won't let me keep my stash. He forces me to fish the bag out of the garbage and he reminds me that he's watching. *Always.* And then he sends me a link to a fucking David LaChapelle photograph of Whitney Houston called *Closed Eyes* and this is the first item that doesn't show the cost. *Price upon request.* And I should be buying this for *you* not for Minka but really I should be buying it for no one because no one needs to own this fucking photograph.

Riffic trots into the room and hisses at him. *Good cat.* "Sorry," I say. "But Oliver, this is getting out of control. I buy you every little 'antique' you want and you break into my house because I go for a *ride*?"

It's like a bolt of lightning hits and Oliver the artistic and Oliver the detective become one. "You seem to forget that I have video of you holding a dead body, my friend."

I DID NOT KILL HER. "I didn't forget. But you said we were in this together."

"Joe," he says. "I'm a little disappointed in you. I thought you were smarter than that . . ."

FUCK YOU, OLIVER. "I have you on a loose leash because when people feel free . . . when they feel *relaxed* . . . they fuck up. And now I know what you're up to—and now you know that you can't go out and cop a score. It's not just about your health. We are in this together, my friend, and if you blow your money getting high . . . that's no good for my art fund, is it?"

The pills weren't for me and Oliver is never going to believe me and I contact the seller and request the fucking price of *Closed Eyes* and now I have to wait for an answer and Oliver is watching me, Mary Kay. He really is. More than I knew. The worst and most dangerous eyes in this world are the private ones and I could stand up and knock him out and end his life but then his brother would end my life.

"Well," he says. "They hit you back yet? What's Whitney gonna cost us?"

By *us* he means *me* and I dream of my sunken living room imploding, pulling him into a sinkhole, but like my plan of Phil testing the waters with M30s, it's not gonna happen. I refresh the 1stdibs app and think of what Dr. Nicky would say right now. Something trite but true. *Everything happens for a reason.* I am a good guy and good guys find the bright side—it's like that Stephen King quote on the sign by the gas station near (RIP) Beck Road—*It was the possibility of darkness that made the day seem so bright.*

Maybe that's true. Maybe the universe sent Oliver into my life to teach me a lesson. He picks up Licious and Licious doesn't fight him and you were right, Mary Kay. Licious is a stupid fucking name. "Well?" he says. "Any word yet?"

"The guy says he'll get back to me tomorrow."

He takes a selfie with my cat and sends it to Minka. Ugh.

Oliver is an asshole, yes, but he's trying to make his girlfriend happy by fixing up her home. My heart races in the good way. Not paranoid about fentanyl in the air. (I googled. I'm fine.) I have to be like Oliver.

When he leaves, I bring my kitten-cats into my bedroom and give them a loose roll of toilet paper. They play on my bed—so fucking cute—and I send a video to you with a simple, honest *Guess I have to get more toilet paper.* You like the video and send me a smile and now you've seen my bed. We need these moments because you maintain your distance at the library—I get it—but I won't let you forget that you love me. I *exist.*

I hightail it down to my Whisper Room to watch you. You're in bed next to your rat—he's only taping his shit show *three* nights right now and he doesn't go downstairs until Nomi is asleep—and you're eating tortilla chips out of the bag—yes!—and he pokes you. "Do you have to be so loud, Emmy?"

You shove chips in your mouth. *Chomp. Chomp. Chomp.*

Your rat rolls over and you pick up your phone and scroll and then my phone pings.

@LadyMaryKay Likes your photo.

You fucked up. The picture is old. You *unlike* it and hang your head and Stephen King is the Master of Darkness but I am the master of *your* darkness. I turned off the lights inside of you and your rat reaches for your body and you swat him away. No more breakup sex. No more makeup sex. You don't want him. You want me.

25

We're making so much progress, Mary Kay. Oliver got invited to an *extended bachelor party* in Vegas. It's one of his best friends from home and he whined about *FOMO* and I stole a page from RIP Melanda's playbook and worked him over with reverse psychology.

Sucks you can't go. That's life being a Quinn bitch.

Poor Boys Club rules: Gambling is for trust fund kids who don't know the value of money.

Imagine Ray's face if he found out you left me here on my own. Not that I'd ever tell him but man. He would SNAP.

So of course, Oliver is *in* Vegas to prove he's not a *Quinn bitch* and we're in this "together."

☺

I promised to be good and I'm a man of my word, Mary Kay. You've been going to couples therapy somewhat religiously twice a week for two weeks and your shrink, Layla, should be disbarred. She's oblivious to the pain you're hiding. And she leaves the window of her office open as if there isn't an alley right by the building that's a fucking echo chamber.

I'd expect more from an MSW who lives in a semi-city, but at some point in life, I'll learn to expect less.

Layla advises you and your rat to "fill the well" and "nest" and I know what she means—talk, *bond,* fuck—but you don't want to talk to him. You don't want to have sex with him. You just want to buy a whole bunch of new fucking furniture. You loved "nesting" when you were preparing for Nomi to arrive and you're extrapolating like crazy, claiming that you and Phil *nest well together*. Your therapist thinks this is *positive teamwork*—such an idiot—and Phil made his feelings about material things clear a hundred years ago when he lambasted you in song about *a crate in a barrel, a barrel in a gun, remember the summer, the end of all your fun. (Repeat 10X.)* The trouble is, he doesn't want to lose you, so he sits in the therapeutic box nodding as you wax on about "the symbolic value" of buying a new dresser like the heartless slab of phony baloney that he is.

"Whatever it takes, Emmy. Anything for us."

So you bought a brand-new blue dresser and it wasn't made in America—Nice job, China!—it doesn't have cedar linings or metal undermount drawer glides. It weighs less than two hundred pounds and the "wood" is manufactured. They take real wood and disintegrate it and then mash it back together with artificial additives. Like your marriage, it's not real. It arrived a week ago and your cheap lazy husband wouldn't spring for the white glove delivery and assembly. So it waits for you, for him, in two giant boxes of unassembled slabs of fake wood on your back deck, where all the passing hikers and tourists can see it sit there festering, growing moldy. Dank.

Symbolism, much?

I watch from the Whisper Room as you stare at those wilting boxes. Phil's around more these days because of "therapy" and you nag him about the dresser. He's avoidant—*Just ask your buddy Seamus, he gets off on that kinda crap*—and he tells you he's too *worked up* from an NA meeting.

Part of "working on your marriage" means focusing on your past. The rat won't go to the meadow with you and he won't hike up to the bunkers at Fort Ward—*you know I have lower back issues, Emmy, and I can't take a pain pill, obviously*—so you've resorted to other shit. Sadder shit. You're hosting a *Reality Bites #TBT* screening for couples in the library's garden. (Gross. Sad. Just no.) All you need him to do is agree to show up and yet he grouses—*Aw man, are you trying to put me in an early grave?*—and you counter—*It's just one night*—

but he wants to go out that night because *the boys are back in town.* He picks up his pen—*That's a good line, I gotta write that down*—and he puts down his pen—it's someone else's good line, you moron.

Nomi stomps downstairs. She can't concentrate with all this bickering—Don't worry, kid, the Edward Albee shit ends soon—and you lower your voice to a hiss—*I need you to grow up, Phil*—and he tells you to *chill out, Emmy. Don't take out your Melanda shit on me. I'm not your whipping post.*

I clap my hands. You tell her, Phil! You steal from those Allman Brothers and drive her right into my arms!

You groan, you tell him that *he's* the one who needs to grow up. He can't choose his *boys* and *some band at the Tractor* over you and your *work.* He huffs that *the bands are playing new songs and you're playing old movies* and he snaps his fingers—*That's a song*—and he picks up his Gibson and he's strumming and you miss me. Your cell phone rings and you want it to be me but it's Shortus and Phil stops singing to give orders—*Please tell me that asshat's not coming over, Emmy, I can't listen to him go on about CrossFit*—and you are an obedient child bride. You send Shortus to voicemail, which means that he texts *me.*

Shortus: *Isla later?*

Me: *Sure!*

See, Mary Kay. Unlike your rat husband, I have empathy for single dudes who may not have the most scintillating personalities. I know it's hard to be alone, so I'll suck it up and have a beer with Shortus because I feel for him. It was *Friends* when RIP Melanda was around. It was okay for the three of you to be together, waxing nostalgic at the diner, always "popping by," but two is not three. And now that she's gone, you ice out Shortus.

Phil resumes playing his nonsong and you pour wine—*Did you fix the stove?*—and Phil is a child—*Right after I finish this song.*

You hate your life and you plod upstairs to your bedroom. It's a minefield. Your old dresser is in the front yard—what must your cul-de-sac neighbors *think?*—and your sweaters and your tights are mixed up with *his* clothes in big black trash bags. You can't deal with those fucking trash bags and you close your door and climb onto your bed.

You read your favorite parts of Murakami—*all but sucked inside*—and you look at my Instagram—I can't see but I know—and then you put on a silk sleep mask. Your hand delves into *your* Murakami and you tap your Lemonhead and I'm not a pervert but this sex fast isn't easy.

You climax. I climax. For now, this is good enough because it has to be.

The next day when I get to your house, I climb onto your side of the marriage bed and I put on your sleep mask and I imagine you here and when I finish I'm dizzy. I smack my knee into your end table—*Fuck!*—and I rummage in a trash bag for your tights but I wind up with his shit-stained man-panties—*Double Fuck*—and I rush into your bathroom to wash my hands.

I'm getting tired of this shit and I dry my hands on a plush new hand towel—you are trying so hard—and I check your Instagram and it's all *#TBT* of you and your rat. Your nostalgia is misguided, you should be looking toward the future—me—but here you are, circa the late nineties hanging all over your *man*. Instead of being sad about Melanda and the state of your life, you are snarky. You take a picture of yourself in your puffy nineties prom dress.

This is okay to wear to work, right? #RealityBites screening tomorrow night! See you crazy kids there! #DateNight

You really do need to get some boundaries, Mary Kay. This is your personal page and public library events have no place here. We need boundaries, both of us. My alarm on my phone goes off—it's almost 1:45—and it's time to get to work. The work I'm doing now is not unlike my work at the library—nobody is paying me to do this—but the feeling I get from helping you is payment enough. I open my notepad.

DIMARCO HOME RENOVATIONS: DAY EIGHT

-Pour Phil's almond milk down drain, return empty carton to refrigerator.

-Delete *Monterey Pop* from DVR.

-Loosen screws in the leaf of dining room table.

-Jack up heat on thermostat.

-Disable Phil's bullshit fix on the stove.

-Move charcoal to deck so it gets rained on.
-Hide the coasters.
-Turn on all the TVs. High volume. VH1.

Yes, I'm your *handyman*—you're welcome—and you don't know that I'm the prop master, staging things to advance the plot so that you blame each other when things go awry, when you come home to a hot house and he *swears* he turned down the heat before he left. I like the way he flies into an indignant rage, accuses you of being *crazy*. I hate the way you recover—*I know I'm moody, I'm still in shock over Melanda*—but soon you will jump off the building, away from your forty-five-year-old man baby. And he is a baby. Of all my tricks, it's the milk that drives him to slam cabinets and rail on about his vocal cords, your selfishness—*It's not like I ask for a lot from you, Emmy. Jesus Christ. I need my almond milk!*

I finish my projects and I get home and I fix dinner—old pizza from Bene—and I head down to the Whisper Room and turn on my TV to settle in for my favorite sitcom: *You*. Things are especially ugly in your house tonight. I signed you up for Pottery Barn catalogues, Restoration Hardware, and of course, *Crate & Barrel.* The rat is on a tear—*What is this shit?*—and you can't find your favorite sweater in your trash bags—I moved all your things around—and you want him to assemble that dresser *now* but he can't because he threw his back out at the Guitar Store—ha! Thanks for playing, Phil—and he can't take a pain pill, he *won't* take a pain pill—right on, brother!—and Nomi is fed up—*I can't wait to get out of here*—and congratulations, Mary Kay. You're in the twenty-years-later sequel to *Reality Bites* and there's a reason why that movie doesn't fucking exist. In real life, Troy and Lelaina split up three months later and Lelaina realizes that Ben Stiller actually loved her but Troy only wanted to control her.

Right now, your poor man's Troy Dyer picks up his Gibson and you grab it out of his hands and is this it? Are you gonna ask him for a divorce? You sigh. "I don't want to fight with you."

He reclaims his guitar and strums. "Then don't."

You stare at his Michelob Light. It's not on a coaster because I hid your coasters. You walk into the kitchen and tear a paper towel off the roll, you pick up his beer to move it onto your makeshift coaster, and he kisses the back of your hand—*Sorry*—and you rub the top of his head—*Me too*—and I scream at my TV—*NO!*

For a little while you coexist, living your separate lives, but then you try to start dinner. You turn on the stove but nothing happens.

"Phil!"

"Writing!"

"The stove's out again."

"Nope, fixed it, Emmy."

He did, but I *un*fixed it today and this is the final act where it all comes together because the pot isn't boiling, you can't cook, and now he's playing the almond milk card—Good boy, Phil—and he shoves a Pottery Barn catalogue in the trash and you grab your phone. Do it, Mary Kay. Lawyer up!

"What are you doing, Em?"

"I'm gonna find someone on Craigslist to assemble the dresser."

"Oh, come on. I dig the trash bags, it's like the good old days."

You groan—*kick him out*—and you collapse onto your old blue sofa. Did you finally give up? Do you finally *see* what needs to happen?

"Okay," you say. "Should we just order Sawadty? I'm exhausted anyway."

You can order all the beef and broccoli in the world but it won't satisfy your desire to eat beef and broccoli with *me* and Phil is fine with Thai, fine with anything, and you lecture him like he's your indolent teenage son—*We do have to finish the house before Nomi graduates*—and he huffs—*It's only March, I'll stick the boxes in the garage*—and you are calm—*We have a hundred people coming to this house*—and he is a child—*To hang out in the backyard, Em, in two months. Relax.* No one likes being told to relax and you harangue him about the minefield in the bedroom. He snickers—*The party's not in the bedroom, Em*—and grabs his guitar—*That's a good line. That's gold.* He buries his head in his music—*I'll take care of the dresser tomorrow*—and you pour more wine—*I'll hold you to it.* But you won't hold him to it, Mary Kay. You never fucking do. You go upstairs and masturbate and I shut off this bad TV show: *frumpy husband and foxy wife, how original!* I don't have it in me to jerk off. Not tonight.

I have to work harder.

Oliver bugs me for an update—he's easier to deal with when he's out of town—and I tell him I'm at home—the truth—and I don't bitch at him for stealing my M30s because Ajax sold me some heroin and sadly, we're gonna have to use it now.

I am back in your house less than twelve hours later and I am retracing your footsteps. You're always sniffing around his nightstand because you are *Married, Worried.* I plant a baggie of horse in the copy of *Catcher in the Rye* that he keeps in his nightstand. There's a sticker on the cover—PROPERTY OF BAINBRIDGE PUBLIC HIGH SCHOOL—and oh Phil, grow up. I cross the room and slip another bag under an amp—who keeps an amp in the bedroom?—and then I walk over to *your* nightstand. This is where you keep a little book that I can only presume must be your diary. I know I shouldn't read it. But we're in a rut so I open your drawer and I pick up your diary. The first few pages are to-do lists—*almond milk, sell dresser, find one that comes assembled*—and you are a fox. Sneaky. The good stuff is in the back.

The dresser, the damn dresser. It's like a box of Joe and it's like he's on my porch in those goddamn boxes and what am I doing? I am punishing Phil because I want to be with Joe and I can't be mad about Phil about Melanda because come on. I knew. And in some sick way I felt good letting it go on because we all know that I really did steal him and maybe I hoped he would leave me for her? But he didn't and now he's never leaving and I can't leave but what about ME? When do I get to be happy? God I miss Joe. But is that only because I want what I can't have? Joe in the bunkers at Fort Ward. Joe in the meadow. Joe Joe NO AHAHAHAHAHAH

The danger of a good book is that it swallows you whole and animals in the wild don't read because if you get lost in a book, you lose sight of your surroundings. You don't hear the predator. For all of Phil's laziness, the fucker did do *one* thing you asked him to do last night. He sprayed WD-40 on your sliding glass door. And I couldn't reverse that fix. That's why I didn't hear the door open.

But now I hear the footsteps above all the TVs. Someone is here, inside this house.

The floorboards on the stairs whinny beneath feet. "Dad? Is that you?"

It's your daughter. It's Nomi, the Meerkat.

26

When I was a kid, my mother didn't read to me. She was always groggy, tired. *I work a double and I get home and now you want me to read to you?* No one was going to read to me so I learned to read to me. You can do that, you can read the story out loud and if the story is good enough, you transcend the limits of your ego. You split. You become the reader and the listener, the child and the adult. You beat the system. You beat your doom. Reading saved my life when I was a sweaty little kid and it saves my life again today because I *always* carry a book. I'm carrying one right now: Robert McCammon's *The Listener.* You gave it to me last week, Mary Kay, and come on, book, work your magic and save my life because Nomi is at the bottom of the stairs clutching her chest.

"You scared the living shit out of me!"

"You scared me too, Nomi."

She grips the banister. "What are you even doing here?"

I walk, one step at a time. "Your mom gave me this book and I was bringing it back. I thought someone was home . . . Do you guys always leave so many TVs on?"

She sighs, the fear in her voice waning. "That's my dad. And they wonder why I always have my headphones on."

I reach the bottom of the steps. "I'm sorry I scared you . . ."

She shrugs. "I thought it was just Seamus," she says and oh that's right, that fucker is like your handyman and she really *isn't* scared, not anymore. She yawns. "Can we go outside? It's such a relief when I have the place to myself."

I open the sliding glass door and it glides—Damn you, Phil—and Nomi and I sit at the table on your deck. It's my first time hanging out here like one of your *Friends* and Nomi picks up my book. "So why didn't you just bring this back to the library?"

I won't let her ask the questions and I smile. "So you're home early, yeah?"

I caught her good—ha!—and she begs me not to tell her parents—I won't.

My phone buzzes and she yawns. "Who's that?"

Oliver. "An old friend from home . . ."

Oliver found a $35,000 bedazzled horse at some gallery in a casino and I tell him it's tacky and he tells me to fuck off and then he fires back.

Oliver: *Being good?*

Me: *Yes. And you do NOT buy art in Vegas, Oliver. Rookie move.*

I look at the Meerkat. Her eyes are glazed and she's puckering her lips and wait. Is she stoned right now? Well, that means she won't tell you about our little run-in.

"Nomi, I'm not a narc but I do have to ask . . . are you high?"

"A *narc*? Are *you* high?"

She laughs and pulls a bong out of her bag. "It's legal," she snaps. She barely knows how to work the thing and her lighter is almost dead and she's awkward. Uncoordinated. She coughs. "They say this stuff makes you paranoid. But I was born paranoid. Maybe it will make me normal."

She shows me the "new" book she's reading—a reissued copy of *In Cold Blood*—and it pains me to see a young woman filling her mind with more darkness, but at least it's not *Columbine* and I smile. "So, then I assume this means you're all done with Dylan Klebold?"

She bangs her bong on the table. "I told you I just like his poems. A lot of good writers are nutjobs." She coughs and I hope she doesn't overdose and she asks me if I live alone—*with all those cats*—and I nod and she coughs through a sigh. "I could never. I would be so paranoid. I would go nuts. And cats can't even protect you."

I won't be insulted. Of course she has issues. Her father is a playboy and her parents aren't in love. "It's not so bad. You get used to it, Nomi. Cats are good company."

She shrugs. "I always told Melanda that she should get a cat." Wrong. She couldn't keep that condo clean as it was. "I think she went nuts from being alone so much." Well, that's closer to the truth. "It's cool to be alone in a city or whatever, but *here*? No offense."

"None taken," I say, and I have to remember that this is a child. A minor. A shit ton of perfectly well-adjusted people live alone, they don't pair off, but *still* the family people act like there's something wrong with us. "So," I say. "Melanda moved?"

She smiles at me in a way that reminds me that she came from inside of you. Her grin is pure Alanis Morissette, a little *too* knowing. "Yeah," she says. "Maybe she took off cuz she was pissed when I told her how much I loved that movie you told me about."

I am the adult. The authority figure. "That's crazy, Nomi. Don't blame yourself. Not for one second."

She's a kid again, scratching her messy hair. "Yeah, she probably just got sick of my parents. They're so annoying." I can't agree with her so I don't respond but I can't imagine living in that house either. "Did you know her?" she asks. "Did you know Melanda?"

I don't like the question and I might be getting a contact high. Paranoid. I steer us back to the safe water, after-school-special seas. "Nomi, your parents aren't annoying. All parents are annoying. That's biological design. Otherwise no one would ever want to leave the nest."

She takes off her glasses and wipes them with a napkin. "I can't wait to get out of here. My parents . . . they act like everything since high school blows, like they'd get in a time machine if they could. It's so sad. I mean life is all about what's *next,* you know?"

I wish you were more like your daughter, Mary Kay, but it can't be me and Nomi talking shit about you, so I defend you and your low-grade nostalgic depressive fever. I remind Nomi that we grew up in a different time, before cell phones and Instagram. "Your mom's not living in the past, people our age just miss the way things used to be."

She huffs. "Well excuuuuuse *me.*"

"No, Nomi, I'm not saying we were better than you. I'm just saying we were better *off*."

"Totally disagree."

I want your fucking Meerkat to *listen* and I snap my fingers. "Think of a meerkat."

"Okay . . ."

"A meerkat in the wild is just living her meerkat life. But a meerkat in a cage, well she needs people to feed her. She tries to do meerkat things but she doesn't have the space. And let's face it. She wants people to look at her because she learns that's the only way she gets to eat."

Your Meerkat gives me a *huh*—she's thinking about my metaphorical meerkat—but maybe not, because now she's staring at me again. Alanis eyes. Piercing. "You want to know something sick?"

No. This is one step too far and I steal your words—"I should probably get going . . ."—but she leans in like the little meerkat that she is. "My mom is so paranoid about my dad that she put *cameras* all over the house." All my blood stops midflow. She knows. *She knows.* Do you know? "So yeah, I think she kind of likes capturing the moment."

I put my hand on *The Listener* and I will McCammon's strength to funnel into my veins. I will not turn red. I will not cave in to paranoia. "Wow. How do you know?"

She rocks back and forth in her chair. "Well I don't *know.* It's just a vibe."

Thank Christ, and I pick up her bong. "The rumors are true, Nomi. This really can make you paranoid. Once I got so high that I thought there was an earthquake in New York. I called 911."

She's a *Listener* and she's backtracking, doubting herself. "Yeah, I guess you're right. And my mom is so bad at technology, she wouldn't know how to work cameras."

We're in the clear—I think—and I take a deep time-to-go breath but she pulls her knees to her chest and keeps talking. "You know my parents started going out in high school? Can you imagine?"

I can't leave, not when she goes there. "I didn't know that."

"Everyone thinks it's so romantic. They have this Nirvana ticket stub framed and she swears she remembers the night and I'm like do you even? Or do you just stare at that ticket stub so much that you *think* you remember it? She acts like her life is so good, like that's how it works, like posting the ticket stub every year isn't pathetic. She's like 'Do you have a crush on anyone at school?' and it's like 'No, Mom. Boys my age are stupid. Do you think that means I'm gonna die alone?' But then I'm like, whatever . . . I don't like the guys and they don't like *me.* I mean Dylan Klebold was like . . . bad . . ."

"Yes."

"But it was kinda like mistaken identity . . ."

No. And I hate drugs. I do. "Okay, Nomi, but—"

"See if *I* had been that girl, that girl he was in love with, I mean I would have gone up to him and like . . . who knows? Eric would have bugged him to help with his psycho mission but Dylan woulda been like no . . . I'm good. I mean nobody *had* to die, you know? Like . . . that girl . . . she could have saved him."

That's a fantasy of a child who thinks that love can cure anything, even mental illness, and I relate on some level. I tried to save Borderline Beck and my parents were like Nomi's parents—minus the *nostalgia*—but there is nothing for me to say to fix the damage that Phil has done to this child. You're complicit, Mary Kay. She's a soulful kid, an artist without a medium, and for all your *Nomi needs me* you don't seem to be getting into it with her and does she fucking know about my cameras?

She yawns. "Sorry," she says. "This is why I can't smoke pot. I get stupid."

"Don't be ridiculous, Nomi. Don't ever be sorry for talking."

She squints, a Meerkat again, a child full of doubt, wonder. "Do you know my aunt Melanda?" she asks again.

She committed suicide in my basement and I nod. "Not so well. I heard she moved."

"Well, do you know why?"

Because she thought she'd never find true love and she realized she's not Carly Simon. "I think it was something about a job."

The Meerkat fights a smile. "That's what she said, but everyone at school says she was . . . you know . . . *doing* this freshman kid and the parents didn't want to press charges so they were like, *leave.* This kid in my orgo class says he saw her sticking something in his *butt* on this trail where we went to release salmon eggs when we were little. I mean *I* believe it. And my mom's not speaking to her and she was always in my face about stuff but now she's like . . . silent. I bet it's true."

"What does your mom say?"

"She says I can't believe everything I hear but I mean I'd go crazy if I was her age alone here too. No offense . . ."

"None taken."

I tell the Meerkat I have to go and she says to wave goodbye to the cameras—chills—and I am offended, Mary Kay, but not in the way you might think. The Meerkat is high, pretending to be so cavalier about her aunt disappearing, but beneath that adolescent bravado, your daughter is in pain. RIP Melanda wasn't perfect, but she was Nomi's fucking *aunt* and she was a regular in your home. The Meerkat misses her aunt and she wants to believe the bullshit story about the freshman because it's easier than thinking that one of the only people on this planet who cares about her just walked out of her life. That would be like if Mr. Mooney had shut down the bookstore on me and skipped town without a word and you just can't fucking do that to a child. I would have gone nuts if I had lost the only mentor in my life and don't you see, Mary Kay? Phil isn't just bad for you. He's bad for everyone. Because of him, Melanda is dead to you—not to mention dead in real life—and you have to cover for her. You have to encourage Nomi to *believe* an outright lie because you're a good mother and you've wondered what's worse: your daughter knowing that your husband fucked your best friend or your daughter thinking Melanda was a sexually deviant spinster child molester.

I get it. You don't want Nomi to despise her father and I know you can't tell Nomi what Melanda did to you, what she did with Phil, but Nomi is in pain. You're in pain. You women suffer while he tries out *guitars, man,* and enough is enough.

It's time for reality to take a bite out of Phil but then I hear the Meerkat in my mind—*Wave goodbye to the cameras, Joe*—and I hope reality doesn't bite me first.

27

It's 12:36 P.M. and I'm at Starbucks and it's one of the stranger things about this island. You'd think people would look down on corporate coffee but it's always packed in here and that knit cap fucker from the ferry is blocking the mobile order pickup spot with his *stroller* and what can I say? I'm in a mood. Oliver's back—four tables away, as if all that trust we built is gone—and my favorite hate-watch TV show is getting canceled—thanks, Nomi—and people get grumpy when they lose their binge shows. I push the knit cap dullard's empty stroller and he glares at me as if his unremarkable lesser Forty is *in* the fucking stroller.

"Sorry," I say. "Just trying to get my coffee."

He looks through me, Seattle freeze style, and I grab my latte and I really am *trying*, Mary Kay. I wait outside and sure enough, Oliver is out the door.

"You seem a little moody, my friend. Do I have to worry about you snapping?"

"Oliver, no one likes to be stalked."

"I dunno about that," he says. "Minka got two *thousand* more followers after this bikini shoot and when those pervs DM her about coming to get her . . . that shit makes her happy."

I laugh and fake a sneeze. "Oh right," I say. "Seth MacFarlane follows her, doesn't he?"

I don't know if Mr. Fucking *Family Guy* "follows" Minka, but it doesn't matter. Seth MacFarlane has the career that Oliver wanted, so Oliver is backing away, muttering about emails that need sending when we all know he's going to take a nice, deep, time-sucking dive into Minka's verified followers.

He waves at me. "Have fun with your cats, my friend. Stay safe."

He's starting his car and opening Instagram—I knew it—and thank God for that because I *do* need my space. I've been trying to make things better for us but your daughter is a paranoid truancy case and I don't have a choice, do I? I have to scale back my renovations on your home as if she issued a STOP WORK order via some state compliance agency. I studied the footage all night in the Whisper Room and Nomi never once looked directly at the cameras, so I do *think* we're safe. I don't think she actually knows about them. But Shel Silverstein's *Whatifs* are upon me and they will not be ignored.

Nomi's at school and you and Phil are with Layla—sorry to miss out on our therapy, but my car needs to stay in the driveway in case Nurse Oliver pops. I slink out the back door of my house, into the woods. I make it to your house—thank you, woods, for the camouflage—and I walk into your house and I put my coffee on the counter. I go room to room and I remove every one of my high-def cameras and it's not fair. Even with this kind of access, you shut me out. I didn't know about your little talk with Nomi about Melanda because that must have happened in your car or at the library and now how am I supposed to *keep up* with you fucking DiMarcos?

I've got all my cameras in a reusable tote bag and I leave the way I came in and I won't be like Phil and allow myself to turn blue on you. I've always been good at lifting myself out of the muck. Okay, so the TV show is over but you know what? I was getting a little sick of watching the three of you anyway. Last night it was more of the same and I can remember it word for word as I walk on the trail by the sea.

You swore you'd get almond milk, Emmy.

You swore you'd assemble that dresser.

Well I would if the Allen wrench was where you said it was.

Are you calling me crazy?

Am I that stupid? Hell, no, Miss Perfect. I know I can't call a woman crazy.

You know what, Phil? Maybe this hiatus is bad. Maybe you should go back to your damn show because your moods are out of control.

Well, maybe I wouldn't be in a mood if there was some coffee in this house.

I bought coffee. I told you it's in the freezer.

Emmy, I've been in the freezer. There isn't any coffee.

Coffee. *My coffee.* I drop my tote bag and the cameras fall out and *oh heck it's up to my neck* and I shove the fucking cameras into the fucking bag and I am backtracking, running faster than I did in New York, faster than I did in Little Compton and this isn't happening but this is happening and it's not as bad as the mug of piss. It's worse. It's a paper cup of coffee with my name on the label and it's on your kitchen counter and this trail is fighting me every step of the way, roots and other joggers—get out of my fucking way—and this is why all you people drink your coffee out of travel mugs because my name is on that cup.

My name.

It's a common name but there's no Joe in your house and now I'm *in* your house and the cup of coffee is a mug of piss, the one that nearly ruined my life. I grab it—*yes*—but *no* because the front door just opened and it's you. It's him. I can't open the slider and I slip into your guest bathroom and there's no shower in here and there's no window and I can't turn on the light because what if there's a fan?

I close the bathroom door—was it open when you left the house?—and what if you have to pee and is this how it ends? Because we're all slaves to caffeine?

"Well," you say to him, not to me, and you should be at work. "Should we do it?"

Oh no. This is not a time for you to get *Closer.* Not while I'm so close. He mumbles and you open a drawer and you riffle with your hands and every sound is an engine in my head.

"Okay," you say. "So the contract. I promise to stop nagging you about stupid stuff."

"Stupid stuff," he says. "Can we get a little definition here?"

"Christ, Phil, don't nitpick already. We have to start somewhere."

No you don't, Mary Kay. You can leave.

He sighs. "Well all right then. But what do we mean by 'stupid stuff'?"

You, rat. You are the stupid stuff and it's hard being a statue, holding this mug of piss. *Coffee.* Coffee.

"You know what it means, Phil. You were there. The dresser. House stuff."

He is silent and the silence is worse than the engines because what does the silence mean? Are you making eyes at each other? Are you noticing that the bathroom door is closed when it's usually open?

Your voice is flat. "Okay, just say it. What's wrong? And don't bullshit me about how it's hard to be vulnerable. This only works if you *are* vulnerable."

I love you like crazy and look at me in here. The definition of *vulnerable*.

"Well I dunno," he says. "I was hoping that 'stupid stuff' was more about . . . Emmy, for fuck's sake, you know I don't wanna go to this movie night thing."

"And you know I do, Phil. You know I planned it."

"I know."

"And I *have* to go."

"Emmy . . ."

"I don't know, Phil. You used to like the way I am . . ." I like the way you are. "You used to say how you needed me *because* I plan things, because I care, because I'm someone who *makes the world go round.* And now . . . it's like I repulse you."

"Em, the guys are only here one night."

"Right. Same way they were here last month. And the month before."

"But they're playing."

"And tonight you're busy. As a lot of married men are every once in a fucking while."

"See, I try to talk and you get nasty."

"You think this is *nasty*? You call this talking?"

You throw your pen at the window and thank God you didn't throw it at my door. You lay into him and you call him out on his bullshit—*yes*—and you remind him that you are there for him. You take care of him. "My whole life, I go to things alone. Open houses at school because you're sleeping or birthday parties at night because of your show. And do I complain? No. And I want *one* night from you and this is how it is."

"Hey now, gimme a little credit. I'm on hiatus. Layla said it, Em. You wanted me to take a break from the show and what did I do? I took a break."

"Right. And that's how you want to spend your hiatus. With the guys."

You're crying now. You miss me so much and you can't take it anymore. You're trying so hard and he's not trying at all, patting you on the back, literally, like you're a dog. He's walking now. He picks up the pen and he signs the little unnotarized contract. "I will go to the movie thing and I will do the dresser so you don't have to keep asking me to do to the dresser."

You sigh, pleased. I think you touch him. "See," you say. "We got this, we do."

No, you fucking don't and he is *not* going to that movie night—contracts are like promises, made to be broken—and he grabs his coat so aggressively that he nearly takes down a chair. "Okay," he says. "I gotta split. I gotta go to a meeting . . ." The manipulation, Mary Kay. What he really means is *My addiction is all your fault, just like my life.* And it's bullshit. He's the luckiest man on the fucking planet.

You blow your nose—probably on a harsh napkin, no Kleenex on your table—and you tell him you're sorry. "But, Phil, sometimes it's like you don't remember any of the good stuff. I mean come on. You know why I chose this movie . . ."

He makes a noise and whistles and this is *TMI.* It's obvious that a hundred years ago you went down on him in a theater and Alanis Morissette would be disgusted—I'm sorry but he's just not a very attractive man—but I am a good guy. It's ancient history and I forgive you. You were young and look at you trying so hard to spice up your bland marriage. You really are a fighter and it's your right to try to save your marriage. I will allow it. I do allow it. Because in *our* relationship, we give each other space to breathe. Like now, you're pushing Phil to leave so that he can go to the hardware store to get a wrench before his meeting as if you know I need him outta here. You have to get back to the library—you told them you needed to run errands and your marriage is an errand—and the front door opens and the front door closes and finally both of you are gone.

I turn on the light and breathe and what a different kind of world it is with you, Mary Kay. In my old world, I left the mug of urine behind and it drove me to the brink, to *Los Angeles.* But in our world, I take the mug with me and the mug is made of paper. It will disintegrate. And Bainbridge is showing off today—gray skies turning blue—and I am safe and there is no urine in this cup. There never was. It's just coffee, and I pour the coffee on the damp ground—always damp, permanently moist—and I recycle the cup and I like our world. I do. I like the squirrel that sits nearby and I like the woman in a North Face jacket and I like her happy black Lab and I am beaming. Smiling ear to ear and this is why people love horror stories: It's not for the gore. It's for the moment when the good guy escapes just like you wanted him to because it means that for once on this unjust, dying planet, the good guy wins.

I feel inspired. I text your rat: *Hey man, I got a buddy in town. HUGE FAN. We're up at Dock Street and if THE Phil DiMarco showed up unannounced. Just sayin' . . .*

Two hours later, I'm sitting on a picnic table in the woods by the dock when your rat's jalopy comes into view. He gets out of the car, more puffed up than he's been in a while.

"Jay," he says. "It's your lucky day. Where's your buddy at?"

"Oh shit," I say. "I should have texted you but my buddy had to go meet up with some chick he met in the airport."

He is a deflated balloon—the poor fucker just *tweeted* about how much he loves to surprise his *Philistans.* He lights a Marlboro Red. "No big whoop," he says. "Good to get out of the house." He leans against a tree by my table. That's Phil. Always leaning. "You been good?"

"Yeah," I say. "Some shit went down with my mom, but it's all good."

Phil feels so sorry for himself right now. He drove here ready to dazzle a *fan* and now he has to listen to me talk about my *mother*. Ha. He has no choice but to ask me what happened.

"Oh shit," I say. "I don't know where to begin . . ."

"Women stuff?"

I nod and he snorts. "Try living with one."

Bingo. "Hard times with the wife?"

"I'm in a fight for my life. It's the kinda shit you can only understand if you've been married for twenty years . . ." Typical narcissist. "We're doing it, ya know, we're in counseling, we've both made some mistakes but tonight . . . tonight my boys are in town."

"No shit? Where?"

He withholds the details. For now. "Point I'm trying to make . . . see my boys *mean* something to me, man. And my wife is acting like she's my mother . . . They do that. They get mixed up in their heads."

"Jesus. She won't let you go see the guys?"

"She wants me to watch a *movie* with her. Says I have to. I been a bad boy . . ."

"Oh come on," I say. "She *married* a bad boy."

He smiles. "This is true."

"I don't know shit about marriage . . ." Yes I fucking do. "But to me, a marriage is kinda like a guitar, right? You need tension in those strings or you can't make any music."

Phil blows a smoke ring. "The protégé makes a good point, yes he does."

I keep going, Mary Kay. I tell him that you *want* him to fight back, to be more like the rebel she married. He flicks his cigarette in the woods—such a fucking asshole—and the suspense might kill me. He blows a smoke ring.

"So," he says. "How'd ya like to meet the band?"

A couple hours later, Phil and I are in the city. Free men. Ready to rage.

He lights a cigarette and I check my inside pocket for my Rachael Ray knife. Of course I brought a weapon. This is the city and as we all know, cities are not Cedar Fucking Cove.

He has to check in with *Ready Freddy* to make sure I'm good to get in and I check up on you. You're making an Instagram story about getting ready for *#DateNight*—the denial is disturbing—and you're dressing up like Winona Ryder in a flowery sack dress—not your look—and Phil finishes up his call with Ready Freddy and sighs.

"Jesus. She's *still* bugging me about this fucking movie night."

"Did you tell her you're not going?"

"I told her I'm in a meeting," he says. "She should know better than to bug me."

We get into an Uber—I order the car, as if it's my honor—and he's lecturing the driver about music—*Huh, I've never heard of "Drake"*—and the driver will be right to give me a shitty rating. I make sure my phone is on mute and watch a new scene in your Instagram story. You changed into a Red Bed red T-shirt and pajama pants. Psychic Hotline Depressed Winona. You look scared. Defeated. You know he's not coming to play husband. Why don't you just give up?

Phil groans. "Another text. Jesus, woman, lay *off*."

I keep my mouth shut and Phil whistles at the driver. "Hey man," he says. "We're gonna jump out right here."

We're two blocks away from the bar and we're on the sidewalk and Phil tells me to stop.

"You okay?"

"Yeah," he says. "I just gotta make a quick call."

He leans against a building and he can't *call* you right now, in front of me. I've managed to keep my life with Phil separate from our life and that's no easy thing in Cedar Fucking Cove. If he puts me on the phone to back up whatever bullshit story he's got planned, we die. He's praying—*don't pick up don't pick up*—and I am on his side for once—*don't pick up, don't pick up*—and he bounces in his boots. "Voicemail!"

He lights a cigarette and he's a hands-free smoker. "Hey, Em, so listen. My sponsor thinks it's not a good move for me to go on the date night thing. The therapy we're doing is great, but it's a lot on me." He's not a musician, Mary Kay. He's an *actor*. "I'm in the weeds and it's not about the boys. I just can't do a big-ass night with book people . . . I love you, Em. I just . . . I can't be your guy. Not tonight." And then he winks at me. "And come on. You said it. It's just one night. You know if I'm not sober, I'm nothing. Dresser gets done tomorrow, I swear. Love ya, babe."

It's a miracle that I don't throw up on the sidewalk and we walk to the Tractor Tavern and it's not what I expected but it's what I should have expected. The goons at the door are right out of central casting and they need dental surgery and you can feel them hoping they get to bust out the pepper spray. There's a poster that makes big promises—*ALL religions. ALL countries of origin. ALL sexual orientations. ALL genders. We stand by you and YOU ARE SAFE HERE*—and I bet these guys piss on that sign every night.

"All right," Phil says. "Lemme do some business first. You'll meet the guys after they jam. You don't wanna meet them now, when they're all nervous and shit."

I happily hide by the bar like a shy fan boy and Phil's *boys* are not happy to see him. This isn't even a real concert, it's a glorified open mic, but the way they suck up the oxygen makes me want to jump on the bar and scream YOU ARE NOT WARREN ZEVON NOT ONE OF YOU. My phone pings. You added to your story and the story is a sad one. *Reality Bites* is a bust. Only four couples showed up—three Mothballs and one we-just-moved-here newlyweds—and none of them are in costume and there you are in a sleeveless red T-shirt, stuck in the movie without Ben Stiller, without Troy. And you know what? Fuck the fecal-eyed multigenerational family and fuck the knit skullcap couple too because how dare they do this to you?

Your rat is begging his *boys* not to go onstage—*You're gonna ruin our name, the acoustics are shit*—and Ready Freddy is mute and Little Tony does all the talking—*Nothing's ever gonna be perfect*—and the three of them remind me of my kittens. *Our* kittens.

The *boys* head backstage to warm up and Phil whistles at me like I'm a dog. I obey and follow him toward the stage as he mutters about how the show is gonna *suck*. One band leads to another band and you've gone silent in your stories and it's crowded. It's loud. I read *Killing Eve* and I saw *Killing Eve* and I could stab your rat with Rachael Ray right here on the dance floor but if I did that, the management would have to take down the sign that promises safety inside.

I'm not heartless. I don't want the Tractor staff to suffer for Phil's crimes.

He elbows me and screams into my ear. "See that bass player dancing? Fuckin' A, man. Never trust a bass player who sways his hips. You feel the music in your hands, not your hips."

I check my phone. No more scenes in your story and you really did give up. I bet you're home by now, crying as you pack his trash bags and throw them out the window. I deserve a fucking *break* so I tell him I need a drink and fight my way through the crowd.

The bartender screams in my face. "Whaddya want?"

He takes my card and I order a vodka soda and he's slow and the glasses are plastic and I look up and no. *No.*

It's you.

You're here. Less than twenty feet away in your costume and my plan backfired. The *rat* will want you to meet his *fan boy* and the bartender has my credit card and you are hugging Little Tony and the band is covering "One."

I did all of this for you and you came here to *forgive* that fucking rat and now you turn around and, Shit, Mary Kay. Do you see me?

28

You didn't see me. Right? Right.

I slipped out the door and caught an Uber to a ferry and I made it home and I took care of myself because no one takes care of me. Now I blast the U2 song on repeat on my sound system—sorry, cats, but Dad needs this right now—and I sit in the shower in a ball of nudity, like David Foster Wallace in the asylum except nobody's watching me because I'm not *special*. I'm not a writer and I'm not a rock star and I saw a side of you I've never seen until tonight. You love being *with the band.* You're probably mounting your rat right now and I put on my pants and I throw on a T-shirt—*Nirvana*—and you "worry" about becoming *your* mother? Well, I *am* my mother, blasting my music and slamming cabinets and wiping my hands on Kurt Cobain's face.

You think Phil is special? Well, I am not a rock star. But I am special. I'm special because I actually take responsibility for my actions. I don't live my life on a wagon and make you think it's your fault every time I fall off. I'm special because I've never even done a line of cocaine, let alone *heroin,* and if you knew anything about my fucking childhood, you'd know that *I'm* the special one. Not him. *Me.*

You are changing in my mind and it hurts but I can't stop it. Even your office looks different to me now. You sit in there and look at pictures of Whitney Houston—*Buried*—and Eddie Vedder—*Married*—because you like to love "special" people from afar. I was your star—*Volunteer of the Month*—and I was your rock—*Fiction Specialist*—and how come I don't know how to make you see that *I* am the special one?

You just don't love me, do you? I keep seeing you in that bar, hugging Phil's *boys*.

I'm not a star and I'm not your star and my doorbell rings—fuck you, Oliver—and I ignore it so now the asshole is pounding on my door and he has some nerve and I will knock his materialistic head off—fuck it, you don't love me, why bother trying to be good?—and I open the door and it's not Oliver.

It's you.

Bono wonders aloud if he asked too much and you tossed your Winona Red Bed T-shirt costume—you're back in your trademark tights—and your arms are two bare branches, no leaves. You're here. Did you see me at the Tractor and am I about to get run over, bitten by reality, and why aren't you saying anything and what do I do and then you open your mouth.

"It's over, Joe. I did it. It's done."

I can't speak. I just said goodbye to you because you went to Phil but now you changed your mind. You've come to me. You throw your arms around me and I lift you up and your legs are vines growing into me, onto me, and the recording of this song is bombastic. Live. There are strings in an orchestra, superior to *guitars,* and it is opera, it is rock, it is *you,* loving me with your whole body, not just your fox eyes but your paws and your toes and your fingernails and your lips—both sets—shoes are off, tights are shredded—and I deliver you to the Red Bed and this time there is no hesitation. No boundary. No *sit.*

This is your one life and we are *one* and you are my soulmate, wet and warm, and I am inside of you, reborn. I shake, you shake, and we are virgins who know what we're doing, we are teenagers in a car—there is steam on the windows all around us—and your Murakami is below and then it is on top and I am a boy and I am a man and you are a girl and you are a woman. We are reverberating, multiplying—you are coming, oh this is a *big* one—and you are special—you know how to touch me—*Oh God, Joe, Oh God*—and I am special—you taught me how to touch you—and then we finish.

"Oh God," you say. "Oh God, Joe."

We are alive and dead and you just keep saying the magic words—*Oh God, Joe. Oh God*—as you tell me you felt me in your toes and your eyeballs and the hairs in your nostrils and in the lining of your stomach and you are funny and gross and it just comes out. I can't help it. "I love you, Mary Kay."

You don't miss a beat. "I love you, Joe."

The L-words drag us down. Heavy as the music, the music that makes it okay for us to be wordless and I can't tell if that's your heart or my heart and I know you love me and I know I love you but it didn't need to be said. The kittens know we're finished and they're making the room theirs again. You laugh and blow a kiss to your favorite and you roll into me and your eyelids hit mine. Your nose too. You're so close that I can't see, that I can see. You aren't getting *Closer* anymore. You are closest.

"Joe."

"I know," I say. "I'm sorry. We can forget I said it. We can . . . we can not say it."

You wrap me up in your branches and you say there is no need to be sorry and you kiss my hair, you kiss my head, and you say you wish you could reach inside my body and kiss my liver and my kidneys, and I squeeze your ass—you are my own little Hannibal Lecter and you laugh—*you are sick*—and I laugh—*Okay, Hannibal*—and you tell me you wanted Hannibal and Clarice to get together and I tell you I did too and you sigh. "I wish I could understand why Nomi can't let go of Klebold."

"Do you remember when it started?"

You sigh. "Maybe it's because I used to joke that Hannibal Lecter is my book boyfriend, which is evidence for my Worst Mother Ever award . . . In the middle of the night I get fired up . . . I'm gonna drag her to a therapist, gonna full-on intervene. But in the morning, I don't have that urgency . . . I should probably do something but I just want it to go away on its own."

"It will," I say. "Don't forget that she's *yours*. You made her . . ." Same way I made my son. "And you're right to trust the day. Nights make everything worse."

You tell me I'd be a good dad and I am a good dad and you laugh. "Wait . . . is this song on repeat?"

You love me so much you didn't notice the music until now and I tell you I'm weird and you tell me I'm *passionate*.

The song ends and it begins again, and the audience cheers and it sounds like a hundred candles lit in the dark and the solo twang of the instrument leads to more cheers and the people in the audience sing along and we sing along too, in our own way, with our bodies, our bodies that we already know by heart.

29

We are three and a half weeks into our show: *The Office: NC-17. XXX.* I am on my hands and knees and I am wiping down the Red Bed and you are ten feet away, clothed. Tights on. *Professional.* But that's not how you were last night!

Oh, Mary Kay, I read about this kind of sex and I thought I had *had* this kind of sex but I was wrong. Your Murakami is my favorite place on the planet. Your buns have given way to ponytails—you had to do *something* to express the new love in your life—and we are a secret for now and there is nothing more fun in this world than a really good, juicy fucking *secret.*

I walk outside to go to Starbucks and Oliver is on my tail. A buzzkill. A housefly.

"FYI," he says. "It's illegal to fornicate in a public library."

I don't kiss and tell and I don't fuck and tell but Oliver is no dummy. We all know when our friends are getting laid. "So call the cops, Oliver. Or arrest me. Can you do that? Or is that just some *Police Academy* bullshit?"

He stops walking. "She has a husband."

"And he slept with her best friend." Oliver is an Angeleno so this doesn't land the way it should. "He slept with her for ten-plus years."

"Yikes," he says. "And the kid? Does the kid know?"

"About the affair? Hell no. Oliver, it's *fine*. They've had problems for years. The kid's on her way to college . . ." It's really hitting me, Mary Kay. Spring has sprung—it's drizzling but the rain has purpose, flowers are blooming, and we really are on our way.

"If he loses his shit and kills you . . ."

"He's not that type of guy. And the woman he had the affair with . . . well, you've seen her. Sort of."

Once in a while I like to remind Oliver that he knows where a woman is buried and it's like those cartoons where you can see his blood pressure rising and then he coughs. He shifts. He tries to be the boss of me. "You say this, but I listened to this *Sacriphil* stuff, my friend, and there's a lotta violence in there."

"Exactly, he's a musician. He has drug issues. He beats himself up, not anyone else."

Oliver yawns. "All right," he says. "I sent you some Eames chairs."

"How many fucking chairs can you *fit* in that place?"

He's placated and I carry on to Starbucks and I buy his stupid chairs and I buy myself a Frappufuckingccino because it's all finally happening. Your rat has moved into your junk room, where he sleeps on a futon—he doesn't even get a mattress but then he did *fuck* your best friend—and we have to take baby steps because of the Meerkat but soon you and the rat will be like Billy Joel's Brenda and Eddie: divorced!

You really are getting a divorce *as a matter of course* and it begins with an indoor separation, behind closed doors so that Nomi can get used to the idea of you two moving apart. You're feeling good about it because Nomi is doing better—*She says she saw it coming and I guess in a way she's lucky because with my parents, I was floored*—and I'm so happy for you and the Meerkat, for us.

Naturally, Phil isn't being a very good sport. You told him that you *can't forgive him* for bailing on you that night and he's *Philin' the Blues* in a major way. Last night, he spent the whole show ranting about how Courtney Love should be behind bars because she *murdered Kurt Cobain* because he knows better than to lash out at you and even the *Philistans* who called in were annoyed.

Phil, man, just play some damn music.

Phil man, you know you'd be up there with Nirvana if the world was a fair place. Can you play "Sharp Six"?

Phil, man, when are we gonna get a new album?

He ignored the requests and degraded himself further, accosting Eric *Crapton* for writing about "Tears in Heaven" *as if the only hell on Earth is losing a child, as if the pansy's ever been to heaven.* Oh, you should have heard him, Mary Kay. "I have a daughter, man, and don't get me wrong. I'd die if something happened to my kid, man, if someone harmed her . . . but Eric Clapton walks around like he cornered the market on sorrow and no he didn't . . . the guy's still going! Still living! Got a wife and a big rehab resort in the Bahamas or some shit and let me tell you a little something about the blues, man. The blues are blue. Not blue as in the Bahamas. They're *midnight,* man. Real blues shut you down and shut you up. Trust me, I know."

Obviously if he really was in a Springsteen kind of blue, in the *grave* of his mind, he wouldn't have the energy to pontificate. He's just in whiny dick mode. "Jay" texted him to check in and he was rude to "Jay": *No offense man, but someday if you have a family you'll understand that family shit eats up the time. Peace out. I'm in the zone writing.*

It worries me to think of you under the same roof as him, but you're right. He's the father of your Meerkat and these things do take time. And I didn't kill him, Mary Kay. You love me so much that I don't *have* to kill him. *You* chose to end it with him, and that's why I'm lying low, why I just have to be patient and listen to you, to the sweet things you say to me all day. You're selling your house and you're talking to real estate agents and you're using the D-word on a regular basis.

The irony is that Melanda was sort of right. We were holding each other back and who knows? If she never left . . . maybe I never would have gone through with a divorce.

I spoke to an attorney in the city. He thinks it's gonna be quicker than that other woman I spoke to, and he had good candy.

I am yours and you brought me candy from the divorce attorney's office and you left it in my backpack because once again, it's a secret. All of it. *Us.* I pop the red-and-white old-school candy into my mouth and I don't have a jacket—it's getting warmer all the time, as if Mother Nature is so excited that she can't sleep—and I head out the door and we have the night off—you have to see your *Friends*—but it's a small island and I'm a restless man. With great sex comes energy so I go for a walk and I pass by Eleven and it's not my fault that the place is all windows and it's not my fault that our attraction is the invention of electricity and you see me. You catch my eye and wave and I wave and we don't text—we are too good in person and we know what we have is special—so you have to wait until the next day to see me, to tell me what I did to you. You lean over your desk in your office.

"Buster . . ." That's me. "When you walked by last night . . . it was like my body and my mind and my soul . . . I know I'm probably not supposed to say this to you but I have to say it because it's all I can think about."

I was right. This is an Everythingship. Not that we need a silly name for what we are. "I didn't sleep a wink."

You smile. "Oh come on. Yes you did. People always say that they didn't sleep but everyone sleeps a little, at least a couple of hours."

This is why I love you and I laugh. "Okay I was up *most* of the night, just sitting on my couch literally doing nothing but thinking about you . . ." Except for the part where I was listening to your husband's show. "But I admit, four to six . . . that's a little blurry. I might have slept some."

You beam at me. "Good," you say. "This is good because I slept a couple hours too, and, well, I like the idea of being in sync with you, Buster."

It's not my imagination. RIP Whitney and Eddie are sparkling for us—I windexed them for you—and you can't touch me, not right now. You wave a hand—*get back to work*—and the day is long, it's a sidewalk that will not fucking end—sorry, Shel—and the bass throbs in my head—*Hare Mary, Hallelujah*—because as it turns out, *you* are my true savior, the reason I'll be in such great shape when my son comes to find me, the reason that for the first time in my fucking life, I feel *excited* about my future. Do good and you get good and the day ends and Oliver's running out of *wall space* and you wish me a safe trip home as if there is any danger, as if anything could hurt me now.

Eventually, night falls.

I go for a walk up Madison and what a different world it is, knowing that we'll be in that movie theater, at that diner, walking these streets until our bodies break down on us. I reach the library and take the steps to our love seat in the garden and whaddya know, Mary Kay. The door to the lowest level is open. You didn't lock up. I walk into the library and there you are on the Red Bed, as promised.

Naked.

You want my hand on your neck and you want my other hand above your Murakami, not on it, not yet, and the silence is deafening, equal parts sex and love and after we finish we are mute. And then it's time to play.

"Okay," you begin. "We would need chain saws."

"And a truck."

"And a dolly."

"A few dollies, Mary Kay. This thing is big."

This is our plan. We're going to steal the Red Bed. I squeeze you. "Do you know about secular hymns?"

You nuzzle your head into my chest and your hair is a scarf, a blanket, a godsend. "You mean songs about religion that aren't quite about religion?"

"Yes."

"Then yes, I know about secular hymns."

"Well, I really like them. I think it's because my parents were messed up about religion, a little Catholic, a little Jewish . . . and my whole life, music was the thing for me, the thing that made me feel connected to something larger, especially secular hymns, or songs that have that theme about the collapse into the dark and the climb back into the light, you know, where you remember that you can't have the rise without the fall."

You kiss me twice and then you speak into the hairs on my chest. "Hallelujah, Joe. I know exactly what you mean."

I kiss you. "Being with you . . . it's like it turns out that there really *is* a crescendo. And it isn't just about sex . . ."

You hold on to me and you are perfect. "I know," you say. "The sex is . . . yeah . . . but it's like the magic is real, as if you really did pull a coin out of my ear."

"I get it, Hannibal."

Your hands are on my head, on my temples, and you purr. "Can I kidnap you and lock you in a basement, Clarice?"

"If you insist," I say. "But a little hint. The best way to kidnap someone and lock them in a basement is to not give them a heads-up about your plan."

You pinch my ears and I move my mouth along your body, down, down, down, where I pull a rabbit out of your hat, your Murakami, your soul.

30

You pulled it off. You took a "personal day"—I love that you didn't call it a *sick day*—and you told me to be in the parking lot of Fort Ward at 11:00 A.M. We take separate cars—*secret lovers*—and I get here first—I wanted to make sure that RIP Melanda is still sleeping—she's right where I left her—and it's not the easiest way to start a romantic day in the woods, but when is anything good ever fucking easy?

I am leaning against Nomi's dollhouse-roof shack when I see your car. The mere sight of you gets me going and I am wearing a backpack—I really am *Cedar Cove* Joe—and you were nervous that we would get caught but there are only two cars in the lot. One is a truck with a trailer—those people are out on their *boat*—and the other is a family truckster with Oregon plates. We are safe and you are in clothes that are new to me, there are stars on your tights—a galaxy in between them—and a long, soft black pullover, a mirror to my black sweater.

You say hello and you hear a branch snap and your pupils dilate but it was nothing, just the woods. You're a little nervous—this makes sense—and I don't take your hand—we're in a parking lot—but I hold on to your eyes. "We're okay," I say. "And remember, if anyone *does* see us, we just bumped into each other on the trail."

My words mean something to you and you nod. "Well, the bunkers are up the hill. But since you're the first timer . . ." Hardly, my night with Melanda is unforgettable. "Do you want to take the long way or the short way?"

"What do you think, Mary Kay?"

You are red. Hot. In love. "Okay," you say. "Long way it is." You look up at the roof. "Nomi used to love this."

"Right," I say, wondering if the door is locked, if it would be too much for us to just go at it right here, in the shed. "She told me about that when we were doing the tech help session."

"Come on," you say, and you're right, Mary Kay. We can't have sex in a house that reminds you of your daughter and we are moving up the hill, on the paved path, and I wonder if the blanket I brought is big enough and you blurt, "Hey, do you believe in heaven?"

"Sometimes," I say. "Do you?"

"Sometimes," you say. "It's more like you lose someone, you want to think that they found something new, something they couldn't find here, you know?"

I picture RIP Beck in a clean, well-kept home finally finishing a book and I see RIP Candace writing songs about how she would do it all differently and I smile. "I hear you," I say. "I think heaven is a great idea."

"Who did you lose?"

RIPCandaceBenjiPeachBeckHendersonFincherDelilah. "No one yet. I'm lucky that way."

"Yeah," you say. "But let's get down to it. Do you believe there's more than all this or do you think that when we die . . . that's it?"

"What do you think?"

"No," you say. "I'm not falling for that trick twice."

You nudge me and you want to know me as badly as I want to know you. "Well, I think it's like Santa Claus."

"How so?"

"When I was a kid, I didn't 'believe' in Santa because I knew no matter how many flyers I left out on the table with the G.I. Joes circled in red . . . I mean my mom flat-out said, *You're not playing with dolls.*"

"Oh Jesus."

I tell you that she was a piece of work and a crow flies overhead and

I wonder if she's dead. "The thing is," I say. "I remember that moment, you know, when you're starting to understand the world . . . and you see some kid at the playground and that kid's *actively* trying to be good because that kid *actually* believes in Santa but then you see his mom and his snacks and his brand-new sneakers and it's like . . . well of course that kid believes in Santa. Santa shows up at his house. He has reason to believe and I guess I always had reason to question things."

You link your arm through mine. You don't care about anyone seeing us, not anymore, and you don't push me for all the gory details about my shitty childhood. You know that I need your warmth and you give that to me and then you sigh. "For me it was Glamour Gals."

"I saw those dolls on your Instagram."

I love that I can say this to you, that there's no implication that I'm *stalking* you and this walking, this talking, this is my reward for being a good man even though the world wasn't good to me when I was a boy. You're telling me about Glamour Gals, *the worst dolls you can imagine, no jobs, just ball gowns and big hair,* and then your grip on my arm tightens.

"So here's one nice thing about my husband."

Ex-husband and this is our date not his but you are you. Always thinking. Always *yeah.* "What's that?"

"Well, that shack with the roof. Nomi wanted it for Christmas and she wouldn't let it go and we told her we can't steal a roof and it was driving me nuts all month because I kept asking her what she wanted and it's *the roof the roof the roof* and Phil's kinda checked out all month but then Christmas morning, he drags this giant present out of our shed. I mean the man had never touched wrapping paper in his *life* . . . and there it was. Nomi's roof. He had the grass, he even planted a few tiny flowers on it. And it wasn't just a present for her, it was a present for me."

My heart is turning white and it used to be red and this is our date and you're staring at the sky when you should be staring at me and I can't go back in time and build Nomi a fucking roof and she's too old for that now and you take a deep breath. "Okay," you say. "I know that was weird just now."

"It's not weird."

But your arm isn't linked through mine. You stop walking and you're stiff. You're going to tell me you can't leave him because of *one* nice fucking thing he did a hundred fucking years ago on a holiday, which doesn't even count because everyone gets off on doing nice things on holidays, glorified fucking Sundays when men get trophies for emptying the dishwasher or building a dollhouse as if one good deed makes up for being an INVISIBLE NONPRESENT SELFISH DRUGGED-UP ASSHOLE every other day of the goddamn year.

But then you take my hands. "Joe, I can't pretend he doesn't exist."

You pretended I didn't exist. "I know that."

"And I don't want to make him out to be the bad guy or anything."

He is. "Absolutely."

"And I don't want to check myself every time I think about him because . . . you know, one of these days . . . in theory . . . you'll meet him."

Already did! "I know."

My heart is pounding and RIP Melanda is in the Whisper Room in the sky and your husband is not. He really *is* here and I really *will* have to meet him and I really do need to tell you that I already did meet him and at least, if I tell you right now, you can't run away because we're alone in the woods, on a trail.

"And all my stories, well this is the weird thing about us. I made up this other version of myself the first time we talked on the phone, when I talked about me and Nomi, about our life . . . I erased him. But most of my adult life . . . he was there or he was nearby. He's a part of all my stories and I don't want to lie to you anymore. And I don't want you to shut down on me every time I say his name."

Most marriages end in divorce and most women don't *want* to praise their vile ex-husbands, but you're not most women. You're sensitive. "Don't be ridiculous, Mary Kay. You guys have a lot of history together and I get it."

You kiss me. "You are fucking amazing, Joe Goldberg."

Yes I am! Phil ruined enough already and this day is ours and we're walking again, lighter on our feet and I smack your ass and you jump. You liked it. I tease you that this is hardly what I'd call a *hike,* and you tell me the hill is gonna get steeper and I tell you I don't believe you and you're flirting up a storm and then my phone buzzes. Fucking Oliver.

You glare at me. "Come on, really?"

"It will only take a second."

"I turned off my phone before I got out of the car, Joe."

"I didn't know."

"Well, that's why *I* like to hike because for me, you turn off the devices and are just in the moment, you know?"

I turn off my phone and you smile—*good*—but then you pull a Polaroid camera out of your purse and I tell you that you're cheating but you are a sly fox. "This is different," you say. "It's not a communication device. Say cheese."

I hate having my picture taken and Melanda is in the trough in the backdrop and the world is full of murder podcast people who *want* to think the worst of people and I see a headline from hell. *ACCUSED MURDERER SAYS CHEESE IN FRONT OF THE SPOT WHERE HE BURIED LOCAL FEMINIST.*

But I didn't fucking kill her, I really didn't, and you snap a picture and whistle. "Now, *that* was a real smile."

Life is for the living—it's a well-known fact—and on we go, and you are my tour guide, telling me about the origins of the bunkers that are *right around the bend.* "They built a base here over a hundred years ago. It was the last line of defense for the Bremerton naval shipyard."

"Pressure much?"

You smile like a teacher intent on finishing her lecture. "This was a lookout and soldiers watched for any warships entering the sound. And then it was a camp for needy kids . . ." *And then it was a place for us to fuck.* "And then it was a camp for sailors . . ."

You glimmer at me the way you did that day when you were pushing Murakami on that old man and I want school to end. *Now.* "You really know your Fort Ward, Mary Kay."

"No questions just yet," you say. "See, it really gets interesting in 1939. This was a radio base where they intercepted messages about the war, trying to protect us from an attack . . . but then they shut all that down in the fifties." You scratch your head *in* your head but you make eye contact to make sure that I'm in there too. And I am. "Well," you say. "That concludes my lecture but I just . . . I love it here because it reminds you of how things change and don't change all at once. I mean look at these fucking bunkers!"

You jump onto a step and I join you and I do what you want. I *look* at these fucking bunkers. "They're still here," I say.

"Yeah," you say. "*Bunker* rhymes with *hunker,* you know? That's what I thought for a long time, that I had to be like those soldiers, you know? Hunker down in the bunker in case something bad happens and well . . . here we are."

I kiss you but you deflect and grab my hand like we're in high school and you just *have* to show me your favorite graffiti—GOD KILLS EVERYONE—and I cringe at the big brown *poop* emoji and you don't like that either and you show me what you *do* like, the lower levels of the bunkers, and I squeeze your hand and you squeeze right back. "I knew you'd get it."

"Well of course I get it. I get you."

There is no more getting *Closer.* Finally we are there. Here. The sidewalk ended and the pavement gave way to dirt and your hair went from a bun to a ponytail to a mane that runs down your back and you lead me down steep, deep steps into a little square cave and it's a filthy, musty, rectangular hole in the ground and you pull off your black sweater and sigh.

"Well, City Boy, tell me there's a blanket in that backpack."

We did it.

Your favorite place is now my favorite place and we've had sex in the bunker at Fort Ward and we feasted on beef and broccoli—I came prepared—and we passed out and woke up and did it again and went back to sleep and the floor is fucking *concrete* and isn't that how you know you're in love?

"Come on," you say. "I can play hooky but I can't disappear."

You want to know where *I* had sex in high school and I tell you about a guidance counselor and you're mortified but I assure you she wasn't *my* guidance counselor and . . . you're still a little mortified and

I let you take more Polaroids and I take some of you and we reach the parking lot—it's just us—and I want to tell you this was the best day of my life.

You hand me the pictures. "You should probably hang on to these."

I unlock my car and you unlock your car. You grab your phone and turn it on and I turn on my phone and you sigh. "I'm so glad we did this."

"Me too."

Your phone comes back to life and my phone comes back to life and my news is no news—Oliver wants more Eames chairs and Shortus wants beer—but your news is bad news. I know because you're listening to a voicemail. I know because you gasp and turn away.

"Mary Kay."

You thrash an arm at me. Bad sign. Did someone see us?

You drop your phone onto the pavement and you turn around and all the red I put into your cheeks is gone. You are white as RIP Melanda and do you know? You scream at the sky and is it your father? Did he have a stroke?

I reach for you but you crumple to the ground and your voice is a horror movie and your hands are in your hair and then you say it, barely yet loudly.

"Phil. He . . . he's gone. He . . . I wasn't there and he's gone and Nomi . . ."

Phil. *Fuck.* I reach out to you and this time you don't just flinch. You shove me away and you run to your car and you are in no condition to drive and you can't even get the door open but you warn me to *stay the fuck away from you right now*—Why Phil? How?—and you are too mad for motor skills and you throw your backpack at your car and you look at that roof and all the rage transforms into sadness—you are sobbing—and then just like that, it turns back into rage.

You point a finger at me. "This day never happened. I wasn't here."

It's not a request. It's an order. It's a *sit.* He's gone—I am in shock, I didn't do it—but the way you peel out of here and leave me in the dust, it's like you think I did.

31

Here's my problem with wakes. You lay out all these finger sandwiches, all these pizzas from Bene and then you glance at me as I'm biting into a tiny slice of the coppa—best on the menu—and you look away as if what I'm doing is somehow disrespectful to your dead husband because now that he's dead, he's THE BEST HUSBAND, THE BEST FATHER, THE BEST MAN. I'm alone at the buffet because I don't have a date—you're his widow—and I spit my pizza into the napkin and what a waste of food and okay, so he made your daughter a Christmas present and it took time—*a whole lot of precious time*—but your living room is a hotbed of lies and FUCK YOU, RIP Phil.

How could he do this to us, Mary Kay? You were doing so good—*leaving him, leaving him behind*—and Nomi was doing so good—she saw the divorce coming a mile away—but that rat fucker had to ruin everything. He didn't get T-boned by a truck on his way home from "writing." No. Your lazy, selfish (soon to be ex) husband had to go and *overdose in your house.* Your daughter had to come home and find him. And nobody will say what we all know: HE KNEW HIS WAY AROUND DRUGS AND HE WAS JEALOUS OF KURT COBAIN WHO DIED OF AN OVERDOSE IN *HIS* HOUSE. You're a woman. So of course you feel like it's

All. Your. Fault.

You're wrong, Mary Kay. Dead wrong.

You should be disgusted and maybe deep down you are, but how would I know? You haven't spoken to me since you fled from the parking lot at Fort Ward. We said *I love you* and we were having sex on an increasingly regular and exciting basis but now we are fucked. Nomi's fucked. I'm fucked. You're fucked. And lazy Phil's dream came true. He's a dead rock star, possibly lounging in heaven reading his obituary in *Rolling Stone*—remember when you asked if I believe in heaven?—and all I can do is stand here in the corner of your living room dipping a triangle of pita bread into what's left of the garlic hummus.

Will I ever hold you again? Will you ever smile again?

I glance at you. You're wiping your nose on a napkin while a Mothball pats your back and your dead-eyed daughter is just sitting on a chair, not touching the little sandwiches on her plate and the outlook for us is grim and *fuck you, Phil DiMarco. Fuck you all the way back to the day you wormed your way into this unjust world.*

You shouldn't feel guilty and I don't feel guilty, Mary Kay. Sure, I bought M30s for him—it was a particularly dark moment in our courtship—but Oliver took them away. And yes, I bought *heroin* for Phil. I put *heroin* in his room because heroin is (was) the devil he knows. But I am a rational person. I know that your rat didn't die because of me. He didn't even die from a heroin overdose. He died because he drove to that shithole in Poulsbo and picked up some of those poisonous M-fucking-30s all by himself. I didn't kill Phil and you didn't either, but you're saying it again right now, telling that sympathetic Mothball that you *pushed him over the edge.*

I want to storm through these mourners and grab your shoulders and tell you to stop it.

People get divorced every day, Mary Kay. There's nothing scandalous about it and your rat was a *brat.* He couldn't wait until he was living in some shit box too-old-to-be-called-a-bachelor-pad to jump off that wagon? Nope! He swallowed those pills in this *house.* All he had to do was drive to the Grand Forest or one of the countless places on this island where people go to do bad things. It turns my stomach, Mary Kay. Even *Oliver* cringed and made aggressively passive-aggressive remarks about my being "the other man." I told him to read the *Basic Fucking Text* and learn that recovery is an uphill battle, that no one is to blame, especially not *me.* He cut me off and told me that my body count on this island is up to two—BULLSHIT, I KILLED NO ONE. What Phil did to this family is terrible, Mary Kay. I could never do something like that. Neither could you. Now you pull at your hair—*How did I miss it?*—and I want to comfort you. I have been trying to comfort you for three days now. But you always shiver and turn away, as if you wish *I* were dead, me, the one who made you happy.

I know. Life isn't fair. But just once, I wanted love to be fair. I did everything right. *Everything.* And now I'm losing you, aren't I?

You knock over someone's glass of beer and you snip. "Damn it, Lonnie, there are *coasters.*"

Lonnie apologizes and you're crying again. "I'm sorry. I just . . . I'm so mad I could kill him."

Lonnie says that's natural—since when is *nature* a synonym for *good*?—and she's encouraging you to let it all out and no! You know better, Mary Kay. You don't want to *kill* him because you read his favorite fucking book and I read it too. We both know that addiction is a disease and these "friends"—you've never mentioned Lonnie, not once—they're not on your side. They're not helping and if anything, they're making it worse by validating every mistruth you speak and in that way, they're like Phil's fucking family.

What a bunch, Mary Kay! His mother and father are already gone, as if they have somewhere else to be, and the brother never even *came.* Classy. According to the obituary, the brother is a *well-known life coach,* which might be why he couldn't afford a fucking plane ticket. *Well-known* is code for 21,000 followers and Tony Robbins he is *not* and I want things to go back to normal. I want Phil's parents to get on a plane and go back to Florida. Maybe they'll leave tomorrow. They didn't show up at your wake party tonight—*We're mourning privately*—but oh fuck you, Phil's family. Nobody likes hospitals and nobody likes funerals but we all know that sometimes you have to suck it up and *go.* And if they were decent people, you might not be quite so bad off.

You're so guilt-stricken that you're rewriting history and hiding behind your invisible, brand-new rose-colored glasses. "He really was amazing . . ." Oh come on, Mary Kay. "People don't realize, he gave up his career to be home . . ." Lie. He couldn't get along with his bandmates and he had songwriter's block. "He was the best dad, we had all these great day trips to Seattle . . ." That's another lie. He was your teenage son storming off to play with guitars while you and the Meerkat wasted money on *tchotchkes.* You blow your nose into a cocktail napkin. "And I just should have known."

The Mothball takes you in her old lady arms and you're weeping again and now *I* feel guilty for being so hard on you. I know it's hard to lose someone, but Jesus Christ, Mary Kay, you should lean into your rage because you're right to be mad. Addiction is a disease, yes, but he was a husband and he was a father and instead of getting help, instead of taking care of himself so that he could stay alive for his daughter, he jumped off the wagon. You slip off to *powder your nose*—poor choice of words, considering—and you cry more. You know it was a poor choice of words and the Meerkat is still in a coma on the sofa. Staring at you. She's not crying. She can't cry because you won't *stop* crying. I grab another slice of Bene pizza, a bigger one this time, and I fold it in half and pop the whole fucking thing in my mouth.

Shortus elbows me. "'Sup. Where you been? I haven't seen you at the gym."

That's Shortus for you. We're at a fucking funeral luncheon and he's talking about CrossBore. He picks up a celery stick and chomps. "Don't be letting yourself go," he says. "Don't wanna wind up like *this* guy."

The insensitivity of this poor dolt, and I pick a red pepper flake out of my mouth. "It's just a little pizza."

"You ever try it?" he asks. And then he drops his voice to a whisper. "Heroin?"

"No," I say. "You?"

"I never would." He shudders. "I don't get it . . . Don't these people know about endorphins? Honestly, don't they know about *sex*?"

It's the worst thing to be forced to imagine right now, Shortus sticking his Shortus inside some toned, nerve-ending-less CrossBore addict and it's a reminder that three days ago, in another lifetime, I was one of the happy people on this planet. I was having sex with you. I scan the room and you're not back and in the library, you never slip out without letting me know where you're going.

You're crossing over and it's like I don't exist, like you don't *want* me to exist and the Meerkat isn't on the couch anymore. She's gone too. I pick up my plastic glass of Eleven Winery wine. "I hear you," I say, because I learned my lesson and I won't waste my time debating with another stubborn, irrational dog. "I'm gonna get some fresh air."

You're not in the powder room and I can't go upstairs—we're still a secret, even if you haven't kissed me or talked to me since you deserted me at Fort Ward—and I step out the side door because maybe you are smoking. You did that with the rat long ago.

"Hey."

It's the Meerkat and she's smoking, ripping on her bong. "Nomi," I say. "I realize it's a stupid question, but how are you?"

"Fucked in the head. You?"

I sip my plastic wine and she motions for the cup and she's underage but she saw a dead body for the first time in her life—been there—so I give her my plastic chalice and she gulps it all down, too much, too fast. "Are your parents alive?"

"Honestly, I'm not sure."

"What did they do to you that was so shitty that you don't know?"

"They ignored me."

She nods. "Fuck 'em."

"Nah," I say, Good Joe, Compassionate Joe. "I used to feel that way. But you get older, you realize that you don't really hate anyone, even your shitty parents, because everyone's just doing the best they can."

She coughs. Still not good at working that bong, still doesn't have any friends. I counted two teenagers inside and one was here with her parents and the other was here for the wine. "That's deep, Joe."

"Not really," I say. The last thing I want is for your Meerkat to feel that on today, the second-worst day of her life, she has to be polite and grateful. See, Mary Kay—I wish you could see me right now. I am Jack Nicholson at the end of *Terms of Endearment*. I am stepping up with your kid and I am ready to be a stepfather. I am here to *help*.

She puts her bong in an empty planter and she yawns and her arms are outstretched above her head and she bursts out laughing. I don't laugh with her and I don't judge her and soon she's doubled over—*I'm gonna pee my pants*—and I tell her it's okay to do that, it's okay to do anything right now.

She rolls her eyes and snorts. "Yeah right."

"I mean it, Nomi. It's hard to lose someone. Your mother knows that."

We hear footsteps and the door opens. *Shortus*. "Oh," he says. "So this is where the party's at."

It was his way of trying to ease the tension—fucking idiot is scared of real emotions—and Nomi doesn't laugh at the joke and he throws his arms around her.

"I'm so sorry, Nomi. I just know that he loved you more than anything on the planet."

Except for heroin, the sound of his own voice, a woman's mouth wrapped around his *Philstick,* and his music, but that's funerals for you. They bring out the stupid in everyone, especially the stupid.

Nomi pats him on the back—"Thank you, Uncle Seamus"—and he pulls away the way he should because he's not really her fucking uncle and the girl needs her space. "Tell you what," he says. "When my mom died, everyone was like, watch TV, binge, relax, but none of that worked for me . . ." Because you have no attention span, you lightweight. "What did help me was endorphins."

That's the second time he's used that word in twenty minutes and he will never get married, will he? "Thanks," she says. "I'll remember that."

He takes a deep breath and looks up at the trees. "I'm gonna go do a Murph in honor of your old man," he says. "I know he'd like that."

Phil was a lazy fuck who never broke a sweat deliberately and he would not like that at all. I smile. "That's so nice, Seamus. Seriously."

The second he's gone it's like he was never there and the Meerkat goes right back to where we were. "Do you really think I can do *anything* I want right now?"

"Yep."

"And my mom won't be pissed?"

"Nope."

"Well, in that case, will you tell her I went to Seattle?"

I never offered to be her accomplice but she's wearing a Sacriphil T-shirt and her *Columbine* is poking out of her backpack and it's one thing to have a birthday party and have no kids show up but this is her father's *funeral* and she has no one in there. I know that feeling. When someone you loved in spite of their imperfections is dead and no one in the world seems to care about what that's like for you.

"Do me a favor, Nomi. The bong stays here."

She salutes me like JFK Jr. at his father's funeral and takes off through the backyard to the trail.

Inside, the guys from Sacriphil have picked up their instruments—I knew it was only a matter of time before we had an *Unplugged* Phil-less jam session—and there is an acoustic *shark inside my shark*—and I have a purpose now. I have to find you. I worm my way around the room, skirting my fecal-eyed multigenerational neighbors and for you this is a sad room, but for me this is a hot zone. *Mrs. Kahlúa* is here and this cannot, will not, *must not be* Jay's coming-out party.

I cut through the kitchen but I'm fucked here too. The young woman who warned me about Phil is standing in front of your refrigerator. The door is blocking her face—thank you, door—but I recognize her hand. Two diamond engagement rings. She's having small talk with a court-ordered older alkie I've seen at Isla and I am trapped and the guest bathroom door opens and I slip into that bathroom again.

I close the door. Safe.

Someone knocks on the door. "If it's yellow let it mellow. The pipes are taking a beating!"

I run the faucet and eavesdrop on the NA people whispering about how long they have to stay—GO NOW GO—and they are going—yes!—and I flush the toilet—oops—and I exit the bathroom and here you are, in your kitchen, surrounded by second- and third-tier Melandas. I clear my throat. "Mary Kay," I say. "You got a second?"

You're mad at me but it's not like I walked up to you and kissed you and there is no way to put the toothpaste back in the fucking tube. We *did* go to Fort Ward and you *did* mount me in a bunker—twice—and Dr. Nicky's blog is right: I have feelings too and I am allowed to have feelings.

You excuse yourself, and my palms are sweating. What I say now matters and is it possible to say the right thing when you're not yourself? You open the side door and now it's you and me by the planter and you light one of the rat's cigarettes and blow a smoke ring and who knew you could do that? "I don't want to do this right now, Joe. I can't do this right now."

"I know."

"You don't know, Joe. You don't know what this is like for me."

"I know."

You look at me. Validated. And then you blow smoke in a poisonous straight line. "I had no business turning off my phone. I have a child."

"Let it out."

You grit your teeth because it would be so much easier on you if I was being an asshole right now but I'm not gonna do that for you. "All we had to do was wait. You don't know Phil . . ." Yes I do. "You don't know that we had something of a deal. I looked out for him and he . . ." Did nothing for you but drag you down. "He needed me. I knew he was down and there I was off running around with some fucking guy I barely know behind his back while my own *husband* was dying inside."

That was cruel but I am strong. "And you must feel horrible about that."

"Well I feel like the biggest piece of shit that ever lived. He deserved better from me."

And you deserved better from him but this is the other thing I hate about funerals, about wakes. We don't get to blame the Deathday Boy. He's like a bridezilla. It's *his* day and he gets to whine and cunt out about every stupid thing in the world. "What can I do to help?"

You flick the cigarette on your own lawn and shrug. "Nothing," you say, your voice flattened by Klonopin and semi-Melandas and all the pressure of hosting people in your home while *you just die underneath*. "There's nothing anyone can do or say to bring him back and honestly, that's all I want. Anything you do is a waste. Anything you say is a waste. Right now all I want in this world is the one thing I can't have. One more day with Phil to tell him that I know he's hiding heroin in his nightstand, under his amp, to take all of it and flush it down the toilet and force him into a car, into a rehab clinic so that my kid doesn't have to go the rest of her life without a father, so that she doesn't have to go through the rest of her life being the one who found him. I'm a big girl. I know that I can't have that. But that's where I am right now."

You don't touch me. You don't make eye contact. You are a zombie with a *second set of teeth* and they're *his* teeth, constant proof that he was alive, and I will be patient. I've been there, Mary Kay—I know what it's like to lose someone who was bad for you. I know you're bleeding inside. That pain you're in gives you no right to hurt me but I won't make this about me.

Unlike your dead rat, I am a strong man. A good man who's able to put you first and respect the reality that his death is harder for you than it is for me. But you're a widow now. You're anointed with a new title and I *too* could kill that fucking rat for what he did to us. His *guys* finish playing the one and only true hit song that Phil ever wrote and the clapping is loud, too loud. You start crying and shutting the slider behind you, leaving me on your deck alone and if you had any intention of a future with me, you wouldn't have closed that door.

32

I went home. I pigged out. I played some Prince, I played some Sinéad and I was bracing myself for *seven hours and fifteen days* without a word from you. But I was wrong, in the best way possible. You called me last night at 1:13 A.M. and you cried and I let you cry and soon you were talking about Phil's parents—*They always treated me like I wasn't good enough and they think it's my fault*—and then you were crying again—*It's all my fault*—and then you were angry—*How could he do this to Nomi?*—and then you were guilty—*I should have been there for him, I should have known this was too much.* I was so good to you, Mary Kay. I encouraged you to let it out and you fell asleep and I did not end the call. I stayed up all night until you were coughing.

"Joe?" you said.

"Morning."

"You're still here."

"Of course I am."

You said it was the kindest thing anyone ever did for you—fuck that stupid grassy dollhouse roof—and it's been almost two weeks. You're in mourning, still guilt ridden. And I get it. Your separation was a secret and it's *complicated* but you texted me that you forgot to buy toilet paper—it's always something—and I went to the store and bought you toilet paper and you're tearing the plastic.

"Huh."

"What?"

"This is the right kind."

I know because I've spent a lot of time in your house and I shrug. "It's the best kind, so of course it's your kind."

I make a note in my head: Buy Mary Kay's overpriced toilet paper before she comes to *my* house and then the sliding door opens and it's Shortus, who's somehow become my unworthy rival in this irritating episode of our *Cedar Cove* life. He cracks his knuckles and he cracks his back and sighs. "Your gutters are officially clean, MK."

You're a grieving widow and obliged to your *Friends—Thank you, Seamus, you're a godsend*—and you rummage around the refrigerator. "Okay, boys," you say, as if I am your son and Shortus is a friend I brought home from school. "Who's hungry?"

He plops into a chair and he is not a man, he is a fourth-grade boy. "I burned a lot of calories out there, MK. I can eat!"

I wish he would go away. He's different since RIP Phil died. It's like one of those fucking reality shows where the loser thinks he has a shot because the guy in the lead pulled a muscle and backed out of the race. Shortus is actively competing with me to be the man of this house and that's not what *I'm* doing. I love you. I miss being inside of you and I am your *boyfriend* but he's a lonely CrossBore, a real patriarchal sexist who acts like you need us menfolk and what bullshit, Mary Kay. You don't need *men*. You need me.

I pull *The North Water* out of my bag and set it on the table. "Almost forgot," I say to you, not him. "This is that book I was telling you about."

In other words, *GET OUT, SHORTUS,* and he huffs. "Jeez, Joe, I don't think the woman can *read* right now. We're still reeling, ya know?"

He didn't even *like* your husband but I can't fight with him because he's your *friend* and if he wasn't here, we would be talking about Ian McGuire, but he is here so you just smile at the book—*Thanks, Joe*—and then you're on your feet, dealing with the casserole. This is a critical time for us. You're processing so many emotions and we need to get *Closer* and I'm not stupid, Mary Kay. I know you want a buffer.

That's why you let Shortus come over and have an open-door policy for the semi-Melandas who "pop by" with casseroles—No one likes that shit when they're alive, why would they want it after someone died?—and Shortus jumps up and pulls a chair out for you.

"Young lady, I insist that you take a load off and sit."

He is the patriarchy and I want to smash him and where is RIP Melanda when you need her? You don't want to sit. You shovel lasagna onto his plate and he passes the plate to me. "That's way too much for me, MK. Let's give this to the bookworm, see if he can't get some meat on those bones!"

You like my body just the way it is and Nomi hesitates in the hallway. "What's that smell?"

"Casserole," you say. "You want some?"

She groans. "I'm going to Seattle."

"Nomi . . ."

"I wanna see Uncle Don and Aunt Peg."

I met Don and Peg at the wake. They're Nomi's surrogate ex-hippie grandparents and they own a guitar store and you told me about them the day we walked to the diner, the day you *almost* told me about Phil. You pick at your lip. "But honey, you've been over there a *lot*."

Nomi is unmoved. "So?"

"So maybe you could hang out here . . . with us."

Nomi grabs at the straps on her backpack. "Are they sick of me or something?"

"Nomi, no, I just think it might be nice for you to be at home a little more."

"Mom," she says, and we're all thinking the same thing right now. That the rat died in this house. That Nomi found the rat.

You hug your Meerkat and Shortus scoops a heap of lasagna that's actually bigger than my portion and you walk Nomi to the door and he chews on the lasagna with his mouth wide open, like a bachelor, like a pig, and you'll never know that he ate more than me and now you're outside. There's another fucking *Friend* popping by and I don't blame Nomi for jumping on that ferry every day. You come back glum, holding a cheesecake.

"MK," Seamus says. "Do you do that tracking thing on E's phone?"

You dig into the cheesecake, right into the center. We haven't had sex since Fort Ward and you're going crazy, too. "Huh?"

"You know," he says. "Just so you can know where she is."

You dig your fork into the cheesecake and that's my girl. "I don't stalk my daughter, Seamus, if that's what you mean."

"Well, you can never be too careful. Do you know what she's up to? Do you even know that she's in Seattle?"

Do it, Shortus! Piss her off with your *Father Knows Best* passive aggression.

You are seething. "Honestly, Seamus, if there's one thing we did right, it's Nomi. She's always liked to get away and spend a night or two with Peggy and Don."

He runs his paws over his Cooley Hardware shirt and adjusts his Cooley Hardware hat and how was I ever "friends" with this guy? "I'm just trying to help, MK. My shop's covered. I got a workout in this morning . . . so it's no skin off my back if you want me to see where she's at."

You just lost your husband and he makes it all about *him* as if he's the saint and you pat his arm. "I appreciate it, but we're fine."

I might spit up my lasagna and he pats your arm back. "I know you are, MK."

"Honestly, I don't blame her for getting away. It's been like Grand Central in here and the memories . . ."

And it really *is* Grand Fucking Central because there's a dog barking and another intruder. You jump out of your chair to greet the latest *Friend* and lo and behold it's the fecal-eyed monster mommy. Finally, we are properly introduced and her hand is a dead fish and her yellow Lab still loves me and see that, Mary Kay? Dogs know good people.

Fecal-Eyed Nancy is fresh from a *hike* and she can't stay long and you offer her cheesecake and she makes a face, as if you have cooties, as if the widow doesn't have a right to stick a fork in her own cheesecake.

Fecal Eyes repeats herself—*We just popped by, I can't stay*—and you clear a chair for her and she sits. "Should I ask or should I leave it alone?"

The dog rests her head on my lap. I pet her and you sigh. "I haven't heard from her," you say. "But like I told you, we had a falling-out."

Shortus turns his Cooley Hardware hat backwards. "Oh man," he says. "I didn't know how to tell ya."

All eyes on Shortus, just like he wants, except for the dog, who only has eyes for me. You sip your coffee. "Just say it. Have you talked to her?"

"Yes," he says. "Melanda called me a few days ago."

Fecal Eyes balks and you balk too and no she fucking didn't. She's dead. There are rumors about her because this is an *island* and even at the wake, I heard a couple people whispering that Melanda *had an affair with a student* but I don't care about that. Melanda is dead and dead women don't talk on the phone. Alas, Seamus wants attention, he wants to feel special, and pretending to be a conduit to your friend Melanda is one way to get it.

Fecal Eyes picks at the cheesecake and this is what she came for: gossip. "Unbelievable."

Shortus scratches the logo on his shirt. "She asked me to tell you and Nomi that she sends her love."

You snort and do a good impression of her. "How nice."

"I know," he says. "She would have come back, but you know how it is. Everyone's talking about her 'inappropriate behavior' with that kid at school . . . She didn't want to steal the spotlight."

Fecal Eyes picks up your fork, not afraid of cooties anymore. "So it *is* true. That woman slept with a *student.* I knew it, and I'm sorry, but I can't really say I'm surprised."

Thank God for the fecal-eyed dog or I might throw the cheesecake at the fucking wall.

Finally Fecal Eyes is on the move—*You guys, I just have so much to dooo*—and Shortus looks at his phone and lets out a big sigh. "Rats," he says. "Actually, I can't go to Seattle even if you wanted me to go. The girls need me at the store."

I almost feel bad for him as you shove him out the door, the way he had to refer to his staff as *the girls.* It would be awful to be so intimidated by women, so insecure that you have to make up gossip. He can't even look me in the eye, he just waves—*Maybe a beer later?*—and I nod and he manipulates you into one more *Thank you* as you give him a casserole to take back to the shop, as if he shouldn't be the one thanking *you*.

And then he's gone. You *lock* the door and come back to the table. "He means well," you say. "But he's doing a 5K for Phil and he put up the banner. Did you see it?"

Yes. "No."

"Hang on," you say. You pick up your phone and dial. You bite your lips as it rings and then your shoulders drop. "Oh, Peg, I'm glad I caught you . . . Nomi's on her way there . . . Oh, she is? Oh good. Okay, well, I wanna thank you guys . . . I know, but I still want to thank you . . . Okay, sounds good, thank you, Peg. Bless you, Peg."

I care and I ask the right question. "Nomi get there okay?"

You nod. "She called them from the ferry . . ." Your mom duties are fulfilled, and right now, you just want to bitch about *Shortus*. "So that banner . . . Seamus plastered the Narcotics Anonymous logo on it in this great big can't-miss-it font and it really rubs me the wrong way, as if that was all there was to Phil. And Nancy . . ." Fecal Eyes. "She means well, but her in-laws do *everything* for her and Phil's parents . . . they haven't even called since they went back to Florida . . . Tell me to stop."

"No. Let it out."

You sip your coffee. "I don't want to trash everyone I know. It's not them, it really isn't. I'm not even mad that Melanda didn't call or anything. When it's over, it's over." You sigh. "I think I'm just peopled out."

My heart is racing and it's just the two of us and I throw out my line to you, my bait. "Look, I get the whole peopled-out thing and any time you want me to leave . . ."

Your eyes suckle mine, kittens to the teat. "No," you say. "I want you to stay."

I do what you want. I stay. But I can't make a move. You're in mourning. I have been cautious. Respectful. No mention of Fort Ward. No Red Bed talk. I know that you did love him. I know that you did hate him. I know that permanent separation is shocking and I know that the guilt is eating you alive and I know you need to let it out.

I stroke your hair and I let you cry. I let you be. I do what none of your *Friends* let you do. I support you quietly, wholly, and so you are able to cry loudly, wholly, and when your phone rings—it does that too much—you see that it's your dad and you tell me that you *should probably* take it but you don't have it in you. He feels so bad about missing the funeral but he had to miss it. He had back surgery. You send him to voicemail and that's my cue, Mary Kay. I kiss your hand. "Come on," I say. "Let's go upstairs."

We did it. We made love in your marriage bed and we've been in your room for the bulk of the past twenty-four hours. It's been fun. You worry about my cats and I tell you about the automatic feeders that dispense food and you tell me how *caring* I am, how *responsible,* and this is how you heal. This is how you learn to love me out loud, without feeling guilty about it.

You pull the duvet over our heads and I am the man of your dreams, repeatedly offering to go, and you are the woman of my dreams, bringing my hand to your legs, to your Murakami. We break the laws of physics and travel through time and slip into our future and I hold you knowing that I will hold you forever, that this is our sneak peek at Forever.

I kiss your foxy hair, tendrils all over my bare chest. "Do you want coffee?"

You run your hand through my hair and sigh. "Mind reader, Joe. Truly."

RIP Phil never did nice things for you. No breakfast in bed, not even a fucking cup of coffee. But then you glance at one of his trash bags and you're crying again, guilty. "I'm the worst woman in the world, if anyone knew you were here . . . We can't jump into this. You know you can't be here when Nomi gets back."

"I know." I kiss your head, the most patient man alive. "You want me to take some of these bags down?"

You pull away. "Whoa, slow down there." You pull the covers over the part of your shoulder, the skin that I just kissed. "Way way *way* too soon."

"I'm sorry, I was only trying to help."

You bite your lip. You won't let the past wreck our future. "I know, but right now I really just want coffee. And I'm sorry. I didn't mean to jump all over you."

I kiss the top of your head. "Don't worry about me."

I put on pants and a shirt—the Meerkat really could come back at any time—and bound down the stairs and I can't fucking wait for you to get rid of this house, this albatross. You're jumpy because you're here. In your head, this house belongs to your dead husband. And I get it. Everything will be better when we get you out of this place, when my house becomes *our* house. I can already see us on the sofa, watching our cats preen under the Christmas lights that will be up all year, on at all hours. I love you, Mary Kay, and I open the freezer of casseroles we'll never eat because these casseroles are like Phil's trash bags, like this house. They also need to go.

I find the fucking coffee—finally—and close the door and flinch.

There's a man standing there, staring at me as if *I'm* the intruder and did Oliver send him? His face is familiar but he's too old to be Oliver's brother and he's wearing a Rolex so he's not a cop.

He breaks the silence. "Who the fuck are you?"

I turn that shit around. "Who the fuck are *you*? And how did you get in here?"

He clocks the sink full of dirty dishes. "I'm Phil's brother. I have a key," he says. Blithe. Cold. "And I guess you do too, huh?"

33

This no-show, middling *life coach* starts washing your dishes like he owns this place, like casserole dishes don't need to soak, and he's a straitlaced version of Phil and I want him gone—we don't need this right now—and I hear you upstairs. You're scrambling into your clothes and washing your face and now you bound down the stairs. You smell of soap. You washed me off.

"Ivan," you say, breezing right by me, putting your arms around Phil Part Two. "You're here."

You should hate him—he skipped the fucking *funeral*—but you don't hate him. You're obsequious. You thank him for doing the dishes as if they aren't still scabbed and you fawn on him for pouring dish soap into the compartment in the scrub brush—oh, *please*—and you treat him like a human gadget. Like he's Mr. Fucking Fix-It. We have the iPhone, the iPad, and now we have the motherfuckering i*Man*.

Yes, your brother-in-law Ivan is a textbook *Ivan*—entitled, arrogant, *starched* on the bottom and wrinkled T-shirt on top—and he's the missing piece of the puzzle, *the shark inside Phil's shark.* Better nose. Smarter. Colder. He's only Phil's *half* brother—they share a mother—and we should be talking about Phil, but it takes eleven seconds or so for *Ivan* to announce that he's been *taking things to the next level* with his "life-coaching business." It sounds like bullshit and you're busy doting on him so I google him and yes. Okay. Ivan's getting some press and he's "trending"—that word needs to die—but anyone can see that his entire "career" is driven by his desire to be a *rock star* like his brother. Can you stop salivating over this fucker and remember the facts? He showed up *after* your husband's funeral—what a monster—and a life coach should have compassion, not to mention a fucking shirt with some buttons.

But look at you, still being so nice to him! The two of you are *catching up* and I'm in a chair in the corner of your kitchen reading about *Ivan* and the mental health situation in the Separated States of America is bad because of people like him. He followed up his BA with a PhD—he's a doctor but he couldn't save a life on a plane—and he made his fortune by greasing the wheels for big, bad pharma. And what does he do with all that extra money? Does he start a nonprofit? Does he build an *incubator* to ensure that the future is female? Nope. He builds a website—well, he *pays* someone to build it—and declares himself a life coach. I watch a short closed-captioned video of him "presenting" his "philosophy."

You took the first step. You're here. I'm here to help you take the next step. Ready, Ladies? Because I'm about to blow your mind. (A long dramatic stare.) *Don't trust your feelings.* (Another long, even *more* dramatic stare.) *Your whole life you've been told that you have feelings. What if the people who told you that you're emotional had told you that you're smart?* (He puts on a baseball cap that reads THINKING CAP and ugh, he made *merch.*) *Welcome to a new world where you don't trust your feelings. You see them for what they are: Cobwebs. Quicksand. Clutter. I'm here to make you think.*

No wonder there are so few views and yet look at you right now, pouring vinegar into your coffeemaker because *he* said to do it. Like his dead brother, he brings out the worst in you and I *dislike* the fucking video to focus on the show in here. He has an excuse for everything.

Why wasn't he at the funeral? *I had twelve hundred clients with flights booked, hotels prepaid. I had to be there.*

Nope! He *paid* to attend a seminar on social media branding for life coaches and he did not *have* to be there.

Why wasn't he here for wake week? For the casserole parade? *I had a sit-down with* GQ *in New York. I begged my agent to let me do a phoner, but they wanted the whole shebang, a photo shoot, the X-factor when I walk into the lobby of the Four Seasons, all that good stuff.*

The story was for *GQ dot com* and the story is only online and sorry, Ivan, but you didn't have a *sit-down.* It's a piece about CEOs with "second acts"—Ivan hired a *publicist* after his brother died and that publicist used RIP Phil DiFuckingMarco to get Ivan some press. I am a good guy and Ivan is a bad guy, a fake-it-till-you-make-it motherfucker who uses words like *shebang.* And again I say it: WHAT KIND OF A LIFE COACH SKIPS HIS BROTHER'S FUNERAL?

He looks down at the coffee you hand to him. He looks down at you. "You better not be beating yourself up for what happened, Emmy. You know it's not your fault, right? You know there's nothing you could have done."

I don't have a *PhD in Psychology* but this is projecting and you are fawning—*Thank you for all those flowers, Ivan, they really did make the funeral*—and I butt in. "What a good brother," I say. "That's generous, considering you couldn't be there."

"Well, they're half brothers," you say. "And Ivan's so busy in Denver . . ."

He claps his hands and he almost hits your nose. "Stop that, Em. There is no half or whole. He was my baby brother. End of story." His phone buzzes. He smiles and walks to the front door and you and I follow, like sheep.

Nomi is on the street, running faster than I've ever seen her move.

You are puzzled. "She said she was gonna stay in Seattle."

He is smug. "I told her I was here."

That selfish bastard pulled Nomi away from people who actually love her and she hugs him and he says she looks so grown-up and I don't like his Rolex, sliding around his wrist so we can't forget it's there. "All right," he says. "Where are we headed in the fall?"

Ivan's got his arm around Nomi and they're walking into the house and do I stay? Do I go? You wave at me—*come on*—so I follow you but this is all wrong. I'm more in tune with this family than this Ivan Come Lately but he's the one Nomi is excitedly telling about NYU.

"You're going to love New York," I butt in.

We're all back in the kitchen and there's an awkward silence.

Ivan looks at you, not me. "Sorry, MK . . . who is this guy?"

You rub your collarbone the way you do when a Mothball asks for help with a fucking *e-card* and Nomi answers the question. "Joe's a volunteer at the library. And he's from New York, so of course he's biased about NYU." She tears at a loaf of bread and laughs. "Also he has three cats."

I don't need Ivan to know about *our* cats and I was a mentor to Nomi. I listened to her talk about books. I helped her discover how rewarding it is to help *old people* and this is how she repays me? You lighten the mood by pouring coffee and there are three of you and one of me and I'm not even allowed to be mad that you didn't tell Ivan I'm your boyfriend because oh that's right.

Our love is a secret. Nomi doesn't know either. She thinks I'm a loser like Shortus.

You open the freezer and retrieve a casserole and Ivan claps his hands again and you and the Meerkat freeze up like this is a fucking improv class and he is your teacher. "Rule One," he says. "Those casseroles go in the trash. That food is something that other people needed to provide in order to express their condolences. But that food is not for you to eat, girls." *Girls* and he's just another insecure prick, a tall fucking Shortus. "Rule Two," he says, on his feet now, rolling up those sleeves like he's about to manhandle a baby at a political convention. "Same logic applies to Phil's things."

"Ivan," I say. "You don't want to go there."

You don't look at me. Your eyes are glued to him and he puts his hands on your shoulders. "Emmy, I know you . . . Trust me when I tell you that death is a part of life. We are animals and we have to move forward. Your feelings are intense. But feelings aren't real." He points at his head and I wish his finger was a gun. "We have to use our heads to protect us from the spontaneous, *reactionary* urges of our hearts."

The word is *reactive* and he's talking about me, Mary Kay. He may as well pick me up and shove me in one of RIP Phil's fucking trash bags and he is wrong. Your feelings for me are not a *reaction* to that dead rat—we've been falling in love for months—but what do you do?

You tell him that he's right and you are gonna gather Phil's things *today* and I offered to get rid of those fucking trash bags less than an hour ago and you bit my head off. You're all hugging and I may as well be back in the woods, on the trail, behind the rock. My chair squeaks when I stand. "I think I should get going."

You keep your head where I can't see it, buried in Ivan's chest, and your voice is muffled—*Thanks, Joe*—and Ivan pats you both on the back and offers to walk me out as if this is his house. You and the Meerkat hide in the kitchen and he opens the front door before I can get my hand on the knob.

"Thanks for helping out around here . . ." His voice drops to a whisper. "But you and I both know that a recently widowed woman needs time on her own."

"Of course. I just came by to help her with some stuff around the house."

He mad-dogs me and my fucking shirt is inside out and does he still smell you on me? "Well," he says. "That's what I miss about this place so much, all that generosity . . ."

I leave and there is nothing I can do because his presence doesn't change anything—our love is a secret, it's too soon—but his presence changes everything. No more lingering in the bed with me. No more working through your grief the right way, behind closed doors, with me. Right now, you're in that house and you're regressing at ninety miles an hour, putting on a proper widow show for your dead husband's no-show brother. You were Phil's muse, and that was a problem, but this is worse, Mary Kay. Now you're the one onstage.

34

One day passes. No word from you. I buy Oliver a violin. Minka is taking classes.

Another day passes. No word from you. I buy Oliver a fucking *piano.* Minka didn't like the violin.

Another day passes. No word from you. I bite Oliver's head off when he calls and he laughs. "I know," he says. "But there's this Casio on 1stdibs. It's super eighties, my friend. You don't have to learn how to play it. It's intuitive . . . or sort of intuitive? Whatever it is, we want it."

I buy Oliver his *non*-intuitive Casio—am I ever going to see you again?—and my doorbell rings. Yes! You! I run to the door and I open the door and no. Ivan. I wish I wasn't in sweatpants and I wish Riffic was a fucking Rottweiler.

Ivan laughs at my cats. "Sorry to surprise you."

"No worries. Did you want to come in?" *So I can lock you in my Whisper Room?*

"Actually," he says. "Nomi mentioned that you live here . . ." Nomi. Not you. "And I know how helpful you were last week . . ." Someone had to be, you prick. "I wanted to invite you over for supper tonight. It's the least we can do to repay you for being such a good neighbor."

The word is *boyfriend,* you asshole, and he better not tell you about all the cat hair on my sweatpants. "I'm always happy to help and that sounds great, but unnecessary. I don't want to intrude."

"Don't be ridiculous." He tells me he'll see me at six and I start to close the door and he snaps his fingers. "Oh, one more thing," he says. "Feel free to bring your partner, if you have one . . ."

I hate the word *partner* and I picture Rachael Ray riding one of her knives into the center of his chest and I smile. "Thanks," I say. "But it's just me."

A couple hours later you call me and you are hiding in the garage, whispering, as if you're the guest in his house. You are *so sorry* for all the *radio silence* and you say it's *so complicated.* "See, Ivan and Phil didn't have the best relationship and I feel like you got stuck in the middle of some ancient history."

"Mary Kay, I'm gonna say what I always say. Don't worry about me. Really."

You blow me a kiss but I hear him in your voice and it's so much better in my house, no fucking *Ivans* clogging the pipes. I go down to my Whisper Room to get ready for *supper* (a.k.a. read up on Uncle Ivan) and here's my conclusion, Mary Kay.

He isn't a life coach. He's an aspiring cult leader.

He claps and women stop talking and women *pay* him for his authoritative "coaching." The man is the real fake deal. But let's be honest, Mary Kay. He's a bad guy, and this is the problem with the fucking Internet. Thanks to his publicist, women are *watching* his videos and every hour he has more followers and "converts" than he did the hour before. It doesn't hurt that he's not a bad-looking guy who enforces a *one*-strike rule—that's so cult—and stares into the camera and tells women what they want to hear, what we all want to hear: *You deserve better.*

No, Ivan. Most people are pretty shitty and they don't *deserve* better and I wish RIP Phil would come back from the dead so that I could tell him that I get it, *man*. If this was my brother—God help me—even half brother, I would've been popping pills and singing about sharks, too.

Ivan's also an Instagram junkie—women who love guys like Ivan also love Instagram—and here's a brand-new post, a photo of a vintage BMW in his parents' garage at their summer home in Manzanita. The caption is sexist, directed at you: *Good to be home, baby. Missed you.*

You are not a car and he went to Yale and is there anything worse than a forty-nine-year-old man still identifying by the college that accepted him before he could legally buy beer? Ivan isn't famous-famous (yet). He's not John Fucking Stamos. Three years ago, he was flying from one self-made bubble to another, speaking to "crowds"—trick photography—of women who then swarmed him in the lobby bars of various Marriotts all over the country. And this year, even before your husband died, Ivan has hit his fucking stride and the lie is coming true.

A guy couldn't so easily become an Ivan twenty years ago—fuck you, Internet; fuck you, images—and I put on your favorite black sweater and I can do this. Your brother-in-law didn't invent the snake oil game and I can make nice with him.

And if not I can . . . well, no, I can't.

I turn the corner on the trail and Ivan is on your deck, dumping charcoal into the grill. I hoist my bottle of Bainbridge vodka and he waves his tongs, longer than my bottle, and he stares at my vodka. "Wow," he says. "Hard stuff on a school night. Yikes. You don't see a lot of the hard stuff in wine country." We're not in *wine country* and you like vodka and it says BAINBRIDGE on the bottle. "I don't drink it. It's like they say, perfume going in, sewage going out."

It takes a lot for me to punch someone with an *actually,* but I do it now. "Actually, Ivan, that's what they say that about champagne. Not vodka."

He doesn't cop to being wrong even though he was wrong and he sighs. "When did you say you moved here?"

"I didn't." Pause for dramatic effect. "A few months ago."

He wants to ask more but here you come in a Red Bed red sundress and I shrug, affable houseguest, changing the subject, and you keep your distance from me but Ivan watches, assessing our body language like the unlicensed pervert that he is. You pour wine and Nomi puts a cheese board in the middle of the table and Ivan starts telling some long, boring you-had-to-be-there story about the time you and him and your rat had an olive-eating contest and Ivan nods at me. "Go ahead, Joe. Have an olive."

This isn't your style. I've watched your sitcom and I know you.

You're not a foodie. You binge on Tostitos in bed and you let the frost bite your salmon and I pick up a piece of white cheese. "This is quite a charcuterie board."

"Nicely done," he says, clapping like this is NA. "A lot of people can't pronounce that word . . ." As if it's surprising that I *can*. "Do you not like olives, Joe?"

I hate olives, but I pop one in my mouth—I belong with you—and my body recoils and you're all laughing at me. He hands me a napkin. "Just spit it out. You do you, Joe."

You bite your lip and sip more wine and Nomi opens her *Columbine* and she's telling *Uncle Ivan* about the book, and Ivan *knows* Dylan Klebold's mother, he met her at a *publishing lunch* at a restaurant and he loves the *resy* app—*Resy* isn't a word, you prick—and he shows us an email confirmation that begins with empty validation: *You're popular*.

I know you're just as disgusted as me and I laugh. "Imagine taking that personally."

You don't laugh—you can't, our love is a secret—and Ivan puts his phone away and Nomi jumps out of her chair—she has to pee and she says so, the way girls her age do—and now it's just us. Adults. "So," Ivan says, as if he's your father and I want to take you to the prom. "Emmy tells me you're a volunteer?"

He was too happy to use the word *volunteer*, so I tell him about my book business and he's Tom Brokaw and I'm the terrorist and he slaps me on the back. "Don't be so self-conscious, guy."

I'm not *self-conscious* but I remain calm. He says he was thinking about writing a book—aren't we all, Ivan—but opted to go with a website instead. *Yes, Ivan, because you could never write a fucking book* and you are drinking too much, too fast, and you praise the olives and ask where he got them—YOU DON'T FUCKING CARE ABOUT OLIVES AND YOU DON'T EVEN LIKE THEM—and you wash down those pungent things with wine.

"Sorry," you say. "I get these waves . . . I can't *believe* Phil is gone."

That's more like it, Mary Kay. You don't need to please this man and compliment his fucking cheese board. You just lost your *husband.*

He nods. "There are gonna be waves, Emmy. Ride them. Stay strong."

He says this like it's a grand fucking insight and he flashes his put-me-on-TV eyes at me again. "So, Joe, what's your take on all this?"

I don't have a *hot take* on your life because you're a human, not an issue. "I think it's been a really rough couple of weeks on the family . . ."

Meaning the family that Ivan is not a fucking part of, and Nomi opens the screen door and looks around the table. "Wait," she says. "Mom, did you tell him?"

You rub your forehead. "Nomi . . ."

"Uncle Ivan, you know Mom and Dad were gonna get divorced, right?"

Ivan frowns. "No? Emmy, is this true?"

You cough. "Nomi, it's a little more complicated than that. Let's not get into it, okay?"

"Why?" she says. "I mean he was sleeping on the couch for like two weeks, right?"

I should have stayed home and you slam a plate and march into the house and order Nomi to follow you and Ivan motions for me to follow him. "Joe, do you eat lamb?"

I shake my head no and he wants to know if it's for political reasons and I laugh him off. "I just don't like the taste."

He lays his lamb shanks on the grill and inside, you and the Meerkat are screaming and I can only hear bits—she says you broke his heart, you say he wanted to leave *you*—and Ivan closes the lid on the grill.

"So," he says. "You never met my brother, is that right?"

I nod. He opens the lid of the grill and flips a helpless lamb and I want to flip *him*. "That's a shame," he says. "He wasn't perfect . . . but he was a good guy. Emmy and Nomi, they were *everything* to him . . ." Not true. "Joe," he says. "I don't want to pry . . ." Liar. "But what exactly is your relationship with Mary Kay?"

"Ivan, look, I think we got off on the wrong foot. I live around the corner, things were *bad* . . . you can imagine how bad, Nomi finding him . . . Mary Kay just *reeling*."

A normal person would let the guilt bomb hit him but Ivan just flips his *shanks*. "It must be hard for you right now . . . your girlfriend feeling so guilty about cheating on her husband . . ."

"Whoa, Ivan. That's not what's going on."

"Relax," he says. "I'm not here to judge. I see the guilt eating you alive . . ."

I never said I felt guilty and again he flips a little chunk of dead lamb and I miss the silence of *our* lambs and I can't tell if you and Nomi are fighting or making up and he calls me your *latest adoptee, another orphan from the library,* and I am not your project and we take care of *each other* and you are crying and the Meerkat is crying and I want to go inside and help you but I can't. Ivan flings innocent dead lamb parts onto a platter. He is the shark inside Phil's shark circling, finding someone new, me. "I'm gonna make this easy," he says with a smile. "We're gonna eat lamb. You don't like lamb. Why don't you call it a night?"

Two days later, and I still haven't heard from you.

My cats are all over me. They feel my pain and I feel your pain too. You're in mourning. You and Nomi need to heal and our love is a secret and my hatred of Ivan is a secret—I wouldn't burden you with my opinions right now—but time is passing. You are nesting with another man and I'm alone. Oliver went back to L.A. to see Minka and he's bugging me about David LaChapelle's *Jesus Is My Homeboy,* which costs thirty-five *thousand* dollars. I buy it—ouch—and he says he'll see me on *Menopause Island* soon, but when will I see you?

Ivan is staying in your house and luring you into his cult and I can't blame you for it because you lost your fucking husband and your daughter discovered her own father on the floor.

Dead.

You are the two most vulnerable women in the world and men like Ivan . . . this is what they do. They hunt for women like you. Nomi shares too many pictures of Denver, the city that Ivan calls home, and you don't call me. You just send me questions via *text* and I hear Ivan's voice in your voice.

You, infected by Ivan: *Question. How did you get into rare books?*

Me: *I worked in a bookstore in New York. My mentor was amazing. It takes years to build contacts and learn how to read a book, to spot a fake. My eyes are permanently tired!*

You say nothing. You don't laugh at my joke. But read between the lines, Mary Kay. I *worked* for my position in this world. I didn't buy my way in like *some* people.

You, infected by Ivan: *Question. How come you don't have a website?*

I placate you—*My business is purely organic, people tell people about me*—and you are turning cold on me—*Thanks*—and you're sharing photographs of Ivan's *homemade duck-fat fries* and your mind is turning to duck fat and of course he knows how to cook, Mary Kay. All sleazy bastards learn a few dishes to seem like *husband material* and you are not that woman who lives online but here you are on Instagram, defiling your non-brand brand and talking about . . . *him.*

You're not going crazy. You're going sane. @IvanKing #Wordsof Wisdom

You're not *going sane.* You're going crazy. Nomi is too:

Denver here I come! #GoingSane

That's a big decision—she belongs in New York—and I should not find out about big decisions in our family-in-the-making on *Instagram.*

Oliver interrupts me with a DM: *Instagram is bad for your mental health. FYI.*

He shouldn't *know* that I'm online but he hacked my account and changed my settings and I change my password—fuck you, Oliver—and I let two hours pass, as if I'm some fucking child with overbearing paranoid parents.

I go back on Instagram and Ivan's been busy. There's a picture of the three of you in brand-new matching baseball caps on the ferry to Seattle.

Bye-bye, feeling caps. Hello, thinking caps. #FamilyisEverything

I grab *my* hat—fuck you, Ivan—and head out my door. Family is everything, Mary Kay. But he's not your family. I am. And it's time I helped you remember that.

35

I walk to Pegasus. It's a free country, it's a small island, so I keep strolling, as people do sometimes. I turn onto your street and then into your yard—we're *Friends,* we pop by—and I enter through the side door—you didn't lock it, *tsk-tsk*—and I toss my coffee cup into your recycling bin with all the other Pegasus cups and I walk upstairs and go into your bedroom. I take a deep breath. Okay. This is good news. You're not sleeping with Ivan. I would smell him.

But there's something you're not telling me and I pick up one of your trash bags. My phone buzzes and it's an electric shock to my nervous system—leave me alone, Oliver—but it's not Oliver. It's fucking Shortus—*wanna go for a run?*—and no, you asshole, I don't want to go for a run. I tell him I already *went* for a run today and he calls me a pussy and I shove my phone back into my pocket and pick up a trash bag. This one isn't soft like the others because this one is full of journals. It's time for me to learn about what you *really* think of Ivan and I lie on your bed. There are so fucking many of them and it's mostly you beating yourself up about not being a good mother, not being a good wife, wishing Melanda would find someone, wishing you had left when you had the chance. I can't sit here all day and you're a *fox,* you're wily, so I pick up a yellowing notepad of grocery lists and errands. My heart is beating. I turn the pages. And sure enough, twenty-three pages into your errand book, I find the *real* diary, the one that doesn't have a fucking sunset on the cover. The one where you use a pencil instead of a pen.

-Nomi ballet slippers?
-Phil therapist or couples therapist
-dry cleaning
Oh god I am going to hell and it will be an olive garden only not a restaurant. Just olives. Something shifted. He gave me an olive . . . and I slept with him. Am I a monster? I just feel so drawn to him and he's so together and oh God I am a monster. I want him. But you can't do this in life. You can't leave your husband for his brother but they're half brothers and oh god what is wrong with me? I want olives. I want Ivan.
-yams, salmon, chips, diet coke

Nothing was wrong with you, Mary Kay. You were young, married to an unstable man.

Two days later, you used a sharper pencil, and my eyes thank you for that.

-return ballet slippers
-DRY CLEANING
-pickles, frozen pizza, that mac and cheese thing that Nomi likes
Well that's that. Big news! I'm not good enough for Ivan. HAHA shock of the century right? Yep I threw myself at him, so smart, so smart MK! And he told me that it could never work out and yep, go to the head of the class you whore. Well done. And now . . . if Phil ever found out . . . well, good job, me. I sure can pick 'em.
-haircut?

My heart hurts for RIP Phil and I close your secret diary. So this is why Ivan has a hold over you. You slept with him. But it doesn't matter what you did. You were young. We all were once upon a time.

I leave your bed and I open your computer—it's old and big and the password is predictable—LADYMARYKAY—and I open your email. On the fourth day of every month for the last several years, you have written to him:

Dear Ivan,
Someday we will pay you back. I know how that sounds. But I mean it.
Love,
MK

And on the fifth day of every month, Ivan replies to you:

Dear Mary Kay,
We're family. I'm happy to help.
Love, Ivan

I dive into the financial mess of your life and Phil blew his royalties and his trust fund—he didn't like to work—but Ivan was smart. Straight edge. Their parents cut them both off and you and your rat were regulars at the Bank of Ivan and the house really isn't yours. It's his name on the mortgage.

Your house smells like dead lilies and Ivan's sweat and my phone buzzes and I want it to be you but it's Oliver: *Watching you, my friend. Not crazy about what I see . . .*

Days pass and you get worse and you really are in a cult. I go to Pegasus early in the morning and I wait for you—I am reading *The Girls* and I can't wait to say the word CULT to you—and eventually you enter the coffee shop. But you aren't happy to see me.

"Joe, I'm in kind of a rush."

I close my book. "I get it," I say. "But did you ever read this?"

You shake your head no and you don't ask about me or my fucking cats and it's like you don't even *hear* the Bob Dylan playing in the background. You just point at the counter. "I really do have to go . . . I know you probably want to talk but I just . . ."

"I get it."

"We have company and it's crazy at home."

That's the right word, Mary Kay: *crazy*.

"Oh hey," I said. "Superquick . . . how's Nomi? I just hope she's getting through this okay. It's a rough go those first few weeks . . ."

I already know that Nomi is in trouble. She told everyone on Instagram that she's taking a fucking *gap year* and *putting NYU on hold* to intern for *Uncle Ivan* in Denver. The hashtag made me sick: *#ListenToYourHead*

But you don't tell me about Nomi's bad decision. You barely look me in the eye. "That's sweet of you," you say. "And I promise, we're good. Hanging in. Everything is under control."

Yes, Mary Kay. *Ivan* is controlling you and he's controlling the Meerkat and you buy three lattes—none for me—and you leave with a sexless wave—*Bye, Joe!*—and that shark is moving fast and the Meerkat is adrift. Technically, she's an "adult," but she's a young eighteen and she needs someone to tell her that you don't make life decisions when you're in mourning. The iPhone killed romance and turned us all into lazy, nasty stalkers and now Ivan the iMan is killing us.

Three days later, it's like you've gone to the dark side. I really *don't exist* to you. I don't go outside. Oliver's so "worried" about me that he sent me a fucking cheesecake via Postmates, as if one cheesecake makes up for the thousands of dollars I've spent on him.

I've been playing "Hallelujah" on repeat, trying to hate you, trying to think of you as the woman who fucked your husband right in front of me, a semireformed *brother fucker* who didn't catch on when her best friend was pleasuring her husband. I'm trying to accept that something about those men gets to you. Your rat dies and you immediately glom onto his brother. You have been brainwashed and I know that. I do. But I can't stop thinking about you. I can't stop loving you.

So I send you a text: *hi*

You send me a text: *hi*

I send you another text: *is it bad if I say I miss you?*

You don't answer me and eleven long minutes go by—oh, fuck you, clock—and I am the stupidest man on the planet and maybe I should kill your *half* brother-in-law because a man as stupid as me deserves to rot in prison for being stupid.

And then there is a knock on my door and it's you.

"Hello." You're wearing a baggy dress I've never seen and it's cult white.

"Hi," I say. "Come on in."

You enter in silence and you don't notice the music and you don't smile your foxy smile and you don't cry your foxy tears. You are dead-eyed. You're here but I don't know who you are and you won't sit on my Red Bed sofa and now your lips are moving. I follow your gaze.

"Mary Kay, are you . . . are you counting the red stuff?"

"Well, it is a lot of red, Joe. Is this meant to turn your house into a Red Bed?"

Yes. "No, I just like red."

You nod. You're still in there and you know when I'm lying and you tell me this says a lot about me and it does. But then you purse your lips. "You can't make the world red. This was really confrontational of you, Joe. And overbearing."

"Whoa," I say. "Where is this coming from?"

You shrug. And I know where this is coming from. You listened to Ivan's *take* on us. "Look," I say. "I know you're going through hell, but come on. It's me. I love you."

You close your eyes. "Don't say that you love me, Joe. That's just a physical sensation. It's just a feeling."

I recognize that you are in a cult and it is not your fault. The cult showed up on your doorstep and moved into your fucking house and you are in *debt* to the leader of the cult. But you're in there, somewhere, and I have to try and reach you. "Don't take this the wrong way, Mary Kay, but how's that Kool-Aid?"

"Excuse me?"

And off you go, defending that monster who's *just looking out for you* and I never should have brought him into this and you're hiding from me by talking about him. You tell me that you know I didn't *mean* to take advantage of you and I am on my feet.

"I *didn't* take advantage of you, Mary Kay."

"Oh no? You didn't hang around my house knowing that I was weak, that my *husband* just died? You didn't *pop by* with toilet paper and wait for everyone to leave and you didn't prevent me from being alone so that I could take charge of my feelings and put my thinking cap on? You didn't do that? None of it?"

"Mary Kay . . ."

"Because the way *I* see it . . ." *I* as in *Ivan* and he is worse than RIP Steve Jobs, hell-bent on owning the world's most important pronoun, the one that makes you *you*. "Well, Joe . . ." You never talk like this. "I did not come here to fight with you . . ." Yes you did. "I did not come here to explain myself to you . . ." Yes you did. "I came here to hold you accountable for your behavior, your behavior that was very harmful to me, your behavior that, whether or not you intended it, did drive me off course."

The Whisper Room is right downstairs and you are in a cult and you're not eating enough—he's starving you, it's part of the brainwashing—and I want to keep you, save you. I want to wrap my arms around you and you stand.

"I'm not obligated to listen to what you have to say to me because it's not my job to take care of you . . ." Yes it is. We take care of each other. "And yes, I have feelings for you . . . but you can't trust your feelings."

"Mary Kay, do you hear yourself? This isn't you. This is *him*."

"And you don't like him."

I won't lie to you and I can't lie to you so I don't say a word. You look down at your white cult dress. "Well," you say. "I will leave you to process your emotions and do for you what you did not do for me. I will give you the space to feel your feelings about the dissolution of this relationship."

"Mary Kay, what are you trying to say?"

I know damn well what you are trying to say but maybe if I force you to say it, you will change your mind. "You know what I'm saying."

"No," I say. "I don't."

You ignore one of my cats when he marks you as his territory and you tense up on me, on my cats, our cats. "It's over, Joe."

"So you want to break up with me."

"No. People have to be in a serious relationship in order to break up . . ." We were serious to me. We *are* serious to me. "I was in a fog . . ." You are in the fog right *now*. "And Phil might be alive if you and I hadn't been running around . . ." You make it sound like I grew the fucking poppy seeds and you wipe away a tear and the fog thickens. You shiver when I take a step toward you and your tear ducts go into lockdown. "No," you say. "It's over."

Ivan won your head. He reconfigured your heart. I can't give up. I tell you that it doesn't have to be this way and I remind you of how long we've known each other, how hard we worked to get here, and you huff. "Yeah," you say, and you're not Ivan's puppet and I wish you were but no, this is you, the woman I know. "You said it, Joe. And we really did fuck up. But I don't want to hash it out with you." You purse your lips. "And there's no point . . ."

I step toward you and you step back. "I'm moving," you say.

"You're *what*?" No no no no *no*.

"We put the house on the market."

NO NO NO NO NO. Your insanity is supposed to be *temporary*. "Mary Kay, come on. Slow down a minute. You can't tell me you want to move away. Not with him."

"I just did tell you."

"Hang on a minute. This feels a little unfair, Mary Kay. I *love* you. You know that. You said it."

And now finally you do meet my eyes. "I told you, Joe. That day never happened."

That was the best day of my life—I have the Polaroids to prove it—and you cut me off when I try to reason with you. "I'd appreciate it if you would respect my feelings and stay away." You take my doorknob in your hand. You squeeze. "Goodbye, Joe. Good luck."

You close my door—you don't slam it—and I walk to the window and I wait for you to look back—the woman always looks back at the one she loves—but you don't do it, Mary Kay. You don't love me anymore.

36

It's quiet in the Whisper Room and in the great tradition of so many authors on this island, I open Microsoft Word and I open Chrome because the old adages are true: Write what you know and know thy enemy, especially if you're going to write about him.

I open my mind—ouch—and watch a video of one of Ivan's newest female converts—possibly a paid actor, actually let's go with *probably*—and she's wearing her thinking cap and she is energized. "Ivan should be the biggest life coach on the planet," she says. "He changed everything for me. No more pop music, no more Air Supply when I'm PMSing, and no more sappy movies. Ivan taught me to stop feeling my feelings and start leading with my mind."

I dig up Ivan's bio on his website and there he is with his wife and her kids—second marriage—and her name is Alisa and she's a mousy brunette who *tends to everything at home.* She is rigid. She wears a sweater set. She's from another time and she's on Facebook—of course—and she's "busy" raising their sons . . . who are away at college. None of these people showed up at Phil's funeral and Ivan and Alisa met in grad school—bite me—and the quote at the top of her profile would make RIP Melanda feel sick: *"Stop your feelings before they stop you."—Ivan King, my husband*

Ivan really wanted his new career to happen, and at some point, an intelligent woman *must* have gotten on his nerves and told him to back the fuck off.

I google #MeToo Ivan King.

Nothing. Which makes sense. He's only been officially selling his snake oil for a couple years. But then, there are older videos, some of them from his early days, when he didn't know about bounce boards and lighting. Surely he made a mistake at some point, and I'm not talking about technical shit.

I google gross things: *Ivan King blow job. Ivan King affair. Ivan King rumor. Ivan King harassment.* But it's the same every time. *Ivan King decent. Ivan King loyal. Ivan King ally.*

There's no way, Mary Kay. I remember my old life in L.A., fighting with RIP Forty about our screenplays and the one good piece of advice he gave me—*Trust your gut, Old Sport. It's all in there*—and I do that now. I trust my gut and I know I can be stubborn about technology. I hate the name. I hate the clear intention to shrink our attention span even more. But I do it. I go on fucking TikTok.

This is the miracle of the creative process. Of inspiration. *You.* Because I love you, I am in touch with all the narrows of my soul, my talent. *I didn't think someone like you existed.* You found me and I do exist and my instinct was right—good job, gut—and I find Megan.

Megan isn't very popular on TikTok—she doesn't shoot her whole face, only her mouth—but I like her for bucking the shallow, image-obsessed system. I like Megan's voice, too. She's indignant. Brave. Rattled. It takes a few *TikToks* to tell her whole story—San Francisco tech fucks, you can do better—but I listen to the whole damn thing. And then I play her videos again and *this* time, I write it all down:

> *This is pretty scary. My #MeToo isn't famous but he isn't not famous but that doesn't matter. What matters is what he did to me. The part of me that loves Ivan King says that I'm acting with my feelings, not my brain, because that's how men kept women down for so long, by telling us that we feel too much. But I do have feelings and I can't hold it in anymore. I met Ivan King at his workshop. He told me that I had true potential but that I lacked confidence. He told me he could tell that I had never had an or-*

gasm with a man and at the time it was true and I told him that wasn't true and he knew I was lying because if you know Ivan, you know how he is. How he just KNOWS. He said that sex is an activity. The single most important activity. He said that without good sex I would never reach my true potential. He could tell I had never been in love. I cried a lot. He said I wasn't attractive because men have intuition too. They can tell when you haven't been loved correctly, when you've faked too many orgasms and blamed yourself. So I did it. I took my clothes off. I know I did this myself. He didn't hold me down. He didn't "make" me do anything. I put my "thinking cap" on and I kept that hat on during sex. He abused his power. I know I can't be the only woman who got played. He makes it so hard to come forward. He makes us blame ourselves for having feelings. But I am sick of pretending that I don't. Because if you ask me, no one has more "feelings" than Ivan King. If this happened to you, please tell me. #MeToo is good, but it's not perfect or Ivan King would be on the way down, not on the way up. I saw him in GQ *and well . . . I just had to speak up.*

My fingers are numb and my left eye is twitching and I wrote it once and I doubled back to check for accuracy—as Megan's megaphone amplifier, I owe it to her to nail every word—and then I do what Megan should have done.

I dump Megan's manifesto on Reddit, where people like to pay attention to every word.

And now I wait.

We live in strange times—refresh, nothing—because for all the men who are exposed, there are plenty of bad men who carry on in the shadows because they know how to convince women that they're *emotionally* responsible for whatever the men did with their dicks—refresh, nothing—and I forgot about how *good* it feels to tell the *truth* and help a wronged woman seek justice—RIP Melanda would be so proud of me—and I refresh.

Nothing.

But I am patient. I believe Megan. I believe in her so much that it wouldn't surprise me if she called me right now to thank me for sharing her story. (I linked the transcript to her TikTok. Unlike RIP Forty Quinn, I give credit when credit is due.) Megan has dirty blond hair—refresh, nothing—and slouchy shoulders and credit card debt from Ivan King—refresh, nothing—and I find her other accounts and I learn about her overdue bills from personal trainers and therapists and . . . grad school. Yes! She's a grad student—sadly, snobs care about shit like that—and she's relatable, fiercely intelligent in the classroom, but less confident when it comes to her personal life. She contacted Ivan because she thought he could help make the pain go away and he made it worse and she's not alone and that's why he should be *canceled*. I refresh.

Nothing.

I feed my cats—cats were made for moments of tension like this—and they want to sleep but I get some yarn and fuck with them and they're just like me. They want that yarn *so* bad. And then they get it. And then they run because it's more fun to chase the yarn than it is to have the yarn.

I go back to my computer. Refresh. Nothing. Fuck you, Internet!

I walk to Blackbird and I order the toast my fecal-eyed neighbor likes so much. I wait for the toast—come on *#IBelieveMegan*—and I go on Instagram and the women in my life are a wreck. Love is trying to teach Forty to play golf—he's a child—and you are next-level insane, allowing Ivan to preach to a small group of women at the library.

"Joe!"

That's my toast and I get my toast and I eat my toast and I wipe my hands. Calmly. Thoroughly. I pick up my phone. Refresh. *Something.*

But it's not something good. A brainwashed user named *ClaireSays* has come on here to attack Megan. Claire calls Megan a liar—the fucking *nerve*—and Megan is not a liar. When someone says something you don't like you can't just declare their voice illegitimate and Claire is racking up *approval* because people love to hate. She accuses Megan of being paid off—fucking conspiracy theorist, Claire—and she says Megan needs *help*. And then she contradicts herself and says that Megan should be in prison for slander and WHICH THE FUCK IS IT, CLAIRE? I want to jump into the screen and throttle *Claire* and put her in a basement to teach her the danger of fake news but I can't do that. And I don't even need to do that because what's this?

It's a user named *Sandra2001* and Sandra says what I needed to hear: *He did it to #MeToo. I didn't even know who Ivan was. A friend (witness) dragged me to his "seminar" at a Marriott and there were so few of us that Ivan said drinks were on him. He paid for the drinks. My friend had to go. He told me he had "literature" in his hotel room. I said he could bring it to the lobby. He said that I was being unfair, treating him like a predator. So we got in the elevator and he took his pants off and I kicked him and got out on the 44th floor. That was ninety-one days ago today. I blamed myself. I got in the elevator. But Ivan should go down. Thank you, Megan. #IBelieveMegan #DethroneIvanKing Also, he sent me dick pics the day after. He said it was "fun."*

I stare at the screen and it might be the only time in my life that a hashtag made me smile. Sandra wants justice and Sandra adds another comment.

Dear ClaireSays and all other women throwing shade. You're not as bad as the men. You're worse.

Sandra wants a revolution. She wants to save other women from Ivan the Predator and she wants it all to start right now.

#MeToo, Sandra, *#MeFuckingToo*.

37

The world moves fast on a story like Ivan King. There have been nineteen more accusations and Ivan is now *trending* on Twitter. Seven hours and eight minutes after *#MeganIsSoBrave* spoke her truth on Reddit, my phone rings. It's you.

I follow the news, so I answer with *empathy.* "Mary Kay, are you all right?"

Ivan is screaming in the background—way to cave in to those emotions, Ivan—and you are quivering. "Joe," you say. "I had *no* idea."

"Do you want me to come—"

"Yes," you say, cutting me off. "Joe, please come over. Now."

I grab my coat—*Here I come to save your day*—and I'm on your street and I spot a For Sale sign planted in your front yard—not anymore!—and I don't fight the big fat smile that comes from deep inside.

I saved you from making a terrible mistake and if the noise in your house is any indication—it is—you won't be abandoning our home to join Ivan's fucking cult. Even on the edge of your property, I can hear him screaming. He's on the phone with what sounds like a lawyer—this is no job for a publicist—and I knock once—polite *and* heroic—and you wave me in. Ivan is out of sight, in the kitchen, and what a relief it is to be here, to see you, Mary Kay. You're you again, in black tights and a black skirt and a purple V-neck sweater. You touch my arm and lean in. "He's . . . going . . . crazy."

"Don't worry," I say. "I'm here."

The Meerkat is stretched out on the sofa with her security blanket—what's up, *Columbine*?—so I sit in RIP Phil's chair while you join the Meerkat on the sofa.

Ivan kicks your wall. "But that bitch is lying, Jerry! Do something to shut these cunts up! They are gonna kill my brand!"

Ivan wanted to be in *GQ* and now he's in *GQ*—the headline of the *hot take* think piece made me happy: THE POWER IS OUT . . . BUT WAS IT EVER ON? Yep, Ivan is a dark star now and his Wikipedia page is blistering: *Ivan King—Middling "life coach" and half brother of Sacriphil front man Phil DiMarco. King rose to infamy when dozens of women came forward and outed the "coach" for destroying their lives.* Ivan still isn't famous but he sure is infamous, and the next time he's in a Marriott lobby bar packed with women, they won't be trying to get into bed with him.

They'll be trying to kill him.

There's more good news, Mary Kay. Ivan's wife, Alisa, started a Twitter account last night and her first tweet was a good one: *#MeToo.*

Ivan throws his phone at your wall and *just* misses a framed photo of you, RIP Phil, and the Meerkat and you snap. "Ivan. That's enough."

"Right," he snorts. "Because that's you, Emmy, always looking out for your *family.* Just calm the fuck down and let me *think.*"

Megan was right, Mary Kay. Ivan is a fucking pig.

I must be patient. You're a lot like Love Quinn, drawn to these bad men, prone to enabling them even when they're abusing you. You should have kicked him out but instead you're providing safe harbor, as he mouths off in front of your daughter—*that Megan came on to me*—and he picks up an empty can and tosses it on your carpet.

"Where's the fucking beer in this house?"

You jump off the sofa and run out to the garage and Ivan continues defending himself by attempting to discredit all *nineteen* women who have joined *#MegansArmy.* It's a classic excuse, the code of dishonor that keeps men like Ivan in control. He grabs his phone off the floor (finally) and shows us a picture of a woman named Wendy Gabriel. "See this one?" he snarls. "I didn't lay a hand on her. *She* grabbed *my* hand and put it on *her* leg. But they don't tell you *that* part of the story." He spits at the article in his phone. "Fuck you, fake news!"

You return from the garage with two beers and he groans—*This is a Michelob Light*—but he pops one can and shoves the other in the freezer and goes back to screaming at his lawyer about how he never harassed anyone. Ever!

I'm worried about Nomi. She's been staring at the same Klebold poem in her book for several minutes now and I'm a protective step-father. I pick up the remote and turn on the TV. She looks at the TV. "Can you put on a movie?"

"Sure. What do you feel like?"

She stares at the ad for an antidepressant. "Something soft."

I go to the guide and see *Cheaper by the Dozen 2* and I click on it and she grunts. "Well not *that* soft. Do they have that *Hannah* movie you told me to watch?"

We're not going there now and she opens her book. "Whatever," she says. "I'm reading."

Ivan is still screaming at his lawyer and we need to get him out of this house. *Ask him to leave, Mary Kay. Do it.* You chew your upper lip and crack your brass knuckles and Ivan says he's *sorry* and it's a hollow apology and his voice peters out as he slams the bathroom door. I get out of Phil's chair and toss the remote to the Meerkat and you follow me into the kitchen.

"Mary Kay," I say. "You don't need to let him stay here. You know how it goes with these things. It's only gonna get louder."

"It's not that simple, Joe."

Nomi opens *Columbine*—*regression* is the word of the day—and you sigh. "This is embarrassing but this house belongs to him."

This is good, you're opening up to me and I nod. "Okay . . ."

"It's a long story. Phil and I weren't the best with money."

"So the house is in Ivan's name?"

You are embarrassed and you shouldn't be and we're so close, Mary Kay, inches away from true freedom. Words away from it.

Ivan slams the bathroom door and he's on the phone again. "You call yourself a lawyer? You wait four *hours* to call me back and you pooh-pooh me when I suggest we offer these girls some money? Since when did all these women become allergic to money? Before or after they became allergic to dick?"

Nomi closes her book and picks up her phone. "I'm gonna go see if I can get back into NYU."

See that, Mary Kay? That's good news and we're already back on track. But then Nomi tosses her phone onto the sofa and sighs. "I don't know who to email about school and maybe I won't even bother with college." She grabs the remote. "I mean why bother when our whole family is so messed up no matter what we do?"

She makes a good point, but she won't feel so dismal once you and I start *our* family. You try to sit by her and she pushes you away. "Nomi, damn it, look at me. I love you. I promise things will get better."

She's crying but she's still fighting you, pushing you away, the way she did when she was inside of you, hesitant to leave your womb and enter this nightmare of a world. The third time you try, she lets you envelop her and she is back in your womb now, crying softly into your bosom.

It's a tender moment between mother and daughter and I remain silent, respectful, but Ivan slams his phone on your table. He spills beer on your hardwood floor. "Well, the witches are winning. Good job to their dads and *great* job to their moms."

"Ivan," you say, reminding him of his own fucking niece. "Come on, now. I'm asking you to cool off."

He whines that he can't *cool off* because there aren't enough places to *sit in this fucking house* so I jump out of RIP Phil's chair. "Ivan, please. Have a seat."

He doesn't thank me and he doesn't move. "I can't sit around while there's an active witch hunt." And then he contradicts himself and takes my chair. The living room is silent, except for the family on the screen. Ivan starts to cry.

My work here is done—you know it, I know it—and I put on my coat and wave goodbye to the Meerkat so that you can send Ivan on his way, which you will. The crying was a white flag and the man knows he is a goner.

But then Ivan sits up and says, "Well there is *one* piece of good fucking news."

You look at Ivan and Nomi looks at Ivan and I *don't* look at Ivan because I don't want to know that he *booked* an appearance on some daytime talk show to defend himself.

He grabs the other beer out of the freezer. "I will be able to cover my attorney fees . . ." He pops the can.

All eyes on Ivan, even mine. And he grins. "Because I sold the house."

Your face says it all. You don't speak. You turn white and you never *really* wanted to move and he's cavalier. Heartless. This is your home and he's boasting about a *cash buyer* and you're looking around the living room—this is where you *live*—and your Meerkat looks at you and snarls, "So what now, Mom? Are we homeless?"

38

You're not homeless. And if any man on this island deserves to be sainted, that would be me. I opened my home to you—Generous Joe!—and you live with me now!

Sort of. It's funny how life comes full circle. When I chose this house, I was in *prison.* I showed it to Love because I thought she'd be happy about the guesthouse, a place for her parents to stay when they visited. She scoffed at me—*That's way too small for them*—but I stuck to my guns because I *loved* my house. It's on the water. It has character. It's not an L.A. *Craftsman*—I got so sick of those houses—and they're popular in L.A. because they keep the heat out. But on Bainbridge, we get weather. You want a house with a lot of windows, a place that lets you soak up the sun. I thought my guesthouse would be empty until Forty's old enough to leave his matriarchal prison, but now you and the Meerkat are in my guesthouse.

It was a rough month, Mary Kay. You had no time for me, too busy pleading with iMan to reconsider and cancel the sale. But that narcissist fuck wouldn't budge, especially when his dutiful wife filed for divorce.

☺

I had to tread lightly. Ivan left to go to rehab—copycat much?—and you began hunting for a new home. You were more exasperated every day, agitated by well-heeled Mothballs making passive-aggressive remarks about your spending, as if going without your lattes would have made you a millionaire. I was polite. And then, two weeks before your pending homelessness, I knocked on your office door.

"How you holding up?"

"Terrible," you said. "Lunch?"

I insisted on taking you out—*That's what friends are for*—and we had a nice, long, *lingering* lunch at Sawan. I mentioned my guesthouse in passing and one week later, you insisted on taking *me* to lunch. This time, we went to Sawadty and *you* mentioned my guesthouse. It was your idea to move in—it *had* to be your idea—and you insisted on paying rent. We haven't been sleeping together—moving is stressful—and my phone buzzes: *Are you awake?*

It's your first night in a new house and new houses can be scary. It's after 2:00 A.M. and I'm your landlord—you *insist* on paying rent—so I respond, as any good landlord would.

Me: *You okay?*

You: *Yeah. This bed is good. Do you have the same kind?*

You're in my guesthouse but you want to be in *my* house and the Meerkat is asleep and your rent check cleared and I tell you to come see for yourself.

Three minutes later, you are knocking on my door and I am opening the door.

You pick up Licious and promise him we'll do something about that *god-awful* name and he wriggles free and that leaves you with free hands. A free body. A free night.

You walk up to me. Slowly. "I'm not here."

I walk up to you. Slowly. "And you're not allowed to sleep over."

Our mouths are close. We are close. Your daughter will graduate from high school in a matter of weeks and that's a big goalpost for us. You'll be one step closer to freedom from being the good day-to-day mom. You tremble. Sore from moving all those boxes onto my property. "And you're not allowed to tell anyone I was here."

You lean into me and bring my hand to your Murakami and you send me to your Lemonhead and you missed me. You want me. I kiss you on the neck. "Mary Kay," I murmur. "How could I tell anyone that you were here when you're not here?"

You wrap your legs around me and I carry you to my bed—YES—and you wiggle out of my arms and jump onto my bed and you bounce. You feel the mattress with your hands and smile at me. "You're such a liar."

"Why do you say that?"

"Joe," you say. "Your bed is *much* nicer than the one in your guesthouse."

First you want me on top of you and then you want to be on top and you grab my hair. "I'm sorry."

"Are you kidding? I'm not complaining."

I am inside of you and I am holding you and you hold on to me. "I just want all of it," you say. "I want all of you all at once."

Sneaking around is fun and we're good at it, Mary Kay. You "loved" the first night that we got back together, but you're right. It's too risky for us to be in my bed when the Meerkat is right next door. So we improvise. You come home for "lunch" and you go to work and "forget your phone" so that you have to rush back home to me and you *always* let Nomi go to Seattle to visit Peggy and Don because Peggy and Don have so many pictures of Phil and so many stories about him. Their shop was a shrine to Phil before he even died and I agree that it's good for Nomi to be with people who loved her father.

There's truly nothing sleazy about our sneaking around. We're looking out for Nomi. I'm happy. You're happy. Hell, even Oliver is happy—*When Minka and I have a kid, I'm gonna pitch this whole two-house setup*—but the Meerkat is having a hard time, she is. And I get it. She misses her house, she misses her father—she's been wearing the same *Sacriphil* T-shirt since the two of you moved in—and sometimes, like right now, you get nervous. One minute ago we were laughing, but then the dark clouds roll into your eyes and you sigh.

"I'm worried she knows."

"Nah," I say. "She doesn't know. And school's not out for another hour and twelve minutes. I set an alarm." You smile at that—you like me—and I tickle your leg but you pull away. I stop. I pull away. "Do you want to stop?"

"Yes," you say, as you caress my fucking leg. And then you bang your head on my leg and groan. "You know I don't *want* you to stop but I'm her mom . . ." And I'm her stepdad. Almost. "She just lost her dad. Maybe she'd be okay with this, with us, but if she *wasn't* okay with it and it made her feel *worse* than she already does . . . Well, Joe, I would feel like such a fuckup that I wouldn't even want be with you. I'd hate myself too much."

"I get that, Mary Kay. And if it's easier to stop until she goes to school, you know me. You know I'd be happy to wait."

I offer to wait and you respond by straddling me right here in the living room, as if the mere notion of us breaking up is so terrible that we have to fuck it out of our systems. After we finish, you button up—so cute—and you stop at my front door. "You want to know my dream?"

Yes. "Yes."

"It's pretty simple. No more changes for Nomi right now. She gets a few months where it's all status quo. We stay in the guesthouse, she has a nice summer, and she goes off to school. Then, before she comes home for Thanksgiving, I tell her about us and she has time to process it before she has to see us together."

I kiss your right hand. I kiss your left hand. "I promise your dream will come true."

You leave and I'm a man of my word and a couple hours later there's a knock on my door. It's the Meerkat.

"Nomi!" I call. "Come on in."

"Can I use your oven?"

"Of course you can," I say. "And I meant what I said. You don't have to ask. I know the kitchen in your place needs work."

"You can say that again," she says, carrying a Pyrex container of brownie mix. "The fridge is loud and the windows are fogged over and I know the cats don't go in there but it really smells like they do . . ." Her father just died. Let her vent. She gulps. "But it just feels weird barging into your house so I'm gonna knock first, okay?"

"You got it, Nomi."

The kid's not wrong about the guesthouse. It's in rough shape because I thought I had years before Forty would show up. The main house has three bedrooms and you and the Meerkat could live in *my* house—and you will soon—but right now, we're all about boundaries, and that's why I love you, Mary Kay.

Nomi preheats my oven and sighs. "Why do you have so many books?"

"Well why not?"

"My mom *hates* when I say that when she asks me something."

I pull out a copy of *The Road.* "You ever read this?"

She takes the book. "I saw the movie."

"The book is better and it does really help after you lose someone you love."

"Who did you lose?"

I look at the oven and nope, not hot enough just yet. "My uncle Maynard."

"Who was he?"

In truth, I only met my "uncle" Maynard once. I asked him if I could move in with him and he said he would pick me up the next day and I packed a suitcase and he never showed up. He just ghosted me and then a few months later he was dead but I know the kid wants to picture me with a family. "Well, he was a ghostwriter. Pretty cool stuff."

"Was he nice?"

"He was the best. We'd go to bookstores and he taught me to play pool and he had this harmonica. You would name a song and he could play it. And he wrote books for famous people who wanted to tell their stories but couldn't do it on their own."

The lie makes me feel good, as if I really did have an uncle like that, and the lie makes the Meerkat relax. The oven beeps and I'm closer, so I put the brownies in and set the timer and Nomi sighs. "My favorite ghost story is about this hotel in Concord where there's one room that's haunted and it used to be a slaughterhouse downstairs." She gets distracted, fucking phones, and loses all interest in me, in ghosts, and asks me to text her when the brownies are done and this is rude, but this is good, less crap for me to remember in case you ask about my "uncle" and she's gone and I text you: *Hi*

You: *Hi*

Me: *Later?*

That's code for "Do you want to fuck in the Whisper Room?"

You: *Well, I don't know. What did you just say to her? I REALLY think she's onto us.*

I never get impatient with you because you have an active imagination. And I love how much you care about people, even when it's a *little* fucking annoying.

Me: *I promise you. She doesn't know. She was just here and believe me, I can tell.*

You: *I don't know . . . I think I was wrong. It makes me too paranoid. We have to stop.*

That's not fair.

Me: *That's fair.*

You: *You're really okay with it? I feel bad . . . You know what I said, I don't want to stop but ahaahhaha. I can't live with this paranoia.*

Our relationship is your mug of piss and it takes every ounce of empathy in me to appease you. I know what I said. I know I said I would *wait*. But this is fucking ridiculous and we are adults and the buzzer goes off. I forgot about the Meerkat's brownies and I did *nothing* wrong—she doesn't know and if she does know it's not because of me—and I grab a pot holder and I take the brownies out of the oven and how the fuck are we supposed to make it through a whole summer?

And then my door opens.

It's the Meerkat but you're right behind her and you're not smiling and why are you here? If you really do want to stop sleeping with me then you shouldn't tag along when the Meerkat comes to pick up her brownies and you barely look at me and the Meerkat barges into my kitchen and picks up a knife. You stay by the door and the Meerkat holds the knife but she does not slice into the brownies.

"Honey," you say. "Don't burn yourself."

I reach for the pot holder and offer it to Nomi but she just holds on to her knife. "I'm *fine*."

Your hands are on your elbows and your eyes are on your feet and no, Mary Kay. *No.* This is not how you play it. You don't come in here and act like you're fucking mad at me—what better way to confirm that we are fucking is there?—and I told you she doesn't know about us and I promised she won't find out. But her eyes are sharp like the knife in her hand and all those knives are aimed at me. "Do you think I'm stupid, Joe?"

"Of course not, Nomi. I think you're exceptionally smart."

She digs the knife into the brownies and you're still by the door, as if you already got *your* punishment. I reach for a pot holder and she hisses. "Don't *dad* me, Joe. We all know *you're* not stupid either so you should know why I'm pissed. How long did you think you could pull this off?"

"I swear to you, Nomi . . ." *No, Joe. Don't fucking lie.* "I'm sorry."

She is shaking the way kids do when they're forced to think of their parents as sexual beings and she clenches that knife, my knife.

You walk into the room now, as if on cue. "Nomi, he said he's sorry."

You're looking at her, not me, and she drops the knife in the sink. "No, Mom. I want him to tell me. I want to know how stupid he thinks I am. My dad just died and that's bad enough but you guys run around together behind my back and now he wants to stand here and *lie* about it."

You rub your forehead—bad sign—and Nomi's shoulders are shaking and is she crying? I made your daughter cry and you're never gonna forgive me and I need your help and I look at you but you're . . .

Laughing.

The Meerkat turns around and she wasn't fucking crying. She's laughing too and she raises her knife and winks at me. "Gotcha!"

You. Fucking. Bitches. "Wait," I say. "Did I just get played?"

You are bowled over by the door, possibly peeing your pants, and the Meerkat picks up the pot holder and carries the brownies to the table. "Mom, omigod, I swear, you almost ruined it with your little 'don't burn yourself.'"

You are Red Bed red and you are kissing me on the cheek. What the fuck is happening? "I know," you say. "I don't know why I said that."

"I'm a little confused," I say, because of the kiss, because of the laughter.

"Well," Nomi says. "I'm not retarded."

You sigh. "Nomi . . ."

"Sorry," she says. "But anyway, I asked Mom about you guys . . . not that I *needed* to ask, but she told me and I was like . . . okay. What's the big deal?"

I look at you. You smile. "Outta the mouths of babes."

You're happy because your kid is happy and your kid is happy because she pulled off a prank on me. We're not gonna be like the fecal-eyed bores next door. We're gonna have *fun.*

You check in with me—*Sorry if that was too much*—and I tell you the truth—*You guys got me*—and we're in flow, Mary Kay. This works. This isn't the dream—your dream was unrealistic, like most dreams—and this is real life. Real us. So much fucking better and this is what it means to be part of a family. I get the plates and the Meerkat cuts the brownies and you pour milk into glasses and we sit around my table like the family that we are, going over it and over it, how funny it was, how good you were, how *stupid* I was to fall for Nomi's little trick. This is love. This is love I never knew and we stuff our faces with brownies and you sigh. "What a relief."

"You're welcome," Nomi sasses. "I mean no offense, but you guys are so stupid. I will say, though, it was kinda fun watching you think you're so sneaky and I am sorta gonna miss it."

It occurs to me that the Meerkat might be covering her real feelings with her snarky, no-fucks-to-give jokes and I look at you—*Is she really okay?*—and you nod at me—*Yes, we talked.* You smile at me and I smile at you and the Meerkat looks at you, she looks at me, she looks at the brownies, and she sighs. "I think I'm gonna puke."

When you stand up to get more milk, you squeeze my shoulder and your touch is different now. Better. You love me openly, right in front of your daughter, and it's the first surprise party of my life and it's the best surprise party there ever was.

"Okay," Nomi says. "Can we please talk about something that's actually important?"

You nod. I nod. Such great fucking parents!

"Joe," she says. "I know I'm supposed to say it was nice of you to let us move into your guesthouse, but it's also kind of *not* nice of you because I mean . . . have you been in there? It's so freaking musty and it smells like old people!"

"Nomi, it smells fine," you say.

"Oh come on," I say, looking at you, looking at your daughter. "Why do you think I stopped working on the renovations? Part of me thinks we're just gonna have to burn the thing down."

It's our first collective plural and you laugh and Nomi clamps her hands together. "Okay so can we please, please, please stop this stupid charade and just move in here already? I mean if Mom and I stay in there, I feel like we're gonna die of some fast-acting lung cancer or whatever. Please, you guys. *Please.*"

We laugh like a family and Nomi gives us space to talk and you are the future cofounder of the Empathy Bordello. "She's being dramatic, Joe. It's not *that* bad and please don't feel like you have to say yes."

I too am the future cofounder of the Empathy Bordello. "Well, I was more concerned about you," I say. "I won't be hurt if you're not ready to live with me just yet."

You punch me. Gentle fox. "Oh, please, Buster. You know I'm ready."

We call the Meerkat back inside—she gets the Whisper Room—and we pack boxes like a family and our first family hug happens naturally. It feels right. This is the story of life. People move on. After we move your things, we cook together and we eat together—burritos and salad!—and the Meerkat puts my cats on her Instagram—*our cats, our house*—and then the two of you hang out in the Whisper Room—women need to talk, about this, about me—and I'm not your codependent husband. I tidy up the house and I deal with the litter box and I turn off the light and get into bed to wait for you, hoping that you and Nomi aren't sinking into some mother-daughter slumber party. And we really are in sync because I'm not in bed five minutes before I hear the door close downstairs and it's real. That's you on the stairs. This is you in my bedroom, our bedroom.

"Well," I say. "How's she doing with all of it?"

"I mean . . . she's great. I don't know why I was so worried."

"I do," I say. "Because you care."

"Yeah," you say. You stroke my hair. "I liked it when you looked at me at the table, when you wanted to make sure that it wasn't just bravado on her part, that she really *was* okay about us being together."

I take your hand. "Well, I like it when you read my mind."

You air-kiss me and pick up a jar of face cream and rub cream on your neck as if you think we're going to *sleep* and you gaze at my empty red wall. "I mean . . . can you believe this day? Can you believe we're actually here?"

"You really had me going there for a second, so I'm *doubly* happy we're here."

You rub some of that cream on *my* face and that's more like it, Mary Kay. "Oh come on," you tease. "We had you going for a full *minute*. You were scared."

I take that jar of antifucking cream and put it on the nightstand and I take your wrists in my hands. "If you must know, yeah, I've never been more scared in my life."

After we make love—this is our life now!—you wash your face and reapply your *night cream* and you are a woman, so you feel the need to rationalize your decisions. You tell me things I already know, that Patton Oswalt got remarried only a few months after his wife passed away, that he has a daughter, that no one gets to tell anyone how long the grieving process goes on. You take a picture of us and you crop the picture—we don't need people to know we're in bed—but we are Red Bed official and we are Instagram official and the Meerkat is the first one to *like* it and more likes are pouring in, so much love, and you like those likes and it's our first night as a couple and the Meerkat texts you. She wants to know if she can take the blanket off my sofa and I tell you that she doesn't have to ask.

"This is our house, Mary Kay. My stuff is all of our stuff and you can both do as you please."

You kiss me on the cheek. "You're my mind reader, Joe. I love you."

And you do. You do.

39

Yesterday I preordered two copies of a new Murakami because this is our life now. You've lived here with me for twenty-two sleeps in our house, where *we make the rules* and your books are all mixed up with mine. Your Murakami kisses mine and your Yates leans into my Yates and you are there, on the steps to the sunken living room, our sunken living room.

"I don't know if you know this, but we do have access to a library."

"No shit?"

"You're funny, Buster."

"Well, someone moving in . . . blending the books. It's new to me."

There are times when I am a kid again, too young, and you are the *Sassy* creature who is too old for me, but then your hand finds the back of my neck. "Remember, we're less than ten years apart so . . ."

"So I'm the same age."

You kiss me. "I never did this either, you know? Phil . . . well he wasn't much of a reader." And then you sigh. You sit on the Red Bed sofa. "I think I did something wrong."

"What did you do?"

You put your feet—always in socks, something I know now that we live together—on the coffee table and it still astounds me, you being here, Nomi down in the Whisper Room watching *Dirty Dancing*, your dirty dishes in my sink, your shoes lined up on my doormat. I sit by you and kiss you the way you kissed me in the window at Eleven Winery last night. You remind me that Nomi is downstairs and I laugh. "I'm just trying to find the logic. It's okay to make out in full view of everyone at the winery on Winslow and put a selfie on your Instagram for the whole world to see . . . but this is too much? She's downstairs."

You jab me. "Don't make fun of my Instagram."

"Rest assured, Mary Kay. I will *always* make fun of your Instagram."

This is why we're good, because we're different. You're a show-off. A fox who wants everyone to know about the wolf in your den, and I'm helping you remember that the best thing about happiness is that it's yours. Ours.

"Okay," I say. "Fess up. What did you do that's so awful?"

You look down at your iPad. "Do you have anything going on later this week?"

"Nothing major, why?"

You hand me your iPad and you didn't do anything *wrong*. You planned a trip for us and we're going to another island that you describe as *Cedar Fucking Cove: The Victorian Version*. You promise that Port Townsend is a Victorian paradise of old homes and you tell me that we'll have *Victorian sex*. You keep saying that you're relieved that I'm excited and how in the hell would I be anything *but* excited? "You'll love it, Buster . . ." I love that sometimes I am Buster and other times I am Clarice and I kiss the top of your head. "This is fucking perfect, Hannibal."

"Is it? It's just two nights but honestly, two nights is enough and there are people there that *live* like Victorians and I just . . . I can't wait for you to see it."

This is the second surprise party you've thrown in my honor and the Meerkat emerges from the basement. "Hi, guys. Bye, guys."

"Where you going?" you ask.

"Seattle," she says. "Peg's friend has this daughter . . . I dunno, she's okay and her friends don't suck. Whatever. I have to go."

Your Meerkat is off *Columbine* and she's wearing a new T-shirt and you tell her to take a jacket and she groans. "I'm not eleven."

She slams the door and you laugh. "Is that my child?"

I tell you that all change, even good change, is hard, and we go at it on the Red Bed and I tell you to put *that* on Instagram and you laugh—*Such a sicko*—and we eat our beef and our broccoli and we go to bed full, satiated, but the next day you wake up screaming. This happens sometimes, you have nightmares. I try to take your sad song and make it better but you won't tell me what you dreamed about. My phone buzzes while I am spooning you.

"Who's texting you?" You're never at your best after your nightmares, and your voice is full of suspicion as if I would ever lie to you.

My new friend Oliver. "My old friend Ethan."

"You should invite him up. He has a girlfriend, right?"

I open the 1stdibs app and inquire about another David LaChapelle and I don't want you to meet my *friends* and I squeeze you. "A wife," I say. "And that's a great idea."

I put my phone away and you pull away and walk into the bathroom naked and you turn on a song—"Hallelujah"—and oh. You were dreaming about your rat and I go into *our* kitchen and turn on *my* music and I am a good guy. You are allowed to mourn in your own fucked-up way and I pour milk onto eggs, onto flour and I dream too, Mary Kay. Sometimes whether I like it or not I see RIP Beck in the cage and RIP Candace in the water at Brighton Beach, alive, swimming in a sea of blood.

"Mmm," you say, dressed now. Ponytail low. Did you rub one out in the shower? "I'm starving."

I flip a pancake and you smile and stretch your arms above your head and hold them up there. Cracking elbows. Twisting. "Who is this?"

"Rilo Kiley. 'With Arms Outstretched.'"

You laugh and I laugh—your arms remain outstretched—and you say, "Do you know how fucking happy I am right now? Because I just . . ."

I stretch my arms, just like you. "I love you so fucking much."

"Good," you say. "Because I'm really liking this whole life-is-a-gift thing we have going on."

You are walking to the door to head to work—you go in every day but for me it's only three days—and you reach for the doorknob. But then you let go of it. You stare at a box of trash bags. "When did these get here?"

Yesterday at 4:12 P.M. "I don't know. Does it matter?"

"I told you I was gonna get trash bags. I completely forgot."

I walk up to you. *Closer.* "And I ordered some online. It's no big deal."

You cluck. I reach out to you but you don't want that. "Look," you say. "You've never been married. You've never lived with me. I'd tell him I'd pick up almond milk and I would *mean* to pick up almond milk . . ." AND YOU DID PICK IT UP. "But then I'd forget."

"I don't care about ordering trash bags."

"Not right now," you say. "This is all brand-new. But here's the thing. Next time I forget to pick up trash bags, and there will be a next time, you won't realize it, but things like that . . . they build up and then before you know it, you'll resent me. And I'll resent you because like you say . . . we're talking about something as mundane as *trash bags.*"

"Mary Kay, I don't give a fuck about trash bags. I will never give a fuck about them."

But you look at the trash bags. "Every day, I drive in to work on a high, you know? Because this is a dream, being with you. But then when I'm about to head home, I get nervous. Is this gonna be the day that he's just fucking *sick* of me?" You gulp. "Is this gonna be the day that I'm just fucking sick of *him*?"

That last part was a lie. You're afraid because you know you'll never be sick of *me* and I hold your hands. "Can I say something?" You answer with your eyes. "Look, Mary Kay, I'm not a dream come true. I'm not perfect . . ." I used to have *terrible* taste in women. "But I want you to know that I am never leaving you. And I know that sounds trite."

"It doesn't."

"I don't have a crystal ball."

"No," you say, warming up now. "You don't."

"But just so you know, every day, when I know you're on your way home . . . well, that's my favorite part of the day." You raise your eyebrows. Playful. "Well, I say, it's my favorite part of the part of the day when I'm not in the same room with you."

That was all you needed and I fixed it and we put our heads together. Our foreheads. I can feel your cells commingling with mine. I can feel our hearts pushing, wanting to get *Closer* as in closed. Fused.

"Joe," you say. "Promise me you're in this for the long haul."

"I promise you, Mary Kay. I'm not going anywhere. You're stuck with me."

You laugh and hum a little of that old Huey Lewis song and then you turn serious. You clamp your hand around my forearm and you don't let go. You squeeze to seal the deal, the greatest deal of my life. "Good."

40

Here's the thing about us. It just gets better. The library is fun. It's slow, and that gives us time to play our own subtle game of hide-and-seek. I love feeling you watching me when I push Dolly Carton around the first floor and I love when you slowly go down the stairs toward the Red Bed, making sure that I know to follow. You were right about this—it's a fucking *blast*—and you are right about everything and it's hard not to throw the books at the wall and scream at the top of my lungs I FUCKING LOVE YOU, MARY KAY DIMARCO.

The day drips on and the quietude is eerie. It's dead lately, which gives us time to hatch plans for our Bordello. But sometimes quiet is too quiet and you whisper at me—*I think our sex vibes pushed everyone away*—and you are right. Love is powerful that way, and finally, it's time to go home. We feed our cats and we fuck our brains out again—yay!—and once again we're naked and sweaty, wrapped up in each other. Coming back to Earth.

"What a day," you say. "And I can't wait to get away for a few days. Is that awful?"

"Not at all," I say. Because it isn't.

"Hey, have you heard from Seamus?"

"Not much . . . I think he's out of town on some CrossFit thing . . ."

"Does he seem off to you?"

Stupid, yes. Shallow, yes. Off, no. "Well, I think it's to be expected. It's hard for people who are alone to see two people fall in love."

"Right," you say. "Everyone says that love makes the world go around but it also makes the world a cruel, exclusive place, like a book club that tells you there's no more room at the table."

You are so smart and I kiss your forearm. "I'd be depressed if I was in his shoes."

"Oh no," you say. "He doesn't like me like that . . ." Of course he does. "I just worry."

"I think that's natural. When things are really good, you worry more than normal."

You are vulnerable and there is goop in the corners of your eyes. "Yeah."

"But tomorrow we're gonna go to Victorian Cedar Cove."

You grin like a kid. "Yeah."

"And everything is gonna be fine. Assuming that Victorian sex isn't dangerous."

You laugh. "Victorian sex is perfectly safe, I promise."

"No, Mary Kay. You and I are perfectly perfect."

Soon you are asleep, snoring and even *that's* not annoying. I'm too happy to sleep. I order some more balloons for Nomi's graduation party next weekend—I bet *Phil* wouldn't have ordered balloons—and I pick up one of your Murakamis and I'm half-reading, half-daydreaming about you as you dream on my body. I love to look down and see you there. I love that you want to be here with me and I feel like I can see the neurons firing inside of your mind, forging new pathways, everything leading to me, to happiness.

I'm hungry, so I go downstairs to fix a snack. We're out of eggs so I grab a Hostess Cupcake—RIP Melanda had good taste in junk—and I tear off the wrapper and the cupcake tastes like childhood, like sugar.

And then my phone buzzes. I have one new text message, and that message is from Love Fucking Quinn: *We need to talk.*

She never writes to me and my legs fill with pins and needles. I put my phone on the counter and no. This is not happening. I'm hallucinating—I should have gone to sleep like you—and my screen is black and maybe I *was* hallucinating.

But then my phone lights up again. One new email from Love Fucking Quinn.

She's never texted me and she's never emailed me but she is the *mother of my son.* All the worst thoughts flood my mind at once—*Forty fell down the stairs, Forty drowned in the pool, Tressa stole Forty*—and I grab my fucking phone and I walk outfuckingside and I call Love Quinn on the phone.

The phone rings once and she doesn't pick up and I see my son in the arms of some pervert who played the Injustice System and got a job at Disneyland. The phone rings again and I see my son with half his face torn off by a Rottweiler—Love trusts bad dogs, I don't—and the phone rings a third time and I don't know where my son is right now. Did he just crawl out of an open window in a high-rise in New York City and are my tears from heaven? Did he die without ever getting to meet his own father?

"Well, hello," she says. "I thought you'd be sleeping."

"Is Forty all right?

"Aw, I'm good, Joe. Thanks for asking."

"Is he sick?"

"I think I have new allergies, but I don't have it in me to get tested. All those needles . . ."

The level to which I did not miss the sound of her voice . . . I cut her right off. "Don't fuck with me. Is my son okay? Yes or no."

"Joe . . . He's fine."

"Thank God."

"Well, okay, but maybe more like thank *me* because I'm the one who actually takes care of him . . ."

"What's going on, Love?"

"I sent you an email. I bought you a plane ticket and you're coming to L.A. tomorrow."

I say nothing because that's what she deserves: nothing.

"All right," she says. "It's simple, Joe. I need to see you. *We* need to see you. So I bought you a plane ticket."

If I ask her to wait until Monday she might hang up on me. I want to see my son. I want to be with you, Mary Kay. My neurons are being torn in half.

"Joe?"

"I'm here."

"Good. And you'll be here tomorrow because if you're not . . . Well . . . you're doing *so* good with your girlfriend and her daughter. I mean I know you'd *hate* for them to find out about the family you left behind . . ."

She knows. How does she know? And she's doing it again, twisting all the facts, and I want to climb into the phone and choke her out and it's twenty-fucking-twenty-one and WHY CAN'T WE TELEPORT? I am steady. *Breathe, Joe, breathe.* "I didn't leave you, Love."

"Oh yes you did," she says. "You got into a car my parents gave you and you drove to a house my parents bought for you and those are the facts. I'm sure you've twisted it all in your head to make yourself some kind of victim slash martyr . . . but I know things. And if you want me to keep my mouth shut . . . Well, I'll see you tomorrow. Today actually. So you better go back to bed. The car will be there soon."

She hangs up on me and I *can't move, I can't breathe, I just die underneath* and she is the shark inside my shark. She cut me open and extracted all my secrets. I puke off the side of the deck and I look upstairs and the lights are still out in our bedroom.

I get in my car—*a car my parents gave you*—and I call Oliver and I get voicemail and I text Oliver—*911*—and I call again and it's soothing in some demented way, like knitting while the person you love is in surgery. Finally he picks up. Groggy. "Joe, it's a little late."

"What did you tell her?"

"What did I tell who?"

"Love called me, Oliver. She sent me a plane ticket. And we had a fucking deal."

"Slow down."

"I bought every piece of *art* you wanted and you said you had my back. You said you'd keep the Quinns out of the picture."

"Joe."

"What?"

"Are you calm?"

"Am I calm? She bought me a fucking *plane* ticket."

"And what did you do before that?"

"Oliver, you've been stalking me and watching my every fucking move and you know I did *nothing.*"

He sighs. "First of all, I don't know anything about a plane ticket."

"Bullshit."

"Second of all, if my ex-girlfriend who is the mother of my *child* was both well-heeled and . . . well . . . a little dramatic, I think I'd think twice about bragging about my brand-new fucking make-a-family on a public forum."

"I did *not* post a picture of Mary Kay. I only post books."

But he railroads. "I wouldn't let the whole world know that I'm in love with a woman and I wouldn't want my *ex* to see me playing dad with another family because I'd be smart enough to know that my ex wouldn't like that, my friend."

"Oliver, for fuck's sake, I didn't post a goddamn thing about Mary Kay."

"Ah," he says. "But your MILF did."

I take the hit and Oliver laughs and I hear Minka in the background. "See," he says. "Minka says this is a double fuckup because your lady friend tagged you. Which makes it seem like you thought you were being coy, ya know, posting without posting."

It's no use fighting him because Oliver is right and Minka is right and I never should have let you throw us to the wolves. But I did let you do it, didn't I? It's not your fault for *wanting* to post a fucking selfie but it's my fault for going along with it. You make me so happy that I got stupid. I did this to myself and I was doing so good. I did not kill Melanda. I did not kill Phil. I did not kill Ivan.

But I might have just killed us, Mary Kay.

The call ends and I can't feel my feet and my eyes are twitching. I walk upstairs to our bedroom. You're still sleeping but in the morning you'll wake up and I won't be here. I pick up a notepad on my nightstand. I grab one of your tchotchke pencils. Virginia Woolf's head in place of an eraser. The absurdity of this moment. The horror. I don't know what to tell you and my flight is in a matter of hours and I just promised to be *here.* With you. I scribble lies on a notepad—my bullshit words are sticks that will hurt you—and the last two are stones.

Love, Joe.

You know I love you, but you don't know that I can't avoid Love Quinn. I pull the covers back. I get into bed and you are in a deep sleep, but even in this state, you are drawn to me, moving into me as you make room for me. Such a good fit. The only true fit I've ever known. I hate that you'll wake up tomorrow and realize that RIP Melanda was right all along, that men always let you down, that they bail on you because men do fucking suck. But so does Love, Mary Kay. So does love.

41

Bon Jovi said that true love is suicide and he was right. Love is trying to kill us, Mary Kay. I got off the plane and I got into the black car she sent for me and now I'm at the door to a *honeymoon suite* at Commerce Fucking Casino. She's in the room. She's listening to my George Harrison—*Hare Krishna, Hare Forty*—and I knock on the door like an ABC prime-time *Bachelor*-brained loser, like I want her rose. She opens the door and she is thin, thinner in person than she is on Instagram and she's wearing a Pixies T-shirt, as if she likes the Pixies, and see-through panties. I smell kombucha and salad water and *matcha* and did I really love this creature or did I only love what it felt like to be *inside* this little creature?

She doesn't kiss me. "Come on in, Joe."

There are rose petals on the California king bed and the bathtub is full of *Veuve* and she thinks we can go back to that first night we fucked, in the tub full of pissy bubbles and I didn't want that then, I don't want that now, and I hate rose petals. I hate overpriced champagne and she doesn't get me, not the way you do, and that's when I feel something dig into my back.

A gun.

This is not a duel—I don't have a gun—and Melanda was right—A GIRL IS A GUN—and if anyone should have a weapon it's *me.* She stole my child.

"Ah," she says, as she makes eye contact with me in the mirror. "So you don't miss me."

"Love, put down the gun."

"Just say it. I know you. I *feel* you not wanting me. You don't love me. You're not excited to see me."

"You have a fucking gun on me."

"Oh please. That doesn't scare you. Don't forget, Joe. I know you."

She doesn't know me. She knows things about my past and I am not that man anymore and I slowly turn around and face the woman who made me a father. "Love, it's a two-way street. Don't forget that I know you too."

She grunts. "Like hell you do."

"Love, you don't want me back. You can't do what you did to me and then tell me that you 'love' me with a bed of fucking *rose* petals."

She grunts. "You're such a snob. You really are, Joe."

"See that. There it is. All of this . . . I don't know what it is, but it sure as hell isn't a grand gesture and you can't point a fucking *gun* at me and tell me that you want me back."

"I'm just responding to you," she says. "You started it. You don't want *me*."

"You paid me to go away. You . . ." I look around. I want him to be here—he's my son—but I don't want him to be here—she has a gun. "He's not even here, is he?"

"Who?"

"My *son.*"

"Right," she says. "*Your* son. See, it's usually the girl who uses the guy to get the baby. It's usually the woman who loves her kid more than her husband. But then, you're not usual, are you?"

"What are you trying to say?"

"You fell out of love with me the day I told you I was pregnant."

"That's ridiculous. The baby was just as much a surprise for me as it was for you. Just because I was excited about becoming a father . . . Love, put down the gun."

"No."

"Well which is it? Rose petals or bullets?"

"Say it."

"I was in *prison.*"

"And I was pregnant. What's your point?"

"I told you, Love. The only reason I survived in there—the only reason I didn't lose my fucking mind—was the fact that we were gonna have a family."

"Right," she says. "You should put that on a card, Joe, 'I only fell in love with my girlfriend when she was pregnant with my baby and I knew I spread my seed.'"

"How can you say that?"

"Because it's true. Because the minute I told you about the baby, even *before* you got arrested . . . you didn't look at me the same way. You didn't want me. You wanted *your baby.*"

"Love, put down the gun."

"You notice that every time I tell you the truth, you tell me to put down the gun?"

It's true, but she ended all possibility of an honest negotiation when she pulled out that fucking gun and that's the only fucking "truth" that matters right now. She could shoot me, so I have to stay calm. *Gently, Joseph.* "Come on, Love. You know that's not true."

"You're incapable of love, Joe. You couldn't see your face every time I risked exposure to disease and criminals . . . spiritually . . . physically . . . but every time I went to see you, you didn't look at *me.* You looked at my body like I was a fucking piece of Tupperware carrying your *lunch.*"

"Put down the . . ."

She smiles. Evil. Spoiled. *Wrong.* "What did you say, Joe?"

"You're not remembering things clearly. I was worried about you, all the stress . . ."

"Aw," she says. "You didn't think I was durable enough for the job, did you?"

"Yes I fucking did."

"Ah," she says. "So you *did* think of it as my 'job' to carry your offspring into this world. The second you knew about your seed planted inside of me, I stopped being a person to you."

"It's not like that."

"Oh, so what? You go to 'jail' and you think you're so *experienced* and you just fall out of love with me because I'm out shopping for the baby and meeting with doulas and not obsessing over *you* twenty-four hours a day?"

"Bullshit," I snap. "Do you know what I *was* obsessing over in that fucking hellhole? You, Love. I could *feel* you turning on me a little bit more every time you visited. I hated the fact that I couldn't shop for cribs with you or meet the goddamn doulas, but I blamed the *system*. You, on the other hand, you blame *me*."

I too speak the truth but she holds the gun, so she's ranting again, raving about how I didn't love her. This, coming from the woman whose family paid *mercenaries* to get rid of me as if I am the one in this family with all the problems. She's the sick one. She's the one who told me that I didn't kill RIP Beck or RIP Peach because they were both just *using you for their murder-suicide story that began before they even knew you*. And the worst part is that I did fall out of love with her. I *too* was a little less excited every time she visited.

I *wanted* to love her. I did. But I couldn't. It's the big things—she used our *baby* as a chess piece—and it's the little things—she prefers the fake snow at the Grove outdoor shopping mall to real snow—and she's still ranting and she feeds my son *guac* and *cilantro* and I obeyed her wishes. I moved away. I went against the rules of fucking nature to appease her and what does she do to me? She hits me when I'm up—I don't *want* to love you, Mary Kay, I just fucking do—and Love points at the sofa.

"Right there," she says. "And don't try to fight me. I am prepared to shoot you. This thing has a really good silencer . . ." As if I don't know that she can afford *all* the best things, as if that isn't the reason that she's so demented, because money doesn't make anyone happy unless they do something good with it. "I practiced," she says. "I've been spending time at a gun range and if you try to fight back . . ." This, from a woman who stole my *son*. "I mean it, Joe. I will kill you."

"I don't want to fight you, Love. I came here to make peace."

People who have kids like to tell people who don't have kids that there are things you can't understand until you become a parent, that parenthood *changes* you and that you don't know what love is until you become a mother, a father. It's an insulting position that makes you realize how loveless so many people actually are. But they are right about one thing. Motherhood does change women. This isn't Love Quinn. This is Love*Sick,* armed and dangerous.

My phone is off and you're awake by now—I'm sorry, Mary Kay—and Love is pacing, chewing on her fingernails, what's left of them, and is she on meth?

"I'm not happy, Joe."

"Well, I'm sorry to hear that."

"Are you?"

"Of *course* I am. You have every reason to be happy. You have Forty. Is he with your parents?"

"My parents don't know I'm here, Joe. I'm not a teenager. I don't tell them every single thing I do." She cocks her head. "And I don't know why you're pretending to care about Forty now. You always wanted a girl and you *never* wanted a son. Your friend Mary Kay has a daughter, now doesn't she?"

It's a sucker punch and I didn't see it coming and I can't keep up with her. The floor is shaking—there are earthquakes in Los Angeles, even when there aren't—and Oliver was right. *That's* what this is really all about. I remain calm. "Love, I've always loved Forty. I'm thrilled to have a son. And Mary Kay has nothing to do with us. I met her because you sent me away. Let's be reasonable."

"*Reasonable.*"

"Love . . ."

"Joe, you were never *reasonable.* I mean you say that like I don't know what you're capable of."

I grit my teeth. *Was* capable of.

"Yes, I was postpartum . . ." She *is* postpartum. "And I 'sent you away.' But you're you. I thought you'd swim through the moat and throw rocks at my window. I thought you'd fight, that you'd steal him or die trying or blow your brains out."

"You know I'd never blow my brains out or put our kid in harm's way. We put the child first. That's all I did."

"No," she says. *Unreasonable* and more spoiled than ever and imagine what she's doing to my *son.* "All *you* did was stalk me on *Instagram.*"

"What did you expect me to do? You didn't block me."

"I was trying to be nice."

"So you think that's 'nice'? You think I should be content to watch *videos* of my son."

"Well, I know you. I know you're more at ease watching people from afar than really getting close to them."

Not anymore. Not since you, Mary Kay. "That's just not true, Love."

"Well, here's what *is* true. You found your little librarian and you think you get to have your nice little life and still spy on *us*?"

"I never wanted to be a spy. I wanted to be a *dad.* I am his dad."

"You drifted," she says. "You didn't see us at the zoo last week . . ." I was with you and Nomi and it's not *my* fault that stories disappear. "You watch less and less, as if we're not entertaining enough for you, as if you don't need us anymore. I know, Joe. I *always* look at the list of viewers and do you know what it was like to look at that list and see your name less and less?"

FUCKING INSTAGRAM AND NO ONE SHOULD LOOK AT THAT FUCKING LIST. "Love, Instagram isn't real."

"Well, time is real, Joe. And you invested more and more of your time with your *new* little wannabe family, which says a lot about how much you 'love' your little 'savior.'"

"And what about you? You don't have a moat. You're not a helpless fucking princess. You didn't call me up and say *Hey, what happened to you?* What do you want me to say? How can we make this work?"

But she isn't my *co-parent.* "Well, look at that," she says. "Love and happiness agree with you, Joe."

"I'm not happy," I lie.

She laughs. "Are you kidding? You are so *happy.* Most men . . . if you took away their son and the woman they supposedly love, the only woman alive who really knows them . . ."

"You did that, Love. *You* sent *me* away, Love."

"And you left," she says. "Do you even care what it's been like for *me*?"

"Of course I care." But I don't care. Not anymore. I love you, not her.

She picks at the barrel of her gun. "Well, I got jury duty."

"I thought your dad always got you out of that?"

"This time I went," she says. "Like some everyday person with no connections, you know, like a *librarian.*" She has the gun and the money so she gets to play dirty and I stay silent. "I left Forty with Tressa and drove to the Clara Shortridge Foltz Criminal *Justice* Center. They make you park a mile away and I had to walk all the way from Disney Hall but I got there . . ." I wish you were here, Mary Kay, because as my cofounder of the Empathy Bordello you would see what I see, a profoundly lonely woman with no one to talk to, no one to listen to her describe her day. "I brought my chargers, LäraBars . . ." She winks at me and my blood pressure spikes. I told her RIP Beck ate LäraBars and I miss the man I am with *you.* "So then I got selected . . ." She flips her hair like she got a part in a movie. "I went upstairs and I saw this poor guy in these dress pants that are five inches too short with his lawyer, who was *terrible* . . ."

"Love, we both know that the *Injustice* System is rigged."

Her eyes narrow. "Seriously, Bainbridge Boy, can I just tell my story?"

I nod. I have to remember. Love is unloved. Lonely. Los Angeles.

"We got numbers assigned and I was number one . . ." Oh that's right, she's an *actress.* "The judge asked me all these personal questions about my history and he goes around the room asking everyone and everyone's telling their story and I just . . . I feel so close to these people, like we were in this together, like a family, you know?"

No, I don't know. "I get it. That's a lot to take in."

"They sent us home and I went out with some of the jurors because we were all so *shook* . . ." I don't like the word *shook*. It's a fake word, and this is fake news. "And we wound up at this lounge downtown and it was a *really* late night . . ." Her voice drifts in a way that reminds me that Love is perverted. "Anyway I went back the next day but I didn't get picked to be on the jury. I started reaching out to my new friends and they all just . . . blew me off. Every single one of them."

She's so lonely and you would feel bad for her too, Mary Kay, even though she's making it impossible for me to comfort her right now. The gun. The *gun.* "I'm sorry, Love. I am."

"I miss my brother, Joe. I miss having my people. I thought those people could be my people . . ." Los Angeles is the opposite of *Friends* and my heart hurts for Love, it does, but I don't want Love. I want you. "Anyway," she says. "I told Tressa and Mom and Dad that I got picked. For the past few weeks, I've been here, 'sequestered.' "

Living in a casino would drive anyone crazy and I tell Love that we can get her some help and she shakes me off. "No," she says. "I don't need help. I know why I didn't get picked for the jury and I know why everyone blew me off. See, the judge asked us if we could be impartial in spite of our experiences. Most people said no. I said yes. I know how to love people who do terrible things. It's who I am. It's how I was *born.*"

"Well fuck the jurors, Love, because if you ask me, that's a beautiful thing about you. You have an open heart. It's no reason to be sad."

"Do you think I don't know what you did to my brother?"

My nerves go haywire and no. "I did nothing to your brother."

"You were in Vegas with him. You dragged him to the desert."

"Love, you don't know what you're saying."

"I knew it, Joe . . . in my gut. And I kept waiting for myself to fall out of love with you because if those girls . . . Well I didn't know them. But Forty was my *brother.* He was my *twin.*"

"I didn't kill your brother."

"No," she says. "But you didn't save him either."

"Love, come on. No one could have 'saved' him . . ." He was beyond redemption. "You make it sound like I was with him, like I could have stopped him from jaywalking, like I could have stopped that car. I didn't want him to *die* . . ." Of course I wanted to fucking kill him. He was blackmailing me, erasing me from all the work I did. And yes, I almost did it in Vegas, I *wanted* to end his life. But I didn't, just like I didn't kill Melanda or Phil. Wanting is not a crime.

"Julie Santos," she says. "I think of that woman every day."

The name is *Saint* Julie and I nod. "It's not her fault. It's not my fault. Love, you're right. Twins have a bond and nothing can get in the way of that and no one knew him like you. So no one misses him like you and I can't change that, but I can help."

"No," she says. "You can't help. We're the same. You lost your *son* but you're up there bopping around like the happiest guy on earth . . ."

"You saw a couple fucking pictures and I didn't even post them."

"But you're in them, Joe. You don't care about us because you can't care."

"Yes I do."

"No, Joe. See, my brother killed my *dog* and I still loved him. But *you* . . . You lose your son and what do you do? You run off and find yourself a new family. There's something wrong with both of us, Joe. It's a fact."

"No, there isn't, Love. We're not defective. We're survivors. That's a *good* thing."

But she just points the gun at me. "Get up and turn around," she commands, and she is *the shark inside my shark* and she unlocks the safety and I look out the window at the City of Commerce and I won't let her win, not when I'm finally happy, not when I finally have everything I want. I can't do this to you. I tell her that L.A. brings out the worst in her, in everyone, that I'm better because I *left* and that she could be better too.

But she just laughs. "Oh, Joe. I'm not gonna live in your *guest-house.*"

"Love, listen to me. I miss Forty every second of every day and you know I can't be happy if you're not happy."

I started in the truth and swam into a lie and she knows I don't love her and she says she knows I wanted to leave L.A. "You didn't leave because of the *contract.* You left because you were afraid to be a father. You know me. You knew I was never gonna sign on to that *Bainbridge* plan. You might not realize it, but that's why you came up with that dream. To push me away. And I understand it, I do. You didn't come back to find us because deep down, you know that I'm just like you. Bad beyond repair."

Those are dangerous words and when a toaster is *bad beyond repair* you don't break out the screwdriver. You don't try and fix it. You throw it in a dumpster. And there are dumpsters in this building, in this casino. "I'm here now, Love."

"Right," she says. "Just like me."

We don't belong in the same boat and I know where this boat is going: down. I have to paddle. I have to fight. "Love, we're not bad people."

She won't look at me. She won't give me an oar. "You're here because you love them, not me, but I won't let them wind up like my brother, Joe. Like those girls. I can't do that. I won't."

She raises the gun and her finger squeezes the trigger. The explosion is silent, deadly. The circuit breaks. The lights go out all at once and I fall into a black hole.

42

The black hole succumbs to white light and white light reveals white walls and all the beeping tells me that I'm not in heaven. I'm in a hospital and the beeping is incessant and where are you? Where am I? There was a gun. Love had a gun.

A nurse named Ashley runs in and she looks like Karen Minty and I didn't kill Karen Minty. I set her free and she's alive and well in Queens married to a cop, pregnant for the second time in a year. I'm alive too. I lived. I ask West Coast Minty what happened and she smiles. She has long blond hair and she wears too much eyeliner. "You got shot, honey. But you're okay. The doctor will be in soon."

"How long has it been?"

She points to a whiteboard and it's been who the fuck knows how many hours and *thirteen days* and I tear at the sheets because I missed Nomi's graduation—did my balloons arrive and do you think I bailed on you?—and where is my goddamn phone? West Coast Minty wants me to calm down and I have rights. I want my phone.

"Honey," she says. "Your dad has your phone. He'll be back soon. Just take it easy."

I don't have a *dad* and I might not have a girlfriend anymore—Do you hate me? Do you know where I am?—and as promised, as threatened, the doctor is here with a herd of nondoctors and where the fuck is my "dad"? West Coast Minty deserts me and my doctor looks more like a real estate agent than a physician and *I really do fucking hate L.A.* He flips through my chart. "So how are we doing, Joe?"

I tell him I need my phone and the not-doctors laugh and say that my sense of humor is intact. The doctor points at my head. "I have three words for you, Joe. Location, location, location."

He really did miss his calling in real estate and he brags about his work, how he "saved" my life, as if that isn't his fucking job, as if I care, as if I don't need my fucking phone and all the details go in one ear and out the other and I don't care that less than five percent of people recover from this kind of gunshot. WHERE THE FUCK IS MY PHONE?

"We'll keep you here for a couple more days."

In the great tradition of Mel Gibson in *Conspiracy Theory* and countless other survivors who claw their way out of hospitals, I smile. "That sounds good."

"You're a lucky man, Joe. I'm not sure if you're religious, but if there's someone you want to talk to, we have plenty of people."

I want to talk to *you* and I need my fucking phone and he leaves—nice bedside manner—and I'm not *lucky*. Love kidnapped my son and shot me in the head and where is she? Where is my son? Where is my fucking phone?

I press my emergency button and I sit up in my bed. Calm now. "Ashley," I say. "Can you tell me what happened?"

Ashley knows it all.

She *freaking loves The Pantry* and she moved here from Iowa hoping that she would meet famous people and she did. She saw Love's movie and that's why it's so hard for her to tell me what happened but it's also why she's so excited to do it.

"Love shot you," she tells me and then she checks the door for the tenth time. "And you do promise you won't tell them I told you? I don't wanna lose my job."

"Ashley, I swear to God."

She holds my hand and I look at her knuckles and think of your knuckles and then Ashley Minty tells me that Love Quinn is dead.

The words are garbled. My brain won't let them in. My heart flexes. *No.* Love Quinn can't be dead. Love Quinn gave *life* to my son and it's not her time and yes, she was upset. She was down on herself. But we've all been there and she wouldn't do that to our son. She couldn't do that to our son. Ashley is wrong because she has to be wrong.

"No," I say. "That's impossible."

"I shouldn't have told you."

"Ashley, wait."

But Ashley Minty does not wait. She grabs her charts and makes me swear again not to tell anyone and I look around the room. "Who is there to tell?"

She leaves and I start crying and I'm still at it an hour later and Bon Jovi can fuck off because true Love isn't suicide after all. It's attempted *murder*-suicide and my son has no mother, not anymore, and the only thing worse than a bad mother is *no mother.* I have no father—*Your dad has your phone*—and I'm alone, as if I have no son, no girlfriend, no stepdaughter, and my eyes are pounding, my head is throbbing and then my chest is on fire and there is a voice.

"Easy now."

The voice belongs to Ray Quinn, older and a little wider, so many more liver spots on his face. He's standing in the doorway and comes to sit in the chair by my bed. He hands me my phone—*a* dad, not *my* dad. Love's dad.

"All right," he says. "So it's like this. We've told our friends and family that Love had cancer."

"Did she?"

"No," he says. "Let me finish because you need to hear every word I say and make sure you remember every word. Understood?"

I nod. As if I'm in a position to remember anything.

"We told the authorities that you were mugged in that casino."

I wasn't mugged. Love shot me. And then she shot herself. "Okay."

"It's a nasty place, that Commerce, and the drug fiend . . . the shooter . . . well, he knew where the cameras were, so that's why there's no security footage."

I glance at my phone and Ray is old school. "Are you listening?"

"Yes," I say, and I finish my text to you: *I'm sorry. Can I call you?*

"So basically, if I'm asked . . . Love died of cancer."

"Cancer."

"What kind?"

"Women's cancer." *Really* old school and he rubs his eyes. "Cervical," he says.

"And I got shot in the hallway."

He stares at me. "Yes, you did, Joe. Yes you did."

My phone is deathly silent and Love is dead and death is all around me, it's in Ray's hollow eyes. I want you. I need you. You ignore my texts and I get it but I got *shot.* My son is an orphan. This is too much at once and Ray sighs. "If you'll excuse me."

The second the bathroom door closes I call you and I get voicemail. "Mary Kay, it's me. I'm sorry. I got . . ." I don't want you to worry. "I'll be home soon. I'm okay, and again, I'm sorry."

I go on Twitter and sure enough, there's Tressa posting a Beatles song she doesn't know by heart: *This is for you, Love Quinn. Still can't believe it. Kombucha smooches forever. #RIPLove #FuckCancer.* I click on Love's obituary. It's all lies. They don't tell us that she lied about being sequestered with a jury. They don't tell us that she bought a weapon of mass destruction in Claremont and they don't tell us that she tried and failed to kill me, that she succeeded in ending her own life. Los Angeles can fuck off and die because it really is the loneliest place in the world and I stare at the last line of the fake news story.

In lieu of flowers, we ask for donations to the American Cancer Society.

Ray comes back and he must hate himself right now. He had two children and neither one made it to forty. He sits in the chair by my bed, the chair that's meant for the people who love you.

"So," he says. "How ya feeling?"

"I'm in shock. You?"

Ray ignores my question and lugs his body off the chair. He moves like a Mafioso and time hasn't been good to him, shuffling in shiny crocodile loafers. No socks. Doused in cologne, as if that isn't rude to do when you go to a hospital. He locks the door and is that allowed?

"You okay, Ray?"

Then he turns, flying across the room. He takes off his necktie and comes at me and wraps that tie around my neck and *I can't move, I can't breathe, I just die underneath* and I punch the air but I'm weak. Finally he loosens his grip. And then he throws the tie at me and spits. "Dottie," he says. "The only reason I can't do it is Dottie."

I still can't breathe. He said he won't kill me because of Dottie, but he wants to kill me, and if he did, I too would get "cancer." He picks up his tie and he's meticulous with it, looping it around his big fat neck, making that knot just right, casually talking about *his* father, who taught *him* how to properly tie a tie. Ray had a great dad. I had no dad. I still don't know how to tie a fucking tie. But a good childhood doesn't mean shit because I'm not the one in here trying to *murder* someone.

"All right," he says. "You woke up and they warned me that might happen. So how much more is it gonna take to get rid of you once and for all?"

I don't want money—I survived a gunshot—and the "family man" should know better. "I just want Forty, Ray. That's it."

"Forty grand?"

Unbelievable and yet I should have expected it. "My son."

He makes a fist and he lowers his hand. "He's not *your* son. You walked away."

"You pushed me away and I went because that's what Love wanted."

"Icicles," he says. "Icicles in your veins."

"He's my son."

"And you tell me you'd take good care of him?"

"Yes, I would."

"So you're a reformed man. Mr. Community Service up on Bainbridge Island?"

"We'd come to visit once a month. More than that."

"And you've been doing well up there?"

"Ray, I'm the first one to thank you for all that you did for me. And you've seen me. I've been crying all day and I'll *never* get over this and I'll never forgive myself for not getting that gun away from . . ." I don't want to say her name. I'm not ready. "Look, let me do the right thing here. Let me take care of my son . . ."

"Well . . ."

He doesn't say yes but he doesn't say no and I sit up. I look him in the eye. "You know it's what she would want."

"Oh, kid," he says. "You're in no position to speculate about my daughter's wishes. She wanted you to go away."

"I know," I say. "But she made that plan when we were apart. She was, well . . ."

"It's in the genes," he says. "Dottie was postpartum, too." He rolls his eyes and if only *he* could get pregnant and crawl on all fours and bleed and shit and give birth. Maybe then he wouldn't be so cavalier about what it means to have a baby and that's not what I meant but I nod. "Ray, you're right. She made the contract. She wanted me gone. I know this will sound stupid . . . but she didn't block me on Instagram."

"Speak English."

"She made all these Instagram stories, right? And when you make stories . . ."

"Movies?"

"Pictures. Videos."

"Who wrote the scripts?"

I AM GONNA LOSE MY MIND. "They're like home movies. You put them online and you decide who can see them. And it's very easy to block people, Ray. But Love *wanted* me to watch our son growing up. And I think she'd want me to step in and watch out for him."

"She shot you in the head."

I have no fucking comeback for that and I never should have brought her *stories* into this mess.

"I'm a reasonable man, Joe . . ." He just tried to kill me too. "And Dottie and I aren't getting any younger."

"You look great, though."

I count his liver spots and he smiles. "Thanks, son. Now you're up in . . . Mercer Island, is it?"

"Bainbridge," I say. "And it really is a great place to raise a family. The house is terrific, thank you for that. And I have a guesthouse. We could do this together. Forty could live with me. And you and Dottie, well you'd be welcome anytime, all the time."

He reaches for his phone and is this really happening? I can see it now, Mary Kay, you and me and my *son* and your Meerkat and things really *do* work out for the best—Sorry, Love, but maybe you knew Forty needs me now, right now—and Ray is old school, a tad violent, but he knows right from wrong and he knows that what Love did was wrong. He's a father and *I'm* a father.

He tosses his phone onto my lap. "Here's a story that *I* watched recently."

It's like another bullet hit my head, only this time, I don't black out. I'm in the video. I'm lugging RIP Melanda into the hole in Fort Ward and that "movie" is only telling *half* the story. I did *not* kill her. I did not do it. Oliver was supposed to be my friend. He gave me his word. This is not fucking fair and Ray just smiles. "We're the same in that way, Joe. I too call 'em like I see 'em. And I see you."

"Ray, that's not what it looks like. And you can't trust Oliver . . ." And I did trust Oliver. "He must have doctored that footage. I didn't kill Melanda. She committed suicide in my house."

"And I suppose you didn't kill the rock star either . . . the one whose wife you're schtupping up there?"

I'm not *schtupping* you and I tell the fucking truth. "No, Ray. I didn't kill Phil DiMarco. He had substance abuse issues and he took some bad pills."

His liver spots darken. "You're poison, Joe. This Melanda person . . . this Phil you mention . . . Do I need to remind you that both of my children are *also* dead because of you?"

It's not my fault that his kids are fucked up and a lot of rich kids don't outlive their parents and my heart is pounding and did Ashley poison me with adrenaline?

"Now you listen here," he says. "I am a father. You are nothing. You are a sperm donor."

I am a father. "Ray, please."

"I provide for the child. I make the money so I say what goes. And right now, I say you won't get within a hundred feet of my grandson for the rest of his life. My daughter wasn't a good shot . . . but if you try and get near my grandson . . . Well, Joe, my men don't miss.

He slams a contract on my tray table and then he drops a pen. "All right, Professor. Sign."

This is it. This is a moment of my life. This is my second chance, the second time a Quinn bullied me with a contract. "Ray, you're making a bad decision. You have the wrong idea about me and Forty will want to meet his father one day."

"Over my dead body," he says. "No. Scratch that. Over *yours*."

The sun is bright today, showcasing Ray's liver spots. He sees them in the mirror every morning, ominous blotches that remind him that he won't last forever, no matter how well he does with his investments and his tax evasion. I will outlive this American Oligarch and *that's* why he hates me, not because of what he thinks I did to his children. He knows that I know that he failed as a father. This is not a do-over. This is new territory.

He has the money. He has the power. He has guns. This is why it takes time to smash the patriarchy. People like Ray Quinn don't just have the support of the Injustice System. They own it. If I want to live to meet my son, I only have one option: I sign the contract.

I have faith in my son—*Hare Forty, Hallelujah*—and Hare Ray's liver spots, too. Cancer is coming for that bastard and who knows? Maybe it's already here.

43

The doctor and the nurse wouldn't let me leave, Mary Kay. They held me hostage—*If you don't have your health, you don't have anything*—and on my third day of recovery, Howie had a seizure in the library. I read about it on the Bainbridge Facebook page.

I texted you—*I know you're mad, but how's Howie? I'm worried about him*—and I meant it. I was worried about the Mothball. But you ignored me.

I wasted sixteen days of our *life* in that hospital bed because sure, health is fun, but what good is health without love? I called you, Mary Kay. I texted you. You ignored me and then you ignored me some more. I ordered Bene pizza for you and the Meerkat on Postmates and the delivery was *incomplete.* Just like us. I missed Nomi's graduation—unforgivable, like missing the birth of my *son*—and I can't see you on Instagram—you blocked me—and the Meerkat has gone quiet on her own profile.

"Now, there's no refill on this prescription, but these should get you through the worst of it," the outtake nurse says.

I grab the fucking pills and my plastic bag of papers and I bang on the elevator buttons—come on—and I hightail it to Burbank Airport but my flight is *delayed* and I sit there watching planes come and go, listening to Stephen Bishop songs blur into Steely Dan songs and *finally* it's time to board.

We land at SeaTac and now that I'm really here, really close, it's starting to hit me.

You might not ever forgive me. After all, Love never forgave me.

I call a Lyft and I get into the Lyft and I board the ferry and the I AM BROKEN clock is still broken and I disappeared on you. I broke my promise to you.

We reach Bainbridge and the parking lot is buzzing with tourists and bicycles and it's not summer just yet, but the men are in sandals and the mommies are in light little jackets and time has passed. Is it too much time?

I walk all the way home and I turn onto my street and you were right, Mary Kay. This isn't *Cedar Cove.* If it were, you would be watering our flowers and making a visor with your hand and waving at me. *Joe! You're here!*

I walk into my house and it doesn't smell like brownies and you filled the cat food dispensers and Licious stares at me as if he's not sure who I am—Fuck you, cat—and Riffic hisses—Fuck you too—and Tastic doesn't even get off the fucking couch, so fuck him the most but no. They didn't do anything wrong.

I did.

Your shoes are not lined up on the doormat and I call Oliver and a woman with a Lebanese accent says *there is no Oliver* and that's typical. He changed his phone number. He was never my friend and his house is furnished and people in L.A. just use you to get what they want and I walk to my guesthouse and I hope to see your things in here, but my second little house is empty too. You ghosted me and I have to breathe in spite of my pain. You only ghosted me because you think I ghosted you.

I would never do that to you and you know that deep down, don't you?

I am a wounded soldier of Love home from WWIII. I clean myself up and I *should probably* drive to the library instead of walking but I like the idea of you seeing me wounded, struggling and sweaty. When I get there, I hesitate at the front door of the Bainbridge Public Library and then I take a deep, first-page-of-a-new-book kind of breath and I open the door and there you are in the same spot where you were the first day I laid eyes on you. You drop your book on the counter. Splat. Roxane Gay today, a far cry from our Day One Murakami, *all but sucked inside.*

You march across the library and I follow you outside and you head for our love seat. You don't sit—bad omen—and you make two fists and you seethe. "Oh, fuck it."

Now you sit—omen reversed—and I sit too. You cross your legs, tights even today, in early summer, like a widow in mourning, and do I put a hand on your knee to remind you of the heat between us? I don't.

"Mary Kay."

"Nope. Don't even try."

"I'm sorry."

"Nyet."

"I got shot."

"That's nice."

That's *not* nice and I touch the bandage on my temple and you fold your arms. "If you came here looking for pity, you may as well just leave."

"I know I fucked up. I was in the hospital, Mary Kay. I got *shot* and I called you . . . I texted you . . . Hell, I tried to send you guys a pizza."

You nod. "Howie died."

That's not my fault. Howie was a widower hanging on by a thread, by a poem. "I know. I saw. And I texted you when I read about it and I called you . . ." I can't make this about me. "How are you? How was Nomi's graduation?"

You uncross your legs and clamp your hands over your knees as if you don't want me to see them, let alone touch them. Your knuckles are brass mountains. Mute.

"Hannibal, I know I fucked up. I'm not trying to make excuses."

You don't call me Clarice and your voice is new. "I think you should go."

"We have to talk about this. You can't just punish me because I got *mugged.*"

Foxes are nasty, they kill house cats, and you are no different. "You just don't get it, Joe. And I'm going back inside."

"Wait. You have to let me explain what happened."

"I don't 'have' to do anything. And this is our pattern. I see that now. It's always me telling you that you don't owe me an explanation or you telling me that I don't owe *you* an explanation and we tried . . . but it doesn't work."

"This is different."

You shrug. "We're a bad fit. We're always apologizing or making big ridiculous leaps that neither one of us are really prepared for. I don't hate you. But I know this doesn't work."

"You can't do this to me, Mary Kay. You can't refuse to *talk* about it."

"No, Joe. See that's the thing that you don't seem to understand about relationships, about women. Your feelings are not my responsibility."

Yes they fucking are. That's called "love." That's called "us." "I know that."

"So let's be adults. I messed up too. I realize I was coming on way too strong, moving in with you, asking you to never leave me . . ."

"You were not coming on too strong. I loved all of it."

"You don't get to say that after what you did, Joe. Actions speak louder than words. And you sit here and you don't even understand why I'm mad, do you?"

"You're mad that I left. But, Mary Kay, I left you a note."

"A note," you say. "Yes, you left me a note. *Mary Kay, I had to go to L.A. for a family emergency. I'll call you when I land. I'm so sorry. Love, Joe.*"

That is why you're mad at me, that fucking *note.* But you memorized that note and I still have a chance. "I'm sorry."

"I don't care if you're sorry, Joe. I care that you didn't wake me up to tell me what happened. I care that you were vague. When people are *together* they tell the truth. They don't say bullshit like 'family emergency.' They grab your shoulders. They turn on the lights and they tell you *exactly* what happened and they ask you to come with them, Joe. That's what adults do."

"I'm sorry. Look, it wasn't family, not *exactly.* But this girl I dated in L.A., her family is terrible . . ." It's true. "And she got sick and—"

"Joe, it's too late. You're wasting your time."

You say that but you don't move and you're right but you're wrong. "Well, how about seeing it from my perspective, Mary Kay. You were married to someone, *I know.* And God bless him, may he rest in peace, but he dumped every single thing on you every single day. He didn't hesitate to unload on you at 4:00 A.M. and did you ever think . . . maybe I was only trying to let you get a good night's sleep? Did you ever think maybe I did that because I thought that was a good way for me to love you in that moment?"

"Maybe it's not in your nature to love."

Goosebumps sprout on my arms and fresh bullets zing my head, my heart. That's the worst thing you ever said to me and we're on our fucking *love seat* and you sigh. "I'm sorry. This is exactly what I didn't want. I didn't want a fight, and I do hope your ex is all better, but it's over, Joe. And you need to accept that."

I rub my head, just enough to remind you that I am *wounded.* "Well I don't think it is."

"I'm actually happy that you brought Phil into this . . ." I never should have brought that rat into this. "Because it really is about him. The *one* day he needed me to be there . . . I was with you. I'll never forgive myself for that, Joe. And this whole disappearing act, the wounded warrior bit, you're right. It does feel too familiar. I'm not gonna spend any more of my time taking care of a man who walks out on me and comes back wounded and needs me to fix it." You take a deep, end-of-the-book kind of breath, as if you are ready for this damn novel to be over, and then you offer your hand as if you no longer believe in love.

You say that dirty word again. "Friends?"

Love didn't murder me, but she got what she wanted in her psychotic depressive state. She murdered us. I shake your hand—*Friends*—and the power goes out all over my body and I walk to the parking lot. I am in no condition to walk, to drive. I find shade beneath a tree.

"So it lives."

I look up and it's the Meerkat. She aged while I was gone. Or maybe that's just me and maybe I'm in denial because she also regressed again. She's back on *Columbine,* squinting.

"Nomi," I say. "Congratulations, graduate. How you doing?"

"Well I didn't get stabbed in the head."

"Shot," I say. "But it's no big deal."

She wants to see the wound up close and I tell her to stay where she is because if you are watching us—and I hope you are watching—I want you to know that I'm not using my *wound* to get attention and I would tear this *Band-Aid* off my fucking head if I could. She nods. "Cool."

"Look, I'm sorry about disappearing . . ."

"Oh, I've barely been here. I made some friends in Seattle, been at Don and Peggy's a lot. Anyway, are we moving back to your house? Cuz the Marshall Suites is so gross and I *hate* sharing a room with my mom."

You hate me so much that you moved into Oliver's old hotel and damn you, RIP Love Quinn. "Well," I say. "Your mom's not too happy with me right now . . ."

She shrugs. "My mom's never happy. Except when she's with you." And then she rocks back and forth on her sneakers that are too young for her, sneakers that light up. "Seriously, Joe, see you soon. I mean it's fine. It is."

She says that with such confidence and she knows you in ways that I don't. She's known you her whole *life* and she tells me that she's right about you, Mary Kay. You *are* happy when you're with me and that *is* the bottom line and I see you in the library. You see me and the Meerkat catching up. You know this is meant to be. The Meerkat takes off—*Sorry you got shot in the head*—and I look into the window, into your eyes.

You don't wave but you don't give me the finger. You turn your back on me right now and pretend to be busy with a Mothball—you're not—but you're not done with me. I just have to make things right.

The walk home is brutal and my head is throbbing and I *should probably* have taken a cab from the ferry to my house and I *should probably* have lain low on my first day back. I finally give in and pop a pain pill and I pick up your filthy doormat and throw it into the washing machine—I have to get *our* house ready for you to come home—and I watch the doormat go round around—it's the drugs, I hate drugs—and I put my hands on the glass—*see the boats go sailing*—and I am drooling and sweating and my head is full of tainted cotton candy.

These pills are too much and the doormat is a sailboat. I'm hallucinating. I hear Stephen Bishop in the airport, singing about women in Jamaica and then the music that isn't real dies and I am back in my house and my feet are on the floor of my laundry room and these are my feet and the doormat isn't a sailboat.

But I am not alone.

I see a man in the glass. This is *Bainbridge* and it's safe but I was gone for two weeks and criminals do this. They watch houses. He probably thought I was gone.

He takes a step forward and I make a fist and his shadow is clearer now and this is *Bainbridge* and it's probably a misunderstanding, a neighbor concerned about the sudden activity in the house. But Bainbridge is an island in a state in the country of America, and America is violent and if the man were here on a wellness call, he would say it.

I squint like the Meerkat and take a closer look at his reflection. I see a baseball cap and narrow sloping shoulders. He is short. Short as Shortus. I turn around and it is Shortus but he didn't *pop by* my house to make sure I'm okay. He's armed and I'm empty-handed and slow—drugs are evil—and the blow is fast. *Thwack.*

Man down, Mary Kay, one of the good ones.

44

People say that victim shaming is a bad thing, but sometimes, the victim *should* be fucking ashamed. I took a goddamn pain pill on an empty stomach and I didn't lock my doors, as if I'm some fourth-generation Bainbridge bum fuck who refuses to lock his doors because once upon a time the island was safe and you didn't *have* to lock your doors so you know what? I deserve to be tied up by a *sixth*-generation Bainbridge CrossFit lunatic in his Olympic Mountain hideaway cabin.

Shortus didn't do this to me. I did this to myself.

I smell Windex. Clorox. Things that end with the letter *x*, and I can't punch him—my hands are tied—and I can't kick him—my legs are locked at the ankles—and I have a head wound and I don't know karate.

He put a bag on my head. I can't see. He stuffed a sock in my mouth—I think the sock is dirty—and I wiggle my tongue and this is not how it ends for us. Shortus will not *kill* me.

Or maybe he will because he's close now. "You just couldn't stay away, could you?"

I make a sound and he spits at the bag over my face. "You worm your way into that library. You worm your way into our *lives*. That piece-of-shit has-been crybaby drops dead and you worm your way into her *house.*"

I was right. This is about you. I try to *worm* the words out of my mouth but the sock won't let me and he's on his feet now. *Stomp, stomp, stomp.* "And the worst part is, I knew it. I knew you were bad news." You and me both, asshole. "You move here and suddenly all's I hear about is *Joe.* He *volunteers.* He *reads* a lot. In my head, I'm thinking, *Sounds like a fucking pansy.* But she won't shut up about you. So I figure, I gotta meet this guy, see what he's about. And then I get a look at you and you're soft. You got no job. You're a loser. I'm thinking, This poor loser's no *threat.* I get you a deal at CrossFit, I let you tag along for beers, even though everyone thinks you're a fucking snob. But do I worry? Nah. You crash lunch at the diner and you're talking *chick flicks* with Melanda. You're an even bigger pansy than I thought and I think . . . good. Maybe that feminazi will finally shut up if she gets some good dick in her."

I knew that lunch with your *Friends* was a bad idea, Mary Kay, and he's twisting my words and this is Twitter in real life. I am muted. Blocked.

"I let you mope around in your slick sweaters . . ." Cashmere isn't slick, you moron. "I let her go on about how *smart* you are even though you didn't even go to college . . ." Even in Cedar Cove there has to be some asshole talking about *college* and FUCK YOU, AMERICAN CASTE SYSTEM. "But I'm no dumbass, you sweater-wearing volun-fucking-*teer.*" The bump on my head is playing Ping-Pong with a hockey puck in the *hole* in my head and he's close again. Breathing. "She had it bad for you. You got her to move *in* with you." I think I hear his heart. Does he have a knife? "Even then I wasn't worried. You moved in on *her* after the has-been finally croaked and all girls go nuts when they're sad. I wasn't surprised when you split. I told her myself, *You can't trust a man who doesn't take care of his body.* And I was *just* about to get back in there." I smell urine. He's peeing on me. On my legs. "You shouldn't have come back, pansy. And you shouldn't have gone to the library and tried to get her back."

He zips up and *this* is why you kill people, because most people are horrible. He kicks me in the balls and it's so predictable that it doesn't hurt quite as bad as it would have were there an element of surprise and the pain in my balls is another hockey puck and now my balls are in the game with the hole in my head and the bump on my head and is this how I die? From *Ping-Pong*?

"The whining, man. *Joe came back. I need time to think.*" He kicks me in the balls again. "I said, *You're outta your mind. He's a loser, can't even commit to CrossFit.*" Oh God, he thinks he's my *trainer* and he kicks me in the leg and my shin is in the game too now. Ping. Pong. Pain Pong. "I've been working that girl for *years,* and unlike *you,* I never ran away. *Never.*"

That's a kick to my other shin and the Pain Pong is now a tournament, a death match and *signs, signs, everywhere signs* and I missed every fucking one of them. You called him *a saint, truly* and the first time you ever told me about him, you were defending his honor. He cleaned your gutters, an animal marking his fucking territory the same way he marks his body with that Cooley Hardware logo, so that you see *his* last name and think maybe you could be *Mrs. Fucking Cooley.*

He spits in my face. "No job. No muscles. No *nothing.* That's what you are."

You were wrong about him but you were dead-on about me and I *am* bad at reading people and how did I not realize that his hardware store is a jealousy trap? He refers to those women in his shop as *girls* to make you feel old. Endangered. And the reddest flag of all: He gave your daughter a job in his fucking store. No wonder she quit. He probably bugged her ten times a day—*So, how's your mom, Nomi? Tell her Uncle Seamus said hi.*

My life doesn't flash through my eyes, but I remember things I didn't know that I remember, like Melanda's notepad in her phone, how she griped about Mary Kay and Seamus: *MK's attachment to Seamus is so weird. I know she was only seventeen when they hooked up and I know it was only five minutes but eeeew.* I should have known then, same way I should have known when he blasted Kid Rock at the gym—the remake song about the teenage summer fuckfest by the lake. He's been carrying a torch for you since you were seventeen years old.

He growls. Close. "Look at how soft you got. What did you even do for the past few weeks, pansy? Cuz I can tell you weren't working out."

There is no conversation subject more boring than exercise and this is why it's dangerous for women to be "nice" to men, Mary Kay.

He swats the side of my head. Ping Pain. Pain Pong. "You split town. You come back outta nowhere and she's ready to jump your bones. But Saint Seamus is here to make things *right.*" He got Roman on the *Succession* quiz, Mary Kay. He's evil. Pure evil. "Are you listening to me, Jewberg? You're done with her. It's over."

He hits me and he kicks me and it's March Madness in my head and it's the World Series of Pain in my balls and if I get out of this, those Big Pharma fuckwits will be getting a strongly worded letter from me. Their little pain pills don't do shit and he punches me in the face.

"She's *mine,* you piece of pussy-ass Hebe shit." I'm only half Jewish and I whole hate him and you would too if you could hear him right now. "And she's gonna be mine forever and you know why, Hebe?"

I haven't heard that word since I was ten years old and he is close now. Breathing at me. On me.

"Because I'm a man, you bookworm little bitch. And in the real world . . ." Oh, Shortus, Bainbridge Island is not the real world and in the real world, people in situations like this die. RIP Beck died. She *kept a knockin'* but she couldn't get out and am I next? I flex and I push but I can't get out and he's too quiet. I remember that first touch in the library. Your hand in mine. *Don't tell the others.* I didn't, Mary Kay. *You* did. You told the others. You threw us up on Instagram. You are a fox and you wanted to show off, you wanted to kiss me in the window at Eleven Winery and you wanted everyone to know we were living together. You wanted your *Friends* to approve and it's not the pain, it's not the possibility of death, it's the fact that we really could have had our family if you had just thrown your arms around me a few hours ago, when I was in the kind of pain that can be healed with a hug. Now you're going to lose me and I don't want that for you. You've already lost so much.

Shortus yanks me by the neck and my body hits the floor and the

Pain Pong tournament is a melee, hockey pucks hurling on every playing field in my body. "I'm not gonna kill you," he says. "You think it's so 'safe' up here and it is. Our people are good people. But we got animals, Jewboy. We got *lots* of animals and one of them is going to get you."

45

My back is up against bark—he strapped me to a *tree*—and I still can't see because of the bag on my head. Birds chirp and I can't call for help. I'm still gagged and Shortus has a rifle. It's too soon. Love only pulled a gun on me a couple of *weeks* ago—look how that worked out, she's dead—and you called this man the *Giving Tree* and he calls me a *tree hugger* and I can't fucking talk. He is close again, close as in *armed* and for fuck's sake, America, GET RID OF YOUR GOD-DAMN GUNS. "Today's the day you become a fucking *man*."

The good thing about a bad childhood is that it prepares you for hell in the adult world and Seamus didn't cut off my limbs—positive thinking—but he has a bucket of blood—whose blood?—and he's splashing it on me like holy water and this isn't a cold and broken hallefuckinglujah. This is grim. The ropes are tight—naval knots and he wasn't in the fucking Navy but he did go to *camp*—and a lot of people would lose their shit but unlike the coddled Peach Salingers of this world, I don't need help when it comes to self-soothing. I know how to survive and I will survive because he said it himself—you *have it bad for me*—and you want to be with me. You are here for me now, in the blackness of my panic. In my mind I see you on our love seat and you see me and you want me to be okay—you love me—and I don't want you to worry so I try to make you laugh. I sing because you like it when I sing and you know the tune. *How will I know if he's gonna kill me? I say a prayer but I'm tied to this tree.* Shortus breaks my song with a gunshot—pop—and he shoots an animal and I bet it was a rabbit because he spits and grunts, "Sorry, Thumper."

He picks up his bucket of blood again and splashes it on my back, on my skin. "We need some *real* critters," he says. "These bunnies are bullshit."

I can't believe it either, Mary Kay. Your *Friend* is pouring blood on me to lure innocent woodland creatures and so far it's just tiny ones, rabbits and squirrels, but he lets them get close. I am sniffed and I've been nipped and then he kills these living things and I am safe but I am not fucking safe. What if a bear comes? There are bears, if I'm to believe him, and *Dying for love is so bittersweet, I'm asking you how the fuck you didn't see through this psychopath?* You fade. I can't see your face. He kicks the back of my knee. "You pissed yourself like a little bitch."

I hear his Timberlands pounding, he's walking away again and the bucket is in play, more blood on my body and he's howling for coyotes and if they come in a pack—and they do move in packs; they're like *Friends*—we are dead. Both of us. He hoots and he makes catcalls—*Come on, cougars, I know you're out there*—and he is a fourth-grade boy picking out his favorite wild animal for no good reason.

He sits somewhere and he mews at the cougars and are there cougars in these mountains? He laughs. "Are you crying, pussy? Oh man, you know I wish we *did* put some meat on your bones. Cougars gotta eat too!" He mews again and he says that Robert Frost was right and no poetry. No. "Nothing gold can stay, Ponyboy . . . I love that movie, man. I do." It was a *book,* you fucking moron, and he snorts. "Fucking bullshit ending, though, because Ponyboy shoulda croaked like his little bitch-ass friend. The soc's . . . they were the good guys but the movie makes 'em all out to be so bad just cuz they got good families." He shoots something. A bunny? A squirrel? I don't know. I can't know. "See, you're what happens in real life, fucking hoodlum, how long you been here and not *one* friend comes to visit? Fucking freak."

I hate when he talks because I can't hear the branches or the footsteps of God knows what might be approaching and Shortus finally *does* stop talking but then I hear the branches and the footsteps of

God knows what and the theme of my bar fucking mitzvah is death and he's on the move. Running. In my face.

"Don't even think I'm gonna let some little squirrel peck atcha, pussy. You need to bleed. Just like all the little bitches do when they man up and become women."

I *am* fucking bleeding—the ropes are cutting my wrists—and I try to talk and I shake my arms and he spits at my arms. "That's rope burn, you pussy. You need to bleed like a man."

He's on the move again, Timberlands on leaves, *crunch crunch crunch,* and I see you in a hall of mirrors and you sing to me, you want to save me—*There's a man I know, Joe's the one I dream about*—and you are safe in a cushy hall of mirrors where nothing bad can happen to you and I am here in the woods. There are jaws on my leg. *Teeth.* That's my skin cracking and that's my blood leaking onto my pants and then *Pop.* The jaws let go and it's another bunny down but I am wrong. Shortus whistles. "Huh," he says. "I think this fox was pregnant."

He killed a fox and you are my fox and he's doing something different, shaking his phone. "Man," he says. "When I get back down and I see her, I'm gonna tell her she was right to bitch about the shitty Wi-Fi. I can't even get the score on the Sounders game."

You were here with him—how could you do that to me?—and the image of the two of you in these woods is a *shark inside my shark* and he's a liar. Shortus lies. This I know for a fact and I have to decide that you were *never* here so I do that right now. He killed my fox and he drops his phone. He heard something. I heard it too. Something larger than a squirrel and this is the Stephen King book *Gerald's Game* and unlike Gerald's wife, whose husband was dead and bad, I have someone to live for: you.

I beg and I plead with the universe to call off the cougar—or is it a bear?—and I promise if I get out of this I will do better. I will be the best goddamn man on planet fucking Earth and Gerald's wife had it easy. No bag on *her* fucking head. My senses are hot-wiring and I can't hear and I can't see and I feel the tongue of something wild, something incapable of knowing the difference between a good man like me and a scorpion salamander of a man like Shortus and is it a wolf? *Pop* and the living thing whinnies and drops and Shortus sighs. "Duck

duck *goat.* Goddamn hippies and their goats. Just do your yoga and leave the animals out of it."

RIP goat—no supernatural forces coming to save me in this dull fucking neck of the woods—and Shortus drops his weapon. The flies are all upon me now, loud and close. Mundane.

"Whole shit ton of girls out there, Joe, and you just *had* to fix your eyes on mine."

You're not branded. You don't belong to him. I scream into my sock.

"The worst part about all this, oh man, she tells me she wants you and she says that me and her can be *friends.*"

That's your right, Mary Kay, and when you said that to me did I kidnap your husband? No. I accepted your terms and this is what I get for it and I scream again. It's no use.

"One week ago, one fucking *week* ago she was in my cabin with *me* and you come back outta nowhere and boom. Finito. She'd be here right now if it wasn't for you, you bookworm piece of shit."

It hurts to think of you in these woods with him and this is not how I want to die. Knowing that you slept with him when you were seventeen is one thing. But last week . . . no. You should have told me that he pines for you, Mary Kay. We all get weak, we all make mistakes and I could have martyred your *saint* and then I wouldn't be tied to this tree and he digs his rifle into my back.

"Stop crying, bitch. This is nothing compared to what I went through with my soccer team *or* my frat *or* my old man, so man *up* already."

I am caught in the toxic cycle of masculinity, the one quietly tolerated by the American System of Miseducation and he was hazed so he wants to haze me and *Dying for love is so bittersweet*. He shoots another living thing and he whines—*fucking squirrels*—and every dead animal is a reminder that the days really do go too fast. My life is ending and I don't want to die. I don't want my son to be an orphan. He lost his mother. He can't lose me too. I try to picture him older, and I can't, too scared, and I try to remember being with you on our love seat and I can't do that either. The Pain Pong tournament ended and the flocks of rabid fans are long gone. I will die here and I can't even hate him, because like you, I am too good for my own good. The Empathy Bordello has been ransacked and burnt to the ground before it even existed and he heard something and he hisses.

"Hey," he screams. "What is that?"

My eustachian tubes go to high alert. I heard it too. Is it you? You know about this cabin. You rejected him today and you've *been* to this cabin and did you come back?

"I'm warning you, buddy. You're on my property."

My heart pounds and I can't hear so well and I want it to be you—save me—and I don't want it to be you—he could *kill* you—and I don't know what to want. Cops. Yes. Let you be the savvy fox that knows better than to come here alone.

"I'm counting to three," he says. "One . . ." Please, God, let it be her. "Two . . ." Please, God, don't let it be her.

He doesn't make it to the number three. His voice is thwarted by the pop of a gun. Not his pop. A different gun. I can't see and I can't hear but I see dead people because in my heart I know that Shortus is dead. I scream into my sweaty sock for help—thank God for guns—and the footsteps are getting closer but my heart is beating faster. I want my nervous system to catch up to my brain and I tell myself over and over that it's over. *You need to calm down.*

And then the shooter is at my tree. Breathing heavily. Close. He is not a cop because cops are loud. They announce themselves. The bag is still on my head and a police officer would have pulled the bag off my head by now. Here goes my heart again—tick tick tick—and I was so afraid of animals that I forgot about the worst of all predators, the most power-hungry predators on this planet: *humans*.

Urine runs down my leg once more and the shooter puts the barrel of the gun he used to kill my enemy against the back of my head as if I am the enemy. I am crying now, my pleas about my family muffled by the sock in my mouth and then he laughs and drops the gun. "Relax, my friend. Show's over. Score one for the Poor Boys Club."

Oliver.

46

The bag is off my head and it's over. Oliver saved my life. My son won't be an orphan and you won't have to mourn, wishing you'd told me that you love me when you had the chance. Oliver is a hero and Oliver kept an eye on me because he was worried about me. RIP Shortus was a fake friend but Oliver is a real friend and that's what they say, that you're lucky in this world if you have at least a couple of real friends. True friends.

But all friends are flawed and I'm still tied to the tree and he's in Shortus's cabin and this day in the mountains needs to end. "Oliver! Any luck with finding a knife?"

"One sec, my friend!"

RIP Shortus is dead, yes, but the Pain Pong tournament is starting up again, no more nice adrenaline to lift me out of my body, and it's impossible not to think about what Oliver did *wrong.* That fucking video of me and RIP Melanda and I say it again, calm. "Oliver, I don't want to rush you, but I'm pretty bad out here."

He hops down the front steps of the cabin and he's carrying an Atari game set like he didn't just end a man's *life.* "Check it out, Goldberg. I was just looking for one of these on 1stdibs!"

He takes a picture of his new toy but he can't send it to Minka—no Wi-Fi—and my skin suit crawls because oh that's right. My friend

Oliver is a sociopath private dancer slash screenwriter and without him, I die in these woods, just like RIP Shortus.

"Oliver, I don't know how to thank you." *Oliver, move your ass and get me off this fucking tree.*

"No need," he says. "We talked about this. When you win, I win. When I win, you win."

Then why did you show Ray that fucking video? "Well, still, thanks."

He pats me on the back, as if I'm not tied to a tree. "And I'm sorry about Love," he says.

What about THE VIDEO, you fucking asshole? "Thanks," I say. "I'm just still in shock right now."

Oliver begins slicing the ropes and he's no naval-boys'-camp-trained RIP Shortus. He's terrible with a knife—fucking gun people—and he keeps dropping it on the ground and what if he has a heart attack? What if he dies before he finishes his work? "So I got news. I got a new agent."

I AM TIED TO A TREE AND I GOT SHOT IN THE HEAD, YOU ANGEFUCKINGLENO. "That's great."

He drops the knife and it grazes his hand and now he is *bleeding* and how the fuck did he hack it in the kitchen at Baxter's? "Yeah," he says. "And we're taking my show out next week."

And no one will buy it and it won't be because of karma. That's just how it works in L.A. "How's your hand?"

"Oh right," he says, and at least he's back to work on what matters: Me. You. Freedom. "So my show, you wanna hear the pitch?"

I had three "friends" on this planet, Mary Kay. My drinking buddy turned psychopath friend Seamus is dead. Ethan is engaged to *Blythe,* and this one is a malignant narcissist. "Sure!"

"*Cedar Cove* meets *Dexter.*"

The referee in Pain Pong calls a time-out and the blood stops circulating in my body. I look at him and he looks at me and he smiles. "I wasn't lying to you, my friend. We do have each other's backs."

Oliver's "show" is a roman à clef about *my* life—that's stealing—and his protagonist is JOHNNY BATES—"You know, for *The Shining* and for *Psycho*"—and Oliver hasn't just been stealing my money. He's like your dead husband, stealing my pain. Oliver's going to sell his show to FX or HBO or Netflix—not gonna happen, ideas are a dime a dozen and I can't picture him actually writing the fucking thing—and he's so slow with the knife, droning on about *spin-off potential.* You're out there somewhere, thinking I'm not trying to win you back and I snap. "Fucking A, Oliver, why did you give Ray that video? You swore you wouldn't do that."

Oliver stops cutting the rope and that was not the result I was going for. "Well, you know why I did that, Joe. Because the Quinns bring out the worst in us."

It's a child's answer and it was stupid of me to ask and I WANT OFF THIS FUCKING TREE. "Did he hack your phone?"

"Look," he says. "Minka and I have a huge collection now . . ." YOU'RE WELCOME, OLIVER. "And we need more space. Ray was talking like he's about to fire me. He said I'd get a huge bonus if I found something on you . . . I'm sorry, my friend."

He doesn't chase his apology with a *but* and he plays with his fucking knife, the knife that also happens to be the key to my liberation from this truth. "There's a twist, though." Fucking hacks and their *twists.* "Next day, Ray does his research. He realizes that I withheld the video and . . . he fires me. And that's why I came up here, my friend. I couldn't let anything happen to you . . ." Maybe his heart is bigger than I thought. "You're my only source of income until I sell *Johnny Bates*."

He's lucky I'm tied to this tree and I summon the last of my fucking *empathy* and thank him *again* and he goes back to saving me—finish the job, you prick—and describing his *male lead,* as if that's what the world needs, another sociopath on TV—and he says that Johnny Bates is mysterious and well-read but a little rough around the edges. Finally Oliver gets the top rope but my body lurches back, my muscles are broken from Pain Pong and I lose my balance and again he has to save me from falling. Again I have to *thank* him.

"You okay, my friend?"

No, I'm not okay. I got shot in the head and hit on the head and now this fucker is twisting my life into some gleaming, steaming pile of shit for TV. "I'm good. Just really need to rest."

Oliver shuts up about his shit show and he's getting better with that knife and now my legs are free—*Hare Oliver, Hallelujah*—and he clips the zip ties and I have hands again, two feet instead of one stump. I am dizzy and the car is not close and he says we can't think about leaving until we clean things up.

"Come on," he says. "It's not as bad as that dungeon in your house."

My Whisper Room is not a *dungeon* and I'm too weak to help him and he tells me to take a bath and did you fuck Shortus in this tub? I don't know. I don't care. I bathe and Oliver scrubs the floors, periodically interrupting his flow to tell me about his TV show and finally I am clean and the crime scene is clean and we are on foot, walking, limping.

"So," he says. "You wanna come back to L.A. and help me on the show? Ray says he blackballed me but my agent says he's full of shit."

"No thanks."

"Really? I'm offering you ground-floor access, my friend."

Access to what doesn't exist is access to nothing and I shake my head. "Gonna stay here."

"Well, ultimately, I suppose that's best for both of us. Ray doesn't want you in L.A. and this way, well, hey, if *Johnny Bates* gets a third season, maybe we shoot up here."

I can't think of anything to say that he won't interpret as an insult. He stops walking and he huffs and he puffs and he obviously misread my silence. We should be walking, Mary Kay. Animals in these woods don't stop to *chat* but Oliver's too fucking arrogant, human in the worst possible way, having just killed a fellow man. "Listen," he says. "You took a hit back there . . ." Ya think? "But you gotta let that shit go, Goldberg. You've gotta see the error of your ways."

I will punch him. "The what?"

"Hear me out, my friend. You moved up here to get soft and you did get soft . . ." I hate that he has a point but he does. I didn't see it coming with RIP Shortus. "It's like my agent said about my draft . . ." Say the word *agent* one more time, asshole. "There is such a thing as too soft, my friend. You can *rock down to Menopause Avenue* and spend every day in a library . . . but humans are what they are. And if you want something, you have to go hard, my friend. Always."

I let Oliver high-five me and soon we're in his Escalade. We're on the way back to civilization, passing the casino, the tiny bridge that moves us from the mainland to Bainbridge. Oliver is on the phone with his agent's assistant—*I got a new scene for the pilot*—and my friend is a sicko, but he's a sicko who saved my life.

I thank him again—excessively, considering his ineptitude with the knife—and he's on his phone again, probably searching for some *How to Make People Think You Can Write* article and he tells me that we did it. "We got out, my friend. Love . . . I'm sorry about that . . ." No he isn't. "But she can't mess with your head anymore and okay, so I no longer work for that family, but when my show goes into production . . ." Oh Oliver, *my friend,* do you really think that's gonna happen? "Well, I'll be making more money. In the meantime, though . . ."

My phone pings and it's a link to a 1983 Smith Corona typewriter on 1st Fucking Dibs. "I know," he says. "But I gotta tell you, Joe. Ever since I got back to writing, my mom's doing better. She says she never wanted to say anything, but she felt like I gave up and she feels stronger knowing that I'm back at it. We gotta go hard, my friend. That's the only way for the Poor Boys Club to succeed."

There's nothing more annoying than good advice from someone who makes a lot of bad decisions and we're silent until Oliver drops me in my driveway. Goodbye, Oliver, and hello to my empty houses. You and the Meerkat are still not in your guesthouse and I take another shower—I still smell bunny blood—and I put on my black cashmere sweater and I go into my kitchen and stand before my chopping block of Rachael Rays. I choose a smaller knife, the sharpest one I have, and I slip the knife into a book and Oliver is right, Mary Kay.

It's time to go hard.

47

I pop a Percocet—just one half this time—and Oliver has to win over so many motherfuckers if he wants *Johnny Bates* to make it into American homes. He's my friend, in a way, and I really will cross my fingers for him, but I won't hold my breath. That business isn't so different from dealing with the Quinns. He's gotta go hard when they tell him to go hard and then when they tell him it's too hard he's gotta go soft and when they send him notes and tell him they have no idea what he was thinking, that Johnny Bates is *way too soft,* he's gotta suck it up and tell them how smart they are. It's not an easy way of life, and me, I only have to kill it in one room, with one woman: you.

I catch a ferry to Seattle and I do what I need to do and I catch another ferry back to Bainbridge and I go home. I get my car but I don't park at the library—too close and not close as in *Closer*—and I pull my hat down the way people do sometimes, when you need to leave the house but you don't fucking feel like talking to anyone.

I'm too nervous, what with Rachael Ray up my sleeve, about to go where she's never gone before. Can I do this? Can I really *do* this?

I cut through the woods and I'm in the gardens by the library, crouching. The windows need to be washed but I see you in there. You're being you. I'm nervous and I can't risk you seeing me so I carry on through the woods, into the back parking lot. I might vomit. The half a Percocet. The adrenaline. The Pain Pong.

"Hi, Joe." It's the Meerkat and she's on the move and she doesn't stop to talk. "Bye, Joe."

She zooms by into the library and her Instagram said she was in Seattle and I brought Rachael Ray here for us, for you and me and now she knows I'm here—fuck—and will she tell you?

I duck my head and take the path down the steps into the garden and the cupola is empty—thank God—and I move like a mechanic, like Mick Fucking Jagger, maneuvering my broken body onto the ground, sliding my upper body under the love seat. I wanted to do this the right way, with spray paint, but then other people would see and the paint would bleed everywhere so it's just not realistic, is it? I take the knife out of my sleeve and I start to go to work. It's a slow go. I have empathy for Oliver because knives aren't easy and at this rate I'm never going to finish. I've never carved initials into a tree. I don't even know if you'll be moved by this because yes, you love the graffiti at Fort Ward, but will you love the fact that I carved our initials into the underbelly of a love seat that's property of the Bainbridge Public Library? Will you even be able to read my shitty knife-writing?

"Whatcha doing?"

I flinch and drop my knife and the Meerkat needs to be less caffeinated. Less nosy. "There's a loose screw," I say. "I'm just fixing it so nobody gets hurt. Can you gimme a minute?"

"I can give you a million minutes," she says and then she's gone, *clomp, clomp, clomp.*

I have to move fast because the Meerkat isn't stupid and I am defacing public property for my own private purposes and this is only part one of Operation Go Hard and I have to make it to part *two,* the harder part of going hard.

The door opens. It's you. "Okay," you say. "Please don't make me have to tell you to stop vandalizing our property."

The fucking Meerkat ratted me out and I'm not done yet and I had a plan. I was gonna lay down a red blanket and play "One" by U2—our first fuck—and you were gonna lie down and see our initials and life isn't what happens when you're making plans. It's what happens when you get a fucking *head injury* and turn into a sappy dork.

You say my name again. "Joe, come on. Stop."

I pocket my knife and bang my head as I worm my way out from under the love seat. I am standing. Dizzy. My poor head. You just sigh. "I told you. There's nothing to talk about. Go home."

"Wait."

You don't move. Do I get down on my knees? No, I don't get down on my knees. That's not us. I sit on the bench. I don't ask you to join me, but you do. You put your hands on your elbows.

"You were right," I say.

"About what?"

"You told me that it's not in my nature to love."

"I was mad and I told you I was sorry. Can we not do this?"

"Yes," I say. "We can absolutely not do this. I can go home. I can put my house on the market and I can move. And you can go back inside and pretend I don't exist."

"Joe . . ."

"It's not in my nature to love, Mary Kay. And the truth hurts. And you have every reason to pretend I don't exist because you're absolutely right. My note to you was generic and vague. I disappeared on you. And my letter wasn't just vague. It was *bullshit* because you can't open up to someone without opening up all the way and I didn't do that. I got scared. I ran. No excuses."

"Can I go now?"

"Did I walk out on you when you told me about Phil?"

"Are you trying to tell me that *you're* married, too?"

"Believe me, Mary Kay, I thought about running scared. The man was a *rock star.* I was intimidated . . ." I was never intimidated by that fucking rat but certain situations call for certain logic and it's working.

You're listening. The windows of your Empathy Bordello are opening and you're letting me back in, a little.

"Mary Kay, I promise I'll never chicken out on you again. I know I ran away."

You say nothing and of course you say nothing. A liar can't promise that he'll never lie again. You say you *should probably* go back in and I tell you to wait and you throw up your hands. "I *did* wait. I waited all day for you to call."

"I did call."

"Not when you got off the plane."

"I got mugged."

"Oh, do you expect me to believe that you got mugged at the airport? What, Joe? You got . . . *shot* at the Starbucks in LAX?"

"I flew into Burbank."

"I don't care. It's too late."

"Mary Kay, I told you. You're right. I fucked up. And I don't blame you for icing me out that day and all the days after. You had every right to do that."

"You should go."

"No," I say. "I have to tell you something about me."

I have no plan and I'm not a *pantser.* I am a planner. But I'm not gonna win you back with schmaltz—you want me to be vulnerable and you want some fucking *facts*—and I have to tell you everything without telling you everything. "Okay, look," I begin. "I went to this school shrink when I was kid. She talked about object permanence. How babies, if you show them an apple, they see the apple. And if you cover the apple up with a box, they forget the apple was there. They forget the apple exists because it doesn't exist to them when they can't see it."

"I'm familiar with the concept of object permanence."

"I did lie to you, Mary Kay. On our first date . . . I glossed over my relationships . . ." It's true. "I wanted to come off like Mr. Independent. Mr. Evolved . . ." God, it feels good to speak the truth. "But in reality, I moved here because I let my ex walk all over me . . ." More like *stampede.* "I let her treat me like a doormat . . . And I know it sounds macho and stupid but I thought it might turn you off if I told you about what a sucker I'd been."

"Joe . . ."

"See, I thought, here's my fresh start. If I don't tell you about Lauren . . ." I can't say Love's real name because the story online is a lie—she didn't die of cancer—and I'm caught in her family's web of lies. "I thought that if I didn't tell you that Lauren existed, I would feel like *she* never existed, like that guy I was when I was with her, like *he* never existed either."

You pick at the splintered wood. "So you ran back to your ex. And you referred to it as a 'family emergency,' which tells me that she still very much 'exists' to you . . ."

"I know," I say. "Fucking stupid. Inexcusable. And if I could go back to that night, I would wake you up and tell you about Lauren. I would tell you that she just called threatening to commit suicide. I would tell you that I hate myself for not telling you sooner, for not blocking her number . . . but I would also tell you that I never blocked her number because I have empathy for her. The woman has *no one.*"

"Except you . . ."

"Not anymore, Mary Kay." RIP Love. "My empathy got the best of me, but I cut the cord."

"Well, that's nifty."

"Listen to me. I saw her . . ." Truth. "She was on the verge of taking her own life . . ." More truth. "But now it's over. She's with her brother, the only person she really ever loved, and I blocked her number. This *is* the end of the line for us."

Whoever said that the truth just sounds different was right. You're taking it all in and I really *won't* be hearing from RIP LoveSick anymore. She was never the same after she lost her brother and if there's a heaven, she's with him, and if not, well, she can't hurt me anymore. More importantly, she can't hurt my fucking *son*.

You wave at my wounds. "Did her brother do this to you?"

"No," I say, getting off on all this delicious, cathartic *truth.* "But I'm happy it happened."

You sigh and that was too Phil-ish and I correct. "I mean that it was a wake-up call about what a hypocrite I've been, hiding the ugliness of what it was like with Lauren, as if anyone can just 'erase their past,' sneaking out on you with that stupid half-ass *note.* This gunshot, this beating, it was the universe telling me that playing the hero for Lauren, swooping in to 'save' her . . . well, you can't call yourself a hero if you're lying to someone you love. I won't make that mistake again, Mary Kay, I mean that, not with you, not with anyone."

I take the ring out of my pocket. No YouTube-style show. No flowers. No string section rounding the corner to serenade us with U2. I just put it on my middle finger. "I got this on 1stdibs."

"Oh," you say. "Well, that's nice."

"It made me think about why I ran away, what rings are for people. Because some of us . . . we don't ever learn about object permanence, not really. I mean I was with that shrink because I refused to leave my jacket and my backpack in my locker because I thought if I couldn't see them at all times . . . they'd be gone."

"Are you asking me why I didn't wear a ring when I was . . . when Phil was alive?"

I close my hand around the ring. "Yes."

"Well, I don't have one. I lost it when I was pregnant."

"How?"

"I lost it at the beach . . ." You scratch your elbows. "He was *never* home. Anyway, he finished *Moan and Groan,* all these songs where he's complaining about me and the baby ruining his life . . . The album explodes and he was so happy and I was so lonely. I was pregnant. I had homework. Everyone acted like I should be different, *Oh, you're still getting your masters?*" You ball up your fists. "Nomi was born. He bought me a new ring. I told him I lost that one, too. I was lying. I just hid it in the attic. But I thought I was doing a nice thing. I thought he might get a song out of it . . . two lost rings . . . Anyway, a couple years later, Nomi must have been about three . . . Phil goes up to the attic. He found the ring, the one I said I lost. He didn't yell at me. He didn't cry. He left it on my pillow and I know what you mean. *You're just as evil as me.*"

"You're not evil, Mary Kay."

"I'm gonna be completely honest with you."

Good. "Good."

"I loved not telling you about Phil. I got *off* on the danger, the reality that you might find out and hate me. It was a game and I finally got to be the horrible woman that everyone around here secretly thought I was."

"It's not your fault that I was stupid. We've been through this. It's on me, too."

You smirk and I see this new side of you. Haughty. All velvet ropes and there's no one in the room but you and I want in. "Joe" you simper. "You're earnest. And I'm . . . I'm not sure that I'm even a whole person. Sometimes I think that everything I do and say . . . it's all a reaction to what everyone thinks about me . . . *She thinks she's hot stuff because of one album. Her poor husband was right. She dragged him down just like he said she would! And she won't even wear a ring. If she had any dignity she'd leave him and maybe* then *he'd write good music. She acts like she's some kinda saint, keeping him on the wagon, but the man is miserable! And she just walks around that library pretending to be some independent woman. What a joke. What a lie. Who does she think she's fooling? What is she looking for? When's it ever gonna be enough for her?*"

"Now," I say. "This is enough. You don't scare me and with this 'not a whole person' bullshit, either. Good try though. You almost had me . . . almost . . ."

It's time to go hard but not too hard, soft but not too soft. I open my fist and the ring is right there. You spent your entire adult life pulling Phil out of the quicksand of stardom. I won't *ask* you to marry me. You know what the ring means. I go soft so that you can go hard—please, please, please—and finally, you pick up the ring and slide it onto your finger and your face lights up and you are the star, my star.

"Okay," you say. "I get it now. You really do exist."

"I really do exist. And I really did fuck up. But I learned my lesson, Mary Kay, because we're in the same boat. I never thought a woman like you existed either."

You look at me. "And I do."

"Yes you do."

When we kiss, the Meerkat hollers and we look into the library and she's there with a few of the Mothballs and a couple patrons and they couldn't hear us talking but they were watching. Everyone loves a proposal, even one as simple and ass backwards as ours and you're laughing. "Well, I guess I can't take it off now!"

I kiss your hand. "Never."

The Meerkat bursts through the door and she hugs you, she hugs me, and there is clapping, so much clapping, and a Mothball brings a bottle of fake champagne outside and I should be in pain. I was shot in the head. Love tried to kill me and Seamus tried to kill me but your hand is latched onto mine and you are showing off your ring and the

Meerkat is putting us on Instagram and this is it, my happy fucking ending, my happy fucking *beginning.*

"Nomi," you say. "What are you doing under there?"

She's on her back, under the love seat, taking a picture of my *vandalism.* "Reading," she says. "I think he was trying to carve his initials."

"I love you," you say. "But don't fuck with my library, okay?"

I went hard and you went hard and now we're gonna go hard together. "It's a deal," I say. "I will be good to you and your library, especially that big Red Bed inside . . ." It was just dirty enough and you wink at me, my fox, my fianc-fucking- ée.

48

It's been *four weeks and sixteen days* and the love songs were telling the truth. When it's real, it's real and this is real, Mary Kay. You never take off your ring and commitment agrees with us. We worked hard to get here. We sacrificed a lot. Your friend Shortus died in a hunting accident—well done, Oliver—and I don't care if you slept with him in his stupid cabin. He's gone, I'm here, and we ran in the 5 fucking K to honor that racist, diseased little man and then we took a shower together and you didn't fall off the edge of the sidewalk in despair.

You climb into bed with me and you hug me. "Promise me you won't take up hunting."

It's almost like you know that my life was plagued with violence for so long. "I promise."

Everything is different now. Fecal-Eyed *Nancy* put the moves on me when she was drunk at the pub last week and I told you right away and you told me I did the right thing and we had sex in the bathroom by Normal Norman Rockwell's mermaid in the cage, by the shipwrecked sailor and the naked woman of his scurvy-induced fantasies. And then you decided that maybe you *won't* start hot yoga with Fecal Eyes after all and it's easy to grow apart from people. The toast at Blackbird is good but it isn't something we can't live without and it doesn't matter that Fecal Eyes didn't *actually* put the moves on me. I don't like her. I don't want her in our life and it's just better to push her away because I promised I wouldn't kill anyone and I didn't kill anyone for you and I want things to stay that way. I want to honor my first vow to you, the one you don't even know about.

The Meerkat bursts into the room and groans. "Enough with Taylor Swift."

You're the one who keeps playing "Lover" all the time and I get where the Meerkat is a *little* sick of it because love can be repugnant when it's not yours, especially when it involves the woman who birthed you. You do the right thing. You tickle her. "Never," you say, facetiously. And then you promise you'll take the song off the playlist after *the big day* and the Meerkat snaps her fingers. "But it *is* the big day."

Yes it is! You smile. "But the big day's not over yet, honey."

She groans, but she's not *really* mad and we're getting married in a matter of hours. Yes! I'm a good stepfather and I kill the Taylor Swift and the Meerkat is droll. "Thanks, Joe."

"Anything for you, kiddo."

It's Saturday and there aren't many Saturdays like this left. The Meerkat will be away at college soon—take *that,* Ivan—and it's the three of us now, we're the family boarding the ferry and there are no sharks in these waters. I don't ignore you the way your rat did and the *Gilmore Girls* found their Luke and we spend the whole day in Seattle, roaming around looking at tchotchkes, tchotchkes we don't buy because I'm here to remind you that they're tchotchkes we don't need and I love your friends who own the record store and they love me.

They found all the records I was looking for and that is my wedding gift to you: a jukebox, the old-fashioned kind with actual records, the one that you told me you always pictured in your *Empathy Bordello.* You're right, Mary Kay. I *do* remember everything, and I took a hit from Oliver—1st Fucking Dibs—but I do have a nest egg and we are making plans for our bookshop, sending each other links to potential locations on Zillow.

I still volunteer and you still work at the library and the summer days are long, like days in a Sarah Jio book and sometimes it's a shame that your *Friends* weren't good enough for us, because happiness is contagious. It would be nice if RIP Melanda were here to envy us, if RIP Shortus were here to build us a love seat, if your rat were a big enough man to sit in the audience and force a smile when the love of his life chooses better.

Alas, we can't control other people. We can only control ourselves.

We're such a good fucking family that I want us to go on *Family Feud* because we would win, even if it was just the three of us, *because* it was just the three of us. You laughed when I said it last week—*That'll be the day*—but when I went on your computer and looked at your search results, there it was: *How do you get on* Family Feud*?* I knew it. I knew that once I proposed we would all be in a better place. We are on the roller coaster now and there is no jumping off the ride. Our life is the photograph that rich dimwits pay for at the theme park because their memories alone are inadequate. We took the leap of faith and the coaster was slow to start—amusement parks are all aging and dangerous—but we took our chances. We boarded. We strapped on our seatbelts. And now our hands are in the air and we are coasting.

Our guesthouse is for guests—Ethan and Blythe can't make it to the wedding because Blythe caught a parasite from a piece of sushi—but there will be guests eventually. I like it better this way. We are nesting and look what I did for you, Mary Kay! You aren't the town widow who got fucked over by her druggie husband and her sleazy brother-in-law. You're my fiancée. You stashed my guitar in the closet—*I don't want to go down that road again, you know?*—and I do know. I'm not RIP Phil. I don't want to be a *rock star* and it's like you texted your semi-friend Erin, who is vying for Melanda's position in your life: *I always heard second marriages were like this. I know we're not married yet but JESUS. Every day I'm like oh. So THIS is how it can be. So yes. Bring New Guy to the party. Believe in love!*

I didn't sneak into your phone or invade your privacy. You changed your settings and when you get a text the words are right there because for the first time in your adult life, you have nothing to hide from me, from RIP Phil, from anyone. I only look at your back-and-forths when you leave your phone open on the counter because you have to pee and a lot of people look in their spouses' phones, Mary Kay. I'm sure you'd do it to me too if I were more like you. But I'm me. And you're you. And we're not gonna be those unbearable in-your-face assholes who create a *Mr. and Mrs. Joe and Mary Kay Goldberg* account. We're not in denial about our individuality. But in a good relationship, you respect your partner's needs. You're a worrier so you don't need to know that I just blew five grand on a vintage tabletop Centipede videogame formerly owned by a fucking Pizza Hut. You don't need to know that Oliver still didn't sell his show—issues with Johnny Bates's *likability*—but continues to peddle it around that vile no-good city with his agent. To be me is to be aware of all the mugs of urine in the world, in our house. I know where you keep your diary—up high in the closet that's yours now—but I haven't opened it once and I dip my razor in the sudsy sink and the shaving cream clings to the blade.

Perfect.

I pull my skin and the razor does what razors do, it removes unwanted tiny hairs—I don't want your face to burn when we get in bed together—and all is right in this world, in this home, on this razor blade, and you knock on the doorframe. "I'm just so fucking happy. Is this . . . Is this how it's gonna be?"

I dip my razor in the suds and once again, perfection. "Yes," I say.

You nod. You wear socks. And I *tsk-tsk*—my floors are hardwood, slippery—and your floors were different and you can't wear socks around this house and walk safely and you are stubborn—socks are your tights in summer—and you are always stumbling and sliding. I want to protect you. I nag you to wear shoes or go barefoot but you think you're Tom Cruise in *Risky Business*. You imitate his famous sliding dance and I shake my head and tell you what I always tell you when you walk around in socks, that *life* is risky business. "Young lady," I say. "You need to put on some shoes."

You take a step closer and you are over it. "Are you almost ready?"

I like our nagging because it means we are a real family. We're being ourselves. You had PMS last week and I surprised you with O.B. tampons and you laughed—*Thanks . . . I think*—and you ate the leftover pizza I was planning to eat for breakfast and I was annoyed—*I told you one pizza wasn't enough for three people, that's TV bullshit when they do that*—and you were annoyed—*You try getting PMS every month and see how you deal when your own body turns against you*—and the Meerkat was annoyed—*Mom, can you please not talk about your period so much?*—and it was fucking awesome! Because it means we're like Seinfeld and company on Festivus, we're airing our grievances instead of letting them boil inside of us. There are weeds in our garden and they complement the flowers and that's how I know this is real. The flowers and the weeds, I can't tell them apart, but at the end of the day, I love them all. We're not afraid of Virginia Woolf in this house. When we tousle it's a fair fight. Clean.

You blush, horny like the fiancée that you are and you tell me that you'll be on the deck and I breathe you in and you kiss my cheek and shaving cream covers your lips and I wish it was whipped cream. You giggle. Dirty. You reach for me with your hand and the door is wide open but you are a fox. You like the risk and this is who we are now. *Lovers.* You want my hand in your hair and I do what you want and there is no reason for you to know about RIP Beck or RIP Candace—your tongue grazes my shaft—and what we have is real. It's now.

You stand. Dizzy. I zip up. Dizzy.

You are bashful, avoiding your own reflection in the mirror, as if what we just did was wrong. You swat me with a washcloth—*Bad Joe, Good Joe*—and I throw up my hands—*Guilty.* I tell you that you make me feel young and then I take it back. "That was the wrong word," I say. "You make me feel better than young. You make me feel old. I always liked the song 'Golden Years,' and I know we're *that* old, but I get what Bowie meant in a way I never did before."

You like that. And you laugh. "Fun fact," you say. "When Phil proposed, I was sleeping."

I'm used to this by now. When I make a rock 'n' roll reference, you respond by talking about your rock 'n' *RIP* husband. And it's good, Mary Kay. It's healthy. You're remembering all the little things that made him fallible because nothing compares to *me* and I fucking love it when you see the light. I'm excited for the rest of our lives and I grin. "No."

"Oh yes," you say. "He put the ring on my finger and left the house and it took me a long time to notice it and he was so mad . . ."

I do not speak ill of the dead but wedding days are like this. You reflect. I kiss your forehead. "I love you."

You lean your head into my chest. "Yes, you most certainly do, Joe."

And then you smack me on the ass and remind me that we have fifty people waiting downstairs and I salute you. "Aye, aye, Hannibal." And then you change your mind and you close the door. "Or do you prefer *Buster*?"

I lock the door that you closed and I press my body into yours. I run my hand down your back and I pull your panties off and I am on my knees and who gives a shit about the fifty people outside when I am in here, *Closer* as in closest?

49

It's a shame that RIP Melanda didn't live to see this.

Our backyard wedding is just the sort of night she pictured for herself when she read Sarah Jio's *Violets of March* and your high school friends are irritating and the Seattle freeze is on—one asshole showed up in a *Sacriphil* T-shirt, as if Nomi needed that today—because this is our wedding, *our* celebration of *our* love.

The Sacriph-asshole pats me on the back. "He'd want her to be happy," he says. "But ya know . . . it's still weird for some of us."

The asshole is drunk but you come to my rescue. "Paul," you say. "You look like you're freezing. We put a pile of fleeces by the bar. Why don't you grab one?"

He gets the hint and you save this moment, you save me, you save everything. You kiss me. "We did it."

"Yes we did."

You are my conspirator and you rub your nose into my nose. "And wasn't I right? Isn't it kind of more fun this way?"

I tell you that you were right because you *were* right. We fucked up a little. We didn't get a marriage license yet, but you told me that you want us to make it official in private, after all the pictures and the partying, because in the end, it's nobody's business but ours, after all.

You squeeze my ass and whisper in my ear. "If Nancy tries anything funny, I got your back."

"Technically, you have my ass."

You squeeze harder. "Semantics."

And then you're in circulation, as a bride must be, as loving and warm as you are in the library, only this is our house, our life. Everything is in place now. Brand-new Erin truly is the best replacement. She isn't horny and snooty like Fecal Eyes and she isn't a toxic fossil from your past like *Melanda*. It's sad but ultimately good that RIP Melanda isn't here to take pictures of you and put hearts on the unflattering ones, to call out the music for being problematic—*Well she was just seventeen*—and there's so much love in the air that she might have gotten weak and wound up mercy-fucking RIP Shortus or *Uncle Ivan,* not that he came. But you don't miss him. You say you'll never forgive him for ignoring the invitation and if he were here, he'd fall off the wagon and start recruiting Nomi's new friends and that frustrated, fecal-eyed mommy into some new fucking sex ring. I spin you around the tiny dance floor and you turn a little sad as "Golden Years" ends but that's the way of all songs, all weddings, and I wonder what ever happened to Chet and Rose, the newlyweds in the woods where RIP Beck went to sleep.

I kiss you gently. "What's wrong?"

"I'm okay. It'll pass. Just a little emotional right now."

I kiss your hand. "I know."

"It's weird without my core people . . ." Rotten to the core, all of them. "And at the same time, I'm remembering why I lost touch with half these people . . ." Atta girl and I kiss you and we don't need to start having *game night* as you've threatened every now and then. "It's strange," you say. "But in a good way, you know?"

Whitney Houston comes to our rescue and you want to dance and it's not easy to dance. The floor is small. My yard is small. Boring third-tier friends form a messy circle around us. We are *Chet and Rose* and it's *us* in the center. These people aren't our people, they're warm bodies on a late summer night and none of them will be *popping by* tomorrow—not even Brand-New Erin—and Nomi taps your shoulder and we bring her in and we are that family now, that family everyone else wishes they could be and then the song ends and we aren't the center anymore. A slower song begins, fucking reggae, somewhere between dancing and not dancing, and it's too crowded and people are drifting and the three of us keep dancing and you ask Nomi if her friends are having a good time and she shrugs and I tell her that her friends seem cool and she laughs. "Don't say *cool*. You sound lame."

We have a family chuckle and it's just as well because her friends don't really seem all that cool. They're sulking down by the dock like *Philistan* fan girls who don't want to dance with a bunch of old people. But as we know, friends are important, and Nomi finally got rid of the little round glasses. She's swaying hips I didn't know were there and she won't be a *Columbine* virgin forever and my brain hot-wires. I picture my son years from now, a younger me, macking on Nomi in a bar . . . but he's too young for her now and he'll be too young for her then and we are okay. All of us.

The reggae fades into "Shout" and Fecal Eyes and women from your Book Club are calling for you—*Mary Kay, come do a shot*—and it's the part of the song where you slowly get down and what a sight this is, middle-aged mountain bike people trying to twist. We can have game night, fine, but we won't be having any fucking dance parties, that's for sure.

Nomi loses her balance and grabs my shoulder. "So Melanda texted me yesterday."

Impossible. She's dead and Shortus told the same fucking lie and I stumble but I don't grab the Meerkat's shoulder. "Oh yeah? How is she?"

It's the part of the song where we work our way back up and Nomi's talking about Melanda like she's *alive.* This is my stepdaughter. This is a child—she's eighteen but she's a young eighteen—and she grew up in a should-have-been-broken home so I shouldn't be surprised that she's a liar. She lied for the same reason that Shortus lied, because lies make us feel better about ourselves.

The Meerkat pulls a strand of hair off her face and builds a better world. She tells me that Melanda is so much happier in Minneapolis than she ever was here. "She's still mad at my mom for not having her back . . ." In Nomi's fantasy, Nomi is the glue. The secret. The one with all the power. "But I get it and honestly, she does too because I mean that kid was a kid, you know?"

I do know and I nod.

"Anyway, mostly she's just really happy about how you helped me get back on track with NYU and stuff."

"Well that's great," I say and Billy Joel picked one hell of a time to start singing about loving somebody *just the way* they are. I stuff my hands in my pockets. I won't slow-dance with my fucking stepdaughter. She wears a bra and those father-daughter Facebook dances are perverse. That's your *daughter*, you shithead. Alas, Nomi's father was dead when he was alive—*the end of the summer, the end of all your fun*—and she puts her hands around my neck. She wants to dance and this is wrong—eighteen is too close to seventeen—but she leaves me no choice. I rest my hands on her hips and I hit bare skin, but if my hands go lower, they're on her ass, if they go higher, they're on her chest. She looks up at me and there is moonlight—*Are people looking at us?*—and she smiles. "I owe you."

"Don't be ridiculous," I say and I wish Billy Joel would shut up and I wish you would come back. "You don't owe me anything."

"No," she says. "The only reason I get to go to New York is cuz you helped me see that Ivan was a jerk."

I lie to her and tell her that Ivan isn't necessarily a bad guy, that good people go through hard times and that life is long, that Ivan will go back to being good. Her smile is too bright and we need to find this kid a boyfriend. Or a best friend. These new *Friends* of hers are no good—two of them are pouring vodka into red plastic cups—and Nomi looks into my eyes—no—and I search for you, but you're busy by the fire pit with *your* fucking *Friends*. The Meerkat has fingers—who knew—and she runs the tips of those fingers through my hair. I pull away. She claps her hands. She doubles over. She's laughing at me—*Omigod you are so paranoid*—and she's teasing me—*You really do watch too much of that Woody Allen stuff*—and then she turns serious because *I* am too serious. So I muster a laugh. "Sorry."

"You just had a bug in your hair. I was pulling it out."

I scratch my head the way you do when someone reminds you that you have one. "Thanks."

"Don't worry," she says, stepping back, on her way to her bad-influence friends. "I won't tell my mom about your little freak-out. I'm not stupid."

None of our wedding guests saw what happened and maybe that's because nothing happened. I fix a drink—I am of age—and I search the air around me for bugs. Gnats. Fruit flies. Anything. I see nothing. And then you are here, by my side, following my sight line into the abyss. "We really hit the jackpot, huh? No rain."

You make everything better and you stare at the stars above and you sigh. "I saw you dancing with Nomi," you say. "That really made me happy. That's when it all kind of hit me, Buster. We did it. We really did."

We all know the rules. IF YOU SEE SOMETHING, SAY SOMETHING. You saw us dancing and you saw nothing and this is the *good* part of my life so I go with it, I go where you go because I can, because I have to. "Yep," I say. "It made me happy too."

50

Better safe than sorry and I am playing Centipede, just like Oliver and Minka. I play alone—you don't know about my game—and I am winning. The goal is simple: Do not be alone with Nomi. Kill that Centipede every time it appears on-screen. Except in this game, I don't kill her. It's in her nature to want to be with me and there *are* bugs, she might have been trying to take a bug out of my hair. But you just never know, do you? And the Centipede isn't *evil* and we're all just prone to root for the soldier, the player, because the Centipede is presented as the enemy. I am like you—a future cofounder of the Empathy Bordello—and I am able to see things from Nomi's perspective. She lost her father. Her uncle's a motherfucker. Her fake uncle died in a hunting accident and proceeded to be torn apart by wild animals. And now she has a stepfather. It's confusing stuff and the Centipede is on a mission to get close to me and it is my duty to do what is best for the Centipede: to stay the fuck away from her.

This is no way to live, being endangered in my own house, but in four days she goes to New York and that means no more fucking Centipede. At least, not until the *real* Centipede arrives, the two-player tabletop I bought for us. You walk into the kitchen and I pour coffee into your mug and you say you don't have time for that. You have to catch the ferry. Erin is meeting you in Seattle to see a *designer.* I push the coffee across the table. "Oh come on," I beckon. "You can do that later. Stay home."

You sip the coffee. "You are a very bad man, Joe."

I smile. "Yes, I am."

If Nomi didn't live here—just four days and three nights to go—I would pull your skirt off and bend you over the counter but Nomi does live here and she's here now, rummaging in the fridge for a Red Bull. You nag her about her beverage choice—*That will poison your brain*—and she barks defensively—*It's no different than coffee*—and I play my videogame, casually moving my position so that I am on the opposite side of the room from Nomi.

You don't know about my Centipede score. You haven't noticed a change in my behavior since she touched my hair. But I am the top scorer in the game and I have not been alone or within touching distance of your daughter *once* in the past four days.

When you yawn and say you have to go to bed, I follow.

When the Centipede—not a Meerkat, not anymore—*pops by* the library and sees me packing up and asks if I want to walk home, I tell her that I have to go to Seattle to see about a book.

When I am outside flipping steaks on the grill—no more *lamb shanks* for us—and you are inside chopping vegetables and the Centipede opens the door and asks if I need help, I smile—polite—and tell her I'm *all set*.

The Meerkat has *daddy issues* and because I am such a good stepfather, I don't want her to find another bug in my hair. I don't want her to beat herself up for anything when she's in New York, starting over.

You peck me on the cheek and Nomi is in this house and you are leaving this house and I have to stop you.

"Wait," I say. "You're leaving *now*?"

Nomi laughs. "You guys are so gross."

You tell me that you have to get the ferry and the Centipede hops up on the counter and she is wearing shorts and her legs dangle and I tell you I want you to stay and Nomi groans again. "I can't take this anymore," she says. "I'm going to the beach with Anna and Jordan and please don't bug me about dinner later!"

That's what happens in videogames sometimes. The enemy appears on-screen and you're out of position, you can't evade the bullets, but then it slips off-screen and you worried for nothing. You feel my forehead. Such a mother. "Are you okay? You look a little red."

I pull you in because I can do that now that the Centipede is outside—GAME OVER—stuffing a towel in her bag. "Bye, guys!" she calls from the driveway.

"Come on," I plead. "We have the whole house to ourselves. You can see the *dee ziner* any old day."

You kiss me but it's a kiss goodbye. "Erin's waiting for me, Buster. So come on, lemme go. In four days, this is how it'll be *every* day."

"In four days a bomb might go off and we might all be dead."

You sling your purse over your shoulder. "And I think *I'm* the paranoid one."

I try once more. I put your hand on my dick. "Come on, Hannibal . . ."

Your eyes are two foxes, they have teeth, sharper than mine. "No," you say. "And honestly . . . can we cool it with the Hannibal stuff?"

That hurts my feelings but in any relationship, there is growth and I'm not a fucking nickname person anyway. "Whatever you want, Mary Kay DiMarco."

You walk to the door and blow me a kiss. "Be good."

I blow you a kiss. "See you in twenty minutes when you change your mind?"

Your eyes land on the sofa and you fight a horny smile and you love me but you leave me and I sit on our in-house Red Bed and I turn on the TV. Everything is fine. I'm catching up on *Succession*—you were right, it is good, and there's a nickname that you do like: Ken Doll—but I can't focus. I need to zone out so I turn on *Family Feud.* I'm not paranoid, but this is a challenge for me. Things are working out for the first time in my life and sometimes I think about New York or I think about L.A. and I hear Aimee Mann in *Magnolia* warning me that getting everything you want can be unbearable. I am so used to never getting what I want that I don't quite know how to sit on my sofa and be a basic Bainbridge *hubby* in khaki shorts killing time while his almost-wife—it will be *courthouse official* on 8/8, you like that date—searches for curtains and my stepdaughter hits the beach with her *friends.*

The door opens and I turn off the TV. You knew I needed you today and you're here, kicking off your shoes in the foyer. "Did you miss me, Mary Kay soon-to-be-*Goldberg*?"

I look up from the red pillow I just moved to make room for you and it isn't you.

It's the Centipede and this is a new level in the game—a dangerous level—and she pulls a can of spiked seltzer out of the fridge and she's eighteen years old and it's 11:00 A.M. She closes the fridge with one hip and shakes the can before she pops it. She giggles. "Finally, right? My God, I was going crazy."

I clutch my pillow. My armor. "Nomi, you shouldn't be drinking."

She jumps on the couch and I get off the couch and she is the Centipede, on her side now, *legs for days* and who knew she had legs and what is she doing? She's sipping her spiked soda—spikes on a dark road at night, spikes that flatten tires—and she's propping her head on a red pillow. "Whatever," she says. "These things have like no alcohol. Don't worry. I won't be *drunk* or anything."

I hold my Red Bed red pillow and the Centipede isn't moving with her body but she is moving in other ways. Running her hand over her collarbone and the collarbone isn't yours but it is. It came from inside your body. "Joe," she says. "Relax. She's gone."

She takes a sip and fuck you, Woody Allen. You did this. *You.* She's a virgin—isn't she?—she isn't old enough to know what she wants but she says that *I* know what she wants and she licks her lips. "Seriously. She and Erin . . . they live for stuff like this, shopping for *curtains.*" She sighs.

"Nomi, you shouldn't be drinking."

"And you shouldn't be getting *married.* Jesus, Joe. We were set."

The Centipede broadsides me from afar and I lose a life and stutter. "There is no we."

She laughs and did she always laugh that way? "I get it," she says. "You do things the hard way. We were so close . . ." Close as in *the Centipede is winning.* "Mom was all set to be a brother-fucker and go off with Ivan . . ." No you were not. "But you go and bring him down . . ." No I didn't. "And then you go hunting with my ex-boyfriend . . . He told me he was gonna 'teach you a lesson' for trying to steal me away, like it's not *my* choice. Such a jerk."

The game table flies into the air and I duck for cover. She said *ex-boyfriend* and it was her in the woods with Seamus. Not you.

Nomi.

He wasn't pining for you and he was a pedophile and he thought *I* was a pedophile same way RIP Melanda thought I was a pedophile and I AM NOT A PEDOPHILE. The Centipede isn't alone anymore. There are bombs falling from the top of the screen and my control panel is stuck—does she know about the bunnies and the buckets of fucking blood?—and I want to punch the console and scream. "You . . . and Seamus . . . ?"

She shakes like her body is covered in ants and she screeches. "Don't remind me. I know. He wasn't exactly smart. He barely read. But don't be a dick about it. I was young."

"You *are* young."

She blinks and I wish she still wore those unflattering little round glasses. "He could be sweet, though, like driving to Seattle to pick me up from Peggy and Don's to take me to his cabin. I don't think I would have gotten through high school without those weekends."

The cabin. The girls weren't twenty-fucking-two like you said, Mary Kay. The girls were *Nomi* and I beg her to stop and she sighs. "Don't be that way, Joe. Don't be jealous. The cabin was freaking *boring* and it's not like I was ever in *love* with him."

"Nomi, please. Stop it."

"But kids here . . . they're like kids everywhere. They suck. Seamus was just, I mean one day I was bored hanging out by the creek near my old middle school and . . . there he was."

CrossFit is across the street from that fucking middle school and I snap. "He's a rapist."

Now she sits up. "*You* stop it. Nobody raped me, Joe."

"It's called statutory rape. And it's wrong."

She crosses her arms. All one hundred of them. "Oh really, Mr. Morals? Mr. *Hiding in the woods watching me . . .*"

"I was *not* watching you."

"Right," she says. "You just happened to be there with all the time in the world to take this long, leisurely walk to the grocery store with me . . ."

The screen turns from orange to green and I am dying. I did that. But I didn't. "Nomi, please, that's not what that was about."

"Now you're gonna tell me that you didn't push me to watch your favorite movie . . ."

I hate that this is true—I did that, I pushed a teenage girl on Woody Fucking Allen—and I am *one* soldier and she is a reptile on fire.

"Come on, you were worried that I was one of Melanda's little pawns, *so* freaking cute, you actually believed that I never saw a Woody Allen movie. I mean, I live *on* a rock, but I don't live under a rock. And I know when someone is watching me."

"I was not watching you."

"Right," she says. "Same way you didn't *literally* go to my house in the middle of the day when I was cutting school."

"I was dropping off a book."

It is true and it isn't and the Centipede moves swiftly. "Nope," she says. "You were waiting for me. And you didn't rat me out to my mom, which is how I *really* knew we were in this for the long haul."

"Nomi, I am sorry that you misinterpreted things but you are dead wrong."

"One word," she says. "Budussy."

Budussy: the only word worse than *Centipede,* and I shoot her down. "No."

"That whole time you helped me at the library you were making eyes at me all nervous about getting caught and you keep looking to see if my mom noticed. You were so cute, Joe. So cute."

"Nomi, I wasn't making eyes at you. I was making eye contact, and there is a difference."

"Aw, come on. You can be real with me now. Don't fight it."

"Nomi, I'm not fighting anything. You misread things."

"Ooh, I thought of another one of our little 'moments,' that day you almost ran away . . . I saw that box in your car, Joe. I knew you were gonna leave . . . But then you saw me." No. "And you were so cute, worried that I thought of you as one of those old people in the library." No. "I had no idea that you were so self-conscious about your age and I promised to be more sensitive . . ." No. That is *not* how that went down. "And you stayed." She clutches her heart. "The absolute sweetest."

The bomb almost hit me that time and the game is rigged. "Nomi, this is all a big misunderstanding and you've been through a lot and I'm really . . . *sorry* isn't the word . . . I'm horrified by what Seamus did to you but I am *not* like that."

She shrugs. "He didn't 'do' anything to me. I like older guys. You and Seamus like younger girls. Almost *all* guys like younger girls. There's nothing wrong with that. That girl in New York you went out with . . . the dead one . . ."

This time the bomb hits me. The game is over. How the hell does she know about that? I put another quarter in the machine in my mind and I will fucking *win.* I tell Nomi that she has PTSD. She lost her father. She isn't thinking clearly. I remind her that I know where she's coming from. I had a rough childhood. I know how hard it is when your parents are fighting and you don't know who you can count on and I tell her that we can get her someone to talk to, someone who can help her sort through this mess.

But she just smiles. A centipede with eyes. "You remind me of him, you know." Don't say Woody Allen. "Dylan," she says. "Dylan Klebold." Dylan Klebold is a mass murderer and I am your common-law husband—why didn't we go to the courthouse *today*? "You don't just say things. You actually *do* things. I mean the way you gave me that Bukowski . . ."

"Your mom gave you that."

She smiles. "I know. Well done there."

"Nomi, I am not Seamus."

She looks at me and laughs. "Oh come on, Joe. The way you both hung around my house after my dad died . . . I mean it was unbelievable. He wouldn't let me go and you wouldn't just freaking *go* for it . . . and my mom...*ugh*..." You resented your mother and she resents you and a nipple appears under her shirt. "You don't have to be jealous, Joe. I didn't break it off the day I met you but I mean . . . he's gone. We're here. Plus, honestly, when I started up with him, I was a whole other person. I was young so it doesn't even count."

"Nomi, you *are* young," I say again.

She grins. "I know."

I missed it. The man was abusing your daughter and I hear Oliver in my head. *There is such a thing as too soft, my friend.* Cedar Cove rotted my brain and broke my radar and the Meerkat was never a fucking Meerkat and kids grow up faster—fucking Instagram—and they know how to be four different people at once and I took her little round glasses at face value. I thought she was innocent and she was just *playing* innocent but she *is* innocent because HE WAS A FUCKING PEDOPHILE. I said the word out loud—someone has to make this right—and she throws a pillow at me. "Don't use that word."

"Nomi, that's the only word there is right now."

She's quoting RIP Melanda—*It's not history. It's HERstory*—and she talks about Seamus like he was her equal—*He did the salmon egg thing too when he was a kid and he could be sweet*—and I tell her that's impossible. "He was a grown man, Nomi. He had all the power and what he did was wrong. He should be in fucking jail."

She snaps her fingers. "*That's* why Melanda hated you. I thought she was just jealous as usual but you're better than this. You can't tell *me* how I feel. I know you know that."

I tell her she needs to stop and she balks as if we are lovers at war. "Don't tell me what I *need,* Mr. Woody Allen's number one fan. Even *Seamus* knew better than to talk down to me like that."

Seamus was a pervert who tried to kill me and I am the adult. The stepfather. "Nomi, what he did was wrong."

She tells me that in a lot of cultures, girls her age have babies and that I don't get to sit here and take it all back when I've been leading her on since the day we met. "It sucked when you disappeared. But I get it. I know it was too painful for you with me so close but so far away . . ." No. "And it doesn't matter because you came back. You waited for me in the parking lot of the library and once again, I told you to stay. I told you not to give up." She looks at me and the Centipede burns me alive. "And you didn't give up," she says. "Yeah, the wedding was a little icky, but we both know that you're not going through with my mom's little *eight-eight* plan. You're not even really married."

I am down to one life now and she laughs. "Stop being so freaked out. It's *me,* Joe. It's *me.*" But then she stops laughing, like the Centipede she's become. "I almost forgot," she says. "You should have seen your face when I told you Melanda texted me. Another classic."

This is the part of the game where you kill the enemy and the screen changes colors and the enemy is reborn stronger, faster. She says she's not stupid. She knows Melanda's *gone for good* and I tell her it's not like that. "You've been through a lot and if your mother knew . . . if she knew that Seamus . . . that he raped you."

"Jesus, will you let it go? We broke up. It's over. And then the idiot went and got himself killed hunting. Honestly, it's not the biggest surprise in the world . . . He was so depressed about being dumped, he was in no state of mind to be off in the woods, going off about what he was gonna do to *you* . . ."

The Centipede is staring at me, slowing down and daring me to move into defensive mode. I am not stupid. I am quiet. *Does* she know what he did to me? Does she know what Oliver did to him?

She crosses her arms again. "Don't look at me like that. I know he was spiraling. And he got so pissy about you . . ."

He didn't get *pissy.* He tried to *murder* me. She's on her feet—the Centipede has feet—and she pulls at my pillow and I hold on to my pillow and she picks up her bottomless can of spiked seltzer, a drink designed to appeal to children, to make them feel older than they are.

I tell her she has the wrong idea and this game isn't for me because even when I win, I lose. The game gets harder. She *appreciates* me for holding out, waiting for her to graduate, *buying time* for us and I can't beat the Centipede, can I? She takes the pillow out of my hands and hugs me and I am numb. Game Over. I think fast. *Hard.*

Let her hug me. She won't tell you about this. In four days, she'll get on a plane and go to New York and become obsessed with some Dr. Nicky professor type and you don't need to know about this *Feud.* Shortus is dead. Revenge is impossible and *Cedar Cove* damaged *your* brain too. You didn't see it either—you were worried about your husband and there are only so many worries a heart can bear—and I would never judge you for that. I have to let her say what she needs to say so that she can move the fuck on, so that *we* can move the fuck on.

I grab her shoulders. We are close now, so close that I can actually see the innocence in her eyes—she really does love me—and I have been where she is. I have loved people who didn't love me back and I tell her this will hurt—Jude Law in *Closer*—and my voice is firm.

"I don't love you, Nomi. And that's okay because you don't love me."

Her teeth chatter inside of her mouth and her shoulders tremble beneath my hands and the hardest thing about a Centipede is that a Centipede is always moving. That's the nightmare of the game. I stay with her as I fire my bullets because I wish any woman who broke my heart had been so kind with me, willing to be here for me as I realize that I am not loved. My hands are still on her shoulders when you burst into the room. You kick off your shoes and slip into your cozy socks. "All right," you say. "You win, Buster. I'm home."

51

It's been a few minutes since you walked in on every mother's worst nightmare and the Centipede is curled up in a ball on the sofa and she is screaming—*He went after me*—and you are screaming—*I can't take this*—and you are in the game too now but your control pad is compromised because this is too fucking much. You defend me—*Nomi, why are you saying this?*—and you defend her—*Joe, don't say anything right now*—and I abide and the Centipede cries and you cross your arms. "Okay," you say. "Everyone needs to take it down a notch."

The Centipede looks up at you like she wants to be hugged and you don't hug your daughter. You don't run to the sofa and hold her. You don't believe her and you don't know about Shortus and I can't be the one to tell you that she's projecting and she's in a bad place right now—I don't love her and she knows it—and she wants you to hate me and you don't want to hate me and she picks up her can of spiked seltzer but the well has finally run dry. She slams the can on the table.

"Mom," she says. "Can we please leave already?"

There is only one player in the game and it's you. You fold your arms. "Nomi, honey, please stop crying. We're not leaving this house. Not like this."

There's a foolproof way to make anyone cry: Tell them to stop. She's bawling again now and I say your name and you growl at me—*I said stay out of it*—and then you growl at her. "Why the hell are you doing this? Why do you make things up?"

"Making this up? Mom, I forgot my phone and I came home and you saw him trying to kiss me. Are you blind?"

Your heart is beating so fast that I can feel it in my heart and your nostrils flare like RIP Melanda's and you say it again. "Nomi, why are you making this up?"

She rubs her eyes. Part Meerkat. Part Centipede. "Mom. He *kissed* me."

"I didn't!"

You don't look at me. You look at her. "Nomi . . ."

"Wow," she says. "You believe *him*. Nice, Mom. Real nice."

You tell her that you believe *you*. You trust your gut and you don't think I would do that—I wouldn't, but Seamus did, and your child needs you but you don't know what I know—and you are blaming the victim, warning her about the danger of making *false accusations* and she springs off the sofa and the Meerkat is possessed by a barefoot Centipede. She throws her empty can at the wall and calls you a *sicko* because *what kind of woman believes her fucking boy toy over her daughter?* You storm by me and I don't exist. Not right now. This is your *Family Feud* and I am powerless, locked out of the arcade, and you lash out at her. "Do not speak to me like that. We have to be honest."

"Oh?" she snaps. "You want me to be honest? Well, Mom, *honestly* I think you're a fucking sham. Most women *believe* all women and all you ever do is make excuses for *every* single piece-of-shit guy you drag into my life."

"Stop it, Nomi."

"Why? He's dead. Dad's dead!"

This is why we didn't see the Centipede inside the Meerkat, because the Meerkat is like me, she stored all her pain deep inside where nobody could see it. You do that for eighteen years, you get good at it and this chasm was always here, it's the reason RIP Phil was *Philin'* the blues every night. The Meerkat hits below the belt—*You feel sorry for yourself because you're a mother and for that you can fuck off*—and you hit back—*You make it impossible to be your mother be-*

cause you talk to me about nothing—and I sit on the sofa and all I wanted to do was make you happy and look at you now. You're crying and she's crying and you tell her it's not your fault that he's dead and you are right but she blasts you—*Like hell it isn't! You fucked his brother!*—and you respond to the wrong part of what she said—*Don't talk that way about me*—and you don't look at me because you're ashamed and there is no shame in our love and I want you to know it but I can't go where you go, into your nest with your daughter. I am scared for our family and I'm supposed to be the father, the man of this house, but that's a patriarchal thought and RIP Melanda would be right to tell me that it's not about me.

It isn't. I moved here to be good. I *was* good. I didn't kill your cheating husband. I didn't kill your lying best friend and I didn't kill Seamus, the rapist. But I did make a mistake. I wanted to believe that everyone is like us, good, and in that way, I was naïve. You were too, Mary Kay. Your daughter says that you ruined her life and that makes you cry and I can't hold you, I can't go to you and you blow your nose on your sleeve and you won't allow yourself to look at me, to take the love that you so desperately need. Nomi is crying too.

"Nomi," you say. "Why do you . . . why do you hate me so much?"

You are mother and daughter. You stop crying and so she stops crying and I remain where I am, wishing I had turned off *Family Feud* instead of muting it when I heard you come in.

She picks at the hem of her little shirt. "Well, you don't care about me."

"Honey, how can you say that? You're all I care about. I love you. I see you."

The Meerkat is so focused on you that she doesn't point at me to say that you're protecting me and this is good, I hope. This is healing. "You don't see me. You're blind."

"Nomi."

"What do you think I was doing all the time?"

"All the time . . . When do you mean? What do you mean?"

I remember a line from *Veep,* when the tall guy running for president gets his followers to chant: *When are you from? When are you from?* I fight tears—it's not my place to cry, that's the last thing you need—and the *Veep* man was right. We don't come from places. We come from time. From traumatic moments that cannot be undone.

"Mom," she says. "Why do you think I got all those UTIs?"

"Nomi, no."

"Mom," she says. "I read *Columbine* for you. I thought eventually you would force me to go to some shrink . . . and maybe if I talked to some shrink . . ."

"No."

"He told me that you knew. He said moms know it all. And you didn't."

You clamp your hands over your ears like a child and I know it hurts. That bastard raped your daughter and you cry as if you are the one who got hurt because you hurt right now but she wants you to let *her* cry and she's mad at you for that, screaming that it was your fault, that you let *Uncle Seamus* into your house, that you missed every sign that a good mother would see. I want to tell her to stop but how do you tell a teenage girl to stop talking when she's saying what she needs to say?

She slaps you across the face and you hold your cheek in your hand and that was too much but at the same time the fucking two of you need to learn once and for all that life is what happens right now, not what happened years ago and cannot be undone.

I say her name, like a stepfather. "Nomi."

She stops moving and Centipedes don't do that. They don't stop. You tell her to go downstairs where the two of you can talk *in private* and you think I don't love you anymore and it's the opposite, Mary Kay. I never loved you more. This is it, this is our Empathy Bordello and it's one thing to dream about it but it's another thing to live in it.

And you can't do it right now. I feel it slipping away—New York in November, Thanksgiving—and I don't know how to grab it because you don't know that I *know* about New York in November, Thanksgiving. You rub your face—it stings where she hit you—and she pats her hand—it too stings—but you didn't like that and you huff. "So that it, then, huh? You blame me for everything, but I got news, honey . . ." Don't do it, Mary Kay. "The one you should blame for this whole fucking mess is your father."

The Centipede is breathing fire. "Stop it, Mom. Stop it."

"He was supposed to protect you."

"I said stop it."

"Nomi, do you know why your Auntie Melanda really moved? Do you?"

No, Mary Kay. Don't go there. She thinks Melanda loves her deep down and kids *need* that and do I barge in? Am I allowed? You cluck. "Well, I'm done protecting your rock 'n' roll father who never did *anything* wrong and your perfect little miss feminist aunt."

No, Mary Kay. They're gone. You know you should let them rest in *peace* but you feel so guilty about missing what happened with Seamus and you want her to feel sorry for you. I know this game, I do.

"Well," you say. "At some point, we all learn that our parents are flawed. Your *auntie* Melanda was having an affair with your father, okay? Your *father* was sleeping with my best *friend.* So before you go putting them both on pedestals . . . well, that's what your beloved father and your beloved aunt did to *me*."

She says nothing. You say nothing. You know you made a mistake and you are better than this, smarter than this, and I know that being a mother is the hardest job in the world—RIP Love quit too—but the Meerkat didn't need that right now and you're about to apologize—I see it your eyes—but she throws a book at you. A Murakami and you swerve and the book hits the wall and she screams. "I am the child, Mom. *Me.*"

You make earmuffs again and my mother did that too when she was in the weeds, when she got home from work and I was on the floor watching TV and I would look up and say hi and she would wave, no eye contact, *I'm beat, Joe.* I'm beat.

I know where you are. I see you in your mind, kicking yourself. You never ripped up *Columbine* and dragged her to a therapist and you made nice to Seamus and this is why you cry. The guilt. You want the Meerkat to take care of you and she wants you to take care of her and you're crying, she's crying, and you both cry like sharks inside of sharks, deprived of fresh air, freedom. You put your hands on Nomi's shoulders and she leans her head into yours and your foreheads are touching. "Nomi, honey, don't worry. I'm not mad at you."

That was the wrong thing to say and I know it and Nomi knows it and she grabs your shoulders and my floors are hardwood. Shiny. You twist like spaghetti and she hurls you at the wall and your foot slips—socks—and I'm too slow. I'm too late. You tumble down the stairs and the Meerkat screams and I freeze up inside, outside.

I picture the police report that's coming.

Murder Weapon: Socks.

No. There is no murder and you are. Not. Dead. Time is slow and fast and fast and slow and Nomi is still screaming and of course she is screaming. She came home to find her father dead on the floor and now her mother is out cold—Are you dead? You can't be dead—and Nomi shrieks—*Mommy!*—and it's unnatural for a child to see one parent out cold on the floor, let alone two. Your body is in our basement—no, you're not a body, you're a woman, my woman, and I failed to protect you and my heart is in flames and you're the love of my life and you're the love of *our* life and Nomi clamps her hands on the banisters. She's on her way down the stairs but every step is ten miles long and why are there so many fucking steps?

She stops on the second-to-last step. "She's not moving."

I want to rip Nomi's heart out of her chest—this is too much for her, it is—and I want to rip mine out too—this is too much for me, it is.

She takes one step closer and stands over you. She's afraid to touch you. Afraid to feel your hand for a pulse. "Omigod," she says, and she is wailing and I know that kind of warbling sound. She thinks she killed you. She thinks the pain is going to kill *her* and she thinks there is less love for her in this world than there was forty seconds ago.

I lean over your body and hold your wrist in my hand. Your heart is beating.

"Nomi," I say. "She's alive."

I take a deep breath, an end-of-the-book kind of breath, the last-book-the-author-wrote-before-she-died kind of breath. "I'm calling 911."

Nomi nods. But she can't speak. Not right now. She's a Meerkat again, trembling and scared. The operator picks up and asks me about my emergency and Nomi screams—*I don't think she's breathing anymore!*—and the operator is sending an ambulance and they *will* save you, Mary Kay. They have to save you. Not just for me, not just for you, but for Nomi.

She thinks this is her fault and you have to survive so that you can wake up and tell her what she needs to hear, that this is not her fault. You try to love. You try to be good. But ultimately, you wear socks on hardwood floors and Ivan was right. We deserve better, all three of us. Your lips move and Nomi's desperation transforms into hope and she feels the pulse on your wrist and looks up at me. "She's alive."

I stay on the phone—I am the *adult*—and I give my address—our address—and I follow their orders—don't move her—and I say all the right things to your daughter—*It's okay, Nomi, she's gonna be okay*—and I hold your hand and whisper all the right things to you as well. You are lost at sea—*See the boats go sailing*—and my voice is your lighthouse. But I can't say everything I want to say and I can't give you my full, undivided attention. Your Meerkat is too close.

It's not what Nomi said—*She's alive*—it's what she didn't say—*Thank God she's alive*—and was she . . . did she *want* you to be gone? Once I saw her push Luscious off an end table. He landed on his feet but you . . .

I know, Mary Kay. This is no time for doubts. When you wake up—and you will wake up—it's gonna be you and me against the world. I promise. Your eyelids flutter, I think, I hope—I wish we were alone—and I stroke your hair and say it all out loud. "I love you, Mary Kay. You fell, I know, but now you're gonna get better. I'm gonna take care of you every day, I promise. You got me, you're my love. I'm here."

The Meerkat is a Centipede. Quiet.

Epilogue

I left America. I had to. How much tragedy can a person bear? Okay, so I didn't cross the border, but my new home feels like another country. I live in Florida now, smack dab in the center, close to the Kingdom, *yeah,* but I'm not close as in *Closer.* I can pretend it doesn't exist. I am alone. Safe. And I get it now. I'm better off on the wrong side of the tracks. You were special, Mary Kay. You saw something in me. But in the end, you turned out to be like my past coastal elite loves, too tangled up in your blue roots to pave a new road with me. No more hackneyed American dreams of a love that conquers all for *this* Florida man.

The shop is closed, as they say, and I turn on the lights in the Empathy Bordello. It's too dark and it's too bright and I'm trying to move on. Last night I watched a documentary about RIP Sam Cooke—he gets me—and I wanted to know more about his music but it was mostly just speculation about his murder, as if that's all that matters. I am so sick of this obsession with *death,* Mary Kay. What about what we do with our lives? Licious meows—his brothers are back on Bainbridge—and you were right. He is the best cat, a *baffled king* on a perpetual victory march, as if he always *just* composed "Hallelujah" and if you were here, you would say that every suffix needs a prefix and I miss you, Mary Kay.

I do.

I wanted to build a life with you and I did everything right. I was a good man. I volunteered at the library. I opened my heart to you and I believed that we could be happy in *Cedar Cove.* But, like so many *Sassy* American women who trust their feelings, you spoke your truth and got thrown down the stairs. My heart is broken. Permanently.

I can't talk to you so I play a Sam Cooke song, the one where he's sad about a woman who left him. She broke his heart—*she stayed out, she stayed out all night*—and he begs her to come home. He offers his forgiveness. You can do that when the person you love is alive. You got pushed. Life does that to us. But you lost your footing and fell down the stairs because you were wearing *socks*—I warned you—and now you're in a coma and you can't burst into the Bordello to tell me you regret *leaving, leaving me behind.* You're like every woman I ever loved. You didn't walk away. You didn't stay out all night. You left the fucking planet.

You wanted this Bordello before you ever met me and I wanted us to have Christmas together and leave the lights up all year and now you can't even see our jukebox. You can't do the most important thing we do as people: evolve. Apologize to your child for being human, for being a mother, for letting empathy make you go blind.

I look at my phone just to make sure it's real and it is: *They're pulling the plug tomorrow. Thought you should know.*

Nomi didn't even call to tell me about you—she *texted*—and I flip the switch on the pink neon Open sign in my bookstore, where I serve *Cocktails & Dreams* alone. You didn't help me build the Bordello and I can't blame Nomi for being cold and I know she'll be fine in the long run. She's not one for empathy—I still see her hovering over you, I still hear those words, *she's alive*—and it's not her fault, Mary Kay. She's moving on with her life, studying our fucked-up environment at NYU and young, wounded female victims turned sociopaths thrive in New York City and I should know.

I've been hurt by more than a few of them.

I try to stay upbeat. There are people out there who do love me. Ethan might visit—but he would bring *Blythe*—and here I go again, replaying it all in my head. I loved you like no other. The EMTs arrived and they gave me hope. The United States Injustice System cooperated this time around—cause of injury: accident—and there was no biased "investigation," no online crazies trying to blame me for your fall. I tried to be the guy with a *girlfriend in a coma*—we have that book in stock at the Bordello—and I was dutiful. I was there. But every time I went to get a soda I came back to find one of your *Friends* in my chair by your bed. Erin disappeared and Fecal Eyes swept in with her multigenerational family of lookie-loos and I know you wouldn't want me sitting there with that woman who brought out the worst in us.

I loved you. But my love wasn't enough to save you. Now you sleep in a mechanical bed while a machine does all the heavy lifting. I was the man of your dreams—*I didn't think someone like you existed*—and you always wanted to dance with somebody (who loves you). And I did love you and we did dance. But from the moment we met, we were stuck in the middle of the circle. Your *Friends* and family were holding us hostage every step of the way because they didn't want you to be happy. And look how that worked out for them.

Your best friend Melanda is watching movies at Fort Ward.

Your husband Phil is snorting heroin in heaven.

Your brother-in-law Ivan is blogging about his new *gambling addiction.*

Your buddy Shortus is in hell doing CrossFit and your daughter Nomi is alive but motherless.

I play our Lemonheads song and I can't believe I'll never see you again and I wonder what you would think of the tabletop Centipede game by the back wall of the Bordello. But I'll never know, will I?

Acid shoots through my esophagus, all that leftover love with no place to go.

I lug a barrel of empty bottles out back into the dumpster, where the air is thick as bread and Florida makes you believe in the ether, the unknown. Sometimes I get paranoid. I picture you haunting me from within like a ghost I can't escape, *the shark inside my shark.*

But there's no such fucking thing as ghosts. I'm getting older and you're not and it will take some time to adjust to this living arrangement, the one where you're dead and I'm turning on the TV because the music hurts but the news helps.

Naked Ocala woman urinates on customers at Popeyes

Broward County husband tells police: "My wife called my girlfriend a whore! It was self-defense!"

Father and son arrested for selling meth at school bake sale

And then an ad for a new show on Fox: *Johnny Bates: The Man You Hate to Love*

After you fell down the stairs and our family splintered, I thought about going to Ray, trying to get my son back. But I was right about Ray. He has cancer. And if there's one thing I learned from my time with you, it's that Dottie has enough on her plate right now. She's taking care of my son. She opened an Instagram account and I followed her and she followed me right back and sent me one important message: *Ssssshh.*

She doesn't post as much as Love did, but it helps to have an online family museum and I'm happy my son has more privacy now. I also have a Google alert for "Ray Quinn" and "obituary," and that's a thing that keeps me going.

The door of the *Empathy Bordello Bar & Bookstore* opens and it's only 11:32 and we're usually dead until noon—even in these parts, people are shy about morning juice—and I have a customer. She's not a person to me yet. She's a blur in the doorway and she holds the door open with her hip. She's sending someone a text and I can't see her face in the white light. The AC is on and the cool air is pouring out, driving our planet into despair. If I ask her to close the door, I am rude because she's talking to someone—her boyfriend?—and if I let her stay there like that, I am complicit in the destruction of this planet, of my heart.

She moves her hip and the door closes and we're alone in the dark that's not as dark as it seems. My eyes still can't get there and I'm blinking, squinting, as if your eyes cover my eyes, warping my vision. I want to see this woman—I am alive—and I don't want to see this woman—They all leave me, they leave me behind—but it doesn't matter what I want. Eventually, my muscles adjust—the holes in our faces have free will—and like it or not, I see the world clearly, the woman who just sat down at the bar in my Bordello. She says hello and I say hello and it defies all logic—I lost everyone I ever loved, everyone—but somehow my heart is intact. It ticks madly, just like hers.

Acknowledgments

A lot of people helped me put this book in your hands.

My editor, Kara Cesare, responds to my emails, my anxieties as well as my fears. I am so lucky to have Kara on my side, a psychic book friend who challenges me and nudges me and knows what I'm trying to say. I am also grateful for the wisdom and whip-smarts of Josh Bank and Lanie Davis. Thanks for pushing me onto a plane! I'm constantly happy to have the support of Les Morgenstern and Romy Golan. My attorney, Logan Clare, is both hilarious and helpful. I love being a member of the Random House family because of so many warm and compassionate people: Avideh Bashirrad, Andy Ward, Michelle Jasmine, and Jesse Shuman, among others. And I thank Claudia Ballard and her team at WME for their enduring belief in my work, plus all those gorgeous foreign editions.

A lot's changed since I wrote that first draft of *You* in 2013. (I think it's officially clear that Penn Badgley was the right one to play Joe on-screen.) One way in which I don't change is that I still get butterflies when I realize that my imaginary "friend" Joe *exists* in a real, meaningful way for so many people. Case in point: Natalia Niehaus, a Bainbridge-based fan of *You* Netflix who acted as my Bainbridge tour guide and was excited about Joe's new home. I put my hands together for the people who read my books and hang out in the Cage, in the Everythingship squad, and for all those who spread the word about books—I'm looking at you, Mother Horror—because word of mouth, whether written or spoken, is a special thing, an author's dream.

I don't just bug my editors with late-night angsty emails about Joe. I treasure my friends and family, the ones who deal with my incessant screenshots of this page and nerves about that page and are understanding when I disappear. They make me laugh and they make me feel like everything is going to be okay, even when it's July 8, 2020, which it is right now and . . . well, if you're reading this in 2021 or 2061, I hope our world is getting better and doing better.

Love you, Mom, Alex, Beth, Jonathan, Joshua. XOXO

ABOUT THE AUTHOR

CAROLINE KEPNES is the author of *You, Hidden Bodies, Providence,* and numerous short stories. Her work has been translated into a multitude of languages and inspired a television series adaptation of *You,* currently on Netflix. Kepnes graduated from Brown University and previously worked as a pop culture journalist for *Entertainment Weekly* and a TV writer for *7th Heaven* and *The Secret Life of the American Teenager*. She grew up on Cape Cod, Massachusetts, and now lives in Los Angeles.

carolinekepnes.com
Facebook.com/CarolineKepnes
Twitter: @CarolineKepnes
Instagram: @carolinekepnes

ABOUT THE TYPE

This book was set in Caledonia, a typeface designed in 1939 by W. A. Dwiggins (1880–1956) for the Merganthaler Linotype Company. Its name is the ancient Roman term for Scotland, because the face was intended to have a Scottish-Roman flavor. Caledonia is considered to be a well-proportioned, businesslike face with little contrast between its thick and thin lines.